# SECRETS OF THE MIST

Also by KATE RYDER

*Summer in a Cornish Cove*
*Cottage on a Cornish Cliff*

# SECRETS OF THE MIST

Kate Ryder

First published in the UK in 2019 by Head of Zeus Ltd

Copyright © Kate Ryder, 2019

9 7 5 3 1 2 4 6 8

A catalogue record for this book is available from
the British Library.

ISBN : 9781788541114

Cover design © Charlotte Abrams-Simpson

Typeset by Silicon Chips

Printed and bound in Great Britain by
CPI Group (UK) Ltd, Croydon CR0 4YY

Head of Zeus Ltd
First Floor East
5–8 Hardwick Street
London EC1R 4RG

WWW.HEADOFZEUS.COM

*For Helena*
who witnessed the very first spark

# I

As I looked towards the huddle of cottages nestling on the far side of the village green I noticed how still it had become – like an expectant, held breath – and somewhere deep within my soul I felt tendrils of distant memory reach out to me.

The sun was warm on that early summer's evening and yet I shivered. A thick haze hung in the air and the sounds of the pub seemed muffled, as if the world was somehow suppressed; waiting for something to happen. What, I did not know, but my senses were on high alert. Something was coming. Suddenly, from out of nowhere, I detected the slightest breeze and a wisp of air languidly encircled my body as if investigating me.

I looked towards Dan to see if he had noticed anything, but he seemed distant from me, as if I was cushioned and remote from the world. I didn't feel threatened. In fact, I revelled in the sensation of that warm, tender kiss of air as it gently caressed me. As if in some way being guided, I watched the shadows fall across the mellow-coloured cottage on the far side of the village green and shivered again.

Earlier that afternoon, when one of the film crew

suggested a drink after work at a local pub he'd discovered I was only too pleased to be invited. We had endured a hard day's filming; one that proved particularly trying for me, having to deal with a star whose ego was extremely large, and I had already used up most of my diplomacy and patience during the previous three weeks' filming. A bit of good old R&R was in order.

They were a great crowd at Hawkstone Media and I had happily worked there for the past eight years since first arriving in the UK as a fresh-faced, enthusiastic girl from Dublin, full of raw ambition. Ken Hawkstone – the man behind the company – was a demanding, but fair, whirlwind of creative force and he recognised that ambition, offering me numerous breaks along the way. I had worked my way up from continuity girl to assistant director and loved the work, even though it was all-consuming and left little time for anything else.

However, over the past couple of years, I'd found sleep increasingly fitful and was often awake in the small hours battling strange, disconcertingly deep thoughts about the random nature of choice, fate and destiny; thoughts that made no sense at all in the cold light of day. And, although I could never recall the details on waking, I was visited by a recurring dream; one that left a lingering memory of a pair of tender, blue-grey eyes and a feeling of a hand having touched my heart. As the years slipped by, however hard I tried to ignore it, I was aware of an underlying, nagging insistence for change.

The sounds of a busy pub enveloped me as we entered the Blacksmith's Arms – a charming seventeenth-century country inn with flagstone floors and heavily beamed ceilings. It was obviously a popular haunt. Clusters of people sat in private alcoves enjoying an early evening drink and through an open archway I saw tables being set for dinner. We booked a table for eight o'clock and then, having ordered drinks, walked outside into that early summer's evening towards the first moment of my future.

I looked across the village green, beyond the massive oak tree standing proudly at its centre, towards the stone cottage and saw a red and yellow 'For Sale' board erected in its garden. Again, I detected the slightest breeze and as I watched the shadows from the oak fall across the cottage I shivered involuntarily.

'Cold, Mads?' asked Dan, one of the camera crew and my occasional lover.

He was a kindly soul.

'Not really. I've just got this feeling I've been here before. Kinda spooky, in a comforting sort of way, if you know what I mean,' I finished lamely.

He drew me to him and gently squeezed my shoulder. 'Have you ever been to this part of Dorset?'

'No, I've never been to Dorset before. You know me, Dan. The bright lights, the next drink, the latest wine bar, the hippest party! I'm not a country girl, I don't know what I'd do with myself all day, and yet...' I swept my hand before me, acknowledging the village green and the cluster of cottages across the way '...this feels so familiar.'

Tim, the stunt co-ordinator, was listening to our conversation and now joined in.

'Perhaps you lived here in a former life?' he said, tongue-in-cheek.

'Perhaps you were the blacksmith's wife,' contributed

Emma, the newest of the make-up girls and on her first assignment. 'And I bet you lived in that cottage over there.'

She pointed to the 'For Sale' board and the hairs on the back of my neck stood erect.

'Mads, are you OK?' Dan asked, peering at me intently. 'You've gone really pale.'

'I'm OK.' I could see he wasn't convinced. 'Really I am, but I'll just sit for a while.'

I joined the remainder of the crew sitting at one of the wooden picnic benches provided by the pub.

Emma, however, had warmed to the subject. 'I bet you were born in this village and lived here all your life. You married the local blacksmith and brought up a batch of dark-haired children who were all very practical and good with their hands.'

A ripple of laughter reverberated around the table.

'And I bet it's called The Stables,' she finished triumphantly, pointing to the cottage on the far side of the village green.

'No,' I contradicted quietly, 'it's called The Olde Smithy.'

Emma laughed. 'Let's see!'

She ran across the grass, stood at the cottage's rusting gate that opened directly onto the village green and peered at the property. I watched her hesitate and slowly turn; her mouth agape. By now, the rest of the table listened with interest.

Emma ran back across the green. 'Maddie, how did you know? You couldn't have read the nameplate from here. It's hidden by all that foliage around the front door. I could only just make it out from the gate!'

'I don't know,' I muttered, 'I just knew.'

Standing behind me, Dan placed his large hands on my shoulders. 'I expect Mads is just putting two and two together and coming up trumps. You all know how creative she can be.'

There was murmured acknowledgement of my storytelling skills from around the table.

Dan squeezed my shoulders. 'Come on, guys. Time's marching on and I'm hungry. Let's eat.'

So, we filed into the pub and were soon immersed in ordering food and enjoying the merriment of the evening, and the *déjà vu* feeling subsided. Once again, I was Madeleine O'Brien, assistant director at Hawkstone Media, down from London to film a period drama at an elegant country house not far from Dorset's magnificent Jurassic coastline. But, as we left the pub much later that evening, I detected a whisper on the wind and as I climbed into Dan's car I knew The Olde Smithy was to be mine.

It took a further three months to finish filming and by the time I arrived back in London I had purchased the cottage. My colleagues were incredulous and kept reminding me of my city-girl lifestyle, my cosmopolitan attitude and my need of the Underground to ferry me between watering holes. And when I handed in my notice they actually pleaded with me to see sense.

'But what are you going to do there stuck out in the country all by yourself?' Dan asked. 'You said it yourself: the bright lights, the latest wine bar, the hippest party. If you're fed up with your job, join a different production company. If you want change in your life, get a dog! But don't burn your bridges, Mads. Please…'

We'd been to the cinema to see the latest Bond movie

with his sister, Caro, and her husband, John, and were now eating at our favourite Soho bistro. Dan and I were good companions. There was no great passion between us, but life was easy. We made no demands on each other, being free to date other people, and no questions were ever asked. Nothing ever rocked our boat.

I smiled and touched his face. He meant well.

'Dan, it's OK. I know what I'm doing. I'm going *home*.'

He stared at me in surprise.

'What do you mean, Maddie?' asked Caro curiously.

'I can't explain it but when I first saw the cottage it just spoke to me.' I looked at their anxious faces. 'I knew I had to have it…'

'But, Maddie, Daniel Craig speaks to me and I know I have to have him,' Caro exclaimed. 'I also know it's just not going to happen,' she added forlornly.

I laughed but quickly grew serious again. 'When I approached the estate agents they said that despite the cottage being on the market for some time there were only two interested parties. Both pulled out at the last minute. It hasn't been occupied since the previous owner moved three years ago, apart from a few months when it was tenanted. Basically, it's been standing empty all that time.' Their worried faces made me defiantly state, 'It needs to be lived in and brought back to life!'

'Sounds odd to me,' Caro commented. 'Well, you know if it doesn't work out you can always come and live with us, can't she, John?'

She smiled at me. Like her brother, Caro was a generous soul.

'Yes, there's always room for you in Clapham, Maddie,' John echoed his wife's offer. 'No loss of face there.'

'Thanks, you two. That's comforting.'

'And if you ever get bored stuck out in the sticks, I'll always come down at the click of your fingers to entertain you with stories of the latest ego I have *not* had the pleasure of working with,' teased Dan. He squeezed my knee meaningfully under the table.

I smiled at them all. Such good friends amidst the bustle of what could sometimes be a lonely city and, for a split second, I wondered if I was doing the right thing. I gazed at Dan, my dearest friend in whose arms I'd unexpectedly found pleasure, but we were going nowhere fast and, try as I might, I couldn't imagine a future with him. I was on a roller coaster and nothing could halt me now.

And so, one early October morning, I peered out from the third-floor window of my rented Victorian flat at the acres of chimneys stretching as far as the eye could see. Then, taking a final look around the empty apartment, and with a deep breath, I closed the door on my London life.

Following my leaving bash at the local pub the previous weekend, Dan had stayed with me. We hadn't planned it that way but I couldn't remember getting home from the party and when I did wake up the next day, sometime around mid-afternoon, he was there to ease the hangover with cups of strong coffee and soothing, cool hands and, well, he'd sort of remained...

As I said, we were companionable together.

Generously, he agreed to drive me to Walditch. We hired a van on the Tuesday and loaded the majority of my possessions – not that they amounted to much – and decided to leave early the following morning to miss the worst of the commuter traffic. As soon as the outskirts of London were left behind, a sense of well-being replaced any slight hesitation I'd previously experienced, and by the time we joined the M3, Dan commented that the metropolitan girl had been well and truly left at the city gates. When we reached the A31 I had visibly chilled... and all the time a sense of 'coming home' grew deep within me. I couldn't understand it.

I was born in Dublin, the youngest of three girls, to Matilda and Finn O'Brien; successful, self-made business people. My sisters and I grew up in an environment that encouraged us to follow our dreams. For me, this was theatre, film and TV, whereas Mo had pursued her interest in photography to become a successful photojournalist, known for 'the look' of her subjects that no other photographer was able to capture. Martha, the eldest by ten years, had set the level. Having studied interior design, she now owned a fashionable outfit just off O'Connell Street and was often called upon to remodel homes for titans of industry – one particular project being to refit hotels owned by some famous musicians. They were a hard act to follow... my sisters.

Turning my back on a career in the film industry for an uncertain future was not something my family easily understood. However, Mo – the closest in age and character to me – said that if it was something I needed to pursue then I should follow my heart.

It was a beautiful, clear autumn day and an ever-increasing sense of excitement promised to engulf me. We broke the journey for breakfast at a charming café in the

New Forest that Dan had discovered a few years before on a film shoot.

'You've certainly got some colour in your cheeks now,' he said, drawing me to him. Twisting a strand of my hair in his long, slender fingers, he kissed me. 'Don't forget what we have, Mads, will you?'

I was surprised at the mellow tone to his voice.

'Good heavens, Daniel Chambers, you're not going all sentimental on me now, are you?' I teased in the broadest of Irish accents, but was stayed by the look in his eyes.

'I've always had a soft spot for you, Mads, you know that,' he said quietly. 'I'd hate to think this was it between us.'

'Don't be daft!' I punched him gently on the chest. 'This is a big adventure. If you think I'm not going to share it you've got another thing coming.'

He smiled but I could tell he wasn't happy. I asked the waitress for the bill and opened my handbag to take out my purse. Dan had never hinted at any level of commitment or permanency in our relationship before and this expression of feeling was something new. Frankly, it threw me.

'I'll get this,' Dan said in a flat voice, producing his wallet.


We arrived in Walditch late morning, having first visited the Bridport estate agents, Randall & Mather, to pick up the keys for The Olde Smithy. As we pulled up alongside Walditch village green I noticed a few people already sitting outside the Blacksmith's Arms. Casually, I wondered if there might be an opportunity of work in that establishment.

Clambering down from the van, I stretched and rubbed my hands together. 'OK, let's get cracking.'

Over the next couple of hours we unloaded the van, depositing bags and furniture in various rooms. Dan hit his head several times on the low beams of the downstairs rooms, but I had no such trouble. At five feet four inches I was a good ten inches shorter.

'Must have been midgets in the seventeenth century!' he muttered, ferociously rubbing his skull.

According to Randall & Mather, the cottage dated back to the mid-1600s, in part. The property details stated: *A charming, two-bedroom period cottage situated in Walditch, a village set deep in hilly countryside yet only a mile from Bridport and West Bay. The Olde Smithy offers discerning buyers an opportunity to put their stamp on a property steeped in history but with all modern-day conveniences.*

The sitting/dining room, kitchen and master bedroom were in the original part of the building, and all had heavily beamed ceilings and uneven floors, while a two-storey extension, built during the late 1980s, created a hallway, downstairs bathroom and first-floor guest bedroom. A small, overgrown, cottage-style garden to the front opened directly onto the village green and to the rear, immediately accessed from the kitchen, was a courtyard created by a collection of outhouses, one being an outside privy. A pathway led past the outbuildings to a further area of overgrown garden where there were three gnarled and twisted fruit trees, in desperate need of pruning, and the outline of a long-forgotten vegetable bed. To my delight, at the far end, was a neglected pond.

The day passed quickly and we busied ourselves unpacking boxes, stacking shelves and filling cupboards. I had energy to spare. Soon, the cottage soon took shape and by the time the elongating shadows of the oak tree encroached upon the front garden it felt homely. Only the last remaining packing boxes stacked in the hallway and the lack of curtains at the windows declared me a new occupant. I made a mental note to buy fabric during the next few days to remedy this, as I'd been unable to salvage any window dressings from the flat. Being a Victorian conversion, the apartment had tall sash windows to which the landlord had fitted vertical blinds.

As the day progressed, Dan regained a cheerful disposition and his earlier melancholy evaporated. He was busy cleaning the fireplace as I rummaged through a box in the kitchen, searching for elusive teabags. I paused and looked around appreciatively at the beams, the flagstone floor and the view of the courtyard through the small-paned windows. I could already see next spring's hanging baskets on the outhouse walls. I smiled, instinctively knowing that all that had gone before was simply leading to this day.

'Hey, Mads, take a look at this,' Dan called from the sitting room.

I turned and walked to the doorway. A thick haze filled the room and I marvelled at how much dust he'd created. I was about to suggest he let in some fresh air when I noticed all the windows were open wide. I frowned. How strange… The room was full of fog and yet there was a strong breeze blowing outside.

It must have been a trick of the light because, as Dan turned, his blond hair appeared darker and longer and he seemed less tall and lean; an altogether rougher version. I blinked and shook my head, as if brushing away the image. As quickly as he had appeared altered, there he was, once again, the Dan I knew.

'What have you found?' I walked across the room and saw a small opening in the stonework to one side of the inglenook. 'How did that happen?'

'One of the stones was loose. It came away quite easily when I investigated. I think there's something behind it.'

'Clear away a bit more,' I said, enthusiastically. 'It might be a bread oven.'

Placing his long fingers into the gap, he teased away at the stones around the opening. For a moment nothing happened but then one suddenly shifted, coming away in his hand. There was a definite edge to the hole. I peered inside at a hidden void.

'Wow, how exciting!'

Without hesitation, I inserted my hand and felt around, unsure what I expected to find, but apart from a thick layer of dust and rubble, the alcove was empty. Disappointment flooded through me.

'I'll make a feature of it,' I said. 'I'll visit a reclamation yard and find a door that fits.'

'This cottage will give up more of its secrets as time goes by.'

As Dan spoke the words I became aware of an expectant stillness in the air.

'Why did you say that?' I asked sharply.

'Well, these old places always have secrets, don't they? And this one's had four hundred years to collect them.'

Suddenly I felt hot and short of breath. Feeling dizzy, I reached out for Dan, as if trying to hold on to something solid; something I could trust.

He caught hold of my arm. 'Hey, steady, Mads!'

Beads of perspiration pricked my forehead and I struggled to hold back rising nausea.

'You OK?' Dan asked with concern.

'I just need some fresh air,' I gasped.

'Tell you what – let's abandon the tea thing and go to the pub instead.' This was his answer to most things.

'Yeah, I could do with a drink.'

He smiled at me.

'And dinner's on me,' I said weakly, hurrying towards the door.

'Now, there's an offer I can't possibly refuse, but won't that be a tad messy?'


We had visited the pub on several occasions during our time filming in the area and Brian, the landlord, remembered us. He was a jovial, larger-than-life character in his mid-fifties. We'd seldom seen his wife, Vera, as she was kept busy behind the scenes cooking delicious homemade meals for the hordes of people who frequented the pub.

'So you bought The Olde Smithy then?' Brian said, placing a glass of whisky and soda on the bar in front of me. He poured a pint of Badgers for Dan.

'I collected the keys earlier today. We haven't stopped working since.' I picked up the glass and took a sip.

'It's a lovely cottage. Shame it's stood empty so long. The garden was a treat when Mrs McKendrick owned it. There was nothing she didn't know about plants, and as for her old man's vegetables, he swept the board clean most years at the village show. The local horticultural society is a sorrier place without them.'

'I've seen the remains of their endeavours,' I said enthusiastically. 'The vegetable beds are completely overgrown but I'm looking forward to clearing them and growing my own, come the spring.' I smiled, thinking of all the future projects. 'It will be a steep learning curve, though.'

'Mads is a city girl,' Dan explained, rather unnecessarily I thought.

'Ah, you'll have fun learning.' Brian winked at me. 'Excuse me,' he said, moving down the bar to serve a young couple who had just walked in.

We picked up a bar menu and carried our drinks to one of the alcoves. I gazed around. The pub was a clever conversion of an old coach house with private seating areas created out of the original stalls where horses would once have been housed. An array of old farm equipment, horse brasses, tying hooks and hay racks adorned the walls and the Blacksmith's Arms oozed a warm, welcoming ambience, helped admirably by a roaring log fire.

'I guess you'll be in here a lot,' Dan commented.

'I guess so. I'm considering asking Brian if he needs any help.'

'What *are* you going to do?'

'Oh, I haven't really got that far, Dan. Maybe spend a few months updating the cottage and then, in the New Year, think about earning some money. Perhaps I'll start writing again.'

'Well, let's face it, the number of times you've kissed that old Blarney Stone means you're never short of a story or two!' Dan teased.

I smiled. My first assignment with Hawkstone Media was a period drama set in the countryside around Cork, and Dan and I had worked together on it. From the first, I recognised a shared sense of humour and it was fun spending time with him, introducing him to my country of birth. On a rare day off we visited Blarney Castle and I explained that I'd first kissed the Stone at the tender age of eight.

I amused him with tales of visitors being held by the ankles and lowered head first over the battlements in order to kiss it. This was true, but many years before I first encountered the Stone. On the day Dan and I visited, Health and Safety had long since come into play and, though the Stone was still set in the wall below the battlements, to kiss it we only had to lean backwards from the parapet walkway while holding on to an iron railing. Simple… providing you didn't suffer from vertigo or lumbago.

'Maybe I'll offer my services as a film reviewer for a magazine or paper,' I explained, 'but I really want to get the cottage straight first. It needs painting throughout and one of the window frames requires urgent attention. I'm sure I'll find some other hidden nasties.' I smiled at Dan.

'The inglenook would look great with a feature bread oven,' Dan enthused.

For some reason I was annoyed by his interest and my smile faded.

'I wonder why it was walled up?' he continued, unaware of my irritation.

'No idea.'

Why was I being so uncharacteristically defensive?

'Will you concentrate on that first?' he asked, quite reasonably.

'Haven't a clue,' I answered unhelpfully.

Why did I feel he was prying?

'So, you'll get a door for it?' he persevered with a questioning look on his face.

'Probably,' I answered dismissively.

Not wanting to continue the conversation further, I opened a menu and started reading aloud what was on offer that evening. It was a difficult choice as it all sounded appetising. Once we'd decided, Dan went to the bar to order.

Looking around the pub, my eyes alighted on a heavily framed oil painting displayed above the fireplace. The paintwork was dark – probably not helped by the smoke from numerous fires lit beneath it over the years – but from where I sat on the far side of the pub I could just make out the figure of a man shoeing a horse in front of a timber-framed building. With a sudden rush of emotion, I felt my cheeks flush and my heart begin to race.

Rising quickly, I crossed over to the fireplace and peered more closely at the painting. In the foreground the artist had painted an oak tree and I realised it was the view across the village green from the doorway of the pub. The building was definitely The Olde Smithy but an older, undeveloped version. I glanced at the artist's signature but couldn't make it out. If this pub was originally a coach house it would make sense for the blacksmith's premises to be close by. Perhaps the newly exposed void wasn't a bread oven after all. Maybe it was the furnace where the blacksmith heated the horseshoes.

As I observed the man in the painting, I noted the length of his hair, his build and the set of his body. I stood staring at the strangely familiar scene and, even though I could feel the heat from the fire through my denim jeans, I shivered. After a while I returned to the table but kept my observations to myself, not feeling inclined to share them with Dan.

We had a pleasant meal and during the course of the evening the pub grew steadily busier. The front-of-house staff seemed to consist of only two waitresses, one a girl called Janet. Brian worked the bar. I decided to give myself a week or two to settle in and then ask if there were any vacancies.

We left the pub at around ten-thirty. Earlier, as we'd left the cottage, I'd switched on the porch light, which now blinked at us in welcome from the far side of the village green. Lights from the neighbouring cottages also cast their beams across the grass, guiding our way. As we walked beneath the boughs of the mighty oak, I looked up through the branches. High clouds scudded across the night sky, briefly revealing a scattering of twinkling stars and a watery moon.

'Feels like rain,' I commented.

'Better cosy up then.'

I opened the front door and stepped over the threshold into the hallway. There was a distinct chill in the air.

'Brr… Even more reason to cosy up!' I teased.

'Come here, you!' Dan pulled me close and kissed me. 'Welcome to your new life.'

Dan was a thoughtful lover and our subsequent lovemaking was gentle, comforting and familiar. Before long, exhausted from the day's exertions, we fell asleep. As I drifted off I remember thinking how easy it was with Dan, albeit uneventful, which was why I was so surprised to be woken in the small hours from a deep slumber by hot, insistent kisses all over my body.

At first I thought I must be dreaming, but as I looked across at the curtainless windows and saw the inky night sky and the rain lashing against the glass, I remembered where I was. Dan's hands greedily explored my body as if for the very first time and when his mouth found mine, the passion in his kiss took my breath away. The urgency in his caresses was like nothing I had experienced with him before and I marvelled at the way I responded. Our bodies moved in harmony and I delighted at his every touch, melting under his deep kisses.

'Damn you, woman,' he said, nuzzling my neck. 'I am bewitched.'

I thrilled at the emotion in his voice, but surfaced long enough to register that Dan had never previously referred to me as 'woman'. Momentarily he pulled back and I sensed him looking at me.

The moon, emerging from behind a cloud, cast an eerie green light through the window and alighted on my lover's face. His appearance appeared altered – the Dan I had seen earlier that evening – somehow more feral. Suddenly he groaned and pulled me to him. I gasped as, together, we rode wave after wave of pure sensation; an insatiable rip tide of feeling. Afterwards, we held each other close and it wasn't long before I heard his deep, even, rhythmic breathing. My last conscious thought before sleep claimed me was that this heightened passion between us had made Dan's body feel different, somehow more muscular, and that it, too, must have been the reason for his altered scent.

The next morning I rose before he awoke and made my way quietly downstairs. I was unsure how to handle this new dimension to our relationship and decided to let Dan take the lead. Filling the kettle at the sink, I glanced out of the window at the still, wet day. Leaves lay scattered across the courtyard, wrenched from the trees by the terrific winds during the night. I noticed a young, black cat sitting by the outhouse door assessing me. Moving to the back door, I quietly opened the top half and called softly. The cat watched warily for a moment before turning and fleeing into the garden.

*Probably lives next door.*

I returned upstairs with mugs of tea. As I pushed open the bedroom door, Dan sat up in bed and raked long fingers through his wayward hair.

'Morning, Mads.'

With unaccustomed shyness, I handed him a mug.

'Looks like one hell of a storm last night.'

*In more ways than one.*

I glanced at the window overlooking the courtyard. Rain had seeped through a gap in the casement and formed a pool on the sill. It now steadily dripped onto the bare floorboards.

'Don't you remember?' I asked in an even voice.

With my back to him, I rummaged through my holdall. Pulling out a T-shirt, I mopped the sill before dropping the garment onto the puddle on the floor. A sudden movement out of the corner of my eye made me look into the garden and I saw the black cat hunting amongst the long, wet grass at the far end by the pond.

'You know me, Mads, I sleep through anything. It takes more than hurricane-force wind and torrential rain to wake me!'

It was true. Nothing ever disturbed Dan once his head touched the pillow. I considered this now. Had he been in the throes of a dream? That would certainly explain his uncharacteristic behaviour last night, or had his subconscious taken over, like that of a sleepwalker?

'Don't you remember anything about last night?' I asked.

'I remember getting back from the pub and the heating hadn't kicked in.' Arching an eyebrow, he smiled suggestively at me. 'But we didn't have trouble finding a way to warm up, did we?'

I wondered to which round of sex he was referring.

'God, I was bushed though,' he continued. 'Couldn't keep awake for long.'

I frowned. Our enthusiastic lovemaking had gone on for hours. He *must* have been asleep... and yet he had spoken to me. It didn't make sense.

'You know I've always liked this bed of yours,' Dan said, patting the space beside him. 'It's so comfortable. I could spend a lot of time in it with you.'

I sat down where he indicated and sipped my tea, confused by this turn of events. Our passion last night was so uncharacteristic. Surely, he would want to acknowledge it and discuss where our relationship was heading? But it seemed that Dan had no such thoughts.

'And after that?' I asked. 'We can't just stay in bed. There's more to life than sex you know, Daniel.'

He gave me a questioning look. 'You're in a funny mood this morning. You've never worried about life after sex before.'

'Well maybe I should have,' I replied in an irritated voice.

'But that's why we get on so well,' he said in his usual, calm, unflustered manner. 'No pressure, just loads of fun.'

We were silent for a while and there was a distance between us not present before. Neither of us wanted to make the next move. It occurred to me that Dan's easy-going nature and informal manner masked a reluctance to acknowledge the passing of time and his responsibility to me as a person. I, on the other hand, had always believed I was happy with a relationship where the boundaries were vague and non-committal, yet, perhaps this had in no small way contributed to my increasing restlessness and desire for change. So, later that morning, after I'd rustled up a semblance of breakfast from the few provisions I'd brought with me from London, we loaded the remaining empty packing cases into the van. Closing the rear doors, Dan turned to me and kissed me lightly on the mouth.

'Be seeing you, kiddo!' he said casually. 'Don't forget you can phone me any time, day or night.' And with that he climbed into the van. Starting the engine, he lowered the window and blew me a kiss.

I watched the vehicle until it disappeared around the corner and heard him toot 'goodbye'. Then all was silent. In fact, so silent, it was as if the world held its breath and waited to see what I would do next.

I stood there for a while longer looking at the empty road, feeling numb. The previous night's passion had awakened unexamined feelings in me, and yet, here was Dan, driving off, seemingly without a care in the world, nor acknowledging any subtle shift in our relationship. Sighing deeply, I turned and walked back to the cottage. As I did so, I heard increasing birdsong, the distant barking of a dog and, from inside the pub, Brian instructing Janet to lay the tables for lunch.

# 2

The weather during that first week in The Olde Smithy was changeable: high winds and lashing rain one minute; sudden stillness and stubborn drizzle the next. I tackled the kitchen and cleaned the old units as best I could. What I originally thought was a slate floor transformed into terracotta tiles. The walls and ceiling, filthy with grime, scrubbed up a treat with a good deal of elbow grease and sugar soap. Taking a breather, I stood back and surveyed my work, deciding it would be fun to search for replacement, free-standing furniture from the numerous reclamation yards and auction houses around.

On the Saturday I caught the bus into Bridport where an obviously popular street market was in full swing. To my joy, I discovered a stall selling soft furnishings. I spent half an hour rummaging through the pretty fabric and finally purchased two pairs of matching dusky blue curtains, embroidered with lighter blue entwining foliage. I knew that after some nifty alterations these would be ideal for the sitting and dining room windows. Then I visited the hardware stall and bought two large cans of white emulsion, a selection of paintbrushes and a roller. On my way back to the bus stop, heavily laden with my purchases, I stopped at a newsagent and picked up a local paper.

For the next four days I concentrated on painting the kitchen and by the end of that first week it was bright and welcoming, even if the cabinets were not exactly my style. And all the while a pair of almond-shaped eyes watched me curiously from the safety of the outhouse, poised to flee into the garden at the first sign of any perceived threat.

I'd noticed the cat drink from puddles formed between the uneven stones of the courtyard floor. It was an excellent hunter and obviously not going hungry; several forays into the garden resulted in a triumphant return with a mouse. The weather was atrocious that week and, coupled with the fact I was busy decorating, I didn't venture out into the village at all, so was unable to make enquiries about the cat. However, I did ask the postman if he knew whose it was, but he simply shook his head.

'I've only just taken over the Walditch round,' he said. 'Not sure where everyone lives yet, let alone their pets.'

I explained I didn't think it was a stray as it was in such good condition, but maybe it belonged to people new to the area and was disorientated and lost. Personally, I thought it looked as if it knew exactly what it was about. The postman promised he would report back if he heard anything.

During a brief respite in the weather, I put aside scrubbing brushes and sneaked out to the potting shed to investigate further. The door to the outhouse was permanently ajar, hanging off one rusty hinge. Slowly and quietly, I neared the open door and peered in. The interior was extremely dark – the only window filthy from years of grime and cobwebs – and I blinked as my eyes grew accustomed to the gloom.

A rusting wheelbarrow stood propped against the far wall and a wooden workbench under the window housed a large selection of pots, seed trays and two watering cans that had seen better days. Stacked against the opposite wall were several old gardening tools and beside these was a pile of empty compost and manure bags. On close scrutiny I saw the tell-tale indentation, approximately young adult cat size.

'Aha! So this is where you sleep.'

I returned to the kitchen. Grabbing a bowl from the drainer, I filled it with sliced chicken from the fridge and returned to the outhouse, placing the dish by the side of the sacks. As I left the outhouse I glanced into the garden, but there was no movement amongst the long grass.

I'm going to call you Storm. After all, the cat had appeared the morning after the howling gales during that first night in the cottage.

Dan phoned the following Friday to see how I was settling in. It was good to hear his voice. He was light and cheerful and chatted happily about his imminent departure for deepest, darkest Wales where he was to film a documentary about the poet Dylan Thomas. Not once did he make any reference to our night of passion. Stubbornly, I determined it was not going to be me to broach the subject but I was surprised at how wrong-footed I felt when he finally bade me farewell without a murmur.

My sister, Mo, texted from Morocco where she was on a magazine shoot, something to do with the souks of Marrakech. She encouraged me to:

Go for it girl! Email soon. Mo xx

And my parents rang. They were as loving as always and showed interest in my plans for the cottage. I told them I was considering asking the landlord at the local pub if he required any staff. To my intense irritation, I was aware of the need to justify my decision by saying it would be a great way to meet people. They were warm and positive and, not for the first time, I felt fortunate I was a part of the life of such people.

And then, just as we were saying our goodbyes, my father advised, 'Enjoy the adventure, Madeleine, but don't stay in the wilderness too long.'

I said goodbye and replaced the receiver feeling incensed.

Wilderness? It wasn't some wasteland I'd come to. I wasn't on some escapist trip trying to shirk the responsibilities of my life. I had *come home*!

Letting out a groan, I stared at the phone in frustration.

A vibration in the air made me catch my breath. Slowly and seductively, the subtlest of warm currents swirled around my body, as if wrapping me in a loving embrace. I luxuriated in the sensation and was immediately filled with an excited expectancy and the strongest emotion – that of pure joy.

I noticed how quiet it had become and, yet, as I looked out of the window I saw the branches of the oak tree swaying wildly in the wind and a stray plastic bag tumbling across the green on a frantic journey from dustbin to hedgerow. Incessant rain hammered against the windowpane, but there was no sound at all. Slowly I breathed out, savouring the feeling. All at once, as quickly as it had happened, the world returned to normal and I heard the noise of a wet and wild afternoon.

I wasn't alarmed. I felt, somehow, blessed.

'Thank you!' I said, to whom I wasn't sure.

Maybe I was thanking the cottage for giving me such a sense of belonging.


Sunday, late morning. With a copy of the *Bridport & Lyme Regis News* in hand, I walked across the village green and entered the Blacksmith's Arms. Brian was emptying the glass-washer and hanging clean glasses in neat rows above the bar.

'Hello, young lady,' he said, looking over in my direction. 'And how are you surviving over the far side of the green?'

I laughed. It was all of a hundred yards, if that.

'One room decorated, only five more to go.'

'If you need help I know several trustworthy tradesmen. Just ask.' He closed the door of the glass-washer. 'Now, what can I get you?'

I sat at the bar and ordered a cider and ploughman's lunch.

'What I do need are some trusty wheels,' I said, opening the newspaper. 'Can you recommend any garages around here?'

Brian placed a glass of cider on the counter in front of me.

'Well, let's see. There's Masons in Bridport and Bartlett's out on the Dorchester road, though they can be a bit on the pricey side. Depends what you're looking for.'

'Oh, nothing flash. A reliable run-around.'

I glanced down the column of private adverts.

'Janet's cousin sells cars.'

Brian called over to the waitress who had served Dan and me the previous week. She confirmed that her cousin, Bill, had recently started supplementing his job as a mechanic by trading in second-hand cars.

'He'll do you a good deal,' she volunteered. 'He's on the industrial estate. It's easy to find. I'll give you his number.'

I thanked her and said I would give him a call. I also asked if anyone had reported a missing young, black cat and explained it was living in my outhouse.

'Mrs Tomkins next to you has Rex, the ginger tom,' Janet said. 'He's quite old now and doesn't go out much, but he'll probably be in your garden once the weather's better. I've not heard she's got a new cat. And the Evans family next but one to her have dogs and rabbits.'

'No, I've not heard of any new cats in the village, and I hear it all in here.' Brian grinned broadly. 'Sure beats watching the soaps any day.'

I laughed. 'Stranger than fiction.'

'You can say that again! There's not much goes on that doesn't get reported within these four walls. Why don't you put a poster on the village noticeboard?'

A sudden shout from the kitchen sent Janet scurrying through the swing doors at the side of the bar. A few minutes later, she reappeared with my ploughman's and set it on the bar in front of me.

As I buttered a thick chunk of crusty bread I glanced around. The pub had become progressively busier since my arrival. At the far end of the bar, half a dozen loud businessmen ordered a mainly liquid lunch from Janet, or so it seemed to me. An elderly couple sat at one of the tables by the fire with a map spread out before them, quietly discussing an afternoon's sightseeing. At another table, a young couple tried their best to deal with two noisy children determined to throw all their food on the floor. There were also several couples enjoying the seclusion of the private alcoves and I fancied these were clandestine meetings, snatched during brief lunch hours, with Brian the discreet overseer of their secrets.

The doors to the kitchen suddenly swung open and Brian's wife appeared looking harassed. 'Bri, love, can you come here a mo?'

Raising an eyebrow and muttering under his breath, Brian followed her into the kitchen. Their low voices rose rapidly and I concentrated on reading the newspaper advertisements. Presently he reappeared, red in the face, but instantly regained his bonhomie. I cast him a quizzical look.

'Don't ask,' he said. 'It's mayhem back there!'

It transpired the assistant chef had done a runner a couple of days before and hadn't been seen since. They were coping with Janet not only on waiting duties but also helping out in the kitchen as best she could. It was not proving easy and Vera was nearing the end of her tether.

Seizing the opportunity, I said, 'I'm considering part-time work. I had wondered about approaching you.'

He looked at me in amazement. Suddenly, in one swift action, Brian was on the lounge side of the bar and wrapping me in a huge bear hug.

'You excellent girl!' he exclaimed. 'How soon can you start?'

And so it was agreed. I would start that week, helping out behind the bar on Friday and Saturday nights with further evenings and lunchtimes as Christmas drew nearer, if I wanted them.

Feeling happy with the way things were shaping up, I finished my lunch and bade my soon-to-be colleagues goodbye. On the way back to the cottage I checked out the village noticeboard. There were the usual posters for coffee mornings, a new Pilates class starting up, mobile library and bus timetables, and a flyer announcing that there were still roles available for any would-be thespians for Bridport Amateur Dramatics' Christmas pantomime: *Puss in Boots*. But there was nothing about a missing cat.

On Monday morning I phoned the local vet's and the Cats Protection League and enquired if a black cat, aged approximately one year, had been reported missing. Nothing. The receptionist at the veterinary surgery suggested I brought it in to check for a microchip. She laughed when I said there was no chance as I couldn't get within ten feet of it, but I agreed to do so if the cat ever decided to trust me. I then phoned a number from an advert in the paper and ordered a trailer load of logs. A broad Dorset accent assured me I could expect a delivery within the next couple of days. Finally, I phoned Janet's cousin who described the various cars he had for sale and I arranged to visit him the following day.

That night I went to bed early and decided to read for a while. It was *still* raining. Window dressings had yet to be sorted for the bedroom and, as a temporary measure,

I'd pegged bath towels over the curtain rails. The towel at the window overlooking the courtyard billowed as gusts of wind and rain found the gap in the ill-fitting casement. Despite my improvisations, it was a comfortable room built within the eaves of the cottage and I was just thinking how cosy it looked in the glow of the bedside lamp when I heard a thud downstairs. Had a window or door worked itself loose in a draught? I strained, listening further, but all was silent.

I got out of bed and threw on a dressing gown, switched on the landing light and went downstairs. I checked every door and window but all were secure. Where had the noise come from? Telling myself these old cottages were prone to strange creaking sounds and groans – and ignoring the voice in my head that asked, *but a definite thud?* – I made a mug of tea and was on my way up to bed when I happened to glance over at the inglenook fireplace. On the day I moved in Dan had swept the fireplace clean, leaving it neat and tidy, but on the hearth there now stood a stone.

'How did you get there?' I said out loud.

Sure, the wind was strong, but it must have been one almighty gust to dislodge that.

I placed the mug on the table and walked towards the hearth. The opening to the hidden alcove appeared larger and, on closer inspection, I discovered the stone had dislodged from its entrance. I stood looking at it, trying to work out where a gust of wind might have come from. Was the chimney faulty? The wood-burning stove obviously had a flue going up the chimney stack. Possibly, the bread oven/furnace had a separate flue.

As I stood pondering, I had an overwhelming urge to

put my hand inside the opening and, before I knew it, once again my fingers searched the floor of the alcove. Each time I was in the sitting room I was drawn to the bread oven but, as on that first morning, I discovered nothing – just dust and rubble. Unsettlingly, I noticed there wasn't the slightest suggestion of a draught coming from either the inglenook or the bread oven. I withdrew my hand. A chimney sweep or builder definitely needed to investigate further, especially if this part of Dorset was prone to the sort of weather I'd experienced since first moving in.

Replacing the stone in the opening, I picked up the mug of tea and turned to go. I had just reached the door leading into the hallway when I heard another thud. Looking over my shoulder, I saw the stone once again on the hearth. Despite my mind telling me there had to be a reasonable explanation, something to do with downdraughts and gusts, my skin began to crawl and goose bumps appeared on my arms.

'Oh this is ridiculous,' I said, more confidently than I felt. 'You can jolly well stay on the floor!'

Talking to an inanimate object... whatever next?

I marched purposefully upstairs, switched off the landing light and closed the bedroom door firmly behind me. Then, placing the mug on the bedside cabinet, I jumped into bed and pulled the duvet covers tight up around my neck, all the while trying not to notice the tremor in my hands.

The next morning the rain had stopped. I caught the bus into Bridport and found Janet's cousin on the industrial estate. Bill was chatty and the morning passed quickly.

I liked all the cars he showed me but the VW Golf won me over, being the newest and having the least mileage. I was assured it was 'one careful lady owner driver' who'd brought it in for him to sell. Silently, I thanked my late Aunt Aileen, my mother's sister, whose generosity towards me in her will a couple of years before made all this possible; not just the car, but the whole Dorset adventure. Once we'd wrangled over the price and finally agreed upon a sum that suited us both, Bill showed me to his office and proceeded to complete the paperwork.

'What's your address?' he asked, filling in the relevant car details.

I told him and watched as his pen stalled in mid-air.

'The Olde Smithy, Walditch?' he echoed.

'Yes. Do you know it?' I tried to ignore the odd expression on his face.

'My sister's friend rented it for a few months,' he hesitantly said, looking at me with wide eyes. 'With her son.'

Disconcerted by his stare, and for want of anything better to say, I asked, 'Were they happy there?'

He cleared his throat and started to write again. 'Only there a few months,' he said in a rush. 'How long have you lived there?'

'Not long.' He had stirred my curiosity. 'Why?'

'Oh, nothing.' The look on his face changed to one of embarrassment.

'What's nothing?' I asked, intrigued.

He stopped writing and shifted uncomfortably in his chair. 'Things happened.'

I froze.

'What things, Bill?' I needed to know.

He cleared his throat again and said, 'Um... said she heard noises. Felt she wasn't alone. Things like that.' He couldn't meet my gaze. 'Look, it was probably just her overblown imagination. She's always been a bit of a drama queen. I shouldn't have said anything.'

All at once the office felt stiflingly hot.

'Just going to get some air.' I waved towards the door and rushed outside.

The chill of the afternoon was a welcome shock to my senses. Of course there were noises; it was an old cottage. Everything could be accounted for with a logical explanation.

'Are you OK?' Bill called from behind his desk.

'Yes, I'm fine. I'll just complete the paperwork and be on my way.'

I couldn't wait to get out of there.

Nothing more was said about the cottage and we concluded the deal but as I got into the car and prepared to drive off, Brian knocked on the window. I lowered it.

'Don't take any notice of what I said earlier. My sister's friend is unhinged and can make a drama out of anything.'

I smiled and said, lightly, 'Cheerio! See you in the Blacksmith's maybe?'

'No doubt,' he replied. 'That Brian serves a good pint.'

Without looking back, I drove away as fast as I could.

# 3

Over the next couple of weeks I slowly wooed Storm. At first the cat refused to respond to my attentions despite daily bribes of food but, little by little, curiosity won over his wariness. By early November he was happy to come to the back door and eat but refused to come into the cottage and continued to treat the outhouse as his home. He was a handsome cat and I couldn't understand how anyone could have mislaid him or turned him out. I asked around the village but nobody knew where he'd come from.

Then, early one morning, I looked out of the kitchen window and saw him watching me from the outhouse door. There was a change in his demeanour and as soon as he saw me he got up and came to the back door. Not wanting to frighten him away, I opened the door quietly... and that was that. In he came, as if it was the most natural thing in the world and how foolish was I to think otherwise. He purred around my legs while I spooned cat food into a bowl and then he head-butted my hand as I placed the dish on the floor.

'Welcome, Storm!'

And, so, Storm came to live with me. It was as if he had

finally decided the cottage would be a far preferable place to spend the winter than the draughty old potting shed. I took him to the vet's but he wasn't microchipped. His future with me was assured.

Slowly, life took on a rhythm once more. I enjoyed working at the Blacksmith's Arms and was comfortable behind the bar, pouring drinks and chatting to the locals. Many of the regulars were true characters and, soon, dormant creativity began to stir. I was itching to start writing again. I also continued to work on the cottage. The previous owners had wallpapered throughout, as was probably the fashion during their time there. Painstakingly, I worked my way through the layers and made discoveries on a daily basis – like the imprint of another staircase in the dining room.

It was an exciting time and energy coursed through my veins. Storm took over the cottage completely and was often found lying on my bed when I'd forgotten to shut the bedroom door. Charming and cheeky, he liked to be involved in everything and amused me for hours jumping at the strips of wallpaper hanging from the walls. I was busy and happy and not at all lonely, even when Dan phoned and excitedly announced he'd met someone whilst filming in Wales.

'She's a freelance props dresser and has worked on loads of historical pieces. You'd really like her, Mads. She's such fun!'

I declined to comment on that.

'Where does she live?' I asked lightly.

'Bristol for the past four years but it's too parochial for her. She's wanted to move to London for ages to further her career.'

I snorted. So, she was already moving in on him and they'd only known each other just over a month. How naïve men could be...

'Careful, Dan,' I said. 'What baggage does she come with?'

He laughed. 'Usually just an overnighter.'

'You know what I mean.'

'I think there's an "ex" lurking somewhere, but she hasn't got any kids. She's great, Mads.'

I raised an eyebrow at Storm sitting in the chair by the inglenook, watching me. Trying to steer the conversation to another subject, I asked whether any of his contacts were looking for a freelance writer. He'd always been supportive of my creative side.

After a pause he said, 'Do you remember Colin, my old university pal? He's recently launched an "eco" magazine. I bet he wants "green" articles. I'll give you his number.'

Grabbing a notepad, I jotted down the details. I could tell Dan still wanted to talk about the girlfriend and, sure enough, before long the conversation came back to her.

'I've got to tell you, Mads, life's pretty good at present. She's so vibrant and full on. It's sugar for the soul. She's making an old man very happy.'

Old man? What was he talking about? Dan was a mere six years older than me.

'How old is she for God's sake? You haven't gone and got yourself involved with some Lolita, have you?'

'She's thirty-three, same age as you.'

At least I hadn't been thrown over for someone older.

'I just know you two will hit it off,' he continued enthusiastically. 'I really want you to meet her and I wondered if we could come down next weekend.'

The bombshell. Hell! How was I going to get out of that?

'I don't know, Dan. You see, I work Friday and Saturday nights now,' I said, feeling guilty at looking for an excuse.

'We'd be no trouble, Mads. We'll do our own thing and meet up with you when you're free. I really want you to meet – two of the most important women in my life!'

And so I met Lucy.


The following Friday night I was behind the bar, pouring a pint of bitter for one of the regulars, when the door to the Blacksmith's Arms opened and in walked Dan, looking slightly flustered, with a tall, leggy blonde in tow. He smiled at me sheepishly as he quickly covered the distance from door to bar. Introductions followed and I noticed how Lucy stood very close to him, possessively touching him at every opportunity. Slim and attractive, with a wide, generous mouth, she wore jeans and a short white T-shirt that exposed several inches of toned, tanned stomach. Her tousled blonde hair looked as if she'd only just got out of bed.

I was surprised at how easily the thought popped into my head; it was unlike me to be quite so catty. She possessed a winsome appeal which, instinctively, I felt was carefully manufactured, laughed easily – loudly and a lot – and appeared to hang on Dan's every word. She never left him alone and constantly touched his arm, his face, his hand, or fiddled with his hair. Inwardly, I groaned.

It was good that the pub was busy, as it provided me with a legitimate excuse to escape. I suggested they ate in the restaurant and if I hadn't finished my shift by the time they were ready to leave, they could go to the cottage and settle in. This pleased Lucy well. Throughout the evening I found myself stealing glances at their table. Lucy's laugh rippled across the restaurant and they appeared to have no end of things to talk about. Dan seemed enchanted.

It was an unusual situation for me. Dan and I had always enjoyed a casual, companionable friendship but, even though both of us had seen other people during the time we'd known each other, there had never been a 'significant other'. I felt Lucy's eyes boring through me a couple of times during the evening but I refused to meet her gaze. On the occasion she did catch my eye, her gaze quickly slid away.

They left at eleven.

Working the bar beside me, Brian commented, 'She's quite something, isn't she?'

I gritted my teeth and shoved back the fingers of jealousy threatening to choke me.

'Where did he find her?' he asked.

'In Wales,' I said, concentrating hard on stacking dirty glasses in the washer.

'What, up a mountain?' Brian laughed.

'While filming a documentary. She was on the props team, or something,' I said, avoiding his eye.

'Do I detect a slight green note, Madeleine?'

The grin in his voice did not go undetected.

'No chance!' I answered, slightly too swiftly.

He laughed out loud and I looked up smartly, feeling uncharacteristically vulnerable.

'Never a more interesting development in a relationship than when a bit of competition comes along,' he said. As he walked out from behind the bar to collect more empty glasses he looked at me and winked.

It wasn't as if I hadn't had my chance with Dan. We'd known each other for eight years and our relationship had never cemented into anything approaching solid. Surely, if it was going to it would have done so by now? I wiped the counter with extra gusto and tried to rid myself of an uncomfortable, unsettling feeling in the pit of my stomach. I sighed heavily. Ahead of me stretched two whole days with them. Thankfully, I was due to work the following evening.

By the time I finished at the pub it was past midnight. As I walked slowly back across the village green towards the cottage I noticed the light on in the guest bedroom. Before opening the front door, I paused. I knew Lucy's type and was sure she'd be in a hurry to let me hear how well she and Dan were getting on. I let myself in quietly. Dan sat on the sofa, idly flicking through a magazine. He looked up and smiled.

'How you doin' kiddo? You must be exhausted.'

'Oh, I'm quickly getting used to the pressures of being a barmaid,' I answered flippantly. 'As long as I keep moving, my feet don't hurt too much. It's very sociable.'

'Yeah, I could see that. Everyone wants you to serve them,' he replied easily. 'You've obviously made your mark.'

There was an awkward pause.

'Your hair's grown,' he observed.

During the time Dan had known me, I'd always kept my hair at a manageable shoulder length, spending many a minute studiously straightening out its natural curl. But, since moving to Dorset, I'd let it do its own thing. It was now longer and a mass of loose curls.

'It suits you,' he commented. 'You look softer. A true Irish country lass.'

I didn't know what to say. Commenting on my appearance was not something Dan indulged in. And, besides, I wasn't a 'country lass' – I was Dublin born and bred.

'Do you fancy a nightcap?' I asked.

Dan and I seemed out of synch.

'No thanks. I'm bushed. Think I'll turn in. It's been quite a week, what with one thing or another.'

He rose, stretched and crossed the few yards between us.

''Night, Mads.' He kissed me lightly on the cheek.

'Goodnight,' I responded, thinking how only a few weeks ago that kiss would have been directed at my mouth.

With a sudden sinking feeling, I knew sleep would not come easily that night. And so it was. I tossed and turned and kept checking the time, which, irritatingly, progressed only in ten-minute segments. I was hot and restless and the brief moments of sleep that I did manage to snatch were littered with strange images and shadowy figures... and somewhere a child cried. At around five, I gave up.

Without switching on the landing light, I tiptoed downstairs to the bathroom. As I reached the bottom step I had the strongest sensation there was someone else downstairs. Silently, I entered the dining room and glanced towards the open kitchen door. Lucy stood, naked, at the sink with a glass of water in her hand; her body silhouetted in the pale moonlight. She was oblivious to my presence and stared out of the window with a contented smile on her face, quietly humming to herself. I couldn't help but notice the long shapely legs and the lithe, feminine curve of her body, and a sickening knot settled in the pit of my stomach. I retreated and quietly opening the bathroom door, slipped in.

Two whole days!

By the time I emerged from the bathroom Lucy had gone. As I passed the spare bedroom door I heard low voices coming from within. I climbed back into bed and lay there with my mind racing, growing progressively hot and bothered. Eventually, I could stand it no longer. I got up and showered.

The day passed in a blur. Dan and Lucy appeared mid-morning, glowing in mutual contentment, and I busied myself making breakfast and fussing over their needs. True to form, Dan immediately made himself comfortable on the sofa while Lucy joined me in the kitchen. She talked with a light, carefree banter, but occasionally the mask slipped.

'Dan tells me you were the assistant director at Hawkstone.'

'Yes, that's right.'

Placing bowls and a selection of cereal packets on the kitchen counter, I rummaged in the drawer for spoons. Although moving out of the way for me, Lucy watched me like a hawk.

'Don't you find it very quiet down here?' she asked, her voice innocent. 'I mean, when you've been used to London and a life in the media circus, the charms of the countryside must surely wane after a while.'

'Not at all, Lucy,' I replied evenly. 'I can go to London any time but, to date, I haven't felt the need.'

I indicated that she should help herself to cereal and held up a box of cornflakes to Dan, knowing this would be his choice. He nodded. All the while, Lucy carefully watched the two of us. I poured cereal and milk into two bowls and carried them through to the sitting room.

'But what on earth do you find to do?' she asked, continuing her interrogation as she followed me into the room.

I handed Dan a bowl and sat down next to him.

'There's so much going on in the country,' I said, careful to suppress any hint of rising defensiveness.

The look on her face was one of complicity, suggesting she knew I was lying but was prepared to go along with it.

Irritated by her supposed superiority, I said, 'And people make time for each other, which isn't always the case in the city.'

'But being a barmaid must be so dreary after being in the centre of all the action on set?' she persisted, as she sat in the opposite chair and elegantly arranged her legs, knowing exactly the pretty picture she presented.

I sensed Dan's gaze appreciatively travelling up her long shapely limbs, following the toned curve of her belly, savouring the firm, pert breasts before finally coming to rest upon her face. I glanced at him and was taken aback by the lust and adulation in his eyes. But there was something else too; something unsettling. A madness that reminded me of the addict desperate for his next fix – only Dan's 'fix' was Lucy.

I glanced over at Lucy and immediately realised she was fully aware of the power she had over him. Panicked by what was unfolding, I spoke to her as if speaking to a rather dense child having trouble understanding a simple truth.

'No, I assure you, Lucy, I haven't found it to be so. There are so many characters in the pub and it's giving me plenty of material.'

Hearing the tone in my voice, Dan shifted uneasily.

'Mads is writing again, Luce,' he interjected.

With a fixed smile, Lucy studied me a while longer; her eyes cold and calculating.

'Well, I just know I couldn't survive down here in the sticks.' She beamed across the coffee table at Dan. 'I just have to be in London with my Danny Boy.'

As Dan smiled back adoringly, I wondered if I had time to reach the bathroom before throwing up.

Suddenly, I felt the need for wide-open spaces and suggested we went to Chesil Beach. Dan was instantly up for it, enthusiastically informing us that it stretched for more than ten miles from the Isle of Portland to Abbotsbury and, in places, stood as high as forty feet. Lucy looked dubiously out of the window at the grey, overcast sky and opened her mouth to say something. I watched dispassionately as she glanced at Dan and, quickly swallowing her words, feigned excitement at the outing.

The curve of the beach was magical and awe-inspiring. We walked a good way along the shingle bank that was separated from the mainland by a lagoon and Dan bombarded us with facts about the area. Lucy appeared to lap up his every word. Skittishly she ran round him, goading him to chase her across the pebbles. He willingly obliged. Dashing after her and catching her around the waist, he lifted her high into the air and swirled her around. Her laughter was light and flirty above the sound of the sea and the gulls, and Dan glowed in the attention she bestowed upon him. But it didn't ring true with me.

We stood for a while and watched a man and boy line-fishing from the shore, and were soon mesmerised by the crashing waves. The rain kept away until mid-afternoon, by which time we'd returned to the car, driven past the famous

Abbotsbury Swannery and found a teashop in the village in which to while away a couple more hours. It was hard going and I felt sickened by what was unfolding between the two of them.

That evening I left Dan and Lucy at the cottage and walked over to the pub for my shift. I was happy to escape for a few hours and felt comforted by the warm and hearty atmosphere of the Blacksmith's Arms.

'How are the two lovebirds?' asked Brian as I entered the pub. He was not at all gentle with my sensitive soul.

'Cooing nicely,' I replied.

He laughed and then informed me a table of twenty had booked in the restaurant.

'Vera's enlisted Janet's help in the kitchen so you and Gayle will waitress,' he instructed. 'I'll look after the bar.'

He had no idea what he'd asked of me; I was certainly no waitress. However, as the restaurant filled, soon I didn't have time to worry and I became immersed in the role.

The group of twenty turned out to be members of Bridport Arts & Crafts, out for an early pre-Christmas gathering as their tutor, a great-looking guy called Nick, would be in Australia over the festive period. They were a lively, cheerful crowd and teased me mercilessly for my non-waiting skills.

I did my best but had to laugh when Nick asked, 'What is it that you actually do, Maddie, 'cos waitressing certainly ain't your bag?'

I was attempting to balance precariously stacked plates while trying to prevent a wayward piece of cutlery from falling into his lap for the second time that evening. Deftly, he caught the fork and handed it back to me with a smile.

I muttered something about painting and decorating and that I could pull a mean pint.

'Ah, a girl after my own heart,' he said, looking very directly at me.

I felt myself blush.

'Oh leave the poor girl alone, Nick,' said one of the other men with a laugh. 'She'll drop the lot if you're not careful.'

I excused myself and hurried to the kitchen. As I went through the swing doors Brian caught my eye.

'Remind me not to employ you as a waitress next time!' he teased.

At eleven-fifteen the art group began to depart amidst much noise and with a great display of hugs and kisses. I was sitting at the bar, perched on a stool, chatting to Brian who had poured me 'a well-earned drink' when Nick approached to settle his party's bill.

As Brian processed his credit card, Nick turned to me. 'I hope I didn't offend you earlier over the waitressing thing.'

'Not at all,' I replied lightly. 'You're lucky to be leaving unscathed!'

Was it my imagination or did the sounds of the pub diminish and become suddenly muffled, as if coming from a great distance? And where had all the people gone? It seemed to me there were only the two of us in the room.

'You did a great job,' he continued graciously, his clear blue-grey eyes meeting mine. There was an amused glint in those eyes as he added, 'for a painter and decorator.'

I laughed good-naturedly.

There was something distinctly familiar about Nick. Perhaps he'd been in the pub on one of my previous visits when I was there with the film crew. The room beyond appeared undefined and out of focus but there was nothing whatsoever blurred about the man standing before me.

He hesitated… and I waited.

I noticed it all: the fall of his hair; the sharp cheekbones; the shape of his nose; the sensual lips; the set of his chin. And those eyes! I was mesmerised.

Reaching into an inner jacket pocket, he extracted a business card and passed it to me. 'If you ever need a carpenter just give me a ring.'

Instantly I thought of a hundred and one carpentry jobs that needed urgent and immediate attention. Aware that Nick's eyes were on me, I quickly thanked him and mumbled something about it always being useful to have a list of good tradesmen. He smiled.

Turning to Brian, he said, 'Great evening, Brian. Thank Vera for me. She did us proud.'

He looked back at me, smiled again, and then followed the last of his group out of the pub.

I peered at the card.

*Nick Corbin*
*Carpenter & Joiner*
*Bespoke service offered*
*Awkward corners a speciality*
*No job too small!*
*Mob: 07890 538264*

Deep in thought, I stared at the closed door. Suddenly aware of someone's close scrutiny, I glanced out of the corner of my eye and saw Brian leaning on the bar watching me with a huge grin on his face.

'What?' I asked, indignantly.

'I don't know,' he teased. 'You've got one bloke holed up at your place – admittedly with a new girlfriend, though it looks to me she might wear him out before too long – and here you are but a hundred yards away reeling in another!' He gave a deep belly laugh.

'I'm not reeling anyone in,' I exclaimed. 'As it happens, I *do* need a carpenter.'

Despite blushing furiously, I smiled at Brian and attempted to gain some control of the situation.

'Young lady, you have no idea what you're doing. And you certainly have no idea the effect you have on my customers.'

'I do know what I'm doing,' I countered in mock outrage. He arched an eyebrow. 'And the effect I'm having on your customers is, hopefully, encouraging them to come back.'

'Well, that's for sure. Takings were never so good when Bev worked the bar.' He winked at me.

I finished my drink, said goodnight to them all and walked back reluctantly to the cottage. Dan's car was parked at the edge of the village green. Apart from the porch light, the cottage was plunged in darkness, which meant that he and Lucy had either gone for a midnight walk or had retired to bed. I knew which option they would have chosen.

Slowly I climbed the stairs. As I passed the door to the guest bedroom, I heard deep, guttural moans within. Sighing deeply, I opened the door to my room and lay there wondering how I was going to get any sleep with all the noisy activity occurring just a few feet away in the adjacent room, let alone survive another day without losing my composure. I thought of the evening and couldn't help but smile as I recalled my performance as a waitress, and then I thought of Nick Corbin.

Who was he? Why did he seem so familiar?

As I recalled his face, particularly those blue-grey eyes, the bubbling excitement coursing through my body took me by surprise. I wondered if there was a Mrs Corbin and any little Corbins, and I berated myself for not checking if he wore a ring. It was something I never remembered to do but plenty of my girlfriends did, and it always seemed a very wise precaution to take. I sighed again, turned over and closed my eyes. Putting a pillow over my head, I tried to block out the noise, though I was resigned to the fact that sleep would not come easily. But the evening's stresses had exhausted me more than I realised and I was asleep in an instant.

It was some time later that I came to, disorientated, as the covers moved and a body cuddled up to me. Although the room was in darkness, I was aware of a swirling mist, and from the glow of the digital clock I could just make out Dan.

'You've got to be kidding me,' I exclaimed.

'Shhh! You'll wake her.'

He kissed my mouth hard and I felt his longing. Despite my confusion, my body rose to meet his and before long we were entwined as one.

'My love,' he whispered in my ear.

Dan was behaving uncharacteristically fast and loose; this was so unlike the man I knew. He nuzzled my neck, which drove me wild, and then a deep voice filled with emotion whispered in my ear. 'Come to me, my love. Come to me.'

I experienced the same thrill at hearing the intensity in

his voice as I had that first night we stayed in the cottage. But the words were not Dan-speak. I tried to focus on him, which proved near impossible as he had me pinned to the bed. As our passion rose, Dan's body felt more muscular and, once again, I became aware of his altered scent.

Suddenly, we heard a sound from the next room and Dan instantly rolled away from me.

In muffled tones, he said, 'I'll go to her.'

Yes, indeed, you go to her! It will be interesting to hear how you explain away your presence in my room to Lucy.

I lay back and considered what had just happened but an insistent cry from the corner of the room made me sit up. Thinking it must be Storm, I switched on the bedside lamp and couldn't believe what I saw.

In the corner stood a large, rustic wooden cot, the crying emanating from within. Vaguely, it occurred to me that I might be in the middle of a very strange dream. I climbed out of bed and walked cautiously towards the cot and peered in. A very red-faced, hot and sweating child – a boy, aged no more than four – looked up at me. Crying and whimpering, he stretched out his arms. Immediately, I was overcome with a deep sense of sadness and found it difficult to breathe. My vision blurred and a black tunnel threatened to engulf me. I called out, struggling to stay upright, but my legs gave way and I fainted to the floor.

Presently, I became aware of Dan lifting me onto the bed. Lucy, dressed in only a T-shirt, which I noticed showed off her long, shapely legs to perfection, stood behind him watching carefully.

'Mads. What is it?' His voice was full of concern.

'The boy, Dan. He's ill!'

49

'What boy? What are you talking about?'

I didn't know what to think. I was so distressed. Struggling to sit up, I looked towards the corner of the room but it was empty. There was no cot.

I burst into tears and sobbed, 'He's ill! He needs me.'

Dan sat on the bed beside me and gently stroked my hair, making soothing noises. Through my tears, I saw Lucy frown.

Without looking at her, Dan said, 'Luce, go and make Mads a cup of tea.'

She didn't look too happy at being given an order but obediently left the room.

'Hush, Mads, everything's OK.'

His hands were cool and soothing and I clung to him for comfort.

'Dan, what's going on?'

'I think you must have had a bad dream.'

'But earlier...'

'What do you mean earlier?' he asked.

'Earlier tonight. You and me.'

He frowned. 'What do you mean, you and me?'

'You came to me!'

'No, Mads,' he said slowly. 'I've been with Luce.'

I felt as if I was going out of my mind. Was he sleepwalking again? My body told me we had made love and, yet, here he was denying it. And what of that child? My heart was breaking. The boy needed me.

'Dan, we had sex,' I said.

His hand stopped stroking my hair. 'Mads, I've been next door all night. I think you've been in the throes of a very unusual dream.'

A sound at the door made him look up.

Lucy walked in holding three mugs of tea. 'I thought we all needed one,' she said flatly.

Feeling exhausted and so sad, as if I had lost something very dear to me, I started weeping again.

'Don't cry.' Dan placed a cool hand on my forehead. 'God, Mads, you're burning up!'

'Maybe she's caught a fever and is delusional,' Lucy added, unhelpfully. Dan frowned at her. 'It was only a suggestion,' she said, answering his look.

His attention once more on me, he said gently, 'Have a day in bed. We'll stay as long as we can.'

Immediately, Lucy said she needed to get back to London in good time but Dan silenced her with another look. At least she didn't have complete control over him... yet.

'If you're not feeling better by the evening I want you to book an appointment with the doctor first thing Monday morning. Promise?'

I nodded weakly. It was so like Dan to take control of a situation and ease things over. This was the Dan I knew so well.

'Now, do you think you can get some sleep?' he asked kindly.

I nodded again and he helped me into bed, tucking me in like a child. I noticed with some satisfaction that Lucy was not at all happy.

I drifted off into a fitful sleep and found myself in a dark, claustrophobic tunnel, desperately searching for something very important. But, try as I might, I couldn't remember what it was. Each time I came close to its discovery it turned to dust and I was left worrying, knowing that it was imperative I remembered what it was I was looking for.

I awoke mid-afternoon to find Dan at the bedroom door with bread and soup. Setting the tray on the bedside table, he sat on the edge of the bed and felt my forehead again, telling me he believed the worst of the fever had passed. He encouraged me to have some food and watched attentively as I slowly dunked the roll into the tomato soup and tried a few mouthfuls. I lay back exhausted.

'Mads, what you said earlier about us having sex…' He seemed truly uncomfortable. 'We didn't.'

'I can't explain it then,' I sighed.

'I mean,' Dan continued falteringly, 'we couldn't have. You see, Luce won't let me out of her sight.'

I gave him a long look.

'You're not complaining are you, Dan?'

'Hell, no! I mean she's great and we get on really well.'

I ignored the voice inside my head that said we, too, had got on really well.

'It's just, sometimes she…' He broke off.

'She won't leave you alone?' I volunteered. I was amazed Lucy hadn't already appeared at the door.

'Well yes, that. But, that's not all. Oh, this is kind of awkward.' He looked embarrassed and took a deep breath. 'Luce is extremely fit. I don't have the energy for anyone else.'

Dear exhausted Dan!

'Well at least you won't have to renew your gym membership,' I said dryly.

He laughed. 'That sounds more like my Mads. Are you OK now? We need to be on the road soon. Shall I let Brian know you're feeling unwell and ask him to keep an eye on you?'

I shook my head.

Although still reeling from the sadness I'd felt earlier, I put on a brave face. 'Don't worry about me. I'll survive.'

He leant forward and kissed me tenderly on the forehead. 'My sweet Mads.' His long fingers gently stroked my hair.

A clearing of the throat just outside the door announced that Lucy had been eavesdropping. 'Are you ready, Dan?' she called brightly.

'Coming!' He smiled down at me.

Lucy stuck her head around the door. 'It was nice meeting you, Mads, and staying in your sweet little cottage.' I cringed at her sickeningly patronising tone. 'But, darling…' she paused dramatically '…do take it easy.'

I was instantly incensed. I hated anyone calling me 'darling' – unless, of course, I was their darling – but especially by someone of my own age. She smiled at me, a false, sickly sweet smile, before turning and heading downstairs.

'Bye, kiddo, I'll be in touch,' Dan said, trying hard not to laugh.

'Glad you're so entertained,' I muttered through gritted teeth.

Bursting into laughter, he followed his girlfriend downstairs.

# 4

Christmas drew ever nearer and Brian asked me to increase my hours by working a couple of mid-week lunchtime sessions in addition to covering Sunday lunches. I was pleased to have the extra work as the recent experience at the cottage had left me feeling unaccountably bereft and unsettled. I phoned my parents and arranged to visit them in Dublin for a week over Christmas. It promised to be a sociable family event. Our family extended the length and breadth of Southern Ireland and the O'Briens knew how to celebrate. Mo, though, would not be there as she was spending the Christmas period with a boyfriend in New York. I was sad to hear this as I wanted to see her again, but I phoned her and she promised to visit between assignments early in the New Year.

'Are you OK, sis?' she asked before we said goodbye. 'You sound kind of flat.'

'I'm fine,' I said, in a falsely bright voice. 'It's just—' I took a deep breath and soldiered on '—there are some things happening in the cottage and I need to speak to you about them. Not over the phone, though.'

Mo fell silent at the other end. She was a very sensitive soul, which explained why her photography had a different, ethereal quality to it and her images often captured a unique vision compared to those of other photographers. Being a true Irish family, we children had been brought up on Ireland's various myths and legends and these had always resonated very deeply, particularly with Mo. We naturally accepted the fact that she was the member of our family who could tap into abilities that the rest of us did not possess. I wouldn't actually use the word 'psychic', but Mo saw the world we inhabited on a different level.

'If these things don't worry you then you're meant to be there,' she said carefully.

'They don't worry me, as such, but they are emotionally draining.'

'Has anyone else experienced anything?' she asked.

'Well, I've heard rumours,' I said, thinking of Bill's sister's friend, 'but Dan's stayed over and he's never picked up on anything.' I had already told her about Dan and Lucy descending on me.

'Probably because his mind's on other things,' she said in a gently sarcastic tone. I snorted. 'Can you speak to anyone about this?'

I thought of all the people I'd met since coming to Walditch and, surprisingly, Nick Corbin sprang to mind. But how could I talk to him? I didn't know him. 'I don't think so.'

'Oh why am I going away for Christmas?' Mo said in an exasperated voice. 'Such bad timing.'

'Because you really fancy Jeff?' I suggested.

'Well, yes, there's that!' She laughed.

'Don't worry about me, I'll be all right.'

'Look, Mads, if things get too much move into a B&B or

go stay with friends. I promise I'll come to Dorset as soon
as I can.'

'OK, Mo. Thanks. Oh, and don't do anything I wouldn't
do in New York!'

'Well, that leaves me with huge scope then.' She laughed
again.


Later, I drove into Dorchester and had an enjoyable
afternoon visiting various antique shops. I didn't find
what I was looking for but I did find something I wasn't
expecting. As I headed up the main street back to the car
park, I passed a passageway leading to a cobbled courtyard.
A board secured to the wall listed a selection of shops not
immediately obvious from the high street. Always curious,
I walked down the alleyway and discovered a collection
of interesting craftspeople: a glass designer, a potter, an
art gallery, a fabric studio and, in the far corner, a shop
selling pine furniture. I gazed through the windows of the
art gallery and decided that a picture on display would be a
fitting Christmas present for my sister Martha.

As I entered, a bell above the door announced my arrival.
It was bright in the gallery. All the walls and shelf units
were painted white and a number of mini spotlights drew
attention to the various pictures on display. Occasional,
strategically placed, large-leafed plants cleverly broke up
the white canvas. A smartly dressed young woman appeared
from the depths of the shop and I asked to see the painting.
As she lifted it out of the window display she explained
that the artist lived locally and was well known for her oil
paintings of Dorset landscapes but was now experimenting

with abstracts, such as this one, using an acrylic medium. I could already see the picture hanging in my sister's living room and so, without further ado, said I would buy it.

While the assistant wrapped the painting, I perused the interesting *objets d'art* on display and chose a small, bronze moon-gazing hare for my mother. Having paid for my purchases, I thanked the young woman and stepped out into the courtyard with my packages.

'Hello. I thought it was you.' The voice resonated with a soft Dorset accent. 'What brings you to town?'

I turned to my right. Nick Corbin stood in the doorway of the furniture store. My eyes took in the scene in an instant. He was dressed casually in jeans and sweatshirt, which I noticed were covered in a light dusting of wood shavings.

'Hi,' I responded, flustered.

He smiled. 'So what *does* bring you to town?' he asked again, eyes twinkling.

'I— I was looking for something,' I spluttered, my cheeks burning. Frantically, I hoped he didn't think I'd come into town to check him out.

He raised an eyebrow. 'And what *something* was that?' he teased, amusement tugging at the corners of his mouth.

I took a deep breath and tried to gain some composure. 'I'm looking for a bread oven door but none of the shops I've visited have had anything suitable.'

'You need to visit Jamie's reclamation yard,' he said. In the quiet of the courtyard I was again struck by a familiarity, but still I couldn't quite place it. 'It's just out of town. He always has a number of interesting objects. Come in and I'll find his card for you.' He turned and disappeared through the open doorway. Obediently, I followed.

The shop consisted of two interconnecting rooms. The smaller, front room was set up as a showroom displaying select items, while various pieces of furniture in differing stages of completion were stacked in the larger room. An intense smell of pine pervaded the air mingled with a vanilla scent, which I discovered emanated from half a dozen candles arranged on a large Welsh dresser. The space was light and airy due to the full-width window at the front of the shop. In the room to the rear, a pair of French doors opened onto a small, paved courtyard, in the centre of which stood a wood sculpture about four feet tall – an impression of a woman and two children holding hands and dancing in a circle. Beyond this, on the far side of the courtyard, I saw a further building.

Noticing my line of vision, Nick said, 'That's the workshop where all the sweaty stuff takes place. It keeps these rooms dust-free... relatively!'

He glanced down at the shavings covering his body and laughed, and suddenly I was filled with unaccountable happiness at the sound.

'Ah, here it is,' he said, rifling through a drawer.

My cheeks burned ever more fiercely as he handed me his friend's business card.

'Are you in a hurry or have you time for a coffee?'

'Coffee sounds great.' I placed my precious packages on the floor and concentrated hard on the business card. I frowned. It was unlike me to be so 'at sea'.

Nick smiled, his gaze lingering on me for a moment before he turned and walked through an open doorway into a small side kitchen. He either hadn't noticed the colour of my cheeks or had kindly chosen not to comment. From the doorway, I watched as he switched on a kettle, spooned coffee into a couple of mugs and produced a carton of milk from the fridge. I liked watching him; he was so easy on the eye. I hoped I wasn't staring.

'That's lucky,' he said, 'just enough milk for two. Must have known I was going to have company.'

I removed my jacket and, dragging my eyes away from him, hung it over the back of a chair and looked out of the French doors at the sculpture. 'That's beautiful.'

'Thanks. Glad you like it.'

'What wood is it?' It had a wonderful mellow quality.

'Yew. From the grounds of The Hyde, the care home in Walditch,' he explained.

I wondered if it had been modelled on anyone in particular and remembered I needed to check out the ring situation. He came into the room holding two mugs. As he handed one to me, I surreptitiously glanced at his left hand. Instantly – ridiculously – unaccountable relief flooded through me; there was neither a ring nor an impression of one.

Pulling up a couple of chairs, he invited me to sit. 'A couple of years back, a few trees came down in high winds in the grounds of the home,' he explained. 'They offered me the yew as they know I like to work with different types of wood.'

'Is it one piece?'

He nodded. Indicating to the furniture in the room, he said, 'I do this to pay the bills but my first love is sculpture.'

I was feeling ludicrously shy. Me, an Irish girl who had kissed the Blarney Stone several times during her lifetime! I searched my mind for something intelligent to say but I was falling prey to paralysing mental fog.

Thankfully he broke the silence. 'So, how's the waitressing coming along?'

I looked up and saw the merriment in his eyes. 'Brian's put me back behind the bar. Much safer.'

He laughed. 'It's obvious from your lilt you don't come from this neck of the woods. What's blown you our way?'

'A feeling,' I said, surprised at my honesty.

He looked at me curiously. 'A feeling? That sounds interesting.'

I found myself telling him about the months I'd spent filming in Dorset and how The Olde Smithy had spoken to me. 'It just seemed meant to be,' I explained. 'The whole process was so easy and before I knew it I was in possession of the keys.'

'Time to put down roots, maybe?'

'Yes, I think so.'

Glancing at the small amount of coffee that remained in the bottom of my mug, I wondered how long I could string out this serendipitous meeting.

'I've always lived around here,' Nick said without any regret in his voice. And then, exaggerating his Dorset accent, he added, 'Us Corbins go back centuries in these 'ere parts.'

'That's so nice, not having to wander the world looking for work but making it happen in your own county of birth.'

He considered me. 'And where were you born?'

I told him I'd grown up in Dublin and had followed my dreams into film and TV and this had eventually brought me to London. As the minutes ticked by, I became aware of a deep sense of well-being and a delicious peace settling upon my soul. The mug of coffee was long since empty when the phone rang.

Nick checked his watch and quickly rose to answer it. 'Didn't notice the time,' he said into the mouthpiece. 'See you in twenty.' He replaced the receiver and turned to me. 'I'm late and will have some explaining to do!'

Ludicrously, my heart sank. As he held out his hand for my mug I got to my feet and passed it to him, praying my face wouldn't betray me and give away my heightened emotions. I recalled the Bridport Arts & Crafts group had arranged an early Christmas gathering because he wouldn't be around over Christmas. To mask my disappointment, I asked, 'When are you off to Australia?'

'The nineteenth.'

Ten days.

'Can't wait. Visiting my brother,' he explained as he put the empty mugs in the sink. 'Now, there's a guy who couldn't settle locally. Moved to the Gold Coast as soon as he'd scraped together enough money. Been there ever since.'

I put on my jacket and, picking up the packages, walked towards the door.

Nick shrugged on a reefer jacket. Switching off the lights, he followed me out into the main courtyard and locked the door behind him.

It was past six and the other shops were in darkness, but an old-fashioned lamp post cast its yellow light across the cobbled yard. There was a brisk chill to the early evening air. I hunched deeply into my jacket and zipped it up to the neck. In companionable silence we walked up the alleyway and emerged out onto the high street where a passing couple stopped and greeted Nick. They chatted briefly, and the girl coolly looked me up and down. As they walked away, she linked arms with her male companion and looked back over her shoulder.

'Don't forget Greg's on Friday, Nick,' she called out brightly.

'I haven't, Becky. See you there.' Turning to me, he motioned to his right. 'My car's this way.'

'I'm in the car park,' I said, looking in the opposite direction. 'Thanks for the coffee.' Suddenly feeling awkward, and before I knew what I was doing, I held out my hand. He didn't accept it but simply smiled.

'Don't forget to give Jamie a ring,' he said, as he walked backwards away from me down the street.

I worked the following lunchtime shift. It was busy, and by the time I finished it was mid-afternoon. I walked back to the cottage and stood by the phone for several minutes, taking deep breaths and trying to calm my nerves. Twice I picked up the phone and punched in part of the number only to bottle out at the last minute. This was ridiculous. Quickly – before I had a chance to change my mind – I phoned the number printed on the business card, half-hoping there would be no reply.

'Nick Corbin.'

His lovely soft voice resonated deeply within me, and I tried to catch the thought frustratingly teasing my subconscious.

'Hello, Nick. Maddie O'Brien here.'

'Hi, Maddie. You got back OK?'

'Oh yes, thanks. No problem.' I had expected hesitation

while he tried to remember who I was. He had wrong-footed me again.

'What can I do for you?'

'I need a carpenter.' Immediately devastated at how upfront that sounded, I grimaced.

'Well, you've phoned the right number!' Once again, I heard the amusement in his voice.

My cheeks burned. 'I have a faulty window that lets in the weather and I'm also looking for a small dining table and chairs,' I explained in a rush. 'I was hoping to sort it before you depart for sunnier climes.'

'Four- or six-seater?' he asked.

'A small six if possible. If not, a four would do.'

'No trouble. I've got a couple tucked away out back. Good weight chairs too. I'll have to come out and measure up for the window and I could bring the table and chairs with me then. When's a good time for you?'

I paused, not wanting to sound too eager. 'Well, let me see. I'm working tomorrow lunchtime but any time after that would be fine.'

He said he'd visit as soon as he'd closed up shop and I explained where the cottage was. After he'd rung off I stood outside the back door in the courtyard to cool down. I'd been standing there for a few minutes, deep in thought, when I heard Storm hissing and growl a warning. When I'd walked through the kitchen he was happily eating from his bowl in the corner, but now he stood with tail erect and hackles raised, staring through the doorway into the sitting room.

'Storm,' I said soothingly. 'What is it?'

The growling turned more insistent. Entering the kitchen, I crossed over to the doorway and looked through. The room was empty but the cat continued to stare intently at the corner by the bread oven.

'What do you see?'

I moved into the sitting room and was immediately struck by the heavy silence. The room was shrouded in a fine mist and to my heightened senses there seemed a slight vibration in the air.

Who are you?

Once again, I was drawn to the hidden alcove. My fingers searched the oven floor and around the walls as far as my arm could reach. But, as before, there was nothing there.

'What are you trying to show me?' I said out loud.

As soon as I spoke, the room cleared of mist and the sounds of the world returned. Looking back through the kitchen doorway, I noticed Storm once again eating from his bowl. I perched on the arm of the chair, feeling irrationally deflated. I definitely needed to find out more about the history of The Olde Smithy. I shivered as I recalled Dan saying the cottage would give up more of its secrets as time went by. Sadly, I realised I missed him.


The following morning I awoke in high excitement. I worked the lunchtime shift at the pub, merely going through the motions with an increasing sense of anxiety. On returning to the cottage I tried to calm down, but by the time the afternoon drew to a close I was decidedly agitated. At around five, a van pulled up. Glancing out of the window, I saw Nick striding across the green towards the cottage and my heart raced. Taking a deep breath, I opened the front door and forced a smile. He greeted me casually.

'Come in,' I said, moving back from the door to allow him to enter. And there he stood, Nick Corbin in *my* hallway. I turned and he followed me into the dining room.

'I love these old cottages,' he said, looking around appreciatively. 'They're so solidly built and honest.'

I agreed, noticing he wasn't as tall as Dan and didn't have the same trouble with the beams.

'This is where I want the table to go.'

He nodded.

'I hope the one you've brought will fit.' Silently, I cringed. What a stupid thing to say.

'It will,' he replied, with a wry smile. 'But if you're not happy with it I'll make you another. After all, the customer is always right.' He looked across at the glass room divide. 'That's fantastic!'

Partly separating the dining and sitting rooms was a large internal window made up of small-paned, leaded stained glass; the different colours creating a subtle mood in each room. He walked towards it and touched it lightly. 'This is very old glass.'

'I don't know much about it but the estate agents played heavily on it in their sales particulars.'

'If you want to know more about its origins the glassmaker next door to me would be able to help. Pru has a wealth of knowledge.'

As he ran his hand gently over the glass I shivered involuntarily, imagining what it would be like to feel his touch. He glanced at me with a quizzical look. Quickly, I suggested we brought in the table and chairs from his van and, true to his word, the table fitted just fine. The seats of the solid pine chairs were smartly upholstered with a blue and cream striped fabric and I was pleased with the overall effect.

'Would you like a cup of tea or something stronger?' I asked.

Nick was carrying in the last chair from the van, a writing pad, steel tape and pen balanced on its seat. He set the chair down and glanced at his watch. 'Better not. I'm pushed for time tonight. I'll just measure up and see what I can do for you.'

I swallowed my disappointment. He followed me upstairs and I paused outside the bedroom, suddenly overcome with shyness. As I pushed open the door the bed loomed, mocking me; almost filling the room. Once again, I felt the start of a blush. What was happening to me? I was *not* this wilting lily.

'Great use of space,' Nick commented, as he surveyed the room cleverly created within the roof void.

'It is good, isn't it? I'm short of storage though.' Stacked against one wall were a number of packing cases filled with clothes, still looking for a home.

'You could easily fit a wardrobe under the eaves,' he suggested, indicating the far wall under the sloping ceiling. 'That would work. Now, which window is the problem?'

I pointed to the one overlooking the courtyard. He opened the offending casement and started to measure up, jotting down a series of calculations on his pad.

'It's great you've still got wooden window frames. So many of these old cottages have had the life modernised out of them.' He leant out of the window and strained, peering

66

up at the roof. 'This cottage was probably thatched at one point.'

'Do you think so?' I asked, savouring the fit, muscular outline of his body.

'You can tell from the height and pitch of the roof.' He came back inside and closed the window. Glancing at his calculations, he said, 'I can do one of two things. I can either shave off the inner edge of this frame; the two openers will sit snugly together then and keep out the worst of the weather for the time being. I'll pack out the hinges to compensate. Or I can make a new window frame, but I won't be able to do that until after Christmas.'

My thought processes were lightning-quick. If I asked him to 'make good' *and* have a new window frame on his return from Australia, I would have the excuse of seeing him before he departed as well as once he returned. I was about to ask him to do that when his mobile rang. He fished it out of his back pocket and glanced at the screen. Turning his back to me, he looked out of the window.

'Hi.'

Inexplicably, I felt agitated.

'No, I'm in Walditch. Shouldn't be too long, I'm almost done here.' He looked back at me and smiled.

That smile…

'OK. I'll pick up a bottle on my way back.' He slipped the phone back in his pocket. 'Sorry about that.'

I gestured it was nothing but my mind raced with a thousand questions. I was desperate to know who'd be sharing that bottle.

'So, if I come over Monday after work I can get you weather-tight?'

'That's great, Nick. Thanks.'

He followed me downstairs and I thanked him again for delivering the table and chairs.

'No trouble.' With a wry smile, he handed me an invoice. 'Now the painful part.'

I noticed the stylised writing and smiled to myself. Something about Nick reminded me of an older, more chivalrous era, and it came as no surprise that his characters were carefully formed, resonant of a time when these things mattered. I wrote out a cheque and handed it to him.

I said goodbye and stood watching from the door as he walked across the village green and climbed into his van. Why did he always make me so flustered? Sure, he was great-looking and, from what I could tell, his body was fit, but it wasn't as if I was some naïve little wallflower with no experience of the opposite sex. And what made me think that I knew him? Was it just me, or did he share that feeling?

As he drove away from the kerb Nick looked back at me and smiled.

# 5

Monday seemed an age away and so I decided to busy myself in the cottage by further exposing the oven in the inglenook. I searched the outhouse for a bucket in which to collect the stone and noticed Storm busy devouring a mouse at the back of the potting shed.

'And you always make out you're so hungry!'

I started working away at the stones around the already exposed entrance. The stonework was tight. I used a wallpaper scraper and screwdriver to dislodge the render, these being the only implements to hand, and as the minutes ticked by the stones began to work loose. By early afternoon there was a definite opening measuring approximately twelve inches square, and all the time I was aware of a curious, rising excitement. I stopped to make a drink and heard Storm scratching at the back door. As I opened it, he rushed in and dropped the remains of a mouse at my feet just as the phone rang. I was thanking Storm for my gift as I answered it.

'Hi, Maddie. Has someone brought you a present?' asked Dan's sister.

'Caro! So good to hear from you.' I reached across and

deposited the remains of the small rodent in the swing bin. 'Just the cat presenting me with an extremely mauled mouse.'

'Very thoughtful. Is that a delicacy in your part of the world?' She chuckled.

'I'm not that desperate yet,' I replied. 'The pub feeds me quite well, you know.'

We chatted for a while and she asked what I was doing for Christmas. She seemed relieved when I said I was visiting family in Dublin.

'I'll be back for New Year's Eve, though. Brian's asked me to work that evening. Double pay, which will be useful.'

Apologetically, she broke the news that Dan and Lucy were to celebrate Christmas with her and John. I experienced a sharp twinge of regret.

'How is Dan?' I asked. 'I hardly ever get a call from him now.'

'That doesn't surprise me, Maddie. We don't see much of him these days either and when we do I'm always shocked at how shattered he looks.'

I remembered what he'd said. Poor, dear exhausted Dan…

'Hope he's getting what he wants out of that relationship.'

'So far he hasn't complained, at least not to me,' Caro said, 'and John and he talk quite openly and nothing's been mentioned. But I do worry about the swiftness of it all, Maddie. It seems as soon as Lucy arrived in London she moved in with him, though Dan says otherwise.'

I groaned inwardly. This sounded permanent. Dan was always so protective of his space. Rarely had he invited me to stay over, even when we were in the initial stages of our 'relationship'; he'd always ended up staying at my flat. We changed the subject and she promised to visit me in the spring. We chatted a while longer before Caro wished me a Happy Christmas and promised to be in touch early in the New Year. Sadly, I thought of Dan and realised how fortunate I was to have had him as a friend and lover for all those years. How mockingly cruel hindsight can be; I hadn't fully appreciated how lucky I was. Lucy would ensure the distance between us now grew.

To rid me of these depressing thoughts, I returned to the bread oven and began to remove the debris from its base into the bucket. As I worked I became aware of a mounting feverishness and an hour later, having swept the oven clean, I stood back to admire my handiwork. I had discovered precisely nothing and was consumed by unaccountable, overwhelming despair and anti-climax. Sternly telling myself I should not be prey to these unchecked emotions, I found the business card Nick had given me and phoned the number.

'Strippers,' announced a rasping, heavy smoker's voice.

I made a small sound in the back of my throat. 'Hi, is that Jamie?'

'Aye. How can I help?'

I explained that Nick suggested I phone him and asked if he had any bread oven doors amongst his stock.

'Got a few. Just done a reclamation over Bockhampton way. Different sizes too.'

'That sounds promising. Where exactly is your yard?'

He gave me directions and I arranged to visit the following day.

It was raining again and the wind had picked up. With

nothing better to do I whiled away a couple of hours in the bath and, later, lounging around in my dressing gown, I made supper and watched television with Storm on my lap. There was little of interest and at around nine, having flicked through the channels several times, I decided to go to bed and read. Storm immediately jumped off my lap and rushed upstairs. And so we settled in my cosy bedroom, the cat curled up contentedly on the bed, the bedside lamp casting a warm glow across the room and the towel at the window billowing as ferocious gusts of wind found their way through the gap in the casement.

It was shortly after nine-thirty when Storm suddenly looked up and stared intently at the bedroom door with his ears pricked and alert; fur bristling. I laid the book face down, splayed open on the bed, and soothingly stroked him, but he shook off my caress. As he listened keenly, a low growl resonated from deep within his throat. The bedside light flickered and suddenly dimmed and I noticed the digital clock's luminous green numbers displaying 21:33. Despite the rain hammering against the windowpanes, I was aware of an impenetrable stillness lingering thickly in the air. Curiously, even though the wind still gusted furiously outside, the towel now hung motionless on its pole.

And then I heard them – footsteps on the stairs.

I froze. With heightened senses, I sat very still, every fibre in my body straining; my hearing acute. Who – or what – was coming up the stairs?

A sudden chill in the air made the hairs on the back of my neck prick and I shivered. As I broke into a cold, clammy sweat, my heart raced and I was aware of the blood coursing through my veins. Terrified, I held my breath and counted each footstep – six, seven, eight, nine… Who was out there and how had they got into the cottage? The tension in the room was palpable. As if in slow motion, I turned towards the door and braced myself, waiting for it to open.

But it remained firmly closed. Storm still stared at the door, growling quietly. Slipping out of bed, I stood at the door undecided what to do next, and held my breath, as I strained to hear any noise from the other side. Not a sound. I cast around for something that could serve as a weapon but nothing presented itself. Slowly and quietly I lifted the latch and inched open the door but I couldn't see anyone through the crack. I eased it open a fraction more. There was no one there. Walking out onto the landing, I switched on the light and opened the door to the guest bedroom. It, too, was empty. I made my way downstairs and searched every room. Nothing…

I stood in the centre of the sitting room and looked over in the direction of the bread oven.

'Who are you?' I whispered. 'What do you want with me?'

The silence was deafening. Whoever – or whatever – was no longer here.

I stood a while longer until the cold air nipping at my heels sent me rushing upstairs again. I had been downstairs all of fifteen minutes, but as I climbed back into bed I noticed the luminous numbers of the clock displaying 21:35.

'That can't be!'

Perhaps the bedside light had dimmed due to an interruption in the electricity supply. Maybe this had also stopped the clock. But then, surely, the digital reading would have reset to zero?

Suddenly the numbers changed to 21:36.

Storm was still on the bed, relaxed once more; his coat lying smooth and sleek against his body. I put out my hand and stroked him. He stretched, stood up, circled once and immediately settled, curling up with one paw over his face. Outside, it was blowing a gale and I noticed that the towel at the window overlooking the courtyard had resumed its billowing. I was still spooked and peered into the dark shadows in the corners of the room. Pulling the duvet up to my neck, I tried to concentrate on reading again.

I must have fallen asleep, as I awoke around three to find the lamp still on and the book open on my pillow. Placing it on the bedside table, I switched off the light and turned onto my side, nudging Storm with my feet to give me more room. He grunted his disapproval. A disturbed and dream-filled sleep soon came to me – something to do with Lucy, Dan and me – and when the alarm went off at seven, I woke exhausted and unable to recall any detail. It couldn't have been that important.

After breakfast I drove to Winterborne Monkton under a grey, overcast sky that threatened rain. The journey took me through stunning, hilly countryside between Bridport and Dorchester, past the old fort at Chilcombe Hill. At Winterbourne Abbas I turned off towards Winterborne Monkton, following Jamie's directions. Taking a road that skirted the hill with Maiden Castle at its summit – the largest fortified Iron Age hill fort in Britain dating back more than two thousand years – I turned right down a farm lane. After approximately five hundred yards, I rounded a corner and emerged into a yard surrounded by a magnificent range of stone barns nestling in a fold of the Dorset hills.

I pulled up alongside the only other vehicle in the car park – a battered yellow van that had definitely seen better days – and gazed at a sign hanging above an open door. 'STRIPPERS Salvage & Reclamation'. The yard was littered with architectural objects and as I picked my way through towards the entrance, an Alsatian suddenly appeared in the doorway. Silently, it watched my approach. I hesitated.

'Satan, come here,' growled a deep voice from within.

Satan… Great!

As the dog turned and retreated, I continued on once more and gingerly peered through the open door. The barn was enormous, open to the rafters two floors above, and crammed full of a vast array of salvage. Through the gloom I saw a man sitting at a desk against the far wall with the dog at his feet.

'Hi. Jamie?' I called out.

The man looked up. 'That's me.'

Approximately mid-sixties, he wore his long silver hair tied back in a ponytail. I smiled to myself — he wouldn't look misplaced hanging out with the Rolling Stones. Dressed in a pair of faded denim jeans, a black fleece jacket, woollen fingerless gloves and a bohemian-style scarf casually slung around his neck, he was well wrapped up against the cold of the barn. As I walked towards him I noticed the twinkle in the beady blue eyes that surveyed me from his lived-in, weather-beaten face. What was it about these Dorset guys? It appeared they all shared a secret joke. I explained that I'd phoned yesterday and was searching for a bread oven door. He motioned me to follow him through a doorway into another vast barn, again stacked high with reclaimed material.

'Don't worry about Satan,' he said, glancing at me over his shoulder. 'He's a pussy cat.'

I stared at the dog. It stared back.

'I only called him that to deter any overly interested visitors. It seems to work.'

And Satan did prove to be a real softy. Staying close, he accompanied us through the barns, his wet nose occasionally nudging me for attention.

I followed the man past neat rows of architectural salvage – paving stones, cast-iron baths, ancient wooden doors, old fireplaces – and then he stopped at a stack of slates and scratched his head.

'They're around here somewhere.'

As I followed him down a narrow pathway between the slates, a collection of stone gargoyles propped on low beams followed us with their cold, unseeing eyes. On reaching the rear alleyway, the man stopped and pointed to a row of old oven doors propped neatly against the rear wall.

'There's fancy ones and plain ones, little ones and large,' Jamie said in his gravelly voice. 'What size are you after?'

I explained it was an approximate twelve-inch opening and he pointed to a few that might fit. Leaving me to examine them on my own, he called to Satan and, unhurriedly, they walked back to the main barn.

One door immediately caught my eye. Adorned with a shield displaying three horseshoes and three nails, it was highly suitable for The Olde Smithy. I picked it up and turned it over in my hands. It was heavy and in good condition; the black-coloured lead hardly marked. I examined the other doors but there were none as befitting. I'd found what I was looking for. I spent a further half hour checking out the remaining salvage in the barn and knew this was not a one-off visit. Satan and I were to become well acquainted.

When I walked back into the main barn, Jamie was once again sitting at his desk with the dog at his feet. He was rolling a cigarette but paused long enough to clear a space on the desk so I could write out a cheque.

'So you know Nick Corbin then?' He studied me curiously as he ran his tongue down a length of rolling paper.

I felt a warm glow. Suggesting that I knew Nick made me feel as if I belonged to his inner circle.

'Yes. He recommended you.'

'Good bloke that Nick. Salt of the earth.'

I was ridiculously happy that this man should think so and enthusiastically agreed, even though I didn't have a clue whether Nick was a 'good bloke' or not.

The sound of a car pulling up and then voices, as doors opened and slammed shut, prompted Satan to get up from where he lay. Walking to the open door, the dog stood and looked out into the yard; obviously a favourite pastime. I thanked Jamie for the oven door and said I would be back. He nodded. As I walked towards the entrance he called to Satan to move away from the door.

The weekend dragged, despite working at the pub on both evenings plus the Sunday lunchtime shift. I was jittery and on edge and knew it was because I couldn't wait for Monday evening to arrive. Brian asked if everything was all right as I seemed distracted and I attempted to pull myself together and concentrate on the job in hand, but it was hard going. Janet's cousin, Bill, came in with his girlfriend on the

Sunday and was embarrassed to see me behind the bar. I put him at ease, assuring him that the car was running well and I was happy with my purchase. Not once did he refer to our conversation about the cottage, but I could tell it was on the tip of his tongue. At one point he took Janet aside and whispered something in her ear, and although she looked across at me with a quizzical expression, nothing was said.

That evening, still feeling unsettled and wishing the following day would arrive quickly, I had a light supper and retired early to bed. But sleep evaded me and I lay awake as my mind raced. I tried to steer my thoughts away from Nick, sternly telling myself I didn't know anything about him and, although he seemed a really decent guy, I should try and subdue my feelings until I found out more. Easier said than done.

My thoughts then turned to Dan and I resolved to phone him. Even if he didn't think about me any more, Lucy couldn't stop me from contacting him. This, in turn, brought me to thinking about Dan's friend, the eco publisher, and I made a resolution to contact him early in January to discuss the possibility of submitting 'green' articles with a Dorset bias. And then I heard them again and a shiver ran down my spine.

Footsteps on the stairs.

I glanced at the digital clock's flickering display – 21:33 – and, holding my breath, counted the footfalls. Six, seven, eight and nine... I looked towards the door, again half-expecting it to open, but of course it didn't. Switching on the light, I walked out onto the landing and looked in the guest room before going downstairs to check the other rooms. Nothing. Frantic scratching at the back door made me jump but it was just Storm announcing his return. He marched in, prickly with indignation.

'Sorry, boy. Didn't know you were out there.'

Ignoring me, he immediately went to investigate his bowl. I switched off the lights and climbed the stairs, unconsciously counting the treads as I went. I stopped on step nine and stood for an age, as shivers ran up and down my spine and the hairs on the back of my neck stood to attention. There was still one more step to go.

'Who are you?' I breathed.

But there was no reply. Not even a whisper.

Next morning it was raining *again*. Storm, having forgiven me for locking him out the previous evening, enthusiastically joined in with the decorating and chased strips of wallpaper around the room. I was working on the last papered wall in the dining room when the phone rang. Breathlessly, I answered.

'Hi, Maddie. It's Nick.'

My stomach somersaulted at the sound of his lovely, soft voice.

'Hope I'm not interrupting anything?'

'Oh,' I said, taken aback.

'Hoped you'd be home,' he continued. 'I've finished early tonight and wondered if it would be OK to come over now?'

'Oh!' I said again, and glanced at my watch.

'If it's not convenient I can come another time.'

'Oh!' This was getting ridiculous. Get a grip. 'No. I mean, yes.' Taking a deep breath, I reined in my emotions. 'It's fine.'

He laughed and my cheeks flushed as I heard the amusement in his voice.

'I'll see you in thirty minutes.'

I replaced the receiver and groaned. He must think me a gibbering fool. To try and calm my nerves, I returned to stripping wallpaper and it was some minutes later that it occurred to me I probably looked a mess. Downing tools, I ran to the bathroom and looked in the mirror. Great! Not only was I wearing a paint-splattered work shirt but also scrapings of wallpaper were stuck to my face and trapped in my hair. Quickly, I washed my face and was attempting to remove the scrapings from my hair when I heard a knock at the door. I pulled a face at my reflection in the mirror before walking out into the hall.

My nerves were all over the place and I felt sick. Taking a deep breath, I opened the front door as nonchalantly as I could. There he stood with mobile phone in hand, all bunched up in his jacket while trying to shelter from the rain under the small canopy above the front door.

'Hi,' I said, standing back to let him in.

'What weather!' he exclaimed, as he crossed the threshold. 'Can't wait to get to the other side of the world.'

I took his jacket, shook the worst of the rain from it and hung it on a hook in the hall.

'You've obviously been busy,' Nick said, scrutinising me.

'Yes, nearly finished. Come and see.'

Maddeningly, I felt the beginnings of a blush and quickly turned away. As I walked through to the dining room, he followed and placed his phone on the pine dining table.

'Looks like you're winning,' he said, looking around.

Seeing the impression of the other, older staircase clearly

outlined on the wall, he moved closer to investigate. Then, turning, he walked to the window overlooking the village green and looked back at the opposite wall.

'You know, the original doorway was probably here.' He indicated to the window. 'A narrow passageway probably ran front to back with these stairs leading to an upper room.'

'Do you think this is the original staircase then?' I asked, my voice hardly more than a whisper.

'Could be. They were much steeper in earlier centuries. It's only current building regs that demand a shallower tread. The original was probably little more than a glorified ladder.'

I stared at the nine risers clearly marked on the wall and rubbed goose bumps that suddenly appeared on my arms. The air about me turned thick and still. The world seemed to be holding its breath, full of expectation. Nick said something but I didn't respond. I couldn't hear a sound. He turned and looked at me. In the deepening afternoon gloom he appeared as that other man; the one I had seen when I first moved into the cottage. But, as swiftly as it happened, the moment passed. The light was simply playing tricks again.

'What are you going to do with the walls?' Nick was asking.

Quickly, I regained my composure. 'If they're good enough I'll give them a lick of paint, if not I'll plaster them. By the way, I saw your friend Jamie last week.'

'Did he have anything of interest?'

'Yes he did. Look.'

He followed me through to the sitting room. Storm was

curled up asleep in the chair by the wood burner, as yet unlit, and I watched as Nick gently stroked him. Sleepily opening one eye, the cat coolly surveyed the newcomer.

'Cracking cat!' he commented.

I'd propped the bread oven door against the wall beneath the opening. Nick now picked it up and, carefully turning it over in his strong, capable craftsman's hands, examined it with an appreciative eye.

'It's in good condition. I think this shield is part of the Worshipful Company of Farriers Coat of Arms.'

'Perfect for The Olde Smithy then,' I commented.

He agreed and held the door up to the opening. It was a good fit.

'How are you going to secure it?' he asked.

'Not sure. I can turn my hand to most things but I don't think my skills extend that far.' I glanced through the window at the pub on the other side of the green. 'Brian says he can point me in the direction of several tradesmen, so I'll probably ask him.'

Replacing the door on the hearth, Nick turned to me and announced he had better get on with the job he had come to do. I suggested I made tea while he did so and he agreed, telling me he took it white with one sugar. As I busied myself in the kitchen he disappeared upstairs. I heard him switch on the light in the bedroom and then curse under his breath. The next minute he reappeared in the hallway.

'Everything OK?' I asked.

Looking sheepish, he raised an eyebrow and said, 'Left my tool bag in the van.'

Fishing out a set of keys from his jacket hanging in the hall, he opened the front door and sprinted across the green through the rain. As I waited for the kettle to boil his mobile rang. I glanced out of the front window but couldn't see Nick anywhere, so I walked through to the dining room and picked up his phone.

'Hello. Nick's phone.'

Silence.

'Hello,' I repeated.

'Where's Nick?'

The voice was female and had a strong, local accent.

I looked through the window again but still couldn't see him. 'In his van, I think.'

'Tell him the travel agent's just phoned, will you? The flight's two hours early and we have to be at the airport by six.'

Irrationally, my heart pounded as I assured her I would pass the message on.

There was a long pause before she spoke again. 'What did you say your name was?'

I hadn't.

'Maddie. Nick's doing a job for me.'

Another long hesitation. 'Bye then.'

I replaced the phone on the table and walked back to the kitchen, desperate to know the identity of the caller. Distractedly, I noticed it had at last stopped raining. Was it his sister? It was feasible he was visiting his brother in Australia with family – I hoped – or was the caller his girlfriend? A guy like Nick couldn't be single. Despair and jealousy engulfed me at the same time, and I cursed myself for being a slave to such unguarded emotions.

A blast of cold air announced Nick re-entering the cottage, tool bag in hand, closely followed by a flurry of leaves. He looked windswept and I had an overwhelming urge to gather him up in my arms.

'Sometimes I think I could lose my head!' he exclaimed, taking the stairs two at a time.

I finished making the tea and slowly walked upstairs, trying to make sense of my emotions. As I opened the bedroom door I saw him on the far side of the room. Having unscrewed the ill-fitting casement, Nick stood bent over, the window frame between his legs, slowly and rhythmically shaving off the offending edge with a plane. I stared. The scene was strangely familiar. I noticed the length of his hair, his build, the set of his body, and shivered with a strong sense of *déjà vu*.

He was absorbed in his work and so I set the mugs of tea on the bedside cabinet. My conversation with the mystery female caller had taken the wind out of my sails and, feeling deflated and resigned, I sat on the bed and watched him as he worked. He glanced up. Seeing me observing him, he smiled.

My stomach flipped.

'Maddie,' he said, looking down at the window again and concentrating on his rhythm, 'do you have kids?'

'No, why do you ask?'

'I thought I heard a child crying.'

I froze.

'Maybe it was next door,' he suggested.

'Don't think so,' I said slowly. 'Mrs Tomkins is over seventy.'

He gave a small laugh and then glanced at me with a puzzled expression. 'I could have sworn...' The sentence petered out.

'Must have been the wind,' I said.

Straightening up, he tried the casement in the opening. 'That should do the trick, for a while.'

I watched him pack out the hinges. While he screwed them in place, I mentioned the phone call.

'Your mobile went off earlier. Hope you don't mind, I answered it.'

'Who was it?' he asked, without pausing in his work.

'She didn't give her name.' *She'd asked for mine, though.* 'Apparently your flight's been brought forward two hours.'

'Great! That means getting up at some ungodly hour.'

I was desperate to ask who she was, but how could I?

'There, how's that?' He stood back and surveyed his work.

I got off the bed and tried the catch. The window opened smoothly and, when closed, it sat snugly alongside the other opening casement.

'Thanks. Now I won't freeze all night.'

He smiled and I held out a mug of tea to him. As he reached for it, he inadvertently trapped my fingers beneath his. The bolt of electricity between us was astounding.

'Wow!' I jumped back and tea slopped over the edge of the mug onto the floorboards.

I started laughing nervously. Had he felt it too – or was it just me, the gibbering wreck? I tried hard to stop the hysterical laughter and, shyly, glanced at him. Momentarily, I stopped breathing. I'd seen the look in his eyes before… here in this very bedroom. He wasn't laughing, just looking at me in that way.

Awkwardly I said, 'Harness that if you will!'

I handed him the mug again. This time, he took it without

touching me and we drank our tea in silence. Nick quickly finished his and swiftly put away his tools.

'If you've got a brush I'll sweep up,' he offered.

'Don't worry about that. I'll do it later.'

The afternoon had long since turned to evening and it was now dark outside.

'Guess I'd better be going,' Nick said, checking his watch.

'How much do I owe you?'

'Nothing. It's a favour.' He looked at me with an inscrutable expression.

Suddenly I felt very sober. Nick would now be out of the country for at least a month and then who knows when I would see him again. Turning towards the door, I walked out onto the landing and heard him pick up his tool bag and then switch off the light before following me downstairs.

It was cramped in the hallway for two people to stand side by side and I was acutely aware of his presence. I took his jacket from the hook by the door and handed it to him. He appeared to be on the point of saying something but then obviously thought better of it.

'Happy Christmas, Maddie,' he said eventually.

'And you too, Nick.'

He smiled and indicated to the wallpaper scrapings still caught in my hair. 'By the way, I like the look.'

Reluctantly, I opened the front door and let him go out into the cold, wintry night.

# 6

I didn't see or speak to Nick again before he left for Australia. I was due to work the evening shift on the day of his departure but asked if I could cover lunchtime as well, as I was desperate for any distraction. I couldn't forget that shock of electricity between us and the look in his eyes. Pleased to have the extra help, Brian was more than happy to oblige. My imagination was working overtime and I had visions of Nick flying off to the wide open beaches of Australia with a devastatingly beautiful girlfriend, enjoying sun, sea and... I knew I was beating myself up, but I couldn't do anything to stop the thoughts. And to make matters worse the day dawned bright and clear, as if to mock my melancholy humour.

I was laying tables when Brian called me over to the bar.

'See that family sitting over there by the fire?' I nodded. 'The old lady's Mrs McKendrick. She used to own your cottage.'

I looked across to the people sitting at the table and noticed a petite, smartly dressed, grey-haired lady with delicate features. She must have been very pretty in her youth. She was flanked by a younger woman, who looked remarkably like her and whom I assumed was her daughter, and a man of similar age to the woman. Opposite sat three cheeky-looking boys, the eldest about twelve. They looked a decent family.

'Does she live around here now?' I asked.

'No. Lives with them.'

I studied Mrs McKendrick. The estate agent had informed me the previous owners lived in the cottage for over thirty years. Had she ever experienced any unusual happenings?

'Bet she misses her independence,' commented Brian.

As if she knew we were discussing her, Mrs McKendrick suddenly put down the menu she was studying and looked over in our direction. Brian immediately started polishing a glass and I busied myself repositioning the beer mats on the counter. The man sitting next to her said something to her and then called over, saying they were ready to place an order.

'Maddie will be with you in a minute,' Brian replied with a smile.

'Do you think she heard what we were saying?' I whispered.

'Doubt it. Not at this distance. Anyway, at her age her hearing's probably shot.'

I picked up a pen and notepad from under the bar and dutifully walked over to the group. As I grew closer I realised that Mrs McKendrick's prettiness masked her true age and she was older than she had appeared from a distance. She also seemed frail and I noticed a walking stick hooked over the back of her chair. As I took the family's order she watched me like a hawk, her pale blue eyes never once leaving my face, and when I turned to go she placed her hand on my arm.

'You live in the cottage don't you, dear?'

Assuming Brian must have said something, I replied that

if she meant The Olde Smithy then, yes, I did, and I'd been there just over two months.

'Mum and Dad used to live there,' said the younger woman.

I smiled and turned to the elderly lady. 'Where do you live now?'

'With my daughter in Winchester.'

'That's nice,' I said.

'The stairs got too much for her,' explained the daughter, 'and the boys love having their grandma around.'

I glanced at the three young lads, still at an age when they had time for the older generation.

'Grandma's wick-ed!' said the eldest boy, pronouncing the latter word as two definite syllables.

And not to be outdone, the youngest, aged about five, enthusiastically agreed.

'Grandma tells wick-ed stories.'

'How lucky you are,' I said, glancing at Mrs McKendrick and wondering what she thought of being described as 'wick-ed'.

Excusing myself, I took their order through to the kitchen and then returned to the bar and served a couple of walkers who had hiked over from Shipton Gorge. They said they were keen tennis players and that the owners of the B&B where they were staying had told them that Walditch had a real tennis court. They'd come to investigate. While I poured their drinks I gave them directions to the court and said I'd read that Henry VII had played at the site during his visits to the area.

Sensing someone's eyes on me, I glanced across at the family and saw Mrs McKendrick still watching me. I felt uncomfortable under her scrutinising gaze but she was probably just curious to see who now inhabited her cottage. After all, it had been her home for almost as long as I'd been alive. Presently, Vera shouted from the kitchen that the McKendricks' order was ready. I took their food over and, immediately, the boys started squabbling over which plate had the more chips.

'Just catch my attention if you want anything,' I said.

'Thank you, Mary,' replied Mrs McKendrick.

'Maddie,' I corrected with a smile.

She looked at me, her pale blue eyes seemingly addressing my soul. 'Yes, dear, whatever you say.'

I frowned and the man pulled an apologetic face. I moved away from the group, telling myself she must be a little senile and that was probably the reason why she had gone to live with her daughter and son-in-law. Nevertheless, I felt curiously unsettled.

The pub grew progressively busy and I served drinks to several customers and took more food orders before returning to the group by the fire. As I cleared away their empty plates, the boys studied the list of desserts with great concentration.

'Are you happy at the cottage, dear?' Mrs McKendrick asked.

I felt the question was loaded but didn't want to go into it, especially in front of her grandsons.

'Oh yes,' I said lightly. 'It immediately felt like home. But you lived there for so long you must have felt that too?'

'Oh no, Mary, it was always your home. We just looked after it for you.'

I was really confused and glanced at her daughter.

'Don't worry about Mum, she's a bit, um, unclear these days,' she said, choosing her words carefully.

The old lady clicked her tongue but said nothing. She gazed up at the painting hanging above the fire. 'You know that's your cottage, don't you?'

I answered that I'd guessed it was.

'It's always been a smithy,' she continued. 'This is it in the seventeenth century.'

'Not the *actual* smithy, Joyce,' interjected the man. 'An artist's impression of what it might have looked like at that time.'

I was instantly incensed by his patronising tone, but wondered why it was such a personal affront.

Mrs McKendrick tutted again. Ignoring her son-in-law's comment, she pointed to the man in the painting. 'And that's the blacksmith.'

Her intense gaze seared right through me. Contrary to what her daughter believed, I realised there was very little about Mrs McKendrick that was 'unclear'.

Following his father's lead, the oldest boy said, 'Grandma, of course he's a blacksmith. He's shoeing a horse!'

His brothers giggled.

'James, don't be rude,' scolded Mrs McKendrick's daughter.

'Come on, boys,' said their father. 'Make up your minds what you want for pudding. Maddie hasn't got all day to wait on you.'

I jotted down their requests and noted that the adults only wanted coffee. Then, having passed their order for desserts through to the kitchen, I returned to the bar to prepare the coffees. With my mind working overtime, I didn't hear Brian when he spoke to me.

'Penny for them.' Eventually he prodded me. 'Maddie?'

'Oh, sorry, Brian. I was miles away.'

*On a flight to Brisbane – amongst other things…*

'Yes. I can see that! Hope they're nice thoughts.'

Smiling grimly, I said nothing.

The McKendrick party left around two-thirty. As they prepared to leave, the man approached the bar to pay.

'Thanks for being so understanding,' he said in a low voice, jerking his head in his mother-in-law's direction. 'Joyce is a bit gaga these days. She can't walk very far but was determined to come back to Walditch before she becomes totally housebound. We thought it would be fun to have a family trip out.'

I glanced over at the group and saw the daughter helping Mrs McKendrick to her feet.

'I hope she enjoyed her visit,' I said.

He assured me she had. With a wink, he pressed a tip into my hand. I thanked him and watched as he returned to his family. The eldest grandson held out the walking stick to his grandmother and, linking arms, together they walked slowly towards the exit. As she reached the door Mrs McKendrick stopped and turned to look back at the painting. Then, slowly, her far-seeing, pale blue eyes alighted on me.

'Don't stop looking, Mary,' she called out across the room.

Her daughter mouthed 'sorry' at me and the younger boys giggled. As I watched the family depart, I felt inexplicably sad. What did she mean? Suddenly I felt very cold, despite the warmth of the pub.

'What was all that about, Mary?' teased Brian.

'I have no idea,' I said in a voice far stronger than I felt.

I phoned Dan later that afternoon.

'The Chambers' residence,' Lucy announced, in a ridiculously sophisticated voice.

I tried not to choke. Who did she think she was? She was at Dan's flat in Islington, for God's sake, not some country pile! I was incensed before I even opened my mouth to speak.

'Hi, Lucy,' I said, as calmly as I could.

'Who's speaking?' she asked in that stupidly false voice.

'Maddie.'

'Oh hiya, Maddie.' The sophistication slipped a notch. 'How's life in the sticks?'

My blood boiled but I refused to rise to the bait. 'Great! How's life in the big bad city?'

'Fabulous. I couldn't have made a better move.'

Having already run out of things to say, I decided to cut to the chase. 'Is Dan there? I'd like to speak to him before I leave for Dublin.'

''Fraid not, darling. He's away filming until Christmas Eve. We're spending the festivities with his sis. She's such a hon.'

I seethed. 'Perhaps you'd let him know I rang to wish him happy times.'

'Will do.'

Before I could say another word, the line went dead. No love lost there then.

# 7

The following Tuesday, having arranged for Janet to feed Storm while I was away, I drove to Exeter Airport and boarded a flight for Dublin with a suitcase filled with Christmas presents and a few clothes. I was happy and excited at the prospect of spending time with my family and I spent the next week luxuriating in being back in the fold. Being typically Irish, my family knew how to party and it was great craic. On a couple of evenings I caught up with old friends for drinks in and around Temple Bar and by the time I returned to Dorset on the last day of December, I felt both exhausted and rejuvenated.

I had a day to myself before going back to work at the pub and spent it trying to ingratiate myself with Storm, who was most put out I'd gone away and abandoned him. He was asleep on his favourite chair when I first arrived home and although he looked up when I came in, he'd since studiously ignored any attempt on my part to make a fuss of him. I unpacked my Christmas presents and set the fabulous peacock-blue glass mosaic fruit bowl that Martha and her husband had given me on the coffee table. Then I sorted out my clothes and loaded the washing machine with dirty garments.

As I stood in the kitchen I noticed the answerphone flashing. I half-expected it would be a message from Dan, but it wasn't. It was Janet informing me that Storm had been a breeze to look after and very friendly. Glancing into the sitting room, I raised an eyebrow; the cat had now turned his back on me. I sorted through the post that Janet had stacked on the dining table, certain that Dan's Christmas card would be amongst the pile of envelopes. But there wasn't one from him. Irritated that he'd forgotten me, I noticed with dismay that my feelings were also tinged with sadness.

The day passed quickly. That evening, I decided there was no time like the present to start making a list of contacts I intended to approach for freelance writing jobs. My generous parents had given me a laptop for Christmas and I now placed this on the dining table. Then, making myself a cup of coffee, I set to work.

During the afternoon Storm had forgiven me slightly. He now played with the catnip mouse I'd given him as a Christmas toy, flinging it around and noisily racing up and down the stairs. I closed the curtains and started to search the internet for Dorset-based magazines and newspapers. A short while later, out of the corner of my eye I thought I saw a movement in the sitting room behind the stained-glass room divide. I glanced out of the window overlooking the village green to see if an outside light could have cast a shadow in the room, but the night was calm; the boughs of the ancient oak still. How odd...

Returning to my research, I put it out of my mind, but a while later I heard Storm growl. Standing on the stairs, he stared intently through the archway into the sitting room with hackles raised. As I followed his gaze, once again a shadow moved across the internal window. There was an instant stillness in the room and a chill that made the hairs on the back of my neck stand to attention. Holding my breath, I strained to hear the slightest sound. Rising from the chair, I walked to the archway and cautiously peered around the divide. The room was empty.

'This is a new one,' I said to the cat, more confidently than I felt.

He blinked at me and started to play with the mouse again. I texted Mo straight away. I knew she probably wouldn't respond until after the New Year, as she was busy partying in New York, but I felt the need to make contact.

Hi Mo. What are you doing?

Surprisingly, within five minutes she texted back:

Following your advice – enjoying myself! What's up, sis?

I texted a brief outline of the latest twist to the unusual happenings in the cottage. I needed to talk to her face-to-face and asked when she could visit.

About fifteen minutes later she texted:

Sorry for delay. Diary hiding amongst Jeff's mess. He says greetings, lil sis.

Hmm... very familiar! I had yet to meet this Jeff.

Can visit UK 15–18 Jan en route to Geneva. Happy New
Year! Mo xx

I wrote the dates on the calendar that my young nephew,
Sean, gave me for Christmas – sweeping vistas of the West
Coast of Ireland – 'to remind ye of yer true home' he cheekily
explained, before ducking out of the way as I attempted to
cuff him. Feeling lazy, I popped a ready-made meal into the
Rayburn, lit the wood burner and settled down to watch
TV. Storm, having tired of torturing the catnip toy, joined
me in the sitting room and stretched out in front of the fire.
Nothing else happened that night to disturb the peace.

I worked the evening shift on New Year's Eve. It was just
as well because the pub was packed. Brian had booked a
local band and it promised to be a great night for all, even
me, although I couldn't help but wonder how a certain
person was celebrating on the other side of the world. But,
stoically, every time my thoughts turned in that direction I
told myself to focus firmly on the present moment.

'Nice to see you're back with us,' Brian commented with
a grin. 'I was getting worried about you.'

He squeezed behind me, holding several bottles of mixers
aloft, whilst attempting to fulfil orders for drinks at both
ends of the bar.

'Dublin's done you a world of good.'

I grudgingly acknowledged that I might not have been

completely present during my recent shifts but decided not to offer an explanation. It was fun working behind the bar with Brian. He was always so jolly, even when Vera gave him a hard time because she was stressed and run off her feet in the kitchen. They had hired a new assistant chef who seemed a nice enough lad, but he'd been thrown in at the deep end over the Christmas period and was still finding his feet. During the evening, I caught him muttering to himself and stealing copious cigarette breaks and I couldn't help wondering whether he would survive the baptism of fire and how long he would stay.

At around ten, a group of rowdy revellers entered the pub. Amongst them, I recognised the couple I'd seen in Dorchester the day I bumped into Nick. While the girls made their way through the crowd to find tables with a good view of the band, the guys approached the bar and ordered drinks. They were friendly and in high spirits and flirted outrageously while I poured their drinks. The girl I recognised, and now remembered was called Becky, approached the men unsteadily.

'Come on,' she said loudly. 'We're dying of thirst over here.' She eyed me curiously and I could tell she was trying to place me. 'Not causing trouble, are they?' she shouted above the noise of the pub.

I laughed and said no and that if they were Brian would soon kick them into touch.

She picked up the glass of gin and tonic I had just placed on the bar in front of her. Taking a sip, she looked at me slyly over the rim. I could see the cogs furiously turning. Suddenly her face cleared. 'I know where I've seen you before. You were with Nick the other week, weren't you?'

'Err, yes,' I said vaguely.

'Have you heard from him?' she asked, her eyes narrowing.

'No.' Instinctively, I felt she was being devious and wondered where this was heading. I moved away to serve another group at the other end of the bar, but when I'd fulfilled their orders the girl was still there. It was obvious she'd had a skinful and she must have thought I looked fair sport. I was trapped and couldn't escape.

'I had an email from Sarah the other day,' she said, with feigned casualness. 'Said the weather's amazing and they're having a fab time.' She paused to let me absorb this information, not once taking those calculating eyes off my face. 'Nick's brother's place is to die for, apparently. Right on the beach.'

'That's nice,' I said, politely.

'Sarah says they're both coming back with an all-over tan, dirty cow!'

I swallowed hard, acutely aware the girl watched my every reaction.

'She's so lucky being taken to Oz,' she continued. Waving vaguely in the direction of the man I'd seen her with in Dorchester, she sulkily added, 'Mark wouldn't dream of spending that sort of money on me.'

I mumbled something about fortunate people and she took one last punch.

'I think this is it, don't you? I mean—' she paused dramatically '—they've been together soooo long! I bet she comes back wearing a sparkler.' Waggling her wedding finger in my face, she broke into raucous laughter before swaying her way back through the throng towards her friends.

So there it was. The female I'd spoken to on his mobile wasn't his sister.

The rest of the evening passed in an unhappy daze. I smiled when people spoke to me and tolerated sloppy kisses from a couple of the regulars when we counted down the seconds to midnight, but the girl's comments rang in my ears. And when midnight eventually arrived I had trouble fighting back foolish tears. It would already be New Year's Day in Australia. No doubt, Nick had romantically got down on one knee at the stroke of midnight, their time, and proposed. I didn't even feel any sense of smugness when, towards the end of the evening, Becky was dragged out of the pub by her boyfriend and I saw her throwing up outside. I went through the motions, bidding customers farewell and wishing them a 'Happy New Year', and then Janet and I methodically cleared the tables.

A while later, Brian said, 'Go on, you two. Go home to your beds. I'll divvy out tips tomorrow. You've earned every penny tonight. Thanks a million.' Kissing us on the cheek, he waved us off the premises and locked the door. I turned to Janet and hugged her.

'I'm shattered,' she said. 'Not sure I can make it home.'

I gave a small laugh and pushed her gently in the direction of her house, all of five doors along from the pub. 'Happy New Year, Janet.'

As I walked across the village green towards The Olde Smithy I knew I was the loneliest girl on the planet.

I woke the next morning around eleven. I'd forgotten to shut the bedroom door and came to with Storm rubbing his face against mine, insisting he needed food *now*. I rolled over and groaned as the events of the previous evening came flooding back to me, but, surprisingly, instead of feeling desperate, I became angry. Why had I let the bitchy girl get to me so much? And as for Nick, well, damn him. I didn't even know him! How had I allowed him to get so deeply under my skin? And then I thought of Dan. Damn him too. After I'd left a message with Lucy, I'd expected him to return my call while I was in Dublin, but he hadn't. No doubt too tired keeping Lucy satisfied, I thought bitchily. And, so, I decided there and then that I had two options: either to wallow in self-pity or get on with my life.

'Come on, Storm.' I threw back the duvet and jumped out of bed. 'Let's have breakfast.'

I didn't have to report for work until the evening and wondered how to spend the afternoon. For some reason, I decided to walk over to Shipton Gorge. It was a grey, still day – as if the first day of the New Year nursed a hangover – and there was a chill in the air. Throwing on a waterproof jacket and scarf, I strode across the village green and turned right towards The Hyde Real Tennis Court. Storm thought it great sport and came with me part of the way.

Turning left before the court, I took a footpath following the valley around the curve of the hill that encompasses the village. About fifty yards further along the path I passed a couple of horse riders coming in the opposite direction. Storm decided this was far enough for him and a steady rustling in the long grass proved too exciting to ignore. He left me to continue on my own.

It was a picturesque walk and I carried on ever upwards. I hadn't walked in the area before but I'd often overheard customers in the pub discussing the various trails and bridle paths in the neighbourhood. The track, however, seemed oddly familiar. When it forked, I instinctively knew that if I took the right path it would lead me through a farm and on towards Burton Bradstock and that I needed to take the left route for Shipton Gorge.

As I walked, enjoying being out in the open air, I started to hum a pleasant, rhythmic melody with a distinctly old-fashioned lilt. Where had that come from? It wasn't a tune I recognised. The song persisted and finished with a flourish.

It wasn't far to Shipton Gorge, possibly two miles, but the path traversed Walditch Knapp and was steep in places, and by the time I reached level ground I was hot and out of breath. I removed my scarf and tied it around my waist before continuing my journey. On reaching the crossroads in the middle of the village, without hesitation I continued straight ahead. Where was I going with such determination? It was as if my feet were no longer mine to control.

Presently, I came to the fourteenth-century church of St Martin's. I paused at the lych gate and looked up at the tower with its elaborate doorway and smiled at the gargoyles as if they were old friends. I had the strangest sense of having been here before, but I had never visited Shipton Gorge. As I walked through the gate the size of the church confused me, though I wasn't sure why.

'This is all wrong. It's too large.'

I glanced around self-consciously and breathed a sigh of relief. There was no one about. I walked around the outside of the church with a growing sense of disquiet; it was only when I came back to the West Tower that the feeling left me. I tried the door, which was open, and entered.

The church had a wonderfully peaceful atmosphere and I immediately slipped into one of the pews and started to pray. It took me by surprise that I should automatically want to do so, as I hadn't prayed for years; not since attending the local Catholic school for girls in Dublin. Glancing around at the open framework to the interior, I looked up at the ceiling and noticed the carved stone corbels supporting the main timbers in the aisle. I was amazed by the size of the church. As I walked up the aisle, past the stone pulpit with its handsomely carved panel, and approached the font, I knew it would have seven sides. But how did I know that?

In bewilderment, I gazed at the open benches and wondered where the box pews and galleries had gone. Disorientation overwhelmed me. What was I thinking? Feeling foolish, and not without a certain amount of rising panic, I walked purposefully back up the aisle towards the entrance. On a table by the door lay several neatly stacked piles of literature about the church and the parish, and I picked up a pamphlet entitled, *A Guide to St Martin's*. Then, dropping coins into the donations' box, I walked outside into the cold afternoon air.

For a while I meandered amongst the gravestones, idly reading the epitaphs; some were ancient. And then, rounding the corner at the far end of the church, I stopped abruptly. A faint curtain of mist hung in the air and, through it, I saw a man carefully placing flowers at the base of a gravestone. A wirehaired terrier sat at his feet. I kept a discreet distance, respecting his privacy, but something about him drew me and I couldn't help but watch. Aged about forty, he wore his dark blond hair tied back in a ponytail, and it occurred to me he might be one of the actors in the local pantomime as his dress was so unusual: loose cotton breeches, long leather boots turned over at the top, a leather jerkin with large white scalloped collar and a short cloak slung casually over one shoulder. In his left hand he held a soft, felt, broad-brimmed hat.

The terrier remained seated but moved position constantly, in that busy way terriers have, but not once did it take its eyes from its master's face. There was something about the man's stance that I recognised. Was he a regular at the pub? Suddenly, an overpowering wave of despair swept over me and I gasped. The man turned in my direction and I stood rooted to the spot, at once consumed by embarrassment as I saw the utter wretchedness and helplessness shrouding him. And then I noticed his face, wet with tears, and gasped again. He appeared not to see me. His eyes scanned the graveyard and a frown formed on his brow.

My legs buckled from under me. Seeing me fall to the ground, the terrier stood up, stared intently in my direction and started yapping wildly, though I heard not a sound. I sat in the grass gasping for breath. That face! That dear, sweet face! A face so familiar, it was as if it were part of my very soul… and yet, try as I might, I could not put a name to the man.

After a while I found I could breathe more easily. Unsteadily, I clambered to my feet. The mist had cleared and both the man and the dog had gone. I looked around but there was no one about. I walked to the gravestone where he'd been standing; it was very old and fingers of lichen spread across its stonework. I tried to read the inscription but it was difficult to decipher. Ravaged by time, the elements had all but destroyed the letters carved into the stone, but there was a date – 1844 or 1644. I frowned. Why would anyone be so affected by such an ancient grave? I could just make out the letters 'e', 'm' and 'y' but whole words were impossible to read. Looking down at the base of the gravestone, I was surprised not to see the flowers the man had placed so carefully. Neither were there any impressions in the grass where the man and dog had stood.

At once, I realised my mistake. I had the wrong grave. I looked around for a newer headstone but couldn't find one. As I stood a moment longer wondering about the man, a great sense of acceptance and tranquillity settled upon my soul. I was exhausted by the bewildering emotions I'd experienced that afternoon and, yet, I also felt a deep sense of... What? What did I feel? Belonging? Release? I wasn't sure. I couldn't explain it but for some reason I was at peace with the world. All the irritation and sadness I felt over Dan and the bizarrely intense feelings and irrational despair concerning Nick didn't seem to matter a jot.

A few spots of rain made me squint skywards. Dark clouds had gathered from the north and I shivered. It was time to head back to Walditch.

'God bless you, whoever you are,' I whispered into the wind.

# 8

The next couple of weeks flew by and I was pleased with all that I managed to accomplish. I contacted various magazine editors and was encouraged by the number who asked me to send in freelance material, and I spoke to Dan's eco friend. He was keen for me to search out projects in and around Dorset and we negotiated a favourable deal. I also visited Bridport Street Market again and discovered a colourful stall selling country-style items and purchased curtains for both bedrooms, and – having finally finished stripping wallpaper from the downstairs rooms – I started painting the walls. I considered phoning Dan. However, still feeling piqued he hadn't bothered to contact me at all over the Christmas period I decided to leave it to him to make contact... should he ever find the time.

Mo arrived on the evening of the 15th January and I collected her from Exeter Airport along with several bags of camera equipment. Since embarking on her chosen career in photojournalism, there were very few countries she hadn't visited and she was stopping off in Dorset en route to a photo shoot in Switzerland. It was so good to see her again and she hugged me warmly.

'Wow, look at you.' She tweaked my long curly hair. 'Haven't seen you looking so soft and—' she searched for an appropriate description '—Irish, for how long? Years...'

I laughed. 'Well, hair does have a tendency to grow over the course of eight months.'

'No! Is that the last time we saw each other?'

'Yes.' I took her suitcase and started walking towards the car park. 'You visited me in London just before I went on location with that period drama on the Jurassic Coast. That was last May.'

She strode confidently beside me and I noticed several people glance in our direction.

'You looked very much the assistant director then,' she said. 'Wouldn't take any nonsense from anyone, let alone a mere star!'

I laughed again. Was I still that person, or had Dorset softened me out of all recognition?

Mo was just two years older than me. We had always been close, having similar attitudes and sharing the same sense of adventure. We also bore a striking resemblance to each other – though she was a couple of inches taller than me – and were often mistaken as twins. We had inherited our father's hazel-green eyes and curly auburn hair, which Mo kept short, saying it was easier to cope with on assignment. Martha, ten years my senior, was out of a different mould entirely, what with her sophisticated attitude, sleek black hair and piercing blue 'Paul Newman' eyes.

I'd lit the wood burner before leaving for the airport and by the time we arrived home, the cottage felt warm and welcoming against the bitter night air. Storm thought it was great fun checking out Mo's bags and had to jump on each one in turn, sniffing furiously.

'This is so homely, Maddie,' Mo said, as I showed her around the cottage. 'I can see why you fell in love with it.'

We carried her bags up to the spare bedroom and she sat on the bed looking around appreciatively. The guest room had been designed to match the main bedroom and it, too, was built in the eaves with some effective, newly aged, exposed beams. It had a charming country feel and the new curtains added to the cosy ambience. Leaving my sister to settle in, I went downstairs to the kitchen. I'd made chilli con carne earlier that afternoon and I now put this into the Rayburn, together with some crusty rolls. While I waited for Mo to join me, I prepared a salad and poured two glasses of red wine.

'Look who made himself comfortable on my bed,' Mo said from the doorway with a contented Storm purring in her arms.

I smiled. 'Well, you realise The Olde Smithy really belongs to him. I'm just here to open a tin or two.' I tickled him under the chin and handed Mo a glass of wine. 'How was New York?'

'Won-der-ful.' She strung out the word. 'Jeff took me to loads of parties and I made some really good contacts. We had a ball.'

Being an O'Brien, Mo could party like the rest of us. She knew how to have a good time.

I chopped tomatoes and added them to the salad bowl. 'So, this Jeff, he's cool, is he?'

'His Manhattan apartment is pretty cool.' She grinned at me. 'He's red hot.'

I laughed and drank some wine.

'In fact, he's so damn hot we had to spend hours in his Jacuzzi, and the view from there... I could have stayed there all the time and not seen any more of New York than its skyline!'

We had a great evening, chatting and catching up. I told Mo about the unusual happenings at The Olde Smithy and how meeting Mrs McKendrick had completely thrown me.

'Even though her family thinks she's going senile, I disagree. I believe she's far-sighted and knows something about the cottage... or me.'

Mo frowned. Eventually she said, 'If this cottage has anything to tell you, Maddie, it will. It will give up more of its secrets as time goes by.'

A shiver ran down the full length of my spine. 'That's exactly what Dan said.'

'It's true,' she said simply. 'These old buildings have been witness to a lot of life and if momentous things have taken place in them, well... Memories linger, and sometimes we who follow are privileged to learn of them.'

'But—' and I wasn't really sure what I was saying '—it's more than memories.'

'What do you mean?'

'I don't know,' I said in exasperation. I knew my next sentence would sound truly off the wall. 'Mo, I think I'm somehow linked to The Olde Smithy.'

She frowned again. 'Did Dan say that too?'

'No. I haven't discussed this with him.'

She looked at me and was about to say something, but hesitated. 'How is "Dan the man"?' she asked lightly.

'Who knows? The rotten sod hasn't bothered to contact

me for weeks. Obviously too knackered to pick up the phone or a pen.' It still smarted that he'd forgotten to send me a Christmas card.

'Must be quite a girl this Lucy.'

I'd kept her up to date with the Dan/Lucy 'thing'. I refused to sanction it with the term *relationship*.

'According to Caro, the minute Lucy arrived in London she moved in with him. She certainly wasted no time getting her feet under his table.'

'Or into his bed,' Mo said with a laugh.

But I didn't join in. I was still unsure how I felt about no longer having Dan in my life.

It was way past midnight when, having polished off a couple of bottles of wine, we retired to bed. I noticed Storm sneaking into Mo's room and just knew she wouldn't throw him out.

The next morning I was awake before my sister and made my way quietly downstairs. I didn't have to work at all that weekend, as Brian had generously given me time off when he learnt I had family visiting. It was a beautiful morning and it promised to be a good day. I was pleased the weather was fair as it allowed me to show off the area I had chosen as my home. Or had it chosen me? This part of Dorset offered many things to do, but I decided to ask Mo how she would like to spend the time. Floorboards creaked upstairs and I heard the guest bedroom door open.

'Mornin', sis,' Mo called down. 'One hungry cat coming your way.'

Appearing at the kitchen door, Storm immediately went to investigate his empty bowl. Indignantly, he looked at me.

'No point you looking at me like that,' I scolded affectionately. 'Traitor!'

He came over and walked around my legs, rubbing against me and trying to curry favour as I opened a tin of cat food. Presently, I heard Mo come downstairs to the bathroom and I started to lay the table for breakfast. About five minutes later, the bathroom door opened again.

'What do you want for breakfast?' I called out.

'Cereal and toast will be fine,' she answered. 'Just throwing some clothes on. I'll be down in a minute.'

I walked back to the kitchen and poured orange juice into a couple of glasses. As I carried them through to the dining room she appeared in the open doorway leading out into the hallway. I thought she looked pale as she stared back up the stairs with an odd expression on her face.

'Is there something you're not telling me, Maddie?' she asked slowly.

'Don't think so,' I replied, placing the glasses on the table.

'Who was that hunk I just passed on the stairs?'

The hairs on the back of my neck bristled and I noticed Mo was trembling.

'You saw someone?'

'Yes!'

'What did he look like?'

She looked at me strangely. 'Are you telling me, Maddie, you haven't got some dishy man stowed away in this cottage?'

I shook my head.

'Well...' She paused, searching for the right words and eventually settling on, 'Country.'

Instantly, I thought of the man I'd seen at the graveyard.

'What do you mean *country*?'

'Well, he was wearing rough clothes, like work clothes.'

'But what did he look like? How old was he?' I asked, the urgency in my voice shocking us both.

'It was so quick, Maddie, I can't recall exactly,' she said apologetically. 'He had a good aura though.' She said it as if, somehow, that made it all right.

I smiled weakly. Auras were important to Mo. I started to climb the stairs and she followed. I knew there wouldn't be anyone there but I had to check. Of course, both bedrooms were empty. I slumped down on my bed and looked at my sister.

'Why do you think *you* saw something?' I asked.

'No idea. But the figure was as solid as you and me.'

'I've started to keep a diary of all the things that happen,' I said. 'There seems to be a pattern.'

Sitting down next to me, she put her arm around my shoulder. 'That's a good idea, Maddie, but do you think you should uncover the history of this cottage?'

I nodded. 'But where to start?'

'How about breakfast?' she suggested, the colour returning to her cheeks.

We spent the day driving around the countryside and visiting several places of interest. I parked the car at West Bay and we walked along West Cliff to Eype, stopping for a light lunch at the hotel there. Mo took many photographs. Her trained eye captured some amazing shots along the way and I found myself looking anew at the vistas before me. We carried on down the coast by car and eventually arrived at Lyme Regis.

Being out of season, there were very few people about and we wandered around without the crush of holidaymakers that I'd been told often made visiting the town a trial.

And then Mo said she wanted to take photos of me on the Cobb, as my long curly hair reminded her of Meryl Streep in the *French Lieutenant's Woman*. As she directed me in various poses the professional photojournalist came to the fore. She had me looking wistfully out to sea or furtively glancing back over my shoulder, and at one point she draped me in her black scarf and ordered me to look into the camera with a haunted expression. She said all that was missing was Jeremy Irons.

A man walking his dog along the wall asked if I was a professional model to which Mo replied we were doing a shoot for *Vogue*. I thought for one moment she was about to invite him to join in, but, thankfully, she didn't. I couldn't stop laughing. Later, we browsed the various shops in the town and she said she wanted to buy something for me as a late Christmas present. At the back of an Aladdin's Cave we found a large mirror set in a beautifully crafted driftwood frame.

'This will go very well in your charming cottage,' Mo commented, as we placed the mirror in the boot of the car. 'Now, what shall we do for supper? I'm paying and it's not up for discussion.'

We found a little bistro in the town run by a gay couple who had moved down from London the previous year. They were great fun and we had a delicious meal with plenty of laughter thrown in. It was an easy, unhurried day, spent in good company.

Later, driving back to The Olde Smithy, Mo said, 'It's

been good spending time with you again, Mads. My work schedule over the next few months is chaotic, to say the least, and I'm so pleased we've caught up before it's fully under way.'

I gave her a smile. 'Will you fly back to New York at all?'

'Probably for my birthday, but not before. Jeff says he'll travel to wherever I'm based. One of the perks of being a high-flyer in the airline industry. Nowhere in the world is inaccessible.' She smiled at me.

'Is it serious, Mo?' I asked, casting a sideways glance.

'Not at the moment. It's party, party all the way. But who knows what the future may bring.' She laughed. 'But what about you, Maddie? We all thought you and Dan would eventually get it together. God knows he's been a part of your life forever.'

'Oh, you know us. We were so comfortable together there was never any urgency to do anything differently. It was only when Lucy showed up that I wondered if we hadn't been quite as clever as we thought.'

She nodded. 'So, have you discovered any new talent in Dorset?'

Instantly I coloured. 'Well, yes and no,' I mumbled, thankful it was so dark.

'Good God, Maddie, what does that mean?' She turned to look at me.

And so I told her about Nick and my instant feelings for him although they were going nowhere fast, due to a long-standing girlfriend being on the scene.

'Nothing like a challenge to make one inventive in pursuit,' said my wiser, older sister.

I shook my head. 'Not this time, Mo. No pursuit.'

'That doesn't sound like the feisty sister I know.'

I sighed. It seemed as if the weight of the world pressed heavily down on my shoulders. Life shouldn't be this complicated.

'He took his girlfriend to Australia for Christmas and New Year and his friends think he will have proposed to her out there.' Even to my ears I sounded morbidly dejected.

Immediately taking control, in a brisk, no-nonsense voice my sister said, 'Well, don't forget it's a big pond out there, Mads. There's plenty more fish.'

Trouble was, I only wanted that *particular* fish.


Sunday dawned, another beautiful day. We woke late and decided on a leisurely day. We tried the mirror in several locations, eventually choosing the hallway at the foot of the stairs. As I stood back to admire it I noticed the internal stained-glass window beautifully reflected, the different colours of the leaded panes turning the mirror into a work of art in its own right. I started preparing brunch while Mo walked around the cottage with her camera, taking several photographs from the village green and also in the back garden. Storm, her constant companion, put in an appearance in most. As I made coffee and toasted bread on the Rayburn hotplate, Mo lay on the sofa with the cat stretched out on top of her.

'This looks interesting,' she said, flicking through the pamphlet I'd brought back from the church in Shipton Gorge.

'That's the church I visited the other day; the one where I saw the man and terrier at the graveside.'

'Maybe we could visit St Martin's today?' she suggested.

'That's a good idea. The walk over Walditch Knapp will do us good after such a calorie-laden brunch.'

'Ugh, Storm.' She sat up and carefully removed the cat who was trying to lick her chin.

I checked the sizzling bacon in the frying pan.

'It says here,' she said, '*Visible from almost everywhere in the village, the fourteenth-century church of St Martin's stands on a small plateau on the south side of Brook Street. It retains its original fourteenth-century tower with an elaborate doorway but the remainder of the church was rebuilt in 1862, which more than doubled the seating of the old building.*'

A distant memory surfaced, as I recalled how I'd expected the church to be smaller. I tried to catch the thought but it eluded me.

She continued reading aloud, '*The architect was John Hicks of Dorchester for whom Thomas Hardy was then working – and the contractor, from a village of masons, was one of the Swaffield family. There has certainly been a church here for a very long time and the thirteenth-century font is unusual in that it has seven sides. There was likely to have been a partial rebuild in the seventeenth century, which added box pews and galleries. However, apart from the tower, the church was completely rebuilt in the nineteenth century.*'

I stared at the simmering baked beans in the saucepan; my senses sharp. Not only had I instinctively known the font would be seven-sided but also I'd wondered where the box pews and galleries had gone. What did it all mean?

'Storm, you're really cute but I've already washed!' Mo exclaimed. I heard her get up from the sofa. 'That smells good. How's it coming along?'

Shaken into the present, I called out, 'Two minutes.'

After brunch, we walked across the village green and turned right towards The Hyde Real Tennis Court. Mo thought the chapel-like building built of Dorset ham stone was beautiful and took several photographs.

'Apparently, it was built in 1885 to entertain the, then, Prince of Wales who was a real tennis fanatic,' I said.

'Has it always been used for that purpose?'

'No. It was a real tennis court up until the First World War and during the Second World War it was used as an army facility. Since then it's been a vehicle repair shed and agricultural building, or so Brian informs me.'

'Am I going to meet this Brian?'

'We could go to the pub for supper tonight,' I suggested.

She put her hands on my hips and spun me around. 'Well then, we'd better build up an appetite. Come on, race you up the hill!' Laughing, she set off up the footpath at a fast jog with the camera bouncing on its strap around her neck.

I followed in hot pursuit and was immediately transported back to our wild, carefree childhood days in Ireland. The younger O'Brien girls, 'peas in a pod' we were told; the world our oyster and the future stretching tantalisingly before us.

We stopped at the top of Walditch Knapp to admire the view and catch our breath. It was a fine afternoon and high cirrus clouds scudded in from the west. I played the historian, authoritatively informing Mo that there was reportedly a Roman fort above the village. We scanned the landscape looking for tell-tale signs without success. I also explained that the series of terraces along the hillside were known as lynchets and that these were the first signs of arable farming from prehistoric times. My sister was very impressed, but I couldn't keep it up and eventually had to admit that a local historian had visited the pub the previous week.

Presently, we arrived at Shipton Gorge. When we reached St Martin's Church, even though I now knew it had been rebuilt in 1862, I experienced the same sense of bewilderment as on previous visit. How altered the building appeared. As we entered the church, a couple of ladies looked up from their flower arranging and welcomed us in. The older of the two asked if I was the bride for the forthcoming wedding, for which they were dressing the church. I smiled and shook my head. We complimented them on their beautiful floral displays and said what a wonderful church to get married in. Leaving the ladies to their arranging, Mo and I walked around, quietly reading from the booklet I'd picked up on my previous visit. Again, it was very peaceful.

Once outside, Mo photographed the lych gate and the fourteenth-century tower in the winter sunshine, while I walked amongst the gravestones towards the area where I had seen the man. I clearly remembered he set flowers at the foot of a shiny new headstone, yet the graves at this end of the church were ancient. It didn't make sense. I looked over at Mo working her way along the rows of stones, reading the epitaphs.

'Some of these are so sad. Listen to this, Maddie. "*In Loving Memory of Miriam Bowden, born 21st January 1860, died 21st January 1884 and of her beloved husband William Bowden born 18th October 1856, died 8th September 1888.*" She died on her birthday and was only twenty-four.'

'Better for her husband to have passed only four years later than to have survived another twenty without her,' I commented.

As I spoke the words I turned ice-cold, as if someone had just walked over my grave. Briskly, I made my way to the spot where I'd seen the man and his dog, and glanced back at the angle it made with the church.

'I don't understand it, Mo,' I said, as she joined me. 'I'm sure this is the grave where I saw the man but there aren't any new headstones here.'

Grass grew long at the base of the stone, which leant at a precarious angle, giving the impression it would topple over with the slightest push. Together, we attempted to decipher the carved epitaph.

'I can see a couple of names here. I can't read the first one but I think this one says Elisa. There are some more letters so it's probably Elisabeth,' Mo said, pointing to the lower word. I shivered as she spoke the name. 'And the date is either 1844 or 1644. Are you sure this is the one, Maddie?'

I nodded.

She took a photo of the gravestone and we stood in silence, trying to make sense of it all. Behind us, the church door creaked open. I glanced over and saw the younger of the two flower arrangers emerging with a posy in her hand. She turned and headed away from us down the path leading to the lych gate. Quickly, I followed.

'Excuse me, but do you know if there are any recent burials in that part of the graveyard?' I indicated to where Mo stood.

'No. The recent graves are all on the other side. I'm going

there now. My grandmother,' she said, raising the posy she was carrying.

I thanked her and walked back to my sister.

'I don't understand it. There are no recent burials on this side of the church but this is definitely where I saw him.' I looked back at the stone and a thought came to me. 'Mo!'

The urgent tone in my voice made her look up sharply.

'When the man looked in my direction he didn't see me and yet I was only twenty yards away. I assumed it was because he was so distraught, but...' I faltered, not sure whether I dare continue.

'Go on.'

'What if he couldn't see me because I wasn't there?' I said slowly.

Uncomprehendingly, she gave me a puzzled look but then, suddenly, understanding dawned.

'And where are his flowers?' I continued.

Slowly she nodded her head. 'This is important, Maddie. You've got to find out what it all means. I have a friend who specialises in film enhancement. I'll see if he can clean up the photo and decipher the inscription.'

The last of the daylight was fading fast and, all at once, floodlights illuminated the church. In the gathering dusk we walked back to Walditch and by the time we reached The Olde Smithy it was nearly dark.

Later that evening I took Mo to the pub for supper. Brian was charm personified and the perfect host.

'I had no idea there was another stunner in the O'Brien household,' he exclaimed, as I introduced my sister. Mo laughed and graciously accepted the compliment. 'Now, what can I get you two lovely ladies?'

We ordered drinks and I enquired what Vera's 'special' was that night.

'Not Vera's, it's the "assistant chef's special" tonight. I've given Vera the evening off to visit her sister in Salisbury. Now there's a family lacking in the looks department, I can tell you.'

'Brian! That poor woman,' I scolded. 'You work her to the bone and in return she looks after you magnificently. She's given you the best years of her life. The least you can do is support her.'

'That's true, she certainly looks after me.' He patted his belly. 'Can't complain about that, but you must agree she's no oil painting.'

'You're a shocker and you don't deserve her,' I said.

'I know.' He laughed. 'She's too good for me.'

We sat chatting at the bar with Brian, and not for the first time I considered how lucky I was to have found this job only yards from my home. Being a Sunday evening, the pub was not particularly busy but a few people had ventured out. I was vaguely aware of a group entering the pub and moving to one of the private alcoves by the restaurant entrance.

We decided to risk the 'special', placed our orders and debated whether to eat at the bar or move to one of the tables nearer the fire. Suddenly, Mo leant forward with a conspiratorial look on her face.

'Don't turn around, Maddie,' she said in a low voice, 'but a guy over there keeps looking your way.'

I was itching to check. 'What does he look like?'

'Nice. Oh! You'll find out in a minute. He's heading over.'

She leant back and I watched her smile at the approaching man. The next minute I became aware of a presence beside me and heard a voice that was as music to my ears.

'Hi, Maddie. Thought it was you.'

I turned my head and there stood Nick, tanned and gorgeous, and my heart skipped a beat. 'Hello, Nick. You look well.'

He appeared happy and carefree, his blue-grey eyes seemingly all the more intense within his lovely, tanned, open face. He smiled and immediately butterflies took flight in my stomach. Suppressing them, and without missing a beat, I made the introductions. He shook Mo's offered hand.

'I thought you must be family. The resemblance is very strong.'

I was disproportionately jealous that my sister had actually touched him.

'How was Australia?' I asked, attempting to keep my rising emotions under control.

'Good. Very hot and over in a flash. It was great seeing Chris again.' Turning to Mo, he enlightened her, 'My brother.'

She smiled. 'I agree. It is good to spend Christmas with family, although I missed out this year.'

'We've been catching up over the last couple of days instead,' I explained. 'Quality sister time, but it's gone by too quickly. Sadly, Mo leaves tomorrow.'

I noticed his hair was longer and his fringe flopped over his eyes, making him look like a romantic smuggler. It suited him.

'So how do you like our neck of the woods?' he asked Mo, in that lovely, soft Dorset lilt.

'I like it very much. I can see why Maddie has fallen in love with the area and wants to make a life here.'

Had I imagined it or did this news make him smile? I was on edge and stole a glance to see if there was any hidden meaning to Mo's comment, but she was being sincere. It was just paranoia and my heightened nerves playing tricks on me.

'Then we are very fortunate indeed!'

He looked from Mo to me, the merriment dancing in his eyes. Infuriatingly, a blush started to creep up my neck and, inwardly, I groaned. He and my sister seemed so at ease. It was only me out of control.

'How's the window holding up?' he asked.

'Great. No draughts. Very snug.'

Damn! I shouldn't have said that. Now I would have to find some other job for him to do if I wanted to see him again. But in the next sentence Nick paved the way for further meetings.

'Glad to hear that, but it is only a temporary measure, Maddie.' He glanced in the direction of his friends. 'I'd better rejoin my table. Nice to have met you, Mo, and I hope you visit your sister again soon. Enjoy the evening.'

He walked away. Instantly, I felt the chill.

Mo sat gazing at me with a thoughtful look on her face.

'Who's he with?' I demanded. She didn't answer immediately. 'Mo! Who's he with?'

'Can't see who's sitting opposite him but there's a girl there.'

She wasn't giving much away.

The doors to the kitchen swung open and Brian emerged with our order. We decided to sit more comfortably by the fire and as we moved to the table, I took the opportunity to glance over at Nick's table and instantly wished I hadn't. The girl sitting next to him was equally tanned and he sat with his arm draped casually around her shoulders, chatting to whoever sat opposite. They looked comfortable and relaxed together. As I sat down at the table I noticed Mo observing me.

'Oh this is hopeless,' I said in an anguished voice.

'I don't see why.'

'How can you say that? He's with her!'

'Yes, and he needn't have come over to say hello but he did.'

She had a point.

'Tuck in, Maddie, and – as Nick said – *enjoy the evening.*'

I tried to swallow my disappointment. I so wanted to enjoy my last evening with my sister.

'Have you noticed that painting?' I pointed to the picture hanging above the fireplace.

As she studied it, surprise registered on her face.

'Maddie, that man,' she said, not taking her eyes from the oil painting. 'I swear he's the one I saw on your stairs!'

I looked up at the figure shoeing the horse as she turned and looked at me.

Seeing my expression, she added, 'You're not surprised, are you?'

I shook my head. 'It's obviously The Olde Smithy. Every time I look at the painting I feel as if I know the scene. I mean...' I paused, searching for the right words '... somehow I think I'm connected with the scene.' I pointed to the blacksmith. 'This man is very familiar to me and yet I can't place him.'

'Mads, you must discover the history of your cottage.'

I agreed.

We finished our meal, decided against dessert and ordered two Irish coffees. Brian brought them over and announced they were 'on the house', adding with a flourish that as the two best-looking girls in the pub that night, we'd earned the right to have a double whisky in each plus an extra dollop of cream. We laughed.

Presently, I became aware of Nick's table preparing to leave and, surreptitiously, I watched as the other couple emerged from the alcove. It was Becky, the bitchy girl who'd warned me off Nick on New Year's Eve, and her partner, Mark. The two girls happily chatted as they put on their jackets. The tanned girl, who I assumed was Sarah, looked to be in her late twenties and was of medium height and build. She wore her long blonde hair tied back in a loose ponytail and although not overtly pretty, she had a healthy, wholesome girl-next-door appeal. Envy consumed me; for her relationship with Nick and the legitimate time she could spend with him.

Dragging my eyes away, I met Mo's unwavering gaze. I groaned and pulled a face at her, watching as she looked up brightly at the approaching party. Mark passed by and continued on towards the door, but Nick stopped at our table and wished my sister a safe onwards journey. Then he looked me straight in the eye.

'Bye, Maddie. I'll give you a ring in the week to arrange a day and time to deliver the window.'

Deliver the window? I hadn't yet asked him to make a new one! We had only discussed the inevitability of replacing the temporarily patched-up one.

'Great,' I said, wondering if I had lost the plot.

Sarah, standing behind Nick, gave me a quizzical look as he put his arm around her waist and ushered her towards the door. As Becky passed by she glared at me, which made Mo laugh out loud. Momentarily thrown, the girl faltered but quickly regained her composure and pulled a face at my sister before hurrying after her friends. I sat there, a jumble of nerves, trying to work out what had just happened. Mo sipped her coffee slowly.

'Well, this certainly has been a most entertaining evening,' she announced.

'I'm glad you think so. I'm an emotional wreck.'

'Why?' She laughed.

'Because Sarah's got Nick and no doubt they're just about to get married and have lots of babies. In fact, they were probably discussing wedding plans tonight and that couple with them are their Best Man and Chief Bridesmaid.'

'Oh, Maddie, your imagination!' She set her coffee down on the table. 'You are your own worst enemy.'

'But it's probably true,' I wailed.

'Did you see a ring glinting on her finger?' she asked.

Damn, I hadn't looked. I was so hopeless at this and Mo was so together.

'No,' she answered her own question. 'The only thing I saw her wearing was one pretty fine tan.'

'All over,' I said dryly, remembering what Becky had been so eager to tell me. 'No white bits.'

Mo laughed again but I couldn't see the funny side.

'And what's all this about a window?' she enquired.

'Not sure.'

'Well, case closed!' Leaning back in her chair, she smiled

broadly at me. 'Be a good little Catholic girl, Madeleine O'Brien, and have a little faith.'

The next morning I drove my sister to Exeter Airport to catch her flight to Geneva where she was to join the rest of her team. Once she had checked in I found myself strangely tearful.

'Look after yourself, little sis.' She hugged me hard. 'That cottage of yours has an unsolved mystery it wants you to unravel.'

I nodded, unable to speak.

'And as for that gorgeous man…' She squeezed me tighter. 'What will be, will be, Maddie, but if I can give you a little advice based on my seniority—' she arched an eyebrow and pulled a mock-superior face '—have a little faith.'

She picked up her hand luggage and joined the back of the queue working its way slowly towards security. After checking through, she turned, smiled and waved… and then she was gone.

The day had not dawned clear and as I walked back to the car I noticed dark grey clouds ready to deposit their load on the earth. It suited my sombre mood. On the drive back to Walditch, I decided I needed structure to my day and formed a plan. I would visit the museums in Bridport and Dorchester as soon as possible and find out as much as I could about the village and the surrounding area. I also set myself a daily schedule of research, both locally and on the internet. Soon, my simplistic diary of unusual happenings at The Olde Smithy would grow to become a journal with more meat on the bone. However, as I became progressively

KATE RYDER

engrossed in Dorset's history, frustratingly little information came to light about The Olde Smithy itself.

The following Friday was a particularly cold day. I'd just lit the wood burner, made myself a mug of coffee and had planned an afternoon of research when the phone rang. Storm, lying in his favourite chair by the fire, stretched as the shrill ringing disturbed him from his slumbers. I walked to the kitchen and lifted the handset from its cradle.

'Hi, Maddie. Hope I'm not disturbing anything?'

A swarm of butterflies took to the wing.

'Nick!' I swallowed hard. 'Nothing that can't wait,' I added, attempting to sound cool.

'Just wondered if you'd got around to fitting that bread oven door?'

I looked through the open doorway into the sitting room and laughed. 'Nope, it's still where it was before Christmas.'

'Would you like me to come round and fit it for you? I could check the repairs on your window at the same time.'

'That's very chivalrous of you. Yes please.'

'How are you fixed next week?' he asked.

I explained I had started writing on a freelance basis so I'd be at the cottage most days. He sounded interested and asked what writing I did.

'General interest pieces with a Dorset flavour and also eco projects within the county. I don't suppose you know anyone doing their bit for the planet?'

There was a pause at the other end. 'Yes, as it happens. Me.'

'Oh, in what way?'

He described how he was in the process of renovating his

barn, the aim being to create a low-carbon-footprint home that was as self-sustaining as possible.

'That's exactly the sort of thing Colin's after,' I said. 'I don't suppose I could do a piece on it?'

'Sure. How soon do you need it?'

'Sooner rather than later.' The little white lie tripped off my tongue.

'How about this weekend?' he suggested.

I punched the air. 'You'd better give me an address and directions then.'

And so it was agreed that I would visit on Sunday, late morning.

'Look forward to seeing you,' he said.

Did he truly mean that?

I said goodbye and stood for a while taking it all in.

Returning to research, I became so engrossed that I didn't notice the diminishing light as the afternoon faded to early evening. It was only when Storm walked through the open archway between the two rooms to remind me he needed feeding that I realised the time.

'Sorry, boy, you're rather neglected at the moment.'

I made to rise from the chair but stopped. A fine mist hung in the air and then I saw movement on the other side of the stained-glass divide. I froze as a figure appeared in the archway and moved from the front to the rear of the cottage. I was aware that Storm mirrored my stance. Slowly I got to my feet, walked to the archway and cautiously peered towards the kitchen. There was no one there. As the mist began to clear, I glanced towards the inglenook, once again drawn to the bread oven. Was this the figure Mo had seen on the stairs?

I jumped as Storm brushed past. I followed him into the kitchen and noticed my hands were shaking as I spooned cat food into his bowl. However, Storm was, once again, behaving normally and clinging to the belief that animals possessed a sixth sense, I decided to use him as a gauge. Slowly, my heart rate returned to normal.

Walking back to the computer, I opened the file entitled 'Happenings' and noted the time. There was a definite pattern emerging. I described everything I had just witnessed. The figure was a man, aged approximately mid-forties, with a weathered face and shoulder-length, dark blond hair. His clothes were grubby: a shirt, possibly made of linen; loose buff-coloured trousers, equally in need of a wash; and he was wearing a pair of well-worn leather boots. As I typed my observations I realised this was definitely the man I'd seen at the graveside. My rational mind told me it was impossible and, yet, these events were happening. The figure was no fleeting suggestion or spectre on the edge of my vision, and I recalled Mo's words following her visitation on the stairs: *'As solid as you and me'*.

# 9

I turned off the road, as directed, drove past the main house and on towards the farm. Just before reaching the farm buildings I turned right onto a stone track. After another three hundred yards or so, the track rounded a corner and came to a sudden end in a circular parking area to one side of Ashton Chase Barn. Before me, nestling in a fold of the Black Down Hills, was a substantial, traditional stone barn with a cleverly added green oak extension to one end. I parked next to a silver Nissan pickup, switched off the engine and stared at the view. It was simply stunning. The land fell away from the barn in a series of terraces, still under construction, each enjoying uninterrupted views over the magnificent vista stretching as far as the eye could see to the coast and beyond. On an area of lawn immediately to the front of the barn, three dogs romped together in the morning sunshine.

I sat a moment longer, savouring the view, before reaching over to the passenger seat and picking up my bag and camera. As I opened the car door, one of the dogs looked up and started to approach. I hesitated. Sensing someone watching me, I gazed up at the barn. Nick stood at the open door, casually dressed in jeans and sweatshirt with a mug in one hand. He appeared happy and relaxed. The Weimaraner crossed the stone parking area towards me.

'Don't worry about Baron,' he said. 'He likes the fairer sex.'

'Well, that's a relief.'

The dog sniffed my leg and I gently stroked its silver-grey velvety head.

'You're a handsome boy,' I said softly, and the dog pushed his head strongly into the palm of my hand. 'You didn't tell me you had dogs,' I called out, and instantly cringed. I didn't know Nick. Why would he have told me?

He didn't reply but continued to study me.

I took a deep breath and approached the barn. 'This is fabulous.'

Baron followed closely behind.

Nick smiled and moved aside so I could enter. 'It's a work in progress. Hopefully it will be fabulous, but not yet.' Looking back at the two dogs still playing on the grass, he called, 'Casper, Tilly. Come.'

The German shorthaired pointer paused in its rough and tumble game with the Golden Retriever and responded obediently.

'Tilly, come!' Nick called again. 'My sister's dog. Tilly stays with the boys when Helen goes away.'

I smiled and gazed around the amazing space. An open-plan living area about fifty feet long, substantial oak beams rising to the atrium and floor to ceiling glass along the full front elevation created a definite 'wow' factor. However, he was right. It was, indeed, a work in progress and there was still some way to go before the finished product emerged.

'Would you like a coffee?' Nick asked. 'The kettle's just boiled.'

'Thanks.'

He walked to the kitchen, at ease in his surroundings, with the Weimaraner at his heels. The pointer settled down on a well-worn, brown leather couch as Nick's sister's dog disappeared through an open doorway to my left.

'Make yourself comfortable,' Nick called over his shoulder.

'How long have you lived here?' I asked, removing my scarf and jacket.

'Just shy of two years. I should have finished by now but work's taken up a lot of my time recently. Not complaining, though.' He opened the fridge door.

'It's a great spot,' I said, sitting on the couch next to the pointer.

'I was very fortunate,' he said modestly. 'Kate and Simon up at the house are good friends of mine. When they heard I was looking for somewhere to develop they offered me this barn with a couple of acres.'

*Friends indeed.*

'The planners needed a little more persuasion, though.' He approached with a mug of coffee in one hand and a packet of biscuits in the other. 'But once I'd explained my plans and demonstrated how low a carbon footprint the whole project would have, they soon rolled over.'

He laughed, that lovely soft sound, and my heart went into free fall.

Passing me the mug, Nick placed the packet of biscuits on a chunky wooden coffee table and invited me to help myself.

'I'd like to take photographs to accompany the article, if that's OK with you?'

'Good idea. It's a great day for photos,' he said. 'We can get challenging weather here, being so high up. It rolls in from the sea and sweeps across the valley, but this barn has withstood many a storm.'

I looked up at the glass atrium two floors above. 'Isn't it noisy in the rain with all this glass?'

'No, not noisy, more muffled. We've used two sheets of glass, seven millimetres thick, bonded together with a specially formulated resin for the atrium and glass roof panels. It dampens the vibrations and sound waves by forty per cent. It also blocks eighty-six per cent of ultra violet light and transmits sixty-six per cent of visible light. It also has very low solar heat gain, which helps to keep the barn cool in summer and indirectly warm in winter.' He smiled at me and then teasingly asked, 'Got that?'

I laughed. 'I have, actually.'

'I'd say the rain's more of a comforting sound,' he continued softly, 'especially when lying in bed looking up at the night sky.'

The thought of lying in bed with him! I couldn't meet his gaze and concentrated hard on suppressing the embarrassing blush that threatened to break out. Why did he have this effect on me?

'I'll show you around when you've finished your coffee.'

'I'd like that very much,' I said, quickly patting Baron who had come up looking for biscuits.

We chatted a while longer and I took notes. Nick told me he'd carried out most of the work himself with the help of a few friends in the initial stages. His idea was to sympathetically restore the barn using natural materials, where possible, with the ultimate goal a home as carbon-neutral and economical to run as was practicable. I loved hearing him talk. He was so passionate about the project. When he later showed me round, it was obvious that the craftsman in him had cut no corners and even the walnut dining table was lovingly created. It was a unique building and one that was being renovated with great integrity.

We started the tour on the ground floor and Nick laid out his vision for me. I took photographs and wrote furiously on my notepad, as I tried to keep up with his enthusiasm. It was a large L-shaped stone barn with enormous timber roof trusses and he explained that the doors I'd entered through were where the original threshing doors would have been. These had been replaced with glass panels set within a steel framework rising two storeys to the roofline – very contemporary and a *huge* statement.

'These doors face due south,' he explained. 'They're on the sunniest side of the barn so we've used tinted, toughened glass as this absorbs more solar radiation than clear glass.'

The large open-plan living space was divided into a study and living areas, all with oak flooring. A crisp slate flagstone floor defined the dining area and the bespoke kitchen units were also handcrafted from oak.

'The barn is warmed through under-floor heating, powered by an individual ground-source heat pump,' Nick continued, 'and both warm and cooling air is distributed around the property through an energy-efficient, whole-house system of ventilation.'

At the far end, beyond the kitchen, a door opened to what would one day be a utility room and downstairs bathroom.

A staircase led up to two guest bedrooms with large Velux windows that cleverly opened to provide glazed balconies, each taking full advantage of the glorious views down the valley to the sea. This part of the barn, still in the early stages of development, was designed so it could be used as a separate annexe, if required. The utility room doubled-up as a kitchen and one of the bedrooms would transform into a living room.

At the other end of the main living area, centrally situated between a door leading to the study and another accessing a large side porch with downstairs cloakroom, a beautiful wooden spiral staircase led up to the galleried area. As I followed Nick up the stairs, he explained it was made from the yew tree donated to him by The Hyde; the same tree from which he'd created the sculpture in the courtyard at his shop.

I was about to say 'I love yew,' when I realised how it would sound and managed to swallow my words just in time. We emerged onto the galleried area, which was, in fact, an open-plan master bedroom overlooking the living space. It was an incredible room with massive exposed A-frame trusses rising to a glassed apex. One wall, glazed from floor to ceiling with a door leading out onto a balcony above the porch, afforded fantastic panoramic views down the valley and over the English Channel.

Studiously, I averted my eyes from the extra-large king-size bed, but when he showed me the en-suite shower room I could not dismiss the tell-tale signs of a female presence. Neatly arranged on the counter was a selection of make-up, face creams and straightening tongs. I did my best to ignore the obvious confirmation of Sarah in Nick's life and commented on the travertine tiling to the floors and walls and the clever use of neutral colours. The only window in the room was a glazed arrow slit but there was plenty of light as the sloping ceiling was clear glass. Gazing at the large double walk-in shower, I thought how wonderful it must be to bathe under the stars and then immediately had a vision of Nick and Sarah sharing hot, steamy interludes. Flustered, and with despondency nipping at my heels, I asked if I could have a look around outside.

As we descended to the living area, Nick called to the dogs. Accustomed to their master's voice, Baron and Casper rose immediately and waited patiently at the bottom of the stairs. Tilly, however, remained seated by one of the couches, enthusiastically wagging her tail.

'Come on, Tils, old girl. You'll get left behind.'

She clambered to her feet and followed him through to the porch where he took his reefer jacket from the coat rack. Retrieving my jacket and scarf from the chair, I picked up my camera and followed him outside. Even though it was a sunny day there was a cold nip in the air and I wrapped the scarf snugly around my neck.

We ascended steep steps to the rear of the barn, which brought us to a terrace above roof level where two storage tanks were located. Nick explained that private well water was pumped into the tanks before gravity delivered the water to the property. In addition, a rain butt at the far end of the barn collected water from the roof.

The light had a wonderful quality on that January afternoon. I took several photographs that I knew, even by my amateur efforts, would look pretty special. I followed Nick down a side track, noting how Baron always kept an eye on his master.

'Even though Baron runs off with the other dogs, he never lets you out of his sight,' I commented.

'Weimaraners are a one-person dog,' Nick said. 'Although they'll be friendly towards people they tend to be loyal to just one person. And Baron's been with me eight years so we know each other's foibles fairly well!'

We crossed the driveway, past the parked cars, and walked towards a log cabin positioned a short distance from the barn. This housed a diesel-powered generator, which Nick explained provided power to both the dual 240V and 12V lighting/electrical systems. Beyond the cabin was a wind-powered generator.

'The barn stands at seven hundred feet above sea level and it's often windy up here,' he said. 'In fact, there's so much stored energy from the wind turbine that we give a lot back to the national grid.'

*We?* I had tried to ignore it up until then. Was that simply a figure of speech or was it a reference to him and Sarah? It sounded cast in cement.

I attempted to make notes as he spoke and take photos at the same time. Although agitated at the thought of his long-term relationship, I was aware, once again, that in Nick's presence I experienced a delicious calming of the soul.

As we walked down a flight of roughly hewn steps from one terrace to another, I spotted strategically placed life-size wooden animal sculptures. A couple of pigs rooted amongst the trees, there was a preening cockerel and a scratching hen on the middle terrace, and on the bottom terrace, a hissing goose stood at the edge of a large lake. I photographed the sculptures and said I would like to include them in the feature.

'Examples I did for my students,' Nick commented.

'How long have you been tutoring?'

'This is the third year I've run the evening class at Bridport. It's a general carpentry course but last year's students wanted to concentrate on more creative aspects, so I created these to show what can be achieved.'

'They're great in this setting,' I enthused.

'Yeah. I didn't think they looked out of place.'

At that moment, Casper tore past us. Leaping straight off the terrace onto the one below, he bounded into the wet, reedy area at the edge of the lake. Tilly followed closely behind.

'Look at that mad dog,' Nick exclaimed. 'I swear he thinks he's a water spaniel!' He laughed; that good-natured, infectious sound. Jumping down to the terrace below, he called to his dog. 'Casper, get out of there.'

The dog turned and immediately retreated from the water. Tilly, however, waded up to her belly amongst the reeds, obviously reluctant to leave the lake. Eventually, after much persuasion, she emerged draped in weed and vigorously shook herself.

'Argh! Bad girl, Tils,' Nick said, jumping out of the way of the impromptu shower, but he was laughing as he said it. The dog gazed up at him with soulful eyes.

'I'll explain the significance of the reed lake, Maddie, and you'll understand why it's not good for these rebels to go wading around in it.'

He looked up at me standing on the terrace above him and held out his hands and, suddenly, I had the feeling we were about to take a momentous step. As I placed my hands on his shoulders and looked into his open, tanned face and clear blue-grey eyes, I experienced the strongest sensation we had done this before. Holding me under my arms, he lifted me gently down to the terrace below. As he did so, a great hush descended – a deep silence, like a held breath – and I became aware of an incredible light shining from my body. As our eyes locked, I knew this was how it should be. It was as if time had stopped. We were in a place where there was no time; the normal laws of the universe did not apply. Somehow we had stolen back time. And then words came to me, which I did not fully understand.

'Oh, such joy to look upon your face again and feel once more a touch long still...'

As swiftly as it had happened, the moment passed. I heard Nick explaining how connecting to the main sewer had worked out prohibitively expensive, as well as impractical, so a reed bed purification lake was created that naturally filtered all waste water from the barn.

'The pond naturally balances and recycles the waste water. Once processed, it's then pumped back up to one of the storage tanks above the house for re-use.'

As Nick talked, I wondered if he had experienced anything just then. Had he noticed any slight shift in the order of things? He didn't appear to have, but I was certain that when our eyes had locked I'd seen a flicker of emotion and a question forming. I was still pondering this when Nick interrupted my thoughts.

'How are you for time, Maddie?'

I glanced at my watch. 'OK. I'm only working the evening shift at the pub.'

'Would you like to stay for lunch?'

We were standing next to each other but looking straight ahead at the view. My heart started thumping loudly.

He turned to me and smiled. 'Nothing special I'm afraid. My skills lie more in wood than food, but if you'd like to stay I can rustle up something.'

'*Stay,*' whispered my heart.

'*Go!*' screamed my mind.

And so I stayed.

Sitting at the dining table, chatting companionably while he prepared lunch, I noticed how capable he was in the kitchen. Here was someone who could look after himself although, instinctively, I knew there were very few times in his life when he'd had to. I felt myself falling deeper into the abyss and knew that my heart should not have won the debate. I should have put some distance between us and, by now, be heading back to Walditch. But I was powerless. Some greater force directed me and I was merely an actor with but a small part to play.

# 10

I spent the following week working on the article that I planned to submit to Colin for *Eco World* magazine and was pleased with the way it was coming together. I had several good photos to choose from and wanted to have it finished in time for Nick's visit on Thursday when he came round to fit the oven door. I wasn't sure if it was an extra service he'd offered or whether it simply fell in with his normal work ethic. Either way, it was a generous gesture.

I'd just returned from a shopping trip to Bridport and was parking the car when I saw Janet approach from the direction of the Blacksmith's Arms. She held a small brown paper parcel in one hand and waved it at me. I climbed out of the car, opened the boot and grabbed the bags of shopping.

'Hi, Janet. What's up?'

'This came for you at the pub.' She held out the package to me. 'Brian said Mrs McKendrick's son-in-law dropped it in yesterday 'cos he thought you might be working.'

I took the package from her. On it, in spidery writing, were the words *The Olde Smithy*.

'He said his mother-in-law's been dispatched upstairs.'

I glanced at her, perplexed. Then the penny dropped.

'Oh, you mean she's passed away,' I exclaimed, taken aback by the way the man referred to his mother-in-law's death.

'S'pose so.'

'Thanks for bringing it over, Janet. See you Friday.'

Saddened by the news, I continued up the path towards the cottage and wondered what the package contained. After emptying the shopping bags and lighting the wood burner, I made a coffee and settled down in the chair by the fire before Storm had a chance to monopolise it. Then I opened the package. Inside was a small, sealed envelope addressed to Mary and a well-read hardback entitled, *Dorset – the effects of the Civil War*. I opened the envelope and carefully unfolded the letter. The handwriting was frail.

*My dearest Mary,*

*I am so thankful to have met you. I should have liked to have talked with you at greater length but the good Lord has told me I am approaching the end of my life, although my daughter assures me otherwise (she does so try to protect me from the natural passing of time, bless her). I am very tired these days and I do look forward to being reunited with my husband. As you and I know, Mary dear, life goes on.*

*I was very happy living in your cottage for over thirty years, once I had learnt to accept its special ways (Hugh was always unaware and lived within its four walls in blissful ignorance).*

*I wish you every chance of happiness and fulfilment in this life and enclose something that may assist you in*

*your search. Don't give up.*
   *God Bless.*
   *Joyce McKendrick*


I sat for several minutes rereading the letter. What did it mean? I knew her daughter would dismiss it as the ramblings of an old woman with increasing dementia, but I recognised these were true and honest sentiments, however obscure.

I turned the book over and read the back cover. It appeared to be an account of the role Dorset played during the English Civil War. I opened the book and started reading, not noticing the passage of time until I became aware of a deep stillness. A log in the wood burner caught my eye. Almost burnt through, it shifted and threw up sparks and yet I heard not a sound. And then I noticed the dense, fog-like mist around the opening to the bread oven shifting shape, but never taking form. I was not frightened. I simply accepted it. Rising from the chair, I moved towards it and, as I did, the mist withdrew and compacted, as if viewing me as I viewed it.

'Show me your secrets,' I whispered.

The fog swiftly surrounded me, seemingly investigating me before dispersing and suddenly disappearing. Once more, the sounds of my world returned.

'Please show me your secrets,' I whispered again.

I read late into the night, believing that Mrs McKendrick had presented me with a key to a mysterious, closed door, which had opened a fraction. If I could prise it open further, maybe I would see more clearly the way ahead. I went to bed around midnight, the stack of wood beside the wood burner having reduced to a single log by the time I turned in.

That night I dreamt of dark, claustrophobic tunnels. Once

again, I was desperate to discover something important, only this time, when I came close to its discovery, it did not instantly turn to sand. It was as if I was getting closer to the heart of the riddle and I awoke the next morning with the feeling I'd undertaken a long journey, but with a strangely calm acceptance of all that was happening to me.

That afternoon, shortly after four, Nick arrived. I was sitting at the computer when I heard his van pull up. Peering out of the window, I saw him on his mobile. He appeared exasperated and I watched as he distractedly dragged a hand through his hair. I turned away, not wanting to pry, but a minute later I couldn't help but steal a glance. I could tell it was a heated discussion taking place. Suddenly he threw the mobile onto the seat beside him, thumped the steering wheel and stared straight ahead. I turned away and concentrated on my article, which I'd entitled, *Eco Magic in the Black Down Hills*.

Some minutes later there was a knock at the front door. As I walked out into the hall the driftwood mirror caught my eye. No longer was it reflecting the colours of the stained-glass room divide but, instead, a mass of swirling grey smoke and shadows. How strange… It must have something to do with changing light at different times of the day. I didn't dwell on it further because any thoughts were immediately put out of my mind as I opened the front door and saw the strain on Nick's face.

'It's really good of you to come round,' I said.

He acknowledged this with a brief nod and walked into the hallway, setting his tool bag down on the floor.

'I've almost finished the article on your barn,' I continued lightly. 'Have a look and tell me what you think.'

He hung his jacket on the coat rack by the door and followed me through to the dining room. Sitting at the computer again, I motioned him to pull up a chair. As he sat down, he was so close that our legs almost touched and I could feel the heat emanating from his body. I tried hard to concentrate.

Scrolling down the page, I started to read from the screen. '*If you are prepared to invest in great ideas, look at what can be achieved. I recently visited a unique property featuring the latest in contemporary design with extensive use of natural and locally sourced materials.*' I continued reading the article aloud, acutely aware that Nick had casually put his arm along the back of my chair and was now leaning in to look at the screen.

We were very close and the voice inside my head mocked, '*So near, and yet so far!*'

I read to the end of the article. 'Well, what do you think?' I asked, suddenly overcome with shyness.

'I'm blown away, Maddie,' he answered generously. 'If it wasn't already my place I'd be inspired to create it right away.'

I smiled and relaxed… a little. 'I've started choosing photos to accompany the piece. Take a look and see if you agree with my selection.' I opened the photos folder on the screen and rose from the chair. 'Would you like tea or something stronger?'

'Something stronger sounds good.' He shifted into my seat.

'I have Tom Browns. Is that OK?'

'Great.'

I poured the ale and a glass of wine for myself and

returned to the table. Nick was engrossed in choosing photos. We decided on ten, including one of the magnificent views from the terrace, plus a photo of the dogs around the lake with the hissing wooden goose in the foreground.

Pointing to the sculpture, I said, 'You never know, you may get commissions from this.'

He smiled at me, a gentle look now replacing the earlier strain in his eyes. 'We seem to be good at helping each other out.'

I held my breath, aware that this was the first time he'd made any reference to the two of us.

'Talking of which, let me sort your door.' He rose from the chair, practical once more, and after fetching his tool bag from the hallway, he set it down in the inglenook.

As he straightened up my inner voice mocked, *'He looks so right, as if he belongs.'*

I ignored it. From the kitchen, I fetched the bolts and hinges I'd purchased to fix the bread oven door.

'I'd say this is the original opening,' Nick said, as I re-entered the room. He ran his fingers around the entrance to the bread oven. 'Hopefully the stonework's solid enough to get a purchase.'

He felt inside and then leant in further. 'There seems to be a ledge.' Balancing one hand against the outer wall, he inserted his arm up to the armpit. 'There's something here.' He strained to get a better angle. Suddenly, he withdrew and in his hand was a wooden box.

'What is it?' I asked, aware of intense, mounting excitement. I recalled the anticipation I'd experienced when Dan first discovered the opening.

Nick placed the box on the coffee table and carefully

prised open the lid, which was stiff with age. Within, lay a pendant and a ring. Carefully he picked up the pendant; an exquisitely crafted, 3D heart made of badly discoloured, interlocking metal strands. As he placed it in the palm of my hand, I was suddenly overcome with a rush of such happiness and pure joy that it took my breath away. I heard Nick tell me to turn round and hold my hair aloft and, as if in a trance, I did as asked. Gently, he fastened a silk ribbon around my neck. Glancing down, I was astounded to find that I wore a blue dress with a deep neckline trimmed in white lace and a shiny silver heart pendant nestled just above my breasts. The next minute, I felt a tender kiss on my neck and heard the whispered words, 'I made this for you… a token of my love.'

In astonishment, I made to turn back to him but then I saw two children watching and giggling from the open archway between the two rooms. A little boy with a mop of curly blond hair stood next to an older girl and they peeped through the opening where the stained-glass divide should have been. The cottage, though familiar, was altered. A rustic wooden table and bench seats dominated the other room and there was a crude staircase rising to an upper floor. Propped against the front wall was a large stained-glass window, its lead crisp and gleaming and the small glass panes glistening in the firelight, filling the rooms with a kaleidoscope of colours.

I watched as I held out my hands to the children. The boy was no more than three years old and I recognised him as the child in the cot. Immediately, they ran to me. Holding hands, we danced around in a circle and my skirts swirled as we spun ever faster. I had never felt so happy and we laughed with sheer joy and abandonment.

Glancing over at Nick standing in the inglenook in front of an open log fire, I was taken aback by a look of such wonderment, his blue-grey eyes soft and tender, and I felt my heart shift into meltdown. And then I noticed his appearance had altered and though the eyes that gazed at me were Nick's, his features were those of that other, more feral man I'd seen in the cottage.

Suddenly, dizziness and nausea kicked in. I let go of the children's hands and closed my eyes, willing the room to stop spinning. When I opened them again, in a glance I took in the familiar pictures hanging on the walls and the IKEA sofa I'd bought from the Croydon store two years before. I looked down at the dirty pendant still cupped in the palm of my hand and quickly glanced up at Nick.

'Did you see that? Did you?' I demanded in an urgent, breathless whisper.

The look of wonderment was still on his face. 'I don't know what I saw, Maddie. I saw something.'

I sat on the sofa and cupped the pendant tenderly in my hand. What had just happened? I leant forward, reverently placed it back in the box and picked up the ring. Turning it lovingly between my fingers, I resisted an overwhelming urge to slip it onto my wedding finger. It was exquisite, like an Irish Claddagh ring. Decorated with swirling motifs, the shank was designed as fancy sleeves out of which came a pair of hands encompassing a piece of red glass, shaped like a heart.

'Oh this is lovely,' I said. 'But why are they here?'

Kneeling in front of me, Nick cupped my hand and carefully took the ring from my fingers. I was acutely aware this was the first time he'd made such intimate contact with me from choice. Nevertheless, somewhere deep within, there was recognition – the muffled sound of a bell of distant memory. I sighed. It was as if a great many years of angst had just lifted from my soul.

'These are love tokens,' he said, looking very directly at me, 'but how they came to be inside your bread oven, I don't know.'

'But whose are they?'

He shook his head. 'They're very old. You should get someone to take a look at them. Perhaps the museum?'

I agreed. He handed the ring back to me and, rising to his feet, took the pendant out of the box again. Slowly, he turned it over in his hand.

'This is very well made; the work of a true craftsman. I wonder who?' he murmured, as if to himself. A frown furrowed his brow as he glanced at me.

Suddenly business-like, he said, 'This isn't getting anything accomplished. You sit there, Maddie, and I'll get the door fixed.'

He worked quickly and competently, making surprisingly little mess, and within half an hour the door was in place.

'Looks like it's been there hundreds of years,' he said, standing back to admire it.

I agreed.

'Now, what about that window?'

'Well, it's been fine over Christmas,' I said.

'Let's have a look at it anyway.' Offering me his hand, he pulled me to my feet with such strength that I bowled straight into him. I laughed out of nervousness as he steadied me, but when our eyes met it seemed I had known this man forever and there was no need for embarrassment. He smiled and letting my hand drop, followed me upstairs.

It was as though I walked on air.

*'He's only going to look at your window,'* my inner voice taunted. Firmly, I shut it out.

'It's up to you, Maddie,' Nick said, checking his repairs, 'but this window will last a while longer as it is.'

I thought of all the costs I'd incurred since moving in, plus the fact I currently earned very little and my sensible, fiscal voice told me to make do.

'Well, I have had a lot of expenditure recently...'

'Then, see how it holds up through the year and when you're ready we can discuss it again.' He looked at me across the yawning expanse of bed.

With dismay, I realised there was no longer any practical reason for us to see each other again.

'How are you for time, Nick?' I chose the same phrase he'd used when I'd visited his barn. 'Would you like to stay for supper?'

He looked at his watch and frowned. 'Better not. It's getting late and I shall be missed.'

My heart sank. 'Your loss,' I said, as casually as I could. 'Not only do I pull a mean pint but I also rustle up a terrific shepherd's pie.'

He laughed softly. 'Some other time, Maddie. Thanks.'

*'Some other time – never!'* mocked my inner voice.

And so, once again, I said farewell to Nick. I stood at the door, feeling sad and lonely, and watched him walk across the village green to his van.

As Nick drove away he glanced back at the cottage and acknowledged that I was still standing there. This time, however, he didn't smile and I noticed the troubled look on his face.

The next morning, I emailed the article to Colin and received a reply later that afternoon. He was happy with the copy and confirmed the article would appear in the May issue of *Eco World*. My spirits lifted when he suggested I retake the external shots, should the landscape take on a more spring-like appearance between now and publication date. Here was another valid reason for contact. Colin also asked me to source other eco projects and to submit further articles as soon as possible. He signed off with: *Seen anything of Dan recently? He seems to have gone to ground.*

It still smarted that Dan hadn't bothered to contact me since staying in early December with Lucy in tow. Surely eight years of a very close friendship should count for something? He could at least maintain some contact, however fantastic Lucy might be. My inner voice spoke up: *'Why can't you make that move?'* But my pride wouldn't allow it.

I decided to find out about the jewellery. The previous night I'd placed the wooden box on my bedside table, curiously reluctant to be apart from it, and it was the first thing I looked for when I awoke. I carried the box downstairs and carefully placed it on the dining table. Why was it on a ledge inside the bread oven, and who had put it there? And why had the oven been sealed up? What dramas had The Olde Smithy been privy to?

I fetched the book Mrs McKendrick had bequeathed me and reread her letter, but its meaning was no clearer. Then, taking the contents out of the box, I placed them reverently on the table as if they were my most precious possessions. Again, I had the strongest urge to slip the ring onto my wedding finger, and I marvelled at the fine craftsmanship and delicacy of the heart pendant. Even in its sorry, blackened state it was obvious it had been crafted with dedication. 'A love token,' Nick had said, and I recalled the look in his eyes as he'd spoken the words. A thrill of excitement coursed through my body.

'What story do you have to tell?' I asked out loud.

Silence…

I logged onto the internet. Dorchester County Museum's telephone number was easy to find and I quickly made the call. On the third ring a woman answered. I explained my find and asked if she could recommend anyone to look at the jewellery and possibly date it.

'Just a moment.' I heard her rifling through a folder. Eventually she returned to the phone. 'Professor Stephens, Head of Archaeology at the University of Southampton. He may be able to help.'

As soon as we'd finished the call, I dialled the number she'd given me. There was no reply, so I left a brief message outlining my request and my telephone number.

By now, it was early evening and I needed to get a move on if I was to be at work on time. Even Brian, however amenable a disposition, would not accept a 'got held up in traffic' excuse from the other side of the village green! I opened the back door and called for Storm. There was no sign, but when I rushed upstairs to change my clothes I found him curled up on the bed.

'You,' I affectionately scolded, as I pulled on a pair of black trousers, 'sneaking up here when I'm not looking…'

He yawned, stretched, opened one eye and lazily surveyed me. I rubbed the underside of his belly. 'Yes, you. I'm talking to you!'

Rummaging through one of the boxes stacked at the side of the room, I found a clean sweatshirt. Suddenly, from behind me, I heard an urgent whisper. 'Mary!'

I spun round. There was nobody there.

'What?' I called out, alarmed by the fear in my heart. It was more than just the sound of the disembodied voice. 'What is it? Tell me.'

Detecting a faint breeze on my face, I glanced over at the window but it was fastened tight and the weather outside was still. I slumped down on the bed in frustration. Storm got to his feet and rubbed against my arm.

'How are we going to find out more, Storm?' I stroked his head. And then I heard it again. A loud, urgent whisper.

'Mary, come.'

By the door was a suggestion of the fog-like mist I'd seen in the living room. But, as I reached out my hand, it quickly dispersed and evaporated. The moment had passed. Glancing at the digital clock, I swore under my breath. I was now definitely late for work.

# 11

The following Wednesday was Valentine's Day. Brian had already asked me to work the evening shift and I'd enthusiastically agreed, knowing I didn't want to be on my own that night. Not that I was a great advocate of the event, but I was currently feeling vulnerable and a little sorry for myself. The Blacksmith's Arms had advertised a Valentine's Special and the restaurant was fully booked. With a straight face and a serious voice, Brian informed me he was willing to risk his reputation once again and have me waiting on tables as well as covering the bar. The pub had a red and silver theme for the evening and he and Vera asked that we all dressed in these colours. I wore comfortable black work trousers with a silver blouse, which I'd bought from a charity shop in Bridport, and I tied back my long, curly auburn hair with a silver ribbon. The requirement for red needed some thought but, after searching through my jewellery, I found a surfer's bead choker and matching bracelet purchased by Dan on a weekend trip to Newquay early on in our 'relationship'. I finished off the outfit with my favourite native North American silver feather earrings.

On my way out I stopped and checked my appearance in

the driftwood mirror at the bottom of the stairs, childishly sticking out my tongue at my reflection. The glass appeared smoky, as if in need of a good clean, and even though the lights were on in the dining room across the hallway I couldn't see any detail. I moved in to take a closer look and gasped. The face that serenely observed me was mine... but it was not. In the mirror my hair tumbled down around my shoulders, yet mine was tied back, and in the reflection I wore a dark blue cloak. I glanced down at my open-necked silver shirt.

'Who are you?' As I spoke, the vision faded. 'What do you want from me?'

Was there a suggestion of a smile on that rapidly vanishing face?

Swirling grey smoke now gave way to clear glass and I clearly saw the stained-glass window divide on the far side of the room with my open laptop on the dining table. As I met my gaze in the mirror the look in my eyes was not entirely calm. Exiting the cottage, I closed the front door purposefully behind me and made my way briskly across the village green, beneath the boughs of the old oak tree, and entered the pub.

Janet was already there, and Gayle arrived shortly afterwards with Danielle, the latest recruit. I threw myself into work and forgot about that 'other' woman. The restaurant was decorated with helium-filled silver balloons and silver and red streamers adorned the beams. Brian had hired a local band for the night and the four musicians now set up their equipment and carried out sound checks. We laid each table with a red linen tablecloth, placed a vase with a single-stemmed red rose in the centre, and arranged silver-coloured napkins in wine glasses. Standing back to admire the room, we unanimously agreed the end result was warm and welcoming with a hint of stardust magic.

Before the evening got under way, Brian called us over to the bar and explained that Janet was in charge of the restaurant, which he had roughly divided into four, and I was responsible for the three tables nearest the entrance so I could keep an eye on the bar and help out there when necessary. The remaining tables were divided between Janet, Gayle and Danielle. I saw meaningful looks pass between the girls – there were a number of customers to keep happy – but Brian pointed out that Janet would be waitressing all evening. Kevin, the replacement assistant chef, having survived his baptism of fire, was now a fully-fledged member of the team and worked alongside Vera in the kitchen.

'Any questions?' We shook our heads. 'Good. Then let's make this evening a success.'

I checked the restaurant booking sheet and noticed that table ten was reserved in the name of Corbin. As fate would have it, table ten was my responsibility. A mix of emotions coursed through me.

'Janet, I don't suppose you'd swap your table three for my table ten, would you?' I asked quietly.

She was about to agree when Brian interjected, 'No, I want you free for the bar, Maddie. Table ten is closer.'

I resigned myself to the fact and then thought it probably wasn't Nick anyway. After all, he'd told me the Corbins came from the area so it could be any member of the family.

As the musicians ran through a couple of numbers I helped Brian set up the bar. Nervously, I watched as the first of the Valentine's customers arrived and fulfilled their drinks orders as they congregated around the bar before moving through to the restaurant. At seven-fifteen my table one arrived; a sweet young couple, not much older than eighteen. They ordered drinks at the bar and then Janet showed them to their table. A few minutes later, I walked through to the restaurant with their drinks and left them with a couple of menus. As I returned to the bar area my stomach tied itself into a sickening knot. Sarah entered the pub with a woman I hadn't seen before, closely followed by Nick and another man. I watched as Nick instantly scanned the room.

As our eyes met I swallowed hard and managed a smile, despite my nervousness, which now verged on nausea. He looked fantastic in a white shirt, which enhanced his tan, a pair of grey moleskin trousers and a dusky blue casual jacket. Sarah must have been freezing in a pair of silver strappy sandals, a thin jacket and a short black dress – obviously chosen to show off her deeply tanned, bare legs. She talked animatedly to the other woman as they all moved towards the bar.

Fortunately, Brian stepped forward to serve them. Filled with relief, I escaped to the restaurant to take the young couple's order. However, as I returned to the bar area, Janet was leading Nick's party through to their table. Sarah glanced at me as she passed by, her face an expressionless mask, but Nick hung back and stopped me with a light touch on the arm. The look in his eyes stirred those pesky butterflies in my tummy to perform a series of double-somersaults.

'Hi, Maddie.'

'Hi.'

'You look really good to me,' he said softly.

'You don't look bad yourself,' I responded confidently, although I was far from feeling that.

The room suddenly turned hot and I had difficulty breathing. Was this swooning? To cover my confusion, I hurriedly said, 'You'd better brace yourself. I'm your waitress tonight.'

'No!' He groaned teasingly. 'What have I done to deserve this? Twice in less than three months.'

I laughed and promised to do my best not to stab him this time.

'That would be greatly appreciated!' He removed his hand from my arm. 'I'd better go and join the others.' With a smile, he turned and walked through the open archway into the restaurant, but I could still feel the warmth where his fingers had rested.

Before long, I was too busy to fret about anything. As I guided customers to their tables, acutely aware of Nick's eyes on me, I basked in the spotlight of his gaze. Eventually, I couldn't put it off any longer.

'Good evening,' I said, approaching his table. 'I'm Maddie, your waitress for the evening. Are you ready to order?'

Without any concern for my sensitivity, Nick said to the other man, 'I warn you now, Peter, this girl's lethal. She does a mean trick with flying cutlery!'

The man laughed, and the woman sitting beside side him smiled sympathetically.

'But we can excuse her that because she more than makes up for her waitressing shortcomings with her Irish charm.' Nick gave me a mischievous look.

Sarah surveyed me coldly.

'Don't listen to my brother,' the other woman said kindly. 'He's a big tease. I'm sure you're a fine waitress.'

So, this was his sister. How alike they were, both gifted with the same open, friendly face. Maybe this was a family trait.

Nick laughed. 'No, Helen, I warn you, Maddie is *not* a fine waitress but she *is* an excellent journalist.'

With her lips pursing into a thin mean line, Sarah's eyes narrowed.

'Ah,' exclaimed Peter in an easy manner. 'So you're the one Nick's been talking about.'

'And I understand Tilly made sure she was centre stage in all the photos,' Helen added, in a soft Dorset lilt.

She spoke with the same inflections as Nick.

'Ashton Chase Barn is fantastic in its own right, but having the dogs in the shots adds a homely touch,' I responded with a smile. 'It will enable readers to imagine living there.'

'I must remember to get a copy of the magazine,' said Helen. 'When is the article published?'

'It's scheduled for the May issue of *EcoWorld*,' I replied.

'It's a new title,' explained Nick to his sister.

I turned to him. 'Colin has asked me to take some more external photos before publication deadline.'

Sarah slayed me with a look. 'We can take the photos and email them to you,' she said archly.

An awkward silence descended. Nick was the first to speak.

'Don't be silly, Sarah. Maddie has to take them. It's her job.'

She glared at me.

'I'm starving,' said Helen, concentrating on the menu.

'Let's order. I'm sure Maddie has better things to do with her time than talk to us.'

*Not really. I love talking to you because you're part of Nick's life.*

I took their order and rushed it through to the kitchen, informing Brian they had requested a bottle of champagne. Silently, I prayed this was simply because it was Valentine's Day and not because there was something else of importance to celebrate.

Brian was on good form; he excelled at throwing a party. The band was great, playing romantic songs spanning several decades, and the evening went with a swing. I was astounded that I managed not to drop any cutlery when clearing away the empty plates from Nick's table, especially as I was aware of him watching me. Each time I approached his table I had to will my legs to move, as my knees had turned to jelly. It was all I could do to refrain from jumping into his arms!

Helen and Peter seemed a nice couple, open and friendly, and I liked their company. Sarah, however, was interesting to observe. When I was elsewhere in the restaurant serving other tables she joined in enthusiastically with the table's conversation, but each time I approached she fell silent; her jaw set. She leant in to Nick and made sure I noticed their intimacy, all the while shooting challenging looks in my direction. I remembered to check – there was still no ring on her finger. My sister would have been so proud of me. Mo, whose man had flown from New York to Paris to share a romantic Valentine's meal with her before flying back across the pond the following day.

I was serving coffee and heart-shaped chocolates to the

young couple on table one when I heard Sarah exclaiming loudly and excitedly. Even the young couple looked over in their direction and we all watched as Sarah hugged and kissed Nick. Helen and Peter smiled happily at the couple.

Oh God! – I felt as if I'd been kicked in the stomach – surely he hasn't proposed?

'See, he belongs to her. Not you!' mocked my inner voice.

Suddenly I was diverted from my rising panic.

'Excuse me,' the girl at table one said. 'Someone is trying to attract your attention.'

I looked over to where she pointed and saw Brian beckoning me over.

'What's up?' I asked, as I approached him.

'Your mate's here.' He jerked his head over his shoulder.

'What mate?'

'The one from the film company.'

'Dan?' I asked incredulously.

'That's the one.'

I rushed through the archway and there he was, sitting at the bar. Momentarily, I forgot how annoyed I was with him.

'Dan!' I hugged him hard and then checked to see if Lucy was around. He was on his own.

'Wow, you look fit!' He hugged me back. 'Didn't know what sort of reception I'd get.'

Then I remembered he hadn't been in contact for ages. 'What are you doing here?'

He looked thinner and there were dark shadows beneath his eyes. Dear exhausted Dan…

'Just had to come and see you.'

As Brian set a beer on the bar in front of him, Dan stood

up and delved deep into his jeans' pocket, searching for loose change.

'On the house, mate,' said Brian. 'Looks like you could do with one.'

Dan smiled thinly.

'Have you had anything to eat?' I asked.

'Yeah. Had a bite on the way down.' He looked at me and his eyes alighted on my choker. 'Hey, you're wearing the surfer beads I gave you. Didn't think you still cared.'

'Well, you know me, Dan, a sentimental old fool,' I said, slipping easily into the casual banter we had always shared.

'Fistral Beach. Yeah, I remember that weekend well,' he said with a smirk.

'Look, I've still got tables to serve but I'll be back in a bit.'

I returned to the restaurant wondering where the fantastic Lucy was, tonight of all nights. I served coffee and chocolates to table two and then Peter called me over and asked if they could have coffee and liqueurs in the bar area. I told them to come through when they were ready. Sarah was talking vivaciously with Nick. He laughed and put his arm around her. Immediately, she stared up at me with something like victory in her eyes. I tried to shut out the stab of jealousy, reminding myself they were a couple after all.

I walked back to the bar. Brian was in conversation with Dan, but at my approach he discreetly withdrew to the other end of the bar. I sat on a stool and, facing Dan, placed my hands on his knees.

'So, why did you *have* to come and see me after all this time?'

He searched my face. Why did I get the impression I'd done something wrong?

'Well, that's just it – *after all this time*. You haven't been in touch for ages. I needed to know you were all right.'

'What do you mean, I haven't been in touch?' I removed my hands from his knees. 'It's you who didn't return my call.'

'What call?' he asked, looking at me in confusion.

'And you couldn't be bothered to send a Christmas card either,' I added, sulkily.

'I did send a card,' he said defensively. 'It's you who didn't! At least, Lucy told me she'd sent it...' He paused and we held each other's gaze for a long moment. 'I think someone's been making trouble for us.'

'I think you could be right,' I agreed.

'Come here.' Leaning forwards, Dan drew me into a warm embrace. A safe, comforting, familiar act I knew so well.

As I glanced over his shoulder, I noticed Nick and Sarah standing at the bar a few feet away. Nick watched us and I could have sworn I caught a fleeting look of hurt in his eyes before he turned away. Surely not?

'No, *just your pathetic, hopeful imagination*,' answered my unrelenting inner voice.

I extricated myself from Dan.

Brian placed four liqueurs on the bar and as Sarah took them over to the alcove where Helen and Peter were sitting, I called over to Nick. 'This is Dan. A good friend of mine from London. We used to work together.'

'And play together...' added Dan.

'Pleased to meet you,' Nick responded politely. 'Nick Corbin.'

'Nick's helped me with the cottage,' I explained. 'He's sorted out the window for me.'

'No more draughty nights and puddles on the floor then?' Dan laughed.

I watched Nick's face. There was that flicker again, however fleeting.

'He's also fitted a bread oven door, which looks great,' I continued.

'Swell,' said Dan.

'Oh, I've got so much to tell you!'

Dan laughed at my enthusiasm.

Sensing Nick's discomfort, I wondered if I was being presumptuous and overstepping the mark, assuming there was a friendship between us when, in fact, there was none. I was considering how to proceed when Sarah returned.

'Helen and Peter want to know if you'll join us.' Putting her arm through Nick's, she gazed up at Dan with a coquettish look in her eyes. She smiled brightly. Nick shifted awkwardly.

I quickly made an excuse. 'I'm still on duty, but thanks anyway.'

'That's OK, Maddie, go and enjoy yourself,' said Brian from behind the bar. 'I can spare you for a while.'

I gave him a sharp look. Was he enjoying this at my expense? But he'd turned away to stack the glass-washer, and I couldn't see the expression on his face.

And, so, I found myself sitting at the Corbin table, feeling as uncomfortable as Nick obviously did, while Sarah flirted with Dan. Helen and Peter appeared oblivious to any undercurrents... or simply chose to ignore them. When Dan told Sarah he was a cameraman with a film company, she was so excited I thought she was going to burst a blood vessel. Although she appeared to be only a few years younger than me, she seemed quite unworldly and immature. She fell silent when Dan said I was the assistant director at Hawkstone before giving it all up to come and live in Walditch. I might have imagined it, but I thought I saw a look of pride, tinged with sadness, creep into Nick's eyes. Helen – lovely woman – congratulated me on having the courage to give up an established career to follow my dreams.

'Maddie will always be OK wherever life takes her,' Dan commented.

If only he knew. I was taut from the strain of it all.

Dan threw me such a warm smile that I was caught off guard and thought I was going to burst into tears. Frantically, I searched around for some form of distraction. Luckily Peter provided me with one.

'Will you concentrate on journalism now?' he asked.

'Well, I've been commissioned to write more eco-based articles but, first, I have to find some subjects.'

'I could put you in touch with a work colleague,' he suggested amiably. 'He runs an organic smallholding. What with the ever-looming oil crisis, he's turned part of his land over to sustainable woodland.'

How strange life is. Just when everything seems to have reached a dead end something turns up.

'Charlie?' asked Nick, the first words he had uttered for quite a while.

'Yes, my partner,' Peter explained to me.

'Charles Bosworth is a lovable rogue,' Helen said. 'I swear, if he hadn't been ordered by his father to train as a solicitor he would have found himself on the wrong side of the law by now!'

'He sounds quite a character,' I said. 'Thanks, Peter. That would be great. Perhaps you could introduce us?'

Out of the corner of my eye I noticed Sarah move closer to Nick. Laying her head on his shoulder, she gazed at Dan with big, wide, innocent eyes.

'How long have you two known each other?' she asked.

'Oh years,' Dan answered cheerily. 'As soon as I saw Mads I knew we would have history together. She was like a breath of fresh air.'

The look on Nick's face was inscrutable.

'*History* being the operative word,' I said pointedly.

'Well, history has a way of repeating itself,' countered Dan gently.

Suddenly I turned ice-cold and shivered.

Totally ignoring the others around the table, he drew me close and, looking deep into my eyes, twisted a loose tendril of my hair between his fingers. I was incensed. How dare Dan assume he could simply pick up where he had left off just because something might have happened between him and Lucy! And where was the amazing Lucy anyway? Abruptly, I got to my feet and, apologising to the rest of the table, said I had to get back to work. I cleared away my tables and then started to help the other girls clear theirs.

A short while later, Helen and Peter appeared in the archway to say goodbye and promised to be in touch regarding Peter's partner. I followed them through to the bar and watched as they collected their coats from the alcove. Nick held Sarah's jacket open and smiled down at her. I tried hard not to stare as she slipped her arms into the sleeves, turned in the circle of his arms and smiled up at him with a look of adoration. With difficulty, I averted my eyes from this display of affection and quickly joined Vera and Dan who were drinking at the bar.

As the Corbin party walked by, complimenting Vera on her cooking before continuing to the door, I willed Nick to cast me a last, brief glance. But Peter engaged him in conversation and although he hesitated at the door as if to turn back, the next minute they exited the pub. The room suddenly felt cold and empty.

'The event seems a success,' said Brian, returning from the restaurant. 'People are on the dance floor.' Slipping behind the bar, he poured a gin and tonic and pushed it across the counter towards me. 'Here, get this down your neck, Maddie. You deserve it.'

I took a large swig but it did nothing to quash my despair.

'These evenings are turning out well,' Brian continued. 'Maybe we should think about celebrating St Patrick's Day.'

Well used to her husband's enthusiastic approach, in a long-suffering voice Vera said, 'Let's recover from this one first, Bri, love.'

'Yeah, OK, Vera, but we've got our own resident Irish lass right here in front of us. I bet she could tell us a St Pat's Day tale or two!' He winked at me.

I opened my mouth to respond, but Dan interjected, recounting a visit we'd made for the festivities a few years earlier when I'd first introduced him to the wider O'Brien clan. 'That was an experience and a half I can tell you, Brian,' he said. 'Thought I'd died and gone to heaven. Every which way I looked I was surrounded by stunners!'

'I've met Maddie's sister and can well believe that,' Brian said. 'Bet there wasn't a Dublin lad safe during Maddie and Mo's teenage years.'

'You should see the older sister,' said Dan, warming to the subject, 'and as for Mrs O'Brien...' Making a face that suggested my mother was hot, he blew on his fingers. I grimaced. He'd obviously had one too many. 'I will always hold Finn O'Brien in the highest esteem for handling that family and yet still maintaining some semblance of sanity.'

As the two men laughed, Vera peered at me over the rim of her glass and raised her eyebrows.

Deciding Dan had said enough, I quickly downed my drink. 'Come on, Daniel Chambers, I think it's time to go.'

We said goodnight and I went through to the restaurant and waved goodbye to Janet, Gayle and Danielle who were now dancing on the improvised dance floor in front of the band. I waited while Dan collected an overnight bag from his car and then we walked across the village green towards The Olde Smithy. Moonlight, filtering through the boughs of the mighty oak, cast eerie shadows across the grass in an intricate pattern.

It was past midnight and I was bushed, but Dan had found a second wind and wanted to talk.

'Dan, I need to sleep. I've been on my feet all evening,' I pleaded. 'Look, let's make up a bed for you in the spare room and you can talk while we do that.'

He agreed and followed me upstairs, setting his bag down by the window while I pulled out sheets and pillowcases from the airing cupboard.

'Why didn't you phone me to let me know you were coming?' I asked, as we wrestled the duvet into its cover.

'I did,' he said. 'There was no reply, so I left a message.'

'For all you knew I might have been out of the country,' I countered, thinking of Mo and Jeff, 'whisked away on some romantic trip.'

'True. But then I figured I'd take the chance.'

I plumped up a pillow. 'So, where's Lucy?'

He didn't answer at once and I glanced over. To my consternation, I thought I saw tears.

'I don't know,' he said eventually, in a small voice.

I sighed, knowing sleep was a long way off. 'Dan, come downstairs and I'll fix us a drink. Do you want tea?'

He said he'd prefer whisky, and I decided I probably needed one as well. I ordered him to pour the drinks as I removed a tray of ice cubes from the freezer. Hearing scratching at the back door, I let Storm in. While he was still checking out his bowl in the kitchen, I managed to make it to his favourite chair by the fire. I glanced at my watch. It was going to be a long night...

'So, tell me what happened,' I said.

It transpired that Lucy had moved in with Dan the minute she'd arrived in London. He wasn't aware this was the arrangement until he'd woken one weekend and realised she'd been living with him for over two weeks. When he asked himself if he wanted her to go, he'd found the answer was 'no'. As he told me this, I considered how unfair it was that some women could make a move on a man and get what they want so easily. I focused on Dan's tale as he explained how he accepted the invasion on his, up until then, mainly independent, bachelor lifestyle.

'It was great,' he said. 'She fitted right in.'

Storm jumped up onto my lap, circled twice and settled down, purring.

'We didn't go out for weeks, we were just happy to stay in.'

'Both Caro and your friend, Colin, said they hadn't heard from you for ages,' I said bluntly, not sparing his feelings.

He looked guilty. 'As you know, Lucy's full on. She doesn't leave much time for anything else.'

*As if that's an excuse*!

Pointedly, I said, 'And we are family and friends.'

He held his hands up in surrender. 'Peace, Mads, please. You have no idea what it's like. She bowled me over completely.' He raked his hands through his hair.

I looked at him with pity. Dan had always been so laid-back and easy company. I could see he was torn apart by whatever had happened. I took a long sip of whisky.

'Go on.'

He downed his drink in one. 'Do you remember asking what baggage she came with?' I nodded. 'Well, it appears the "ex" is not so much of an ex.'

'Oh, Dan! I told you to be careful.'

'I know, Mads. Don't preach,' he whined.

'How did you find out?'

'Lucy always answers the phone before I get to it.'

Probably fielding my calls…

'On the few occasions I did answer no one ever spoke, but I could hear breathing.'

'Did you question her?'

He nodded. 'She said she'd experienced similar calls, but assumed it was probably a girlfriend of mine who didn't want to talk to her.'

I was right – devious, manipulative and well-practised.

'I had no reason to doubt her... then,' he said.

'So what made you?'

He sighed deeply. 'Lucy's been unable to find work since arriving in London. When I leave for the studio in the morning she's at the flat, and she's always there when I get home. Well, one day I finished at lunchtime and thought I'd surprise her. I got home and let myself in but she wasn't there. I thought she might have an interview and checked the calendar, but the date was empty. Then I wondered if she'd gone shopping, or something, and would be back soon, so I decided to wait for her in bed.' He looked at me sheepishly. 'We're like that...'

'No need to explain.' I had no desire to hear their intimate details. 'Go on,' I said, tickling Storm under the chin.

'Well, as soon as I entered the bedroom I knew someone else had been there. The sheets were rumpled and there was a strong smell of aftershave.'

'Are you sure it wasn't perfume?' I asked. 'And Lucy could have just had a restless sleep-in.'

'When I left for work she was dressed and making the bed.'

'Oh!' I glanced at Dan. He looked wretched. Lucy must be amazing to have this effect on him, I reflected ruefully. 'What happened then?'

'I waited all afternoon and she returned at four-thirty. I know because I was sitting in the lounge timing her, checking to see if she made it back before I was due home.'

'Did you tackle her about it then?'

'No. I didn't say anything. She didn't notice me at first. She had a secret smile on her face.'

I knew that smile. I'd seen it in my kitchen.

'She was shocked when she saw me sitting there. Said she'd been touting around the agents and was tired and needed a shower. I let it ride, even when she stripped the bed and made some excuse about us needing clean sheets, though she'd only changed them a few days before.'

'So, then what happened?'

'Nothing. She was always there when I got home and our sex life was as fantastic as ever.'

'What about the phone calls? Did they continue?'

'They stopped but she was always texting. And then, last Tuesday, Tim asked if Lucy's brother had got the job. When I asked him what he meant he said he'd bumped into her coming out of the Hilton with a man one afternoon the previous week. She'd introduced him as her brother and said he was in London for a job interview. When I told Tim I didn't know anything about a brother, he looked awkward and said he must have got it wrong.'

Tim, the stunt co-ordinator at Hawkstone Media, was diplomacy personified. I knew how awful he'd feel if he thought he'd caused trouble.

'When I arrived at the flat that evening she was there as usual,' Dan continued, 'but I noticed yet another change of sheets and that made me see red. Over supper I asked if she was free for lunch the next day. She made the excuse of meeting a producer about a costume drama, and when I asked for more details she was fairly vague and changed the subject. A while later her mobile went off and she started texting.'

'How could you let her continue living in your flat if you were so suspicious of her?' I asked incredulously. 'The pressure must be unbearable.'

Dan looked so sad. 'If I hadn't come home that lunchtime I wouldn't have known anything was amiss. Everything – and I mean everything – was exactly as it always was. She has a voracious appetite!' He looked embarrassed, but then the next minute said defiantly, 'I tell you, she's like a drug.' He buried his head in his hands.

This superwoman was really pissing me off.

'How did you find out it was her ex?' I asked as kindly as I could.

He groaned and sat up. 'The next day I left as if to go to work, but phoned in sick. I sat in the car just around the corner in Gladstone Street. There's a good view of the flat from there. I didn't have to wait long. A man turned up and Lucy opened the door in just a T-shirt.'

I remembered her standing in the doorway to my bedroom wearing only a T-shirt. Those long, slender legs seemed to go on forever. 'Could have been her brother,' I suggested.

Dan gave me a withering look – justly deserved. 'She kissed him and pulled him into the flat.'

Maybe not…

'So what did you do?'

'I waited about ten minutes before entering the flat. They were going at it like rabbits… in *my* bed,' he said, his voice rising in anger. 'I stood and watched.'

I could see it now, Dan coolly observing the cavorting couple.

'They were so preoccupied she didn't notice me for several minutes.'

I could imagine her shock when she finally did.

'What happened then?' I asked.

Dan rubbed his eyes, as if attempting to erase the vision. 'She tried to cover herself up. Kept saying she was really sorry but could explain.'

'And the guy? What was he doing?'

'What blokes normally do in those circumstances. Looking foolish, hopping around the room trying to get into his underpants.'

I laughed and Dan shot me a look. Quickly, I rearranged my features into concern. But I couldn't help wondering if Lucy's tousled hair, which always looked as if she'd only just got out of bed, was because, more often than not, she just had!

'I ordered him to leave my flat,' Dan continued, 'which he did, and asked Lucy what was going on. She started to cry. It seems that when I first met her, this bloke, Tony, and she had been having an affair for four years, but he'd suddenly found a conscience and gone back to his wife and kids. She said she couldn't believe it when I started paying her attention as she thought a bloke like me would never be interested in someone like her.'

Oh spare me the violins!

'She said she dreamt of making a new life with me and was overwhelmed when I'd appeared to want the same thing with her.'

I was appalled at Dan's gullibility.

'She was full on from the start, Mads. I know I should have heeded your words but she's like a drug. I can't... couldn't get enough of her.'

'Putty,' I said.

He had the decency to look sheepish.

'So why did this Tony come back into her life?' I asked in a matter-of-fact voice.

'Apparently he was never out of it,' Dan said bitterly. 'As soon as Lucy told him she'd met someone else his interest was rekindled.'

Oh very clever. No doubt, she'd laid it on thick about her new man.

'And once she'd moved to London he told her he couldn't be without her. He's a salesman,' he continued, 'so made sure he spent a lot of time in London and the Home Counties.'

Dan looked so lost and deflated. I removed Storm from my lap and went over and hugged him.

'And do you know what the most galling thing is, Mads?'

I shook my head.

'He's spent about as much time in my bed as I have over the past four months.'

It wasn't all fun for Lucy, though. She must have had one hell of a lot of laundry...

'When did all this happen?' I asked.

'Day before yesterday. I told Lucy to go. She pleaded with me to give her a second chance.'

'You haven't, have you?'

He shook his head. 'I almost gave in.'

I had never seen Dan like this; he was always so level-headed and in control. It shook me to the core to see him falling apart.

'Come on, Dan.' I caught hold of his hands and persuaded him out of the chair. 'It's past three and I'm knackered. Let's go to bed.'

The look of panic that swept across his face made me want to burst out laughing.

'In separate beds, Dan. I don't want to jump your bones tonight.'

Embarrassment replaced the panic. 'Mads, you know you're really special to me but what with all this, I... I'm a mess,' he stuttered.

'You don't need to explain, Dan. We're good friends. Let's just get some sleep. It will seem so much better in the morning. When do you have to go back to work?'

He said he'd taken a couple of days off so I suggested we slept in and got up when we fancied. I glanced in the driftwood mirror on the way upstairs, steeling myself in case I saw the 'other' woman, but the glass was clear. On the landing I turned to Dan and, standing on tiptoes, kissed him lightly on the mouth. His lips responded out of familiarity but the look in his eyes was one of sheer terror. Poor Dan!

I lay in bed considering everything he'd divulged. I was so angry with Lucy. He didn't deserve to be treated so flippantly. Dan was a decent man. I resolved that should our paths ever cross again Lucy would definitely get a piece of my mind.

Sleep came to me eventually, but it was filled with dreams of shadowy figures coming and going in the night and horses – many horses – below in the courtyard. I awoke and glanced at the clock – 05.53. I sighed and opened the bedside cabinet drawer, checking that the precious jewellery was still in its wooden casket. Once satisfied, I turned over and instantly drifted off to sleep. Immediately, I returned to the dream.

In the corner of the room stood the large, rustic cot and I heard crying emanating from within. I walked over and peered in. It was the little boy who had danced with me in the sitting room. He was hot and flushed with fever. Looking up, he whimpered and stretched out his arms to me. I leant over and picked him up, and he clung to me desperately as I tried to comfort him. I glanced out of the window. The courtyard was full of horses. Aware of another presence, I looked across the room and saw the young girl peering out of the window that overlooked the village green. She was aged about seven and I noticed her long, curly auburn hair was not dissimilar to my own.

'Come away from the window, Elisabeth,' I whispered urgently. 'Come away now.'

She moved an inch or two, but stayed within range of the window.

*That daughter of mine is so headstrong. It will get her into trouble one of these days.*

Daughter of mine? What was I thinking? And yet I knew it to be true.

'Elisabeth, come here!' I hissed in a louder whisper. She ignored me and continued to gaze out of the window.

Leaving the boy crying on the bed, I crossed the room in three strides and roughly grabbed her by the arm. She cried out in pain, the hurt reflecting in her eyes, and I pulled her away from the window, but not before one of the soldiers below looked up and saw us standing there. He had a round and ruddy, not unkindly face and wore his hair short under a metal helmet. He stared at us in surprise and I noticed his leather tunic and metal breastplate. He turned to say something to the soldier standing next to him, but did not.

As we withdrew from sight, I saw him glance back up at the bedroom window.

It was dusk and raining hard. From the safety of the room I looked out at the village green. It was full of soldiers and horses; the ground trampled and poached. A huddle of men stood sheltering beneath the boughs of an immature oak tree, and on the far side of the green I saw the Blacksmith's Arms... only it wasn't. It *was* a tavern – a sign swung from its front stone elevations – but whereas the Blacksmith's roof was tiled, this roof was thatched, and an archway led through the centre of the building to a stable yard beyond.

'When I say come, I mean come,' I scolded.

Elisabeth pulled a face. Returning to the bed, I cradled the boy once more in my arms. He was covered in an angry rash and burning up. Lovingly, I stroked his forehead.

'Hush, my child. Hush...'

I was frantic with worry, and the girl sulking in the corner of the room wasn't helping matters. I could stand it no longer.

'Elisabeth. Go to bed.'

She glared at me and stomped off to the opposite corner of the room. With a dramatic flourish, she threw aside a sackcloth curtain hanging from the ceiling and disappeared behind it.

'I was only looking at the horses,' she said petulantly.

'I know,' I replied more gently. 'But it's best the soldiers don't know we're here.'

I knew I had to be strong for the children but I was gripped with a deep sense of foreboding. The boy moaned and wriggled in my arms and attempted to sit up. As he started thrashing around, I felt so helpless and tears of frustration pricked my eyes.

'What's wrong with Francis?' asked the girl, looking out from behind the curtain.

'I don't know,' I said, briskly wiping away a tear.

'Mother, are you crying?'

'No. Go to sleep.'

She mumbled something that I couldn't catch, but climbed into bed without further ado. I stroked the boy's face and started to sing quietly; a pleasant, rhythmic melody with a distinctly old-fashioned lilt. Eventually, he slipped into a feverish sleep. I lay on the bed with the little boy and listened to the rain. An acrid smell lay thick in the air and I heard the rhythmic clang of a blacksmith's hammer on anvil.

Above the constant murmur of men's voices, one voice, louder than the rest, suddenly issued an instruction. There followed a series of shouts and, the next minute, the sound of horses' hooves clattering away down the stony road. As I lay with my son in my arms I tried to block out all around me. A while later I heard weary footsteps on the stairs – six, seven, eight and nine. Suddenly, I was alert. Whispering came from the other side of the sackcloth curtain.

'Goodnight, Father.' Elisabeth's clear, sweet voice drifted across the room as someone climbed onto the bed beside me.

'Be careful, Mary. We must be vigilant,' a low voice cautioned. 'Those men have thunder in their hearts.'

I turned and looked into the face of the man I'd seen at the graveside. The moment I saw him I was filled with such intense emotions that I struggled to breathe. His face was sweaty and grimy and filled with misgiving.

'The boy is sick,' I said. 'I've tried Culpeper's herbs to no effect. He needs a doctor.'

The man leant across me. Placing his hand on the sleeping boy's forehead, he nodded and looked at me. The soft, tender eyes that gazed into mine were Nick's and yet his features were more pinched and angular, brought about by an altogether tougher existence.

'Try and sleep a little, Mary.'

Gently he kissed my cheek and I sighed. Fear lurked within the darkest corners of my being but with this man at my side, maybe – just maybe – it was not as oppressive as it seemed.

'I love you, Nat,' I whispered, relaxing under his loving touch.

He swallowed hard. When he spoke, his voice was husky with emotion. 'And you, my love, are my life.'

# 12

I awoke the next morning to a harsh ringing sound. I sat up and a splitting headache immediately took hold. I felt truly awful and decidedly nauseous. I heaved myself out of bed, threw on a dressing gown and rushed downstairs, reaching the phone just before it rang off.

'Hello,' I said breathlessly.

'Miss O'Brien?' a man's voice enquired.

'Speaking.'

'Professor Stephens returning your call.'

'Oh Professor Stephens, thank you so much for phoning.'

My pleasure. Now, how can I assist you?'

I explained that Nick and I had found the jewellery in the bread oven and we both thought it was old. He agreed it sounded intriguing and was keen to examine it further.

'No time like the present,' he stated. 'I have a rare afternoon off today. Would that be convenient?'

'Yes,' I said, excitement bubbling. 'That would be just fine.'

He gave me his address, which I scribbled down on the notepad by the phone, and said he looked forward to seeing me at three. 'In time for tea.'

I filled the kettle, threw teabags into a couple of mugs and spooned cat food into Storm's bowl, although he was still curled up asleep in his favourite chair. As I waited for the kettle to boil, I drank a glass of cold water in the hope it would quash the nausea and glanced out at the courtyard, remembering my dream. Last night, it was full of horses. As I looked more closely at the outbuildings I wondered at their original use. I thought of that other man, the man who seemed to mean the world to me, and then my thoughts turned to Nick.

With dismay, I recalled that Valentine's evening had not been a success. Nick and Sarah were very much a couple. I also recalled Dan intimating strongly that he hoped to get back with me – although I very much doubted that now, having heard his sorry tale. Suddenly, the inscrutable look on Nick's face at hearing the news came to me. Nick confused me. Although he was friendly and open, each time there was the slightest chance of us getting closer the chasm between us yawned deep and wide.

I made tea, carried the mugs upstairs and knocked softly on the guest bedroom door. I heard a groan.

'Morning, Dan,' I said cheerily, as I entered.

He lay on his back, one hand covering his eyes. 'Can't be that time already? God, I feel rough.'

'Snap. I've got some Resolve somewhere.'

He groaned again, pushed himself up into a crumpled sitting position and took a mug of tea from me. He did look awful and I suspected it was more than just a hangover. No doubt he'd tossed and turned for most of the night, beating himself up over Lucy. I sat on the bed beside him and asked if he planned to stay another day or two, or immediately head back to London. He fumbled for his mobile phone. There were no messages or missed calls.

'I'll stay on, if that's OK?'

'No trouble, but I have an appointment with Professor Stephens this afternoon. You can drive me there.'

He agreed. When he didn't ask who the professor was I knew he was still in the doldrums and wasn't listening.

'Shall I run you a bath?' I asked.

For a minute, he stared straight ahead and I wondered if he'd heard me. But then, turning to me, he smiled a sad smile.

'You're a good friend, Mads. Caro always told me I should have made our arrangement permanent.'

'It wasn't meant to be, Dan, however good your sister's intentions were.' I thought he was going to cry, so I gave him a friendly nudge.

'Missed opportunity,' he said quietly.

However fond I was of him, the days ahead promised to stretch very thin if this sombre mood didn't lift. I finished my tea.

'I'll find that Resolve and run you a bath,' I announced, more brightly than I felt. 'There's plenty of hot water. Take as long as you want.'

For good measure, I took the Resolve as well.

By the time Dan emerged from the bathroom it was past noon. I made tea and toast – neither of us could face anything more – and then found a map of the area and checked out the route to Professor Stephens. He lived at The Manse, in a village called Hermitage, and this proved to be a pleasant drive of some twenty miles amongst Dorset's rolling hills. During the journey, I read extracts from a book I had on the area and it wasn't long before Dan's inquisitive nature shook him out of his gloom and he began to notice the countryside we drove through.

'Listen to this, Dan. *Although situated only four miles from Cerne Abbas, Hermitage seems to delight in being a forgotten place. In Sir Frederick Treves' book, "Highways and Byways in Dorset", it is described as a Rip Van Winkle village lying at the foot of the grassy slopes of High Stoy, a lovely hill 860 feet high, about six miles south of Sherborne. One cannot imagine a greater solitude for the Order of St Augustine whose hermitage once stood here, yet the monks left as long ago as 1460. In 1583 a landslide caused three acres of land to slip and block the highway to Cerne Abbas. Treves, with dry humour, comments: Since this date nothing in Hermitage has moved and it is a question now if even an earthquake would rouse it.*'

I glanced at Dan. He wore a faraway look.

'I wonder if Professor Stephens will be roused by my find,' I concluded loudly.

'What find?' Dan asked suddenly.

So, he was listening.

'Why are we going to see this bloke?'

'Took you long enough, Daniel Chambers.'

He gave me a sheepish look. 'Sorry, Mads. I must be terrible company.'

'Not exactly *terrible*…'

We crossed the A37 and followed a country lane until reaching the crossroads in the middle of Hermitage, which, as Sir Frederick Treves had stated, did appear to be a sleepy, untouched, Rip Van Winkle of a village. Immediately ahead of us was a no through road. Following Professor Stephens' directions, I instructed Dan to drive to the end.

We spotted The Old Manse straightaway. A tall, imposing property set in manicured grounds with plenty of shingled parking in front of the house. We entered onto a sweeping driveway through a pair of wrought-iron entrance gates, which opened at our approach. Dan parked alongside an immaculate black Porsche. Belying my earlier consideration that he might be slow to rouse, Professor Stephens was obviously a man of speed. As I stepped out of the car with precious casket in hand, the gates closed silently behind us and I heard a muffled bark resounding from deep within the house.

Suddenly, the freshly painted front door opened and a tall, casually dressed, grey-haired man, aged about sixty, appeared on the doorstep. He was attractive – in a boffinish sort of way – and steely blue eyes peered at me over a large, prominent nose, suitably offset by a wide, generous mouth.

'Madeleine O'Brien, I presume?' he said, the upper-class accent in keeping with the surroundings.

I walked up the tiled steps and shook his large proffered hand. 'Thank you for seeing us, Professor Stephens. This is my friend, Dan.'

'Nice bit of metal on the front drive,' Dan murmured appreciatively, looking back longingly at the Porsche.

'My little indulgence, dear boy. I have so few these days.'

'A 911 Turbo. Top speed 193mph,' swooned Dan.

'Ah, you know your stuff, young man,' replied the professor. 'And 0–62mph in less than four seconds. Not that I point this out to the Dorset police, you understand.'

He beckoned us into the hallway.

It was cool in the house. Looking around, I noted the original black and white floor tiles, the high ceilings with ornate cornicing and dado rails that ran the full length of the hall. This was a house of substance, befitting a man of Professor Stephens' obvious authority and status. There was nothing fake about this man, I decided, and a sense of excitement began to take hold. Perhaps he would have some answers for me today.

'Let us go through to the sunroom. Janice will bring the tea.'

We followed him through a doorway at the end of the hallway and entered a Victorian orangery filled with plants. Some sunroom! Inviting us to sit at an ornate cast-iron table, the professor then disappeared into the house to organise the tea.

'There's obviously money in archaeology,' said Dan, raising one eyebrow. 'I should have considered that when I was thinking of a career.'

'Shhh. He'll hear,' I whispered urgently.

It was a pleasant view from the orangery. The garden, stocked with a large selection of mature shrubs and specimen trees, backed onto open fields that ran into woodland. In the centre of the lawn was a pond built from mellow Dorset stone and a substantial rockery to one side supported a waterfall that cascaded into the still waters of the pool. The grass, I noted, comparing it to my own sorry patch, was mowed to within an inch of its life. Not a weed dared peep its head above the bowling green that masqueraded as a lawn.

Presently, Professor Stephens reappeared clutching a pair of spectacles in one hand, and followed by a black Labrador who was as grey around the gills as his owner.

'You don't mind dogs, do you?' he asked. 'Bertie is no

trouble these days, though in his youth he led me a merry dance, always running off after any bitch, so to speak.'

He glanced at me apologetically, and smiled conspiratorially at Dan.

I assured him I loved dogs, thinking of Baron and Casper in particular. Suddenly, I flushed, but it had nothing to do with the warmth of the orangery.

'Fabulous garden,' Dan complimented.

'Another of my indulgences, dear boy. This has been twenty years in creation. I think it passable now, don't you?'

'Very,' agreed Dan.

The professor shot him an appreciative look.

'Ah Janice. Thank you.' He rose to his feet as a plump, sweet-faced woman appeared in the doorway pushing a heavily laden trolley. It was set with a full silver tea service, fine bone china and a plate of homemade fruitcake. The professor was obviously a bachelor, and I wondered if 'tea' was a ritual for him. He took the trolley from the woman.

'Would you like biscuits to go with Marjorie's cake, Professor?' the woman asked in a broad Dorset accent.

'Oh I think so, Janice. That would be most appropriate.'

She bustled from the room.

'Janice is yet another of my indulgences,' the professor explained, placing the cake plate on the table. 'I guess one could say I do have quite a few these days after all!' He chuckled to himself. 'I think it such a shame more people don't indulge in a "lady who does".'

Dan's eyes sought mine, his left eyebrow twitching ever higher, and I shot him a warning look.

Janice reappeared with a plateful of biscuits which, to my delight, included my particular favourite – chocolate

Hobnobs. In fact, these could be referred to as *my little indulgence*. Inwardly, I suppressed a smile.

'I'll be off now, Professor,' Janice announced. 'I've hung the freshly ironed clothes in the wardrobe and the silver's been cleaned and put away in the sideboard.'

'Thank you, Janice. Most kind. I'll see you next Thursday.' Janice bade us farewell.

Pouring tea into the china cups, the professor nodded at the cake and biscuits and invited us to 'tuck in'. Dan picked up a plate and helped himself to a large slice of fruitcake.

'Excellent choice, dear boy,' the professor commented.

I selected a biscuit.

'Take two. You look as though you could do with a square meal.'

I did as I was told.

Choosing the fruitcake himself, the professor broke off a piece and gave it to the Labrador sitting patiently at his feet. The dog wolfed it down in one, licked its lips and looked hopefully at the man for more, but Professor Stephens had turned his attention to me.

'Now, young lady, what's all this about a treasure trove?'

I explained that Dan and I had discovered the bread oven and, on further investigation, I had unearthed a wooden casket. Delving into my bag, I extracted the box and placed it on the table. Easing open the lid, I showed him the pendant and ring lying within. As he leant forward to examine the contents, without warning, I was overcome with a curious sense of possession, and when he picked up the ring I had to sit on my hands to prevent an overwhelming urge to snatch it away from him.

With careful deliberation, the professor put on his

glasses, resting them halfway down his prominent, bony nose. Tilting back his head, he peered through the lenses and rotated the ring in his fingers.

'Intriguing,' he said, 'very intriguing. What age did you say the cottage was?'

'The estate agent said part of it dates back to the seventeenth century,' I replied.

'I would say they are probably right, judging by this.' Excitement caught at my throat. 'I won't be a minute.'

Replacing the ring in the casket, the professor strode from the room. The Labrador hauled itself to its feet and followed.

Dan shifted in his chair and leant forward to pick up the ring.

'Don't touch!' I snapped.

He looked at me in surprise.

Why had I shouted at him in such a cross, irritated manner?

'I wasn't going to damage it,' he said, defensively. Justifiably peeved, he sat back in the chair and grabbed a biscuit.

'Sorry, Dan. I just think the less we contaminate the jewellery, the better,' I said feebly.

He didn't look at me and furiously chewed. I could tell he was sulking.

Professor Stephens reappeared with an eyeglass. Placing it in his left eye socket, he proceeded to examine the ring. I knew it was childish but when people used eyeglasses it always made me think of cyborgs. I wanted to laugh but managed to swallow the smile.

'Yes, very intriguing.' He placed the ring on the table and removed the pendant from the casket.

'*A love token.*' Nick's voice rang in my ears.

Professor Stephens carefully turned the heart pendant over.

'This has been very cleverly crafted. It's not the work of a professional, you understand, but whoever created it was a very talented craftsman nonetheless.'

Placing it on the table, once again, he picked up the ring.

'If I'm not mistaken, this is a ring in three parts.' He applied pressure but nothing happened. 'I'd like to show these to a colleague of mine, a jewellery specialist.'

Replacing the jewellery in the casket, he removed the eyeglass. A red ring now encircled his eye.

'Oh, I'm not sure I want to let them go,' I said, at once consumed by irrational panic.

Dan cast me an odd look. 'Go on, Mads, let the professor show them to the specialist.'

'I assure you, young lady; no harm will come to these pieces.'

I hesitated.

'I will furnish you with a receipt,' continued the professor. 'If they are what I think they are, well… they are a marvellous find.'

I was racked with indecision. This visit had not produced the answers I'd hoped for. I wanted to discover more about the jewellery, but did I want to leave these precious objects with this man?

'Do you know what metal they are?' I asked, stalling for time.

'Oh, I should say the ring is enamelled gold and, if I'm not mistaken, the stone is ruby.'

I stared at the contents of the wooden casket in astonishment. 'Ruby! I thought it was a piece of coloured glass.'

'Ah, just you wait.' Professor Stephens grinned at me. 'Philip is one of the best restorers I know. He has a very sympathetic touch. Then you will see what a beautiful piece it is. The pendant, on the other hand, is not gold.'

Dan, no longer sulking and having seemingly forgiven my earlier harsh outburst, was once more intrigued. 'Can you date them precisely?'

The professor smiled at Dan in such a way that it suddenly occurred to me he might swing the other way, which would explain his bachelorhood.

'Well, dear boy, the heart became a very popular design during the seventeenth century. If the ring is what I think it is, that would date it to around the same time. I would say the early to middle sixteen hundreds.'

I shivered. Someone had just tiptoed upon my grave.

'Mads, you've got to let the specialist look at these,' Dan said, enthusiastically.

I looked from one man to the other: the older fired up by a love of antiquity; the younger excited by the mystery of the unknown. Reluctantly, I agreed.

Professor Stephens wrote out a receipt and handed it to me. 'I should think it will be another couple of weeks before I have some answers for you.'

I looked at the wooden casket on the table – still unwilling to leave it – and then followed the men down the hallway to the front door. We thanked the professor for tea and headed down the steps towards the car, the deep gravel crunching beneath our feet. Dan paused to look through the darkened glass windows of the Porsche.

'Next time you visit, dear boy, I will take you for a spin,' promised the professor.

I looked over at Dan and raised an eyebrow. Uncharacteristically, he blushed. The professor's interest in him had obviously not gone unnoticed.

That evening I was agitated and couldn't settle, fretting that the jewellery was no longer in my possession. Amused by my agitation, Dan asked why it meant so much to me.

'I don't know. It just does.' I didn't want to discuss it.

He lay on the sofa with Storm draped across his chest. The cat, totally relaxed, purred contentedly as Dan stroked him. Storm was so nervous and wary at the beginning, it amazed me how trusting his natural character was now; he befriended everyone. Not for the first time I wondered what circumstances had brought him to me.

I sat at the dining table with the laptop open in front of me. I tried to access the internet, as I intended to do a search on Professor Stephens and his specialist friend, Philip Harcourt-Jones.

'Oh damn, why can't I connect tonight?' I said in exasperation.

'Try turning your router off and on,' Dan suggested.

'Good thinking.' I got up and walked to the wall where the router was plugged in. As I bent down to switch it off, I noticed a shadow pass behind the stained-glass divide between the two rooms. Straightening up, I watched as

Nat walked across the sitting room towards the kitchen. Moving quickly to the archway, I was just in time to see him disappearing through the rear wall. I glanced at Dan, still languidly reclining on the sofa, oblivious, but Storm sat bolt upright looking intently at the doorway. I hurried to the kitchen and peered out of the window but there was nothing to see. Nat was not in the courtyard.

'What's up, Storm?' I heard Dan say. 'Seen a ghost?'

Walking back to the doorway, I stared at Dan.

'Why are you looking at me like that?' he asked, removing Storm from his chest and sitting up.

'Like what?'

'Like you're expecting me to do, or say, something.'

'Didn't you see it then?'

'See what?'

I had always believed Dan and I could talk about anything. We were always in tune with each other, or so I'd thought, but since Lucy had insinuated her way inside his head we appeared to have lost that connection.

'I thought I saw something,' I said. 'Never mind. Do you want a drink?'

'Jack Daniel's would be good,' he said, as his mobile rang.

I turned back into the kitchen. Stretching up for a couple of shot glasses on the top shelf, I decided that if I was going to make a habit of imbibing I had better move them to a more accessible height. As I poured the drinks, I heard Dan speaking in a low, intense voice. I opened the freezer door and pulled out a tray of ice cubes as Storm wandered through to investigate his food bowl.

Suddenly Dan's voice rose in frustration. 'But why should

I? I don't know how you can ask me that. You obviously don't know me *that* well.'

It was impossible not to overhear the conversation. Hesitating, with drinks in hand, I contemplated stepping outside into the courtyard to give him some privacy.

'Well you'd better shack up with him again then,' he said loudly and very firmly.

I left it a few minutes before walking into the room. Dan sat on the edge of the sofa with head in hands, his mobile discarded on the seat beside him. I cleared my throat. He didn't look up.

'Here, drink this.' I held out the tumbler.

'God, Mads, what am I going to do?' He took the glass from me.

'I guess that was Lucy?' I sat down opposite him.

He nodded wearily.

'What do you *want* to do?' I bobbed an ice cube with my finger.

'What I want to do and what I need to do are two different things,' he mumbled.

'I suppose she's asking to come back,' I said, taking a sip.

'Begging, more like,' he replied. 'Says she can't believe she's cocked up so badly. She wants us to give it another go.'

'Oh, Dan, you've only known her five minutes! For all you know, this might be serial behaviour.'

He screwed up his face. I could tell he was hurting.

'I thought we had something special. Says she can't be on her own.' He looked so troubled. 'Says she doesn't trust herself and might do something silly.'

I was so angry with her for playing that particular card. If she'd been in the room I'd have punched her.

'Dan, listen. I'm going to be brutal. I know I only met her that weekend you visited, but that's all I needed to understand her. She got into your bed within minutes of meeting you; she knows how to play a man and get what she wants. She's not going to do away with herself, if that's what you're worried about. She's not that type. She's a survivor. Don't be fooled by that winsome little girl thing.' In full flow now, I couldn't stop, 'Don't be so easily manipulated.'

He stared at me coldly. 'And when did you become such an authority on the subject?'

Ouch!

'Well I am a woman,' I replied, keeping my voice steady. I couldn't believe how defensive he was. She'd truly got under his skin, and she didn't deserve his loyalty.

He knocked back his drink in one.

'I tell you what,' I said, taking control. 'Let's get something to eat at the Chinese in Bridport. They do a fantastic Peking duck, so I've been told.'

He nodded, though I wasn't sure he'd really heard. And so, hauling him to his feet, I found his jacket and marched him out to the car.

We had a relatively jolly evening and the restaurant was surprisingly busy for a Thursday night in February. There was plenty of noise and laughter from the other tables to distract us and I tried to keep Dan's mind off Lucy. I told him that Mo had met a successful airline executive from New York who thought nothing of flying around the world to join her wherever she happened to be working.

'Good for her. She deserves some pampering.' He had always liked my sister.

And I told him about the freelance writing work that was

slowly beginning to trickle my way and how the editor of the county magazine had invited me to submit a series of write-ups on places to eat for their 'local eateries' feature.

'Well, at least you won't go without a square meal or two,' he teased, the old Dan emerging. 'Perhaps you should include this place? We could get away without paying.'

'I don't want to be seen as some free-loader before I've even started, Dan!'

We split the bill.

It was a cold night. The temperature had plummeted while we were in the restaurant and Dan put his arm around me as we hurried back to the car. As I fumbled in my pocket for the car keys his mobile rang. I knew by the look on his face it was Lucy. He answered it and immediately turned away from me, walking to the far side of the car park. I sighed, opened the door and climbed in. A thin layer of ice had formed on the windscreen and I switched on the heater. Dan must be freezing. I blew on my hands and watched him pace up and down, talking intently. At one point he stopped and gesticulated madly. He didn't look cold. In fact, he looked hot and bothered. I switched on the wipers and watched as they rhythmically smeared ice in a large arc across the glass. Then I switched on the radio. Ten minutes later Dan returned to the car. As he opened the door a blast of cold air accompanied him.

'Get in quick,' I said.

He jumped in and shut the door.

'OK?'

He nodded but said nothing and we drove back to Walditch in silence.

I didn't question him further that night. It was up to

Dan to decide how to handle Lucy but I fervently hoped he would see sense and not take up with her again. On the landing we said goodnight and went to our separate rooms.

A few hours later I awoke… or was I dreaming? When I thought about it later, I couldn't be sure. I was sobbing. Quickly, I sat up in bed and tried to catch my breath. I breathed in slowly and deeply but the ache in my heart was too great.

'Hush… Don't fret so.' A hand gently rubbed my back. 'The boy's in a much better place.' A tender kiss on my neck.

I turned towards the voice. In the darkness I could just make out Dan, though he was altered, and then I saw it was Nat. Immediately, I looked across to the corner of the room. It was empty. The cot had gone. A wave of utter despair engulfed me as I understood what it was I'd been so frantically searching for. My son.

'He's at peace, my love. Let him be.' Nat wiped away my tears and kissed me softly. 'I will give you another,' he whispered.

Despite my heavy heart, the instant I felt his weight a charge surged through me. I couldn't believe how hungry I was for him or the shudders he drew from my body. Our lovemaking that night built to a wild and desperate crescendo, as if our very lives depended on it.

Afterwards, as we lay sated in each other's arms, slipping into sleep, he whispered, 'I will love you for eternity, Mary, my love, my life…'

The next morning I came to, emotionally exhausted. My eyes were sore from crying. As I turned over I saw Dan asleep beside me. The movement disturbed him. He started to wake and I watched as he focused on me, smiling sleepily before closing his eyes again. Suddenly, he sat up sharply.

'What?' he asked, bewildered. 'What am I doing here?'

How do I explain this?

'What's going on?' he demanded.

'I'm as surprised as you,' I answered innocently.

'Hell! How did I get here?'

'Well, if you can't remember I suppose you might have been sleepwalking or something...'

'Oh God!' he exclaimed, holding his head in his hands; a gesture he was doing a lot these days.

I decided to be flippant. 'Well thanks a bunch, mate.'

He gave me an anguished look. 'I don't mean it like that. I mean I'm bloody sleepwalking now.'

'Don't worry about it, Dan,' I said calmly. 'It probably has something to do with being in a strange house.'

Stranger than he could ever imagine.

'You'll be fine once you're back in your own flat.' He didn't look convinced. 'I'm going to make tea,' I said, swinging my legs out of bed.

He grabbed my arm. 'Mads, we didn't, did we?' Panic rose in his voice.

'Don't think so,' I half-lied, unsure whether it was Nat or Dan I had made love to so passionately. 'But, so what if we did? You're not married or anything.'

'Oh Christ!' he groaned.

I started to get angry. 'For God's sake, Dan, it's not as if we don't know each other's bodies inside out!'

'I know, I know. Oh, Mads, I'm in such a mess.'

*And feeling sorry for yourself is so very unattractive. Get a grip...*

I headed for the door, stomped downstairs to the kitchen and filled the kettle. Storm, curled up in his favourite chair by the inglenook, watched me through the open doorway. Suddenly he stretched, jumped down and walked into the kitchen. As I opened a tin of cat food he purred loudly and rubbed around my legs.

'You and me, Storm,' I said softly. 'That's the way to be. Just you and me. So much less complicated.'

I was still irritated as I took the mugs of tea upstairs. When I opened the bedroom door Dan was on his mobile. I assumed to Lucy. Swiftly, I placed the mugs on the bedside cabinet, turned and walked back downstairs to the bathroom. As I peered in the mirror I was stunned by my appearance – swollen face and red-rimmed, puffball eyes – and Dan hadn't even noticed! I splashed cold water on my face. Then I placed a couple of soaked cotton wool pads on my eyelids and savoured the sweet coolness against my burning skin. I'd just finished brushing my teeth when I heard Dan noisily coming down the stairs. Why did he seem such a bull in a china shop these days? He knocked loudly on the door.

'Mads, I think I'll head back to London this morning.'

I opened the bathroom door, toothbrush in hand. He was already dressed.

'That was Lucy. She wants to meet up today.' He took a step back from the doorway, as if to get out of the firing line. 'And before you say anything, I'm not going to welcome her back with open arms.'

'I wasn't going to say anything, Dan,' I said crossly.

He gave me a long, hard, cold and unforgiving look. It was one I hadn't seen before. Who was this person?

Obviously eager to be on the road and away back to Lucy, he said he would make a start on the breakfast.

Dan left around eleven without either of us mentioning Lucy again or his presence in my bed the previous night. Once he'd gone I breathed a sigh of relief. I was sorry to see him so troubled and in such emotional turmoil, but the laid-back, easy-going man I'd known for so long was nowhere in sight.

# 13

I spent Sunday morning working on a piece about the Blacksmith's Arms for the 'local eateries' feature but by lunchtime I felt claustrophobic and desperately needed to get out. Following Dan's unexpected visit I'd been in a strange mood, reflective and quiet, and my usual optimistic outlook had deserted me. As I drove out of the village with no pre-planned destination in mind, I thought it would be interesting to see where I eventually arrived.

It turned out to be the Hardy Monument. Standing tall on the summit of Black Down Hill, high above the village of Portesham, it is visible from many miles away and commands stunning, panoramic views over most of Dorset. Months later I would ask myself why, on that particular day, was I directed to this area, but at the time I was simply enjoying a break in the weather, driving along country lanes that twisted and turned through the beautiful Dorset downland.

It was a crystal-clear day with a wintry sun at its zenith when I arrived at the monument. I parked alongside the only two other vehicles in the car park and, grabbing my camera, took several photos of the monument and the surrounding landscape before finding a grassy hillock a short distance away. Throwing my waxed jacket on the ground, I sat down upon it. The air was so fresh and clear up here and I breathed in great lungfuls, as I tried to rid myself of the strange mood that besieged me. It was like being on top of the world; I could see for miles. The view from the western tip of Chesil Beach right the way along the coast to the Isle of Portland was breath-taking, and I lazily watched two tankers slowly make their way across the horizon of a sparkling, flat sea.

I'd been sitting there for maybe fifteen minutes, allowing the scenery to work its magic and soothe my soul, when way below, in the far distance, three dogs emerged from the edge of the woods. Casually, I watched their rapid journey across the undulating landscape as they raced each other, stretching their limbs to the maximum and covering the ground with athletic ability. The terrier was easily outrun by the two larger dogs.

As I followed their progress, on the periphery of my vision, I saw a man emerge from the trees and call to the dogs. With a start, I recognised the figure – his build, the rough workmanlike clothes and the way he moved. It was Nat. Suddenly fully alert; I sat very still and focused on the scene below. He called to the dogs again and the terrier halted its pursuit. Panting heavily, it looked back at the man, as he strode across the landscape towards the exhausted dog. The two larger dogs still competed with each other and tore up the hill towards the monument. As they drew closer my heart began to race, as I recognised the Weimaraner and pointer. Looking back down the hill I saw that the figure, too, had altered its course and was beginning the steep climb to the Hardy Monument. A couple of minutes later the dogs came bounding over the ridge, their pace now slower and more laboured. They circled the monument twice before coming to a stop in front of me.

'Hello, Baron and Casper.'

Cocking their heads, the dogs observed me. The pointer approached and lay down at my side. I smiled. Baron watched but, being the one-person dog that he was, kept his distance and waited for his master. Maybe ten minutes later Nick appeared, breathing heavily; his lovely face flushed and energised. He stopped in surprise when he saw me.

'Maddie!' he said, in such a delightfully animated tone that it sent a tingle right through me.

'Hello.' I smiled.

Bending double, attempting to catch his breath, he looked up and surveyed me through narrowed eyes. 'Hang on,' he gasped. 'I'll be with you in a minute.'

Baron moved towards him and nudged his hand. Nick gently stroked the dog's head. Again, noticing his strong, capable hands, I suddenly had an overwhelming desire to feel those fingers gently stroking my skin.

With breathing less laboured, Nick straightened up and climbed over the ridge. As he sat down beside me, Baron immediately stretched out next to him.

'What brings you out this way?' he asked.

'Nothing in particular,' I replied. 'I just felt the need for some air, so drove out here.'

'Well, at two hundred and thirty-seven metres above sea level it's certainly a good place to catch the air.' He looked across me at his other dog. 'I see Casper's claimed you.'

At the sound of his name the dog thumped his tail on the ground but remained lying at my side.

'I told you these two like the fairer sex.'

I smiled. At least I was a hit with his dogs.

'The views are absolutely stunning.'

'Yes. It's the only place where you can see the entire length of the Jurassic Coast.' He looked along the coastline and pointed. 'See the Needles? They're clearly visible today.'

I looked eastwards. Shimmering in the far distance were the Isle of Wight's distinctive landmarks.

'They're about fifty miles away,' Nick continued. 'This is the only spot in Dorset where you can see the entire county and all its neighbouring counties.'

'How tall is the monument?' I asked, squinting up at the obelisk behind us.

'Seventy-two feet and built of Portland stone. Did you know it represents the spyglass of a ship?' I shook my head. 'It was built in honour of Sir Thomas Masterman Hardy, Flag Captain of HMS *Victory*. The story goes that Hardy sailed by in 1805 on his way to fight the Battle of Trafalgar.'

I smiled; comforted that Nick should know such things. 'Not Thomas Hardy the writer, then?'

'No, though a lot of visitors assume that. Thomas Masterman Hardy lived in Portesham until he joined the Navy.' He pointed to the village way below. 'Now, what other facts can I conjure up to impress the Irish lass?' Teasingly, he pulled a thinking face. 'Ah yes, the monument receives such a battering from the weather that as soon as it was built in 1844 the stone began to crumble.'

His eyes looked deep into mine.

I was totally disarmed and quickly scanned the escarpment for any diversion.

'That's one hell of a climb.'

'Sure is! And don't believe anyone who tells you the more you do it the easier it gets.' He laughed… that lovely mellow laugh that set me alight.

The quiet, trance-like reflective mood was still upon me and I gazed out to sea. Neither of us spoke for several minutes but the silence was companionable and not at all awkward. Thankfully, for once, I didn't feel the onset of an embarrassing schoolgirl blush.

After a while Nick asked, 'How's that friend of yours?'

'Dan?' I asked, still looking out to sea.

'Yes.'

'OK, but he has girlfriend trouble. That's why he came to see me.'

'Ah,' said Nick. 'We've all experienced that at some time or other.'

'*Obviously very happy with Sarah, though,*' my inner voice irritatingly pointed out, as if I wasn't only too well aware.

I sighed. I didn't have the strength to do battle with my inner self today. Still in the grips of introspective humour, I turned slowly in Nick's direction and caught him studying my profile. Quickly he looked away.

The sun was no longer high in the sky and a cool breeze blew in from the sea. I shivered. Getting to my feet, I picked up my jacket and placed it around my shoulders. Baron and Casper, now rested, started chasing each other around the monument. I bent to pick up the camera and remembered the terrier.

'Where's the other dog?' I asked, looking down the escarpment.

'What other dog?'

'The terrier.'

'Didn't see one.'

'It was running with Baron and Casper.'

Nick got to his feet and surveyed the hillside below. 'Really? It's not there now. Must have returned to its owner.'

I scanned the slopes below but there was no sign of the dog. Somewhere buried deep within my subconscious I knew there wouldn't be, but I was yet to acknowledge the truth of the terrier being long dead.

Nick checked his watch.

*'Just checking how much longer he's got before returning to the girlfriend,'* said my unhelpful, inner voice.

'What are you doing now?' he asked.

'Going home, I guess.'

'Why don't you come back to the barn? There's still enough light for you to take more photos for the magazine.'

'That's not such a bad idea,' I replied, wondering what Sarah would make of me just turning up unannounced, especially as the subject of extra photographs caused her such consternation.

He called to the dogs and they obediently came to heel. As we walked back to the car park I looked around for his Nissan.

'Where's your pickup?' I asked.

'At the garage. Brake problems.' He laughed and pointed to the mauve Ford Ka parked alongside mine. 'I'm driving Sarah's. It's a bit of a squash for these two rebels.'

He opened the hatchback and Baron and Casper jumped in. Sitting huddled together as Nick closed the tailgate, they peered out with their noses pressed against the rear window.

'Do you want to follow me?' he asked. 'Or do you remember where the barn is?'

I remembered all right – how could I not? All roads led to the barn; it was imprinted on my heart. But I said I was unsure and would follow him.

# 14

Turning left out of the car park, we followed the road for a couple of miles heading west. As we neared the Ashton Chase turning, I started to feel nervous at the thought of meeting Sarah again. I knew she would think I'd engineered this visit, even though it was a completely random event. Firmly, I told myself I was more than capable of handling whatever she threw at me and that I would maintain my composure.

We drove past the main house owned by Nick's friends; a glorious, mellow stone, Georgian mansion set in extensive mature grounds. Through the trees, I glimpsed a tennis court and a swimming pool. Continuing along the lane leading up to the farm with its myriad of rambling outbuildings, we turned a corner and skirted the hill that formed the backdrop to Nick's barn. Even though I knew what to expect, I switched off the engine and sat for a moment, savouring the panoramic vista down the valley to the sea beyond. The view would be wonderful in all seasons. It was simply glorious.

By now, the dogs were out of the car and gambolling around the lawn on the top terrace. I waited with bated breath for Sarah to appear at the front door, demanding to know why I was there. But the door remained firmly closed. I grabbed my camera, climbed out of the car and glanced over at Nick. Shielding his eyes, he stared intently at the sky.

'See the buzzards, Maddie?'

I followed his gaze. Two birds of prey wheeled slowly and majestically on the thermals high above the valley.

'How can you tell they're buzzards?'

'They're easy to spot by the way they soar with their wings held in that distinctive shallow V-shape. There's often a white patch on the underside of the wings, too. We always get this pair here,' he added. 'This valley is their special place.'

I focused the camera and took several photographs of the birds and the view, and even managed to get Nick in a couple of shots without him noticing. We watched the raptors a while longer before he turned and walked towards the barn. Extracting a key from his back pocket, he unlocked the porch door. As he entered, he tossed the key into a wooden bowl on a small side table and glanced back at me.

'Feel free to take whatever photos you think necessary.'

'Thanks. I'll take a couple of shots of the barn from the top terrace and I definitely want to get the lake in the late afternoon sun.'

'I'll follow you down. Just need to check the answerphone.'

I stood savouring the solitude. The only sound was the machine replaying its messages. The seclusion was wonderful; it was so peaceful. If I lived here I knew I would never want to leave.

From the top terrace, I took photographs of the barn

at varying angles. The dogs thought it great fun I was still around and came bounding up, charging around my legs and accompanying me down the steps to the middle terrace. As I stood on the edge photographing the lake below, they leapt off and dashed across the lower lawn to its perimeter. Startled by the sudden intrusion, two moorhens called in alarm and hurriedly paddled across the lake's flat surface before disappearing amongst the reeds.

'Casper!'

Nick stood on the top terrace and called to the dog as it waded into the lake. Leaping down the roughly hewn stone steps, he called again. The pointer hesitated, remaining in the shallows.

'Just look at that dog. I know exactly what he's doing. He thinks if he stays at the edge I'll be hoodwinked into thinking he's obeying me, but as soon as my back's turned he'll be after those moorhens.'

I laughed.

'Casper, I'm watching you,' he said sternly.

'He's very handsome,' I commented, 'as is Baron.'

'Yes, they're a good pair and good mates. Casper, come.'

Again, I wondered where his girlfriend was. On edge at not knowing, I half-expected her to appear at any moment. I took a deep breath. 'Is Sarah at home?'

'No. She's gone to London for a few days. Needed a break.'

My heart thumped so loudly I thought he might hear.

'When Becky said she was going up to the smoke to visit her mum Sarah jumped at the chance.'

Why did Sarah need a break? If I had a life with Nick I would be reluctant to leave for any reason.

'It's good to get away once in a while,' I said, trying not to sound too ecstatic.

The light was diminishing fast and, with it, the temperature.

'Sun's going down,' Nick observed. 'Let's go indoors and I'll fix us a drink.' Checking himself, he added, almost shyly, 'if you'd like one, that is.'

I glanced at him, surprised by the uncertainty in his voice. He didn't meet my gaze.

'That sounds an excellent idea,' I answered warmly.

As he turned towards the barn I saw him smile.

Even though it was early, Nick poured me a gin and tonic and a beer for himself and while I sat on the couch with Casper sprawling beside me, he lit the wood burner. At last I started to relax, and the strange, brooding mood that had besieged me all day finally lifted. Baron briefly deigned to place his chin on my knee so I could stroke his head, but as soon as Nick sat down he left me to sit at his master's feet. Outside, dusk swirled around the barn but inside it felt cosy and safe. Warmed by the heat of the fire, I closed my eyes and breathed out slowly, the tension leaving my body for the first time that day. When I opened them again I found Nick studying me.

'You look the picture of contentment,' he commented.

'I do feel very comfortable.' Absently, I fondled the pointer's ears.

'That's good.' He took a slug of beer. 'Do you miss your former life, Maddie?'

I considered his question.

'No, I don't,' I replied truthfully. 'I thought I might miss the wine bars and the constant partying the film industry enjoys, but I've obviously outgrown that.' I sipped my drink. 'I really enjoy working at the Blacksmith's and Brian's a great boss. Maybe it's replaced that particular need.'

'Yeah, Brian's a good bloke,' Nick said, 'and he and Vera have turned that pub around. It was dire a few years back. When they first took it over we all thought its previous reputation might prevent them from making a go of it.'

'Obviously a bad reputation doesn't stand a chance against sheer personality,' I suggested.

Nick laughed. 'That's for sure. He's certainly no shrinking violet.'

'I expect Brian could get a party going at the frostiest of gatherings,' I added.

Raising his eyebrows, he nodded in agreement. I remembered he'd said his family spanned generations in Dorset and I asked if there were still any members in the area. He told me that Helen and Peter lived in a village just outside Poole and his mother still resided at the family home in Melcombe Bingham.

'Dad passed away five years ago and, as you know, my brother flew the nest for a warmer climate many years back. There are plenty of cousins around, though. We get together from time to time, mostly family gatherings.'

'How far back can you trace your family?' I asked.

'When Dad died his brother felt the need to look into the family history. Said he'd traced us back to the seventeenth century.'

'My sister, Martha, researched our family tree for a school project once, but she was unable to get further back than the mid-nineteenth century. We put it down to the O'Briens having a murky past and not wanting to be traced.'

He laughed.

Dusk had now turned to night. Stretching across the couch, Nick switched on a side lamp, which cast a soft light across the room.

'The other week, when I fitted your bread oven door, you asked me what I'd seen,' he said, quietly serious.

I nodded, though he was not looking at me.

'Well...' he paused, his eyes meeting mine '...I saw you and two children dancing in a circle.'

A bolt of electricity shot through me. 'You saw it too!'

He nodded slowly. 'I did, although I couldn't believe it. It was only when I was at the workshop the following day and saw the sculpture in the courtyard that I realised what I'd seen.' He looked troubled. 'It's an odd thing. When I first started working on that piece I had no idea what I was creating. When it finally evolved into the mother and children it seemed to me that the piece had a life of its own.'

I had never felt so alive. There *had* to be some connection between Nick and me; I felt it in my bones. Dan hadn't witnessed any happenings in the cottage. He simply thought I was unwell and hallucinating when I experienced the visions. I was sure this feeling of complete familiarity with Nick was not just down to wishful thinking.

'My sister, Mo, is very sensitive and views life on a different plane,' I said. 'We always tease her she's psychic. When she stayed with me recently she saw a figure on the stairs – a man dressed in rough work clothes.'

He looked at me sharply and there was something in his eyes I didn't quite understand.

'I, too, have seen a man in the cottage on several

occasions and at a graveside in the church at Shipton Gorge,' I continued. 'I saw the same man today below the Hardy Monument. I don't know what it all means but Mrs McKendrick, the previous owner of The Olde Smithy, well... I think she may have witnessed things too.'

Nick listened attentively.

'She told me that although she lived in the cottage for over thirty years she was only ever looking after it for *me*. That's really odd, don't you think?'

The look in his eyes seemed one of recollection.

'Yes, that's an unusual thing to say,' he said carefully.

'And she always called me Mary, although her daughter dismissed this as senility.'

He looked shaken and for a moment couldn't look at me.

'Did you get the jewellery checked out, Maddie?'

I told him I'd taken the pieces to Professor Stephens who had verified they were very old, possibly dating back to the sixteen hundreds.

'He's carrying out further tests,' I added.

'It seems to me there's a story to your cottage. You should write about it. It might begin to make sense.'

'I have been keeping a diary of events.'

He fell silent for a while and then said, 'It may be that whoever is bound to your cottage needs to be given the opportunity to move on.'

The temperature in the room turned to ice and I started to shiver uncontrollably.

'Are you OK, Maddie?' he asked with concern.

'Yes, it's just what you said...'

Opening the door to the wood burner, he threw on another log.

I hesitated before continuing. 'Do you believe in ghosts, Nick?'

'Not the white sheet and two eye holes kind, but I think there's a lot in this world that can't be rationally explained. I like to keep an open mind on the subject.'

'But I wonder why I'm experiencing these things?' I said in bewilderment. 'What am I to the story?'

He shook his head. 'I'm sure it will become clear in time. Maybe you are the catalyst for this spirit to settle whatever remains unresolved.'

I was surprised and pleased to find that I could discuss my experiences so openly with Nick.

'Do you think the cottage needs to be exorcised?' he continued.

'No, it's not an evil presence. It's benign and so full of love, it takes my breath away. But, I seem to tap into very deep levels of emotion that have nothing to do with my own life.' I paused before continuing, 'I know this sounds really far-fetched but I think, somehow, a past life is living again through me.'

I knew how that sounded and hoped he didn't think I was completely mad. But Nick didn't make light of it.

'Promise me, Maddie, if you ever feel frightened you will phone me.'

I was overwhelmed by his concern and a lump started to form in my throat.

'It doesn't matter what time of day or night it is.'

*'So near and yet so far,'* my inner voice taunted.

I swallowed hard and thanked him, thinking all the while that Sarah would be really chuffed if I phoned at two in the morning.

'I mean it,' he said. 'If you ever feel threatened by anything in that property, phone me.'

'I won't ever be threatened by anything there, Nick. It's my home.'

*And a home where you knew a love like no other.* Unbidden, the words popped into my head.

'I know, Maddie, but you never know where these things can lead.' He rose to his feet. 'Here, let me top you up.'

I held out my empty glass across the table.

'And you'll stay for supper?'

Oh yes, you bet! I wanted to shout, but I simply smiled politely and said I'd like that very much.

# 15

It was a wonderful evening. Together, we prepared lasagne and found some part-baked rolls in the freezer, which we heated up in the oven. While I set knives and forks on the beautiful walnut dining table, Nick threw more logs onto the wood burner and opened a bottle of red wine. It felt surprisingly natural and comfortable sharing domestic chores.

Over supper, he brought up the subject of Dan again. 'How long were you and Dan together?'

'Eight years... or thereabouts.'

He raised an eyebrow.

'On and off,' I added swiftly.

'You must know each other very well.'

'Through and through.' I laughed. 'In fact, I definitely know him better than he knows himself, though I can't believe he fell for Lucy the way he did.'

'Are you jealous?'

I knew Nick was under the impression that Dan hoped to rekindle our relationship, but I wondered why he had asked that particular question.

'Not exactly jealous. You see, we have a casual relationship and it's not the first time there have been others, but I never thought he'd make her a permanent fixture.'

'Has he gone back to her?' he asked in surprise.

'I don't think so.' I took a sip of wine. 'And if he has any sense he won't.'

He hesitated and then quietly asked, 'So why hasn't he taken up with you again?'

'She seems to have cast a spell over him. He's completely transfixed.'

I didn't want to talk about Dan; I didn't want him to be any part of the evening.

'He's a fool,' Nick declared, looking directly at me for the first time during the course of the conversation.

I felt myself blush. Hurriedly, I said, 'So his sister tells him. She thinks he should have put our relationship on a more permanent footing. But enough of me, Nick. What about you? How long have you been with Sarah?'

I didn't want to talk about her either but I did want to steer the conversation away from Dan.

'Ten years. I met her on her eighteenth.'

What a great birthday present, I thought despairingly.

'And you've been together ever since?'

'More or less.' He seemed as uncomfortable answering my questions as I was talking about Dan.

It must have been the wine making me less inhibited because, having started this topic of conversation, I thought if I wanted to find out more about their relationship I had better ask now, or not at all.

'Becky was at the pub on New Year's Eve,' I said in an even voice, careful not to give away any feelings. 'She expected you to get engaged while you were in Australia.'

A small frown creased his forehead.

'Sarah wants to get married,' he answered after a long pause.

'I guess it's not unreasonable, seeing as you've been together so long.'

I couldn't believe I'd suggested it. God, Maddie, please don't persuade him it's a good thing to do…

'I know.' He was truly ill at ease. 'It's not unreasonable.'

'So what's the problem?'

Who was this person asking all these direct questions?

He hesitated before answering, grappling with some inner turmoil. 'I don't want to be disloyal to Sarah. She's a good girl. But that's just it!' His voice rose in frustration. 'She can be incredibly naïve, which I found charming… at first.'

He looked guilty for uttering such thoughts and my heart went out to him, even though I was consumed by jealousy at this display of loyalty to his girlfriend.

'It's OK to talk like this, Nick, but we don't have to if you don't want to.'

'I'd rather not.' Smiling apologetically, he picked up the bottle of wine and leant across the table to fill up my glass.

We polished off that bottle and then another. I knew there was no way I could drive that night and when Nick suggested I stay, I did not object.

'We can have a leisurely morning, if you don't have to be anywhere early tomorrow.'

We remained chatting in the warmth of the living room until I could no longer keep my eyes open.

'Well, I guess it's time to hit the sack. You take the bed, Maddie, I'll sleep on the couch.'

I protested and said I was more than happy to take the couch, but he wasn't having any of it. Rising to his feet, he headed towards the spiral staircase.

I cleared the table and stacked the dishwasher, surprised at how unsteady I was. Normally, I could hold my drink. Through a befuddled stupor, I realised Storm would have to fend for himself overnight. Thankfully, the original nest of sacks was still in the outhouse and I hoped he would use his old bed. Holding firmly on to the handrail, I climbed the spiral staircase to the galleried bedroom. On the far side of the room, Nick pulled a sleeping bag out of a cupboard and a T-shirt from a chest of drawers.

'You can wear this if you want,' he said, walking towards me. 'It's an old rugby T of mine. It is clean.'

I took it gratefully, although seriously doubted I'd get any sleep knowing he was in the room below.

He smiled at me and then said in such a gentle voice that I hardly heard, 'You know, Maddie, you're very beautiful.'

Shaken out of my drunkenness, I stared at him in amazement.

'What...?'

The look in his eyes was soft and his voice tender as he repeated, 'You're very beautiful. I can totally understand why Dan hot-footed it down to Dorset to be with you. If the man had any sense he'd have stayed.'

I flushed, but not from embarrassment.

Moving towards me, Nick took my face in his hands and kissed me softly. The deep emotion I experienced was so powerful I could hardly breathe and I pulled back gasping.

'You know, I've wanted to do that from the very first moment I set eyes on you,' he said in a husky whisper.

Was I dreaming?

And then he kissed me again and this time I responded. Nothing existed outside of that kiss and as our passion grew I felt his body grow tense. I inhaled deeply. His masculine scent was familiar and, instinctively, from somewhere deep within, I knew this was *home*. I kissed him hard, moulding my body against his, and felt his growing desire. His breathing turned rapid and he groaned. As he ran his hands down my body, I delighted in his touch.

In one swift action, as if I were as light as air, he picked me up and carried me to the bed. We fell onto it, laughing, but the instant I felt his weight on me a charge surged through my body and I melted under his hot, insistent kisses that promised a wild and desperate crescendo. The hunger I had for this man sent shudders coursing through me, and as his hands greedily explored my body I marvelled at the way I responded to the urgency in his caress. It was like nothing I had experienced before… Suddenly, I thought of that 'other' man who made love to me whenever Dan stayed in the cottage, and I faltered; breaking the spell.

Nick pulled away. 'I'm sorry. I shouldn't have done that.'

No, it's OK, I wanted to say. It's really OK! But my brains had turned to mush and my knees to jelly.

He rolled off me, looking guilty and full of remorse. Sadly, I watched as loyalty and commitment returned to his demeanour. Sarah was one hell of a lucky girl.

Rising from the bed, he picked up his sleeping bag and walked to the spiral staircase. 'Sleep well, Maddie,' he said, avoiding eye contact.

I staggered to the shower room and, holding firmly on to

the basin, met my gaze in the mirror. There was a wild look in my eyes – was it despair?

'*So near and yet so very far...*'

I splashed cold water on my face. Then, squeezing toothpaste onto a finger, I cleaned my teeth as best I could. Finally, I undressed and put on Nick's T-shirt, inhaling deeply as I pulled it over my head and hugged it to my body. Swaying back to the bed, I lay as the room spun madly and listened to the unfamiliar sounds coming from the room below. The porch door opened. A few minutes later I heard Nick call quietly to the dogs. He'd obviously let them out to do their business. My respect for him was already huge but it went up a notch knowing that even when well-oiled he still acted responsibly.

Lucky Baron, lucky Casper... and lucky, lucky Sarah.

In a low voice he told the dogs to settle. Then all was quiet.

I lay for what seemed an eternity with my body aching for him. I looked up through the glass roof at the inky, night sky and thousands of stars winked at me, as if all sharing a huge joke. Never had I felt so wretched and alone. Gulping back a sob, I squeezed my eyes shut to stem unbidden tears. With the bed continuing to spin, eventually I fell asleep.

# 16

It was a hot summer's day and I lay in the long grass of a wildflower meadow gazing into infinite blue. Wisps of cloud tinged pale pink drifted across the sky and I entertained myself making shapes from them. There was a dog, like my sister's spaniel, and surely that was a dolphin... and wasn't that a smiling face? I whiled away the time, running my fingers through the blades of grass, luxuriating in the buzz and hum of insects as they flitted from one wildflower to another, collecting nectar. Butterflies lifted into the air and somewhere, high above, a skylark sang. Shielding my eyes I searched the sky... but the bird wasn't to be found.

I sat up and was surprised to find that I was dressed in only a thin, linen chemise, which barely reached my knees. My legs were tanned and I was barefoot. Where were my outer garments? I smiled wickedly. What would they think of me out here in the meadow, unclothed and without shoes? Unbecoming and abandoned, no doubt. The sun was way past its zenith and I had no idea how long I'd been out there. It *must* be time to return. Freedom over.

Sighing deeply, I rose to my feet. A beautiful, pastoral scene stretched before me. Neat parkland fell away gently towards the edge of a thick forest, and a herd of russet-coloured cattle grazed peacefully in the meadows. I turned. In an elevated position, presiding over the view, stood an Elizabethan gem of a Manor House, its grey stone walls gleaming almost white; the colour of elephant tusks. In the late afternoon sun, light reflected off its many mullioned windows. Built in an E-plan style, the house stood three storeys high with numerous gabled roofs and chimneys, the architectural detail giving the impression of a castle. Instinctively, I knew entry was made through the middle wing of the west front, where the decorated screens-passage was, with the Great Hall off to the right and the Great Kitchen opposite, occupying the north wing of the 'E'. I studied the recently built staircase tower in the space between the original Tudor house and the newly commissioned extension, which now provided means of access to the upper storeys. The builders had done an excellent job and the addition was seamless.

As I set off across the wildflower meadow and approached the Manor, above the entrance porch I saw the family coat of arms carved into the stone. However, I didn't continue across the lawns to the sweeping gravel drive and the steps leading up to the entrance. Instead, I turned left and headed towards an impressive archway. As I entered the grand stable yard I saw my father's three prized hunters tied up against the far wall, their coats gleaming in the sunshine.

Bent over the hind hoof of an impressive grey gelding – my father's favourite – a man held up a metal shoe to its sole. The horse, used to being shod, stood patiently. Although late afternoon, it was searingly hot and I brushed away stray wisps of hair from my face as I watched the man labour in the heat, absorbed in his task. A sheen of sweat accentuated his impressive arm muscles as he nailed the metal shoes to the horse's hooves.

Suddenly he looked up and glanced over in my direction. At once, I noticed how still it had become – like an expectant, held breath – as a pair of tender blue-grey eyes met mine. In that one moment, a thousand words passed between us. Growing hotter by the minute, I was acutely aware of my thin chemise and brown legs on display. The farrier straightened up. Letting the grey's foot drop, he wiped a hand across his brow. Not once did he take his eyes from me, which I noticed danced with amusement.

I should have been outraged – that he had the audacity to consider a daughter of the house in that manner – but I wasn't. Something about the man spoke to me in a way that made me feel not only safe and secure, but also alive for the very first time. It was as if a whole world awaited me and all I had to do was trust in that look, which held such promises. Slowly I turned away, but those blue-grey eyes remained seared into my soul.

I came to, breathing hard. Where was I? Suddenly it all came flooding back. Gazing up through the glass roof, I saw the sky now held the tinge of early morning and dense cloud cover hid the stars from view. I peered at my watch – 6.15 a.m. So I had slept. As I sat up, a raging headache took hold. Gingerly climbing out of bed, I walked unsteadily to the shower room and stared dejectedly at my reflection in the mirror. Pale and sallow; as if all the life had been sucked out of me. I groaned as numerous unanswerable questions filled my head.

Before returning to the bed, I tiptoed to the gallery and looked over. The barn was still and peaceful, filled with the grey light of dawn. Both dogs lay sprawled on one of the couches and Casper looked up eagerly. Baron didn't stir. On the other couch lay Nick, flat on his back with the sleeping bag half off his body. He was sound asleep with one hand resting on his chest; his head nestled in the crook of his other arm. In sleep, he appeared younger and there was a half-smile on his face. I wondered what happy dreams he enjoyed.

I stood gazing at him for a long while, committing to memory every little aspect of the scene below. He was gorgeous and I knew I was lost. Eventually, the cold air sent me back to bed. I snuggled deep beneath the duvet and, soon, the blessed oblivion of a dreamless sleep claimed me.

I awoke to the smell of frying bacon and was suddenly ravenous. I stretched, sat up and looked around. Even though the barn was still a work in progress it struck me there was very little of Sarah on show. There were make-up and bottles of lotion in the bathroom, but apart from this there were very few girlie items around. Beside the bed was a chunky, abstract, wooden root of a table and, on it, a simple slate frame displayed a photograph of Sarah and Nick with their arms around each other, smiling happily into the camera. However, apart from this, there were no other displays of togetherness that I'd seen. It appeared this was very much Nick's place.

The sound of footsteps on the stairs made me turn.

'You're awake,' Nick said, stepping up onto the gallery floor and holding a mug in one hand. 'Thought I'd let you sleep in.'

'What's the time?' I asked blearily. A major hangover threatened.

'Ten-thirty. I've made you tea. You don't take sugar, do you?'

I shook my head and took the mug from him.

Crossing the room, he pulled out a clean sweatshirt from the chest of drawers.

'Bacon and eggs OK?' he asked, glancing over his shoulder.

'Sounds great.' I gave a brief smile.

Despite the many questions swirling around my head, I said nothing more.

We enjoyed a companionable breakfast and it was a relief to find that conversation flowed easily. There was no tension between us and what had passed the previous night did not appear to stand in the way. I left around noon. As Nick walked me to the car I noticed the two buzzards circling high above the valley.

'The guardian angels still watch over you,' I said, and then wondered why I'd said it.

He gave a half-smile, which quickly turned into a small, puzzled frown.

Unlocking the car, I climbed in and fastened the seatbelt, and was about to pull the door to when Nick prevented me.

'I'm sorry about what happened last night, Maddie.' Concentrating fiercely on the ground, he scuffed the gravel with the toe of his boot.

'Nothing to apologise for Nick,' I said quietly.

'That's very magnanimous of you.' A small smile settled on his lips, but when his eyes met mine they were far from happy. Softly he said, 'It won't happen again.'

I smiled sadly as he closed the door.

Driving away with a heavy heart, I watched Nick in the rear-view mirror until he was out of sight. As I rounded the corner he raised a hand in farewell, and I felt my heart fracture; shards of glass piercing my very soul.

# 17

That night I tossed and turned; my mind gave me no rest. As if playing on a loop, I re-examined the last twenty-four hours over and over in my head, but peace evaded me. Eventually – exhausted – I fell into a restless sleep and it wasn't long before I was in the throes of a poignantly bittersweet dream.

Shafts of late afternoon sunlight made their way through the tall windows and, mesmerised, I watched the particles of dust held in suspension. I sat in the Great Hall, clenching my jaw, willing myself to be strong and not to react. On the other side of the room my father paced up and down, puce with rage. His eyes bulged from the emotion and he spluttered and pulled at his collar. I'd asked him to allow me to marry Nat. Concerned he was about to have a fit, I rose to my feet but he brusquely waved me away. I sat down again. Eventually, the colour in his face subsided.

'Mary, you were born into the ruling class,' he said in a no-nonsense voice, 'and you will *not* marry a working man, no matter how well respected. I will not allow it.'

I tried to object but he silenced me.

'Edward will inherit the estate. Therefore, it is imperative

SECRETS OF THE MIST

that both you and your sister make good marriages to
secure your futures. I have entered into an agreement with
Sir Thomas Ramsey and you are to become his wife once
Lady Ramsey has passed, God bless her.'

I stared at him in horror. I'd heard my parents discussing
the gravely ill wife of a distant neighbour and knew it was
only a matter of time before she succumbed.

'Please, Father, I beg of you. Don't betroth me to a man
almost thirty years my senior.' Digging my nails into my
hands, I forced myself to be strong. 'I love Nat.'

'Love!' My father snorted. Batting me away again, as
if my protestations were a mere trifle, he added, 'Love
has nothing to do with marriage, Mary. In time, I'm sure
you will grow fond of Sir Thomas. His name and wealth
will provide you with the security you need. That is the
important consideration here.'

'I refuse to marry him.' I met my father's eyes. 'I won't.'

'I will not have a daughter of mine rise up against
her father.' He strode across the room and, grabbing me
roughly by the arm, ushered me upstairs to my room. 'You
will remain here until you have considered your situation
and come to your senses.'

He left the room. As he closed the door behind him, I
heard the key turn in the lock.

My mother visited me that evening and tried to smooth
over the rift, pointing out the positives of a marriage to
Sir Thomas Ramsey. But I wasn't my father's daughter for
nothing; I shared his strength of character.

'I refuse to accept the fate Father has in store for me.'

'Oh, Mary!' my mother exclaimed. 'Stubborn as always.'
She rose to her feet. 'I will have supper sent up to you, but

if you wish to escape your imprisonment I suggest you consider carefully what your father proposes. You do know he has your best interests at heart.'

My sister, Charlotte, three years my junior, brought my supper. She revelled in the romantic notion of Nat and me and eagerly accepted her role as 'go-between'. Willingly, she passed a message to him.

I was locked in my room for four long days and nights, but by the time I was finally released, Nat and I had hatched a plan. Under the strict, watchful eye of my father, I pretended to acquiesce to his plans. However, a week later, once Nat had made the arrangements, I bundled together a few personal items and some clothing and, early one morning, before the household was awake, I slipped quietly out of the Hall.

It was the hour before dawn. Keeping to the shadows, I made my way stealthily down the long drive towards the stone entrance pillars and massive iron gates. I knew Nat was waiting for me just beyond, out of sight. He was there with the bay mare and he immediately lifted me easily onto Bess's back. I sat in front of him, clutching my bundle, as we rode to Waldyke. Changing our clothes in haste, before Father had wind of anything, we walked out of the cottage hand in hand, eager to embrace our future.

Coming to, briefly, I glanced at the bedside clock – it was just past three in the morning. Far too early to be awake. I turned over and closed my eyes.

'Mary,' I whispered, 'please show me.'

I drifted back to sleep and soon revisited the dream.

It was a beautiful, late spring day and I felt strangely energised. My skin was warmed by a sun riding high in a clear blue sky dotted with cotton wool clouds, and the gentlest of breezes caressed me. I stood in an apple orchard strewn with wildflowers and a dozen chickens scratched amongst the long grass at the base of the trees. As my gaze travelled beyond my immediate surroundings, I noticed a collection of vaguely familiar single-storey outhouses attached to a thatched building, its reeds glowing golden in the sunshine.

Recognising the rise of hills beyond, I realised I was standing in the land to the rear of Nat's forge. As I became aware of a number of figures around me, their features indistinct, I trembled with excitement. Glancing down, I saw long, auburn locks and a string of pearls tumbling over the bodice of my emerald-green and gold brocade dress; the one I only wore for special occasions. Raising my hand to my head, I felt a small clasp of wildflowers in my hair. I gazed around again at the voluminous drifts of pink and white blossom confetti adorning the apple trees; the most beautiful of wedding floral arrangements.

I turned to the person standing beside me. There was nothing indistinct about him. Dressed in his finest outfit, Nat gazed at me in wonder. Suddenly, a cocktail of emotions threatened to overwhelm me – excitement, joy and sadness, swiftly followed by powerful, all-consuming love for this man. He held out his hand to me. As if following a film script, I watched as I rested my hand lightly in his.

A gentleman I didn't recognise stepped forward. He was dressed smartly and possessed an air of authority. Producing a length of beautiful gold ribbon, he proceeded to loosely bind our hands together.

'Blessed be this union with the gifts of the east: communication of the heart, mind and body; fresh beginnings with the rising of each sun; and the knowledge of the growth found in the sharing of silences.'

He wrapped a second ribbon around our hands, this time silver.

'Blessed be this union with the gifts of the south: warmth of hearth and home; the heat of the heart's passion; and the light created by both to illuminate the darkest of times.'

A third length of ribbon, pale blue in colour, was bound loosely around our hands.

'Blessed be this union with the gifts of the west: the deep commitments of the lake; the swift excitement of the river; the refreshing cleansing of the rain; and the all-encompassing passion of the sea.'

Finally, a beautiful pale green ribbon was added to the others around our hands.

'Blessed be this union with the gifts of the north: firm foundation on which to build; fertility of the fields to enrich your lives; and a stable home to which you may always return.'

As the ribbons were looped together as one, I gazed up into Nat's tender blue-grey eyes.

'As this knot is tied, so are your lives now bound,' proclaimed the man of authority.

Then, untying the fastening, he removed the ribbons and laid them neatly side by side on an ornate iron altar. I recognised it at once and glanced at Nat in surprise. I'd seen him working on it in the forge, carefully coaxing it into shape, but he hadn't told me what he was smithing. His eyes twinkled.

'And now it is time for the giving of rings,' the gentleman continued.

I watched, mesmerised, as Nat produced the beautiful ruby ring from his pocket and slipped it onto my wedding finger. It was a perfect fit; but I knew it would be. I, in turn, removed a simple gold band from a secret pocket at my waist and, lovingly, slipped it on his wedding finger.

Nat's eyes were soft and warm, as he said, 'I take thee, my heart, at the rising of the moon and the setting of the stars. To love and to honour through all that may come. Through all our lives together, in all our lives, may we be reborn that we may meet and know and love again, and remember.'

Tears sprang to my eyes and I smiled up at him. His look was one of wonderment; as if he couldn't truly believe we were wed.

All at once the other figures took shape, and I recognised Nat's family and friends. Sadness tinged my joy. Not a single member of my family was present. As people stepped forward to congratulate us, Nat put his arm around my waist and protectively drew me to him.

'Look, Mary,' he said, pointing skywards. 'Guardian angels to watch over us.'

Shielding my eyes from the sun, I gazed up at the clear blue sky. High above, two dark specks circled and I smiled. As long as the buzzards were present in our life, we would be OK.

We continued our wedding celebrations at the tavern across from the forge. It was important there were many witnesses to our joining. We had to prove our marriage was legally binding, for we knew my father would come looking for me once my absence at the Hall was discovered.

Lying with Nat for the very first time, I was gripped by a sudden shyness but as the night progressed I soon became bold. As his hands explored my body I marvelled at the way I responded and when his mouth found mine, the urgency and passion in his caresses took my breath away. I delighted at his every touch and my skin tingled as his fingers travelled the contours of my body. Moving in harmony, we melted under each other's deep kisses.

'I am bewitched, Mary,' he said, nuzzling my neck, and I thrilled at the emotion I heard in his voice.

Momentarily he pulled back and I sensed him looking at me. Emerging from behind a cloud, the moon cast its light through the window and alighted on my husband's face. Suddenly Nat groaned and pulled me to him. I gasped as my body opened to him and, together, we rode wave after wave of pure sensation; an insatiable riptide of feeling. Much later, holding each other close, I lay with my head on Nat's chest, listening to the reassuring beat of his heart. Gently, he stroked my hair and I breathed in his masculine scent.

'I love you, Nat,' I whispered softly, running my hands lightly over his muscular body.

His grip tightened. 'And you, my love, are my life.'

I lifted my head to look at my husband, but it wasn't Nat gazing at me with love in his eyes. It was Nick.

# 18

I was encouraged by the number of magazines that agreed to accept my freelance articles and relieved that writing money would soon start to trickle in. It suited me to work for Brian and Vera on Friday and Saturday nights, but we agreed that if they needed extra staff for special events I would work additional shifts. It was satisfying to know I was successfully building multiple sources of income.

At the end of February I received an email from Mo.

Hi Mads, Sorry for the delay in getting back to you but I've only just got home from whirlwind photo shoot across Europe. Interesting photo No. 11. I've sent it through full size for definition. Tell me what you think? Mo xx

I opened the photos, laughing at those of my impersonation of the French Lieutenant's Woman on the Cobb, and marvelling at the way Mo had captured The Olde Smithy. Her photographer's 'eye' was unique and I totally understood why she was in high demand in her chosen career. And then I reached the eleventh photograph and the hairs stood up on the back of my neck.

Taken from the door to the hallway, it was of the sitting room, with the inglenook fireplace the focal point. She had captured part of the stained-glass divide between the rooms and the bread oven was plain to see. However, in front of the oven stood a fog-like apparition which, on resizing the photo, took shape. As the image became more defined, I focused on the face peering from the screen and found myself gulping back sobs as I experienced a bundle of confused emotions: despair, grief, joy, elation... and love.

It was Nat, whose spirit I firmly believed shared this cottage and who offered me such unconditional love. As the tears flowed unchecked down my cheeks, my fingers stroked the face on the screen. The eyes that looked back at me were full of wonder and tenderness, as those in my dream. With a jolt, which momentarily stemmed my tears, I recognised that very look from only the week before when Nick had held me in his arms.

Nick... I'd tried to put him out of my mind, but I couldn't. The strong emotions he stirred refused to go away and he filled my waking hours. It was so much more than simple, physical attraction and lust. I was drawn to him in a way I couldn't explain and from the moment I'd met him, I felt as if I knew him; body and soul. And his scent... it was so familiar. But how was that possible? He'd said he found me very beautiful and each time I recalled his words, and the tenderness in his voice, my insides turned to liquid desire. In that drink-induced, oh too brief, uninhibited moment, we had responded to each other without pretence. The emotions were real.

But with strength of will I didn't possess, he'd taken control and placed his feelings to one side. I'd got the message. He didn't have to spell it out. In no way was he prepared to abandon his long-term girlfriend. A part of me hated Sarah for the power she had over him, but I also understood and respected Nick even more for his commitment to her. I just had to accept the fact and learn to live with it. But what madness! Of course I could live with it. After all, I'd never been promised anything.

*Haven't you?*

The voice in my head halted my tumultuous thoughts and I frowned. Of course I hadn't. No one had ever promised me anything.

Grabbing a tissue from the bathroom, I blew my nose and told myself to get a grip, but, unlike Nick, I couldn't coolly put my emotions to one side. Neither could I get the look of wonder and tenderness in Nat's eyes out of my head. As I returned to the screen, I noticed his eyes followed me wherever I moved in the room. I found my mobile and texted Mo.

Photo 11 – is this the man you saw on the stairs?

After a few minutes she texted:

Yes!

I texted back:

He's the man at the grave.

I didn't have long to wait for her reply:

Kurt busy but says he will decipher epitaph soon. Have you a story yet?

I responded:

Still working on it.

She replied:

Good luck. Keep me informed. How's the gorgeous man?

I gritted my teeth as I texted back:

Don't ask... Mads xx

She signed off in capitals:

KEEP THE FAITH! xx

I saved her photos in The Olde Smithy file, but kept Nat's face on the screen.

'Tell me what you want from me,' I whispered into the empty room.

Stillness.

'What do you need me to do?' I asked a little louder.

Deep silence.

I sighed and stared at the dear, familiar face on the screen. I don't know how long I sat there but it was only the phone ringing that shook me out of my trance-like state. It was Caro, Dan's sister.

'Hi, Maddie. How are you?'

'Well thanks,' I lied. 'How about you?'

'Good, I think,' she said. 'John's just been told his company is relocating and he's responsible for overseeing the move.'

'Oh, where to?'

'Newcastle. All the departments are moving up in instalments but we're to relocate at the end of April. Seems a long way from London, but I've already checked and there are flights from both Exeter and Southampton so you can visit any time.'

I agreed that sounded a great idea.

'I hear Dan saw you recently,' she suddenly said.

'Yes. I was really surprised. Hadn't heard from him for weeks and then he turned up out of the blue. Mind you, I haven't heard a peep out of him since.'

'No you won't have,' she said. 'The silly old fool's taken up with Lucy again.'

I groaned. Had he lost all sense? And after everything he'd said! What *was* it about that woman?

'I can't say too much to him,' Caro continued. 'He's very touchy about her but as he is my only family now I don't want to lose him. I make sure John and I see them, when they're in a socialising mood, which I must say isn't very often. They're content holed up in that flat of his. I have to remind him there's a bigger world out there.'

I glanced out of the kitchen window and watched Storm chasing swirling leaves across the courtyard. 'He's lucky to have you as a sister.'

'Oh, he's a good soul,' she said, instantly springing to his defence. 'I just think he's lost his way a little. He's totally smitten. But I am worried about him, especially now that I won't be in London. He doesn't look at all well.'

'It's his life, Caro. Only he can make changes if it doesn't suit him.' I didn't really know what to say. I'd witnessed the hold Lucy had over him.

'I know,' she said sadly, 'but she's such a predator and he's so malleable. I can't help but feel protective.'

'He'll be OK,' I said confidently, though privately I wondered if he would be all right. Changing the subject, I asked, 'Will you have time to visit me before you leave for the north?'

'Sorry, Maddie, I don't think so. I have a huge PR launch to organise before I go and I must get the house ready for letting. We've decided to keep it but it needs to pay its way. You could always come up to London and stay with us before we leave.'

'Good idea,' I agreed. 'Suggest some dates.'

We checked our diaries, agreed on the first weekend in April and I marked it on the calendar. We chatted a while longer before saying goodbye.

Opening the back door, I called to Storm, but he didn't want to come in. It was a sunny, gusty day and, with the wind in his tail, he shot off on some private mission. I followed up the path, fighting my way through the foliage and made a mental note to buy a lawnmower on my next visit to Bridport. I paused halfway up the garden and looked back at the cottage.

This was the exact spot where Mary and Nat were married – how different it looked to the scene in my dream. I gazed at the rise of hills; their outline hadn't altered. However, there were fewer trees today. And although the outhouses were in the same position, they had been modified. The cottage, of course, was no longer thatched and the modern extension had changed its appearance, and whereas the orchard in my dream was full of apple trees, there were now only three.

I continued on up the garden. As I approached the pond, I noticed Storm dash through the fence into next door. As it happened, Mrs Tomkins was in her garden and so I called a greeting. She came over and told me that Rex, her aged ginger tom, was ill over the winter and the vet had put him to sleep the previous week.

'I'm so sorry,' I said gently. 'What a horrible decision to have to make. I expect he gave you several years of companionship.'

'Oh yes, dear. He was nineteen years old. My Fred gave him to me as a twelve-week-old kitten.'

I told her I'd just seen Storm shoot through the fence into her garden.

'He's often here,' she said. 'He and Rex were good friends. They would curl up together in Rex's basket.'

'He kept that one a secret,' I said.

'If you ever go away, dear, just let me know. I'll be more than happy to look after him for you.'

I thanked her. What good timing, having just arranged with Caro to visit her in London. We chatted about my plans for the garden and my vegetable plot and she promised to give me some seedlings from her greenhouse to get started.

'That's very kind of you, Mrs Tomkins. Is there anything I can do for you?'

'Well, I don't know, dear.' She turned and looked towards her cottage. 'I am having trouble with my back door. It's become swollen over the winter months and I find it difficult to open, what with my arthritis. Do you know anyone trustworthy who could have a look at it? I don't like to use tradesmen without recommendation.'

'I know someone very trustworthy. I'll get his number for you this minute.'

I ran to the cottage and jotted down Nick's mobile on a Post-it note. By the time I returned, Storm was in my neighbour's arms.

'You don't mind, do you?' Mrs Tomkins asked, her eyes shining brightly.

'Not at all. It's good to know he has so many friends,' I said, realising she must be feeling very raw at the loss of Rex. 'I do wonder where Storm came from, though. Nobody's ever claimed him and he's such a handsome cat. It seems unlikely he hasn't a home of his own.'

She agreed. Purring on cue, Storm nestled against her neck. I left them to it and walked back to the kitchen. I made a sandwich and was halfway through eating it when the phone rang.

'Professor Stephens here. I have some interesting news for you. Your treasure has proven very exciting indeed!' I held my breath. 'Philip has emailed his report and confirmed my earlier findings. If you'd care to furnish me with your email address I will forward it to you.'

I gave him the address.

'You can pick up the jewellery at any time, but I would be most intrigued to see where you found it.'

'Of course,' I said. 'When would you like to come over?'

'I'm free this Thursday morning, if that suits?'

I checked the calendar. 'Come in time for coffee,' I suggested, smiling at the thought of the gossip it would create in the village when he rolled up in his Porsche.

I opened the laptop, logged on, and finished the sandwich as I waited. Within five minutes the email arrived. It read:

**Observations on Jewellery for Ms Madeleine O'Brien:**

**Pendant** – Maker unknown.

Charming 3D Heart ornament of interwoven polished cut steel.

Not fashioned by a professional jeweller (more likely a skilled craftsman).

Dimensions: 4cm x 3.5cm.

During the 17th century and up to circa 1940, brightly polished steel studs fastened to a steel backplate were fashioned into all sorts of jewellery. The studs were riveted or screwed into place. Highly polished cut steel gave the impression of diamonds. Silver later replaced cut steel as the preferred metal in jewellery making.

From 1620 to 1640 fashionable women in Western Europe wore a single large jewel on their bodice, simply stitched to the fabric of the gown. This particular pendant is cleverly crafted to be worn as such, or to accommodate a ribbon necklace, which would originally have been of silk.

Note: Hearts were popular in jewellery design during the 1600s and the heart motif continued to evolve throughout the century and into the next.

**Ring** – Maker unknown.

Copy based on a German gimmel ring.

Circa 1600–1650.

Enamelled gold set with a ruby.

Diameter: 2cm.

A gimmel ring is made of three interlocking hoops. When worn, the ruby heart at the front of the ring is encircled by a pair of clasped hands. This intricate wedding ring is decorated with symbols of love and quotations from the marriage ceremony. The central motif comes from the Italian *'mani in fede'* (hands clasped in faith), which was a popular symbol of love. The three connecting hoops, each with an attached hand or heart, fit together and appear as one band when worn. In this gimmel ring, the ruby symbolises love and the clasped hands fidelity.

The inscriptions can only be read when the hoops of the ring are opened out.

Inscribed: *My beginning and my end; Let no man put asunder; NC & MO, 8 May 1635.*

Note: Hearts were popular motifs for engagement and wedding rings during the 17th and 18th centuries. Such rings often combined rubies (signifying love) and/or diamonds (signifying eternity).

I stared at the screen, my gut instinct telling me this was an important clue: a waymarker to solving the riddle. I read the report half a dozen times. So, Professor Stephens had been correct. The jewellery did date back to the mid-1600s. But I wasn't any closer to finding out whom the pieces belonged to or why they had been concealed in the bread oven.

# 19

The following day I drove into Bridport and purchased a lawnmower. I was eager to start on the garden and wanted to be well prepared for the spring. I parked alongside the village green, as close to the cottage as possible, and was grappling with the mower in the back of the car when I heard a familiar voice.

'Do you want some help with that, Maddie?'

Butterflies fluttered in my stomach and a dull ache settled on my heart. I glanced over my shoulder and saw Nick wearing an amused expression. I swallowed hard.

'It went in OK so it *must* come out!'

He smiled. 'Here, let me.'

I stood back and watched as he manoeuvred the lawnmower out of the car.

'Where do you want it? Round the back?'

I nodded and shut the boot. As I followed him up the path I noticed how easily he carried the mower, though his straining biceps confirmed its weight. We walked around the side of the cottage and into the courtyard where he set it down outside the potting shed.

'Why are you here?' I asked.

He was about to say something, but stopped himself.

'I've come to fix your neighbour's door. Thanks for suggesting me, by the way.'

He looked at me with such compassion that I felt my fragile heart crack a little further.

'No trouble,' I mumbled, the lump in my throat causing my voice to distort.

'So, you're going to start clearing the garden?' He gazed up the pathway leading to the wilderness beyond.

'Can't put it off much longer. I've got to cut that grass before the growing season starts.'

He laughed. 'Like cleaning the house before the cleaner arrives?'

I acknowledged my irrational logic.

'It's probably a good idea to tackle it with a strimmer first,' he said. 'Don't want to knacker the mower before it's had a chance to show what it can do!'

I agreed. It felt so right being with Nick and I found myself smiling, despite the ache in my heart.

Observing the outbuildings that created the courtyard, he peered through the window of the one attached to the cottage. Taking a step back, he squinted up at the roofline.

'These look interesting. The outside privy is a later addition but I would say this building is probably the same age as the cottage.' He slapped the outhouse wall.

I held my breath. This was important. 'Would it have been a dwelling?'

He shook his head. 'More likely animal housing.'

'Do you think there would have been a doorway connecting it to the cottage?'

'Possibly. Is there any evidence of one inside?'

I said I wasn't sure. Opening the door, he walked into the outhouse. It was well built with thick stone walls and ancient, gnarled A-frame roof timbers that had seen better days. I watched as Nick examined the building, pointing out various features I hadn't noticed before.

'That doorway is relatively new,' he said, referring to the door we had just entered through, 'but look at the arch above it, Maddie. It extends half the length of the building. I'd say this was originally a cart shed, or possibly the forge.'

He walked to the wall adjoining the cottage and, peering closely, roughly brushed away the cobwebs. The flaking render came away easily at his touch.

'I think this answers your question. This area's been filled in. Someone's bricked it up at some point.'

Moving closer, I saw the outline of a doorway and my heart began to race.

'This would lead straight into the kitchen,' I said excitedly, recalling Nat disappearing through an invisible doorway.

'And I think you'll find the original front door would have been bang opposite,' Nick said.

I visualised it and realised that each time I'd witnessed Nat walking from the front to the rear of the cottage he was on that very route.

'Oh, Nick!'

In the excitement of this discovery, I forgot what had transpired between us and I hugged him. His arms instantly held me and I melted. Then I remembered. Quickly I turned away before he could see my despair.

'I'm going to check it out.'

I rushed from the building and across the courtyard to

the back door and was about to enter the kitchen when an urgent voice halted me in my tracks.

'Mary!' I turned slowly. 'Mary, I must speak with you.'

A curtain of mist hung in the air and the scene before me had altered. He stood in an open archway and where the outside privy and potting shed should have been there was now a stone water trough. At once, I became aware of an acrid smell. Behind him, in the far corner, a blacksmith's furnace was alight smithing with several horseshoes laid out on the red-hot embers. Tied to the outside wall, a chestnut horse patiently waited.

Nick, though I could now see it was Nat, stood looking at me. He wore a dirty leather apron over rough work clothes and his hair was tied back in a ponytail. Sweating from the heat of the furnace, he wiped a hand over his brow and his long fringe stuck to his forehead. I walked towards him.

'Elisabeth and you must go to the Hall,' he insisted. 'It's not safe here.'

'But I don't want to leave you,' I pleaded.

'Do as I say. For our daughter's sake.' He gently stroked my cheek and I closed my eyes, savouring his touch.

'When?' I asked.

'Tonight. I've had word Cromwell's men will be back before daybreak.'

'Will you come with us?' I asked, my heart heavy, already knowing the answer.

'I will accompany you on the journey, but I must return.'

'Nat, what's to become of us?' I was suddenly filled with the dread of premonition.

He shook his head, deep sadness clouding his eyes. 'Make

haste, Mary.' As I started walking towards the cottage I heard him whisper, 'My love, my life.'

I turned back, wanting one last look. The courtyard was, once again, clear of mist and Nick stared at me from the outhouse door. The look on his face was the same as on the day we'd discovered the jewellery; wonder and disbelief.

'Maddie?'

'Yes.'

'What just happened?'

'Did you see them, Nick?' I asked quietly.

Slowly, incredulously, he said, 'The horse was here!' He indicated the wall beside him. Quickly covering the distance between us, he took my hands in his and looked searchingly into my eyes, his forehead creased in a frown. 'Does this happen often?'

'Yes, but not as vivid. Normally I only see the man, Nat, in dreams.' I was aware he stroked my hands; his touch so familiar. 'But do you remember when we found the jewellery? The children were there and you saw them too.'

He nodded. 'Cromwell... The English Civil War,' he said quietly, as if to himself.

'And this cottage is seventeenth century,' I added.

Through narrowed eyes he observed me. 'Something happened here, or to the people who lived here. That's what all this is about.' He checked his watch. 'I must go next door – your neighbour is expecting me – but, Maddie, I mean it, if you're ever frightened by anything that happens here, phone me... day or night.'

'Well, thanks, Nick, but I'm sure Sarah wouldn't be best pleased if I rang in the wee small hours,' I said in an amused voice.

He looked at me in confusion. Slowly his eyes cleared, as if only now remembering Sarah.

'This is important,' he said, his voice serious. 'She would have to accept it.' His fingers still stroked my hands.

I smiled up at him. He bent towards me, and for one glorious moment I thought he was going to kiss me. Suddenly the stroking stopped. With a troubled expression, Nick dropped my hands.

'I mean it Maddie,' he said, as he walked away.

# 20

On the Thursday, Professor Stephens roared up in his Porsche. I had added the most recent visitation to the 'Happenings' file and on rereading my diary of events, realised a story was, indeed, taking shape. The professor looked windswept and wild, as he entered the cottage carrying a large leather and tapestry holdall. I noticed he was even taller than Dan and was on the point of warning him about the low beams in the dining room when he cracked his head on one. Sitting down at the table, he brusquely rubbed his skull and cursed in that plummy, cut-glass voice of his. It sounded so much more effective than when I swore.

'Are you all right?' I asked. 'That was one hell of a crack.'

He grimaced. 'Silly old fool! I've probably shaken the very foundations of the building.'

I wondered what else he might have disturbed in the process.

'Now, here's your jewellery, young lady.' Still rubbing his head, he produced the wooden casket from the depths of his holdall. 'By the way, did you notice the initials carved into the lid?'

I shook my head and tried not to snatch the box out of his hands.

'They're much worn but if you look closely you can make out the initials "M" and "C".'

I gazed down at the lid and ran my fingertips over the characters, knowing I'd done this a thousand times before. Opening the casket, I saw the magnificently restored wedding ring and heart pendant, which shimmered like diamonds. I let out a sigh of relief. They were in my possession once more.

'Allow me to demonstrate how the ring works.'

Professor Stephens reached into the casket. He picked up the ring and, in one swift movement, untwisted it into three separate hoops, each bearing an inscription. He held the ring out to me.

Carefully, I took it from him and read aloud each hoop. *'My beginning and my end; Let no man put asunder; NC & MO, 8 May 1635.'* As I spoke the words, a shiver ran up the full length of my spine and when I closed the three interlocking hoops to make the complete band, automatically I slipped it onto my wedding finger. It was a perfect fit.

'Well would you credit it,' the professor said. 'Obviously made for you!'

I admired the ring on my hand and experienced the strongest sense of *déjà vu*. NC and MO – I knew who I'd like that to be. But who was the man that had originally given this ring, and who was MO? Reluctantly, I removed the ring from my finger and carefully placed it back in the casket.

'I'll get some coffee on the go,' I said, rising to my feet.

While I filled the kettle and spooned ground coffee into the cafetière, the professor told me that Philip Harcourt-Jones had informed him a German gimmel ring, not dissimilar to the one in my possession, was on display at the Victoria and Albert Museum. I poured boiling water onto the coffee and placed the cafetière on a tray together with two mugs and a jug of milk. Then, adding a plate of biscuits, I carried the tray through to the sitting room. The professor sat on my IKEA sofa and, randomly, it occurred to me he had probably never visited the store. I placed the tray on the coffee table and sat down opposite him.

'Help yourself to biscuits.'

'So, you found the jewels in the inglenook,' he said, selecting a chocolate Hobnob. 'A rather unusual sequestered place.' He popped the whole biscuit into his ample mouth.

I depressed the plunger. 'When I first moved in the bread oven was sealed up,' I explained. 'I wonder if the jewellery was placed there for safekeeping.'

I poured coffee into the mugs and passed one to him. Taking a gulp, he helped himself to another biscuit and chewed, deep in thought.

'Safekeeping, possibly, but to seal up the oven afterwards…? That's more like a hiding place or locking away a memory.'

*Locking away a memory…* The words seemed to hang in the air. But what memory and who had locked them away? And why?

'Well, this is a mystery,' the professor said, eyeing the plate of biscuits again.

'Try the flapjacks. I bought them at Bridport Farmers' Market. They're very good.' I held out the plate to him.

'Well, if you insist.' Selecting a fat, moist flapjack, he bit into it with relish. Eventually he swallowed and then loudly cleared his throat. 'How's that dear boy who accompanied you the other day?'

I smiled to myself. It hadn't taken him long to bring Dan into the conversation.

'He's OK but I haven't seen him since. Dan lives in London.'

'He seemed very appreciative and had enthusiasm. I like that in a young man. Tell him he's welcome to visit any time. I would love to take Dan for a spin.'

I bet he would! There was no denying this man's gender preference.

I didn't want to disappoint the professor but I knew his message would have Dan bolting for the hills. I also wondered how Lucy would react to a rival for her man being male…

My attention returned to the jewellery. 'I wonder how I can find out more,' I said, half to myself.

'Have you tried Bridport Museum?' Professor Stephens asked.

I said I had and explained that although I'd uncovered some interesting facts about Walditch over the centuries, there was nothing specific about The Olde Smithy.

'What about a visit to the local graveyard?'

'I've already been to St Martin's,' I said, thinking of the day I'd seen Nat distraught at the graveside.

'No, not Shipton Gorge. Here in Walditch.'

'The village doesn't have a church,' I replied.

'Oh yes it does,' he countered. 'Formerly St Mary's. I believe it was deconsecrated and is now a comfortable family home.' He drained his mug. 'You can learn a lot from graveyards and you may find there are still a few headstones in the grounds.'

St Mary's Lodge – the house at the top of the village with its unusual half-spire and clock tower. It had never occurred to me it was once a church and I'd passed by the property many times without giving it a second thought.

'I don't suppose you know who lives there?' I asked.

He shook his head and looked at me with a mischievous glint in his eye. 'Most people are happy to open up their homes when an eminent archaeologist is interested in what their property may, or may not, have hidden within its boundaries.'

I wasn't sure if I understood him correctly. Was he being less than ethical and playing the 'professional' card? He watched me closely as I grappled with the idea.

'Professor…?'

He winked at me. 'Young lady, you don't think I have worked hard all these many years to secure a place of standing in the world of archaeology without being able to flex my professional muscles from time to time? Yes, I live for my work, but I do pull the odd string occasionally.'

Well, the old rogue! Now I understood why he drove a Porsche and not some battered 'old faithful'.

And so it was that half an hour later, having witnessed Professor Stephens' silvery tongue in full flow, we were welcomed into the home of Mr and Mrs Rogers. Although the property was no more than a few hundred yards from

The Olde Smithy, the professor insisted on taking his Porsche: 'To give the right impression, my dear.' As he held open the passenger door for me I noticed Janet cleaning the front windows of the pub. I waved at her. Her jaw dropped as she watched me get in the car. In slow motion, she returned my wave. I slid onto the soft leather seat and smiled, determined to savour the three-minute drive up the street to St Mary's Lodge.

It transpired that Mr and Mrs Rogers had purchased St Mary's from the church four years previously, investing a huge amount of money in renovating the property during the intervening period. It was now in pristine order and full of ecclesiastical features. A stunning stained-glass window and an original rood screen dominated the sitting room, and there were a number of Gothic mullioned archways and, of course, the unusual, ornate half-spire rising from the centre of the roof.

The Rogers explained that the upper part of the spire had been in a dangerous state and, rather than repair it fully, they simply had the top half removed and capped with a low clock tower. Professor Stephens enthused over the clever ways they'd incorporated a home within the four walls of the church, and then explained his main interest was in the grounds, particularly the graveyard.

Opening the French doors, Mr Rogers beckoned us to follow him down a stone path flanked either side by well-tended flowerbeds. We passed beneath a rose arbour into a less formal area of the garden and there, in the quiet solitude of a hidden tree-lined clearing, was the original cemetery. At once, I was overcome by a terrible sense of loss and despair.

In muffled tones, as if coming from a very great distance,

I heard Mr Rogers inform the professor that the headstones were mainly seventeenth and early eighteenth century and that later village burials could be found at the church in Shipton Gorge.

'We are interested to see if there are any graves here belonging to former occupants of Madeleine's cottage in the village,' the professor explained.

'You may be lucky,' said Mr Rogers. 'The graveyard is somewhat protected from the elements and most of the headstones are still legible. I'll leave you to look around.' Turning on his heels, he disappeared swiftly up the garden path towards the house.

'I suggest we work our way along each row in a methodical manner,' Professor Stephens said, surveying the thirty or so headstones. He turned away and started to walk along the lines of stones.

I didn't join him. I knew he was heading in the wrong direction.

It was very peaceful in this garden of rest. There wasn't a sound to be heard except for the occasional burst of birdsong. I breathed in the solitude and serenity, and tried to dispel the utter wretchedness that consumed me. Remaining at the entrance, I looked across the clearing. On the far side stood a headstone, larger than the others, and some older understanding told me this was the one I sought.

As I walked across the glade a robin flitted from stone to stone, eyeing me inquisitively. A deep sense of sadness and grief engulfed me; the nearer I drew, the stronger my emotions. It was a very old gravestone and I had to fight an overwhelming urge to lie down at its foot and stay there forever. A huge sob escaped me as, through my tears, I read the epitaph carved into the stone.

*Here Lyeth*
*Nathaniel Carbayne*
*Farrier of this Village*
*2nd March 1612 – 18th December 1664*
*And Cherished Son*
*Francis*
*7th September 1639 – 15th October 1643*
*Rest in Peace*

I began to choke and, gasping for air, pulled frantically at my collar. Suddenly a pair of strong hands gripped my shoulders.

'There, there…' Professor Stephens hugged me awkwardly.

Despite my distress, I was aware this was a momentous act on his part. The bachelor had probably not shown such tenderness to a woman for many a year, if ever. Looking over my shoulder, he read the epitaph.

'I believe we may have found an important piece of the jigsaw.'

His large bony fingers gently rubbed my back and I breathed more easily. Soon, I was able to extricate myself from his embrace. Sobbing quietly, I wiped away the tears with the back of my hand.

'Better now?' The kindly man peered into my face with concern.

I nodded, still unable to speak. Here lay my husband and son.

'I think we may have found previous inhabitants of your cottage. Nathaniel Carbayne,' he said. He looked at me with compassion, without understanding. 'Farriers were very well respected in the seventeenth century, you know. Their skills were more akin to those of our equine vets today. People would ask their advice on all manner of ailments.'

My aching heart swelled with pride.

'Now, his young son, Francis...'

Unchecked, the tears rolled down my face once again. I wondered what the professor must think but, although he shot me a quizzical look, he didn't say anything.

'Only four years old. Hmm...' He stroked his chin, thoughtfully. 'Well, let's see. He could have succumbed to the plague or smallpox. There was a lot of disease around in that century and there wouldn't have been much effective medication. Mortality rates, especially amongst children, were high and sanitation was not at its best. It became more so later in the century but mid-sixteen hundreds...' He trailed off.

It was smallpox. The red face, the hot sweats and the rash. Despite our best efforts, we were unable to save Francis.

As the professor walked away down the line of headstones looking for proof of further inhabitants, I recalled how distraught Nat had appeared at St Martin's. Why was he at the church in Shipton Gorge? I looked around for something to place at the grave but there was nothing suitable, so I removed the blue glass bead necklace from around my neck and hung it from the top of the stone.

'God be with you,' I whispered. Immediately, the greatest sense of pure joy and total forgiveness descended upon me and the lump in my throat eased. From out of nowhere a warm breeze brushed my face, like the gentlest of kisses.

'There's nothing else here that relates to your cottage that I can see,' announced the professor as he returned. He stood beside me and acknowledged my necklace hanging from the headstone.

'That's a nice touch, young lady. I'm sure that Nathaniel and young Francis are more than happy you are living in their home.'

'*Once more*,' spoke a voice inside my head.

That evening, as I entered the latest piece of the unravelling mystery into my laptop, I carefully considered all that had happened to me that day. I was exhausted and it seemed to me the visitations and experiences were drawing ever more urgently upon me. It felt as if something was coming to a close and a great sense of dread hung over me, which I couldn't shake off. I thought of Nathaniel Carbayne and realised he was the NC inscribed on the wedding ring and I assumed that the other initials where those of Mary. But who was she? I was deep in thought when the phone rang and it made me jump. I answered it, feeling jittery.

'Maddie?' enquired a warm, female voice.

'Yes?'

'It's Helen Moore, Nick's sister.'

I smiled. 'Hello, Helen, how are you?'

'Oh very well, thank you. And you?'

I said I was fine, ignoring the disquiet in my soul.

She explained that Peter had spoken to his partner concerning the potential article about his organic smallholding. 'Charles says he is delighted for you to pay him a visit.'

She gave me his number and I wrote it down on the notepad by the phone.

'But, Maddie, I have to warn you. Charles is a lovable rogue. He is very charming and he will love you!'

'You're painting a very interesting picture of this man, Helen,' I said. 'Didn't you say that if he hadn't been forced into becoming a solicitor he would probably be on the wrong side of the law by now?'

She laughed. 'A slight exaggeration possibly, but his family, like ours, is a Dorset family reaching back many generations. There have always been rumours over the centuries about members of the Bosworth family – mainly their involvement with smuggling.'

I laughed.

'Nick mentioned your uncle researched your family tree,' I said, only too happy to be talking about him with someone who knew him so well.

'Yes, that's right. When our father died, Uncle Robert looked into the family history. I believe he traced it back to the sixteen hundreds but we weren't Corbin then. The name has changed over the centuries. We were Carbayne then.'

Blood pumped through my body at an alarming speed and a loud whooshing noise resounded in my head.

'Maddie? Are you still there?'

'Yes, I'm still here. I need to tell you something. I've had a very unusual experience today.'

I took the phone through to the sitting room and sat down on the sofa. I told her about my visit to the graveyard at St Mary's and how I believed that Nat Carbayne had once lived in The Olde Smithy. She listened quietly throughout, only speaking when I had finished.

'That would figure, Maddie,' she said calmly. 'We come from this part of Dorset and all the menfolk in my family have been skilled craftsmen. I have a copy of the family tree somewhere. I'll look it out for you, if you like. Nick said you are writing a book about your cottage and it might help with your research.'

I smiled, happy in the knowledge that he had discussed me with her. But a book... I hadn't considered that. I thanked her and said I would be in contact with Charles Bosworth.

Before she ended the call, she said, 'Peter and I are off to Kenya for a month next week, but when we get back we'd love you to come over for supper one evening.'

I wished her a good trip and said I looked forward to visiting them on their return.

# 21

Two things happened during the second week of March. I received a payment for the article in *Eco World* and although it was nothing compared to the salary from Hawkstone Media, it was all the sweeter for being the first of the freelance money coming into my account. The second was a letter from Nick; a letter I shall keep to my dying day.

I had not slept particularly well and, surrendering to the bright daylight creeping through the crack in the curtains, I'd risen early. I didn't bother getting dressed and padded around the cottage in my dressing gown, trying to decide what to do with the day. I was drinking coffee, looking out of the kitchen window at the early spring day, when I heard a noise at the front door, as half a dozen envelopes dropped through the letterbox onto the mat. I wandered over. Placing the coffee mug on the table, I picked up the post and sorted it into order of priority on the dining table.

'Bill, no thanks. Another bill, no thanks. Credit card statement, no thanks.'

*What's this?* My heart skipped a beat as I recognised the stylised writing on the blue envelope. Sitting down at the table, I turned the letter over in my hands, not wanting to open it. Some sixth sense warned me of its content. I procrastinated and examined the two other items of post. One was from the local Cats Protection League asking me to volunteer my services; the other was a cheap car insurance flyer.

Slowly, I returned to Nick's letter. Fingers of ice reached up from the pit of my stomach and held me firmly in their grasp. Sick with premonition, I opened the envelope and extracted the letter. The silence in the room was palpable. I heard Storm eating from his bowl in the kitchen, but that was all. No sounds penetrated the cottage from the outside world. I was suspended in time, and time held its breath, waiting for something to happen.

*Ashton Chase Barn*
*10 March*


*Dear Maddie,*

*I have to write this letter. Though I have a skip full of mail that demands answers and my day sheet is crammed with a mass of urgent chores and obligations that I have no hope of fulfilling, I have to write this letter. I have a very stern and hard-working conscience, which is giving me no peace at the moment. This letter may quieten its angry clamouring.*

*It is to be a plea for my defence, a token of gratitude and hope for future friendship.*

*First, my defence. I am not one of life's great planners. I do not chart courses or control events. It cannot be said on my epitaph that he knew what he wanted and went* out and got it. Whilst my successful friends bore across life's oceans in pursuit of lofty goals, I bob in their wake, drifting on the tide of circumstance, admiring the scenery that chance presents. Through such aimless navigation I arrive in situations by accident. I know enchanted creeks and peaceful backwaters that the captains of their own destiny will never see. But there are perils that await the drifter, rocky shoals and whirlpools that responsible people steer clear of.

In the same way that I don't control my life, I cannot control my feelings. I cannot be blamed for admiring attractive scenery. That a client happens to be both charming and beautiful should simply sweeten the working day. Where I am guilty is in not heeding the signs that something was happening within. I should have corrected things and started paddling away at the start when I found myself thinking of you too often and too fondly. That I didn't take evasive action was due to a naïve belief in some Enid Blyton Utopia where everyone exists as 'jolly good chums' – a world uncomplicated by the tangle of feelings, relationships, sexuality, envy and jealousy. The outcome is painful. And now I am dangerously close to being in love, if not already.

This is where the gratitude comes in. For the enchantment that your company has brought to my life. It is a nice feeling knowing there is someone around that you really like. Dorchester, Walditch and the Blacksmith's Arms are places that have grown a new attraction for me – that I might glimpse you. I enjoyed dusting off my peacock feathers (though I hope it wasn't too obvious). I did not make a play for you, rather I fell for you. Thank *you for briefly and unwittingly making me very happy.*

*A grey dawn now fills the barn where I am writing this. It heralds a full day. I have used up all the paper trying to write this and there is no more left, and I have not said anything that I really wanted to say.*

*Maddie, I wish you the greatest fortune in your life. May the gods smile upon you and bless you with happiness – and may your friendship be mine.*

*Love, Nick*

Refolding the letter, I slipped it back into its envelope and refused to weep.

That night I was restless. I couldn't get comfortable, however hard I tried, and sleep evaded me. Eventually I went downstairs, heated up a mug of milk and settled on the sofa, pulling a fleece rug over me. A delighted Storm immediately jumped onto my lap and curled up, purring contentedly. I opened Mrs McKendrick's book and started to read. I had already skimmed through it once, but now I believed I owed it a more thorough reading. Francis died in 1643 and Oliver Cromwell was mentioned during the 'happening' in the courtyard Nick had witnessed, so the era was correct. Mrs McKendrick was definitely trying to tell me something.

During the English Civil War, Dorset was mostly Royalist. Everyone from nobility to labourers joined the 17th-century fight between Royalists and Parliamentarians, with villages often split dangerously down the middle.

While Dorset had a number of Royalist strongholds, such as Sherborne Castle and Corfe Castle (both of which were devastated by fighting), many towns, such as Weymouth, were under the control of the Parliamentarians.

By 1644 the Parliamentarians had virtual control of the entire county. The men of Dorset were noted at this time for their lack of enthusiasm for war, and Clubmen – groups of what would now be called conscientious objectors – were formed in substantial numbers.

The hours passed, but I didn't notice. As my eyelids grew heavy, I drifted into a broken sleep. Storm disturbed me once when he turned around on my lap and I snuggled deeper into the cushions, pulling the rug up around my neck. Soon, I was visited by a dream so vivid that when I thought about it later I wondered if I had been transported back to that harsh, unforgiving time.

It was cold, so cold, and not just in the air; my heart was leaden. I sat astride the bay horse with Elisabeth in front of me holding tightly on to the mare's coarse, black mane. I held a bundle of clothes in one hand and cradled my precious daughter with the other. Nat stood at Bess's head, talking softly to her as he glanced anxiously over his shoulder in the direction of the sound of the advancing army. Bess was a cob of solid disposition, but she, too, had caught something of the electrified atmosphere and stamped nervously. We heard the marching soldiers drawing ever closer and an occasional whinny caught on the wind.

'No time to waste,' Nat whispered urgently. 'We must away.'

I urged Bess on and we rode across the village green

towards the track leading to Shipton Gorge. Nat led the cob, keeping pace with her as we steadily climbed. We did not speak. I was sick with worry. The afternoon was quickly turning to dusk and the chill in the air – a chill of impending disaster – penetrated through to the very bone. As my daughter huddled against me, I pulled the cloak around us both. The journey was difficult in the deepening gloom but Bess was sure-footed and, despite her uneasiness, she did not trip on the rutted path.

The trees on either side swayed eerily in a silent wind. It seemed the world was quietly alert; straining to hear the slightest noise. I imagined eyes amongst the dense foliage watching our every move and I heard Elisabeth catch her breath. She was a spirited child, gutsy too, but I knew she possessed a vivid imagination and that in this half-light it would play tricks on her.

'It's all right, child,' I whispered. 'There's nothing to fear.'

Fit though they were, Nat and the mare were blowing hard by the time we passed the old fort, but eventually we emerged from the wooded hillside onto the level approaches to the village of Shipton Gorge. Suddenly Nat stopped. Raising his hand, he alerted us to remain silent. We stared into the darkness, listening intently. Was that a muffled cough? I felt Elisabeth stiffen. Bess's ears pricked and she fidgeted against Nat's restraining hand on the reins. And then a figure emerged out of the gloom. On seeing us, it stood firm with feet apart and a stick in its right hand.

'Who goes there?' a boy's voice called out in panic.

'Nat Carbayne.'

'Oh thank the Lord.'

As the figure ran towards us I recognised Jacob, one of

my father's stable boys. He stopped when he saw Elisabeth and me.

'Mistress Okeford!' he exclaimed, 'I— I mean Carbayne.' He was overcome with shame but Nat placed a comforting hand on the boy's arm.

'It's all right, lad. Where are you away to?'

'Waldyke. The King is at Maiden Newton and the master has been despatched to oversee the royal visit. We had word the Roundhead army was closing. The mistress instructed me to watch their movements and report back.'

'Then Sir Richard is not at home…' Nat said in a worried voice.

'Nay,' confirmed the boy.

Glancing at Elisabeth, my husband lightened his tone. 'We are away to the Hall now. Mary and Elisabeth will be staying awhile.'

I thought I was going to be sick, so deep was my dread.

In low voices they muttered an urgent exchange, which I couldn't catch, and then Jacob bade us farewell and carried on past us down the track. I knew Nat was trying hard not to frighten our daughter, but when he looked up at me his face was etched with concern.

'Father, how long will we stay with Grandmother?' asked Elisabeth.

'A short while,' he replied, squeezing her knee. 'But you must be strong, Elisabeth, and promise to look after your mother for me until I return for you both.'

She nodded and I saw her smile proudly down at Nat, feeling important to have been given such responsibility. 'Aye, Father.'

My throat tightened and I prevented a sob from escaping. I, too, had to be strong… for my last remaining child.

We continued through the village. It was eerily quiet – all the occupants holed up behind closed doors – and stray dogs wandered the streets, scavenging amongst the dwellings, as we made our way silently past the church and down into the valley beyond. Presently, we turned up a track and, after a while, came to the great iron gates and stone pillars that announced Hammiton Hall. I should have felt relief, knowing we would be safe once behind its walls, but, as we passed through the gates and made our way up the drive, some premonition told me that I would never leave this place again. Each step that Bess took brought us closer to our destiny and I had the strongest urge to gather up what was left of my family and flee in the opposite direction.

As we approached the front entrance, I saw Duncan, my parent's faithful manservant, standing loyally beside my mother who was dressed in her finery, awaiting the arrival of her daughter and granddaughter. She looked older, though still handsome, but without the gaiety of spirit she once possessed. This war had made old maids of us all.

'Mary, Elisabeth,' she called.

My daughter slithered from Bess and ran to her. Nat took my bundle from me and put it to one side and then, looking up into my face, he held out his hands. I slid from the mare's back and into his arms. With my back pressed against Bess's warm flanks, my husband hugged me hard. I breathed in his masculine aroma and tried to gain some slight comfort, but the story was unfolding and there was little reassurance to be found.

'Won't you stay?' I asked, already knowing the answer.

'Nay, Mary. Your parents have never accepted me. They know there could have been a better marriage for you.'

I looked deep into his eyes and proclaimed, 'You know that's not true! I loved you before I ever knew your name.' Tears slid down my face. 'As soon as I saw you, you had my heart,' I said in a small voice.

'Hush, my love.' He wiped away my tears. 'It's not safe at the forge, you know that. You are better protected here at the Hall, for the girl too.'

He kissed me tenderly and held me close. The mare shook her head and stamped a hoof, impatient to be on the move.

My heart was heavy with foreboding but I tried one more time, in vain. 'But, Nat, I need you. We need you. If I pleaded with you not to go, would you stay?'

'Cromwell's men demand a farrier. They know where I am and will expect me to go with them.'

'You know I will always love you,' I said, my heart breaking.

He kissed me again, his hand lingering gently on my face. 'Mary,' he spoke the name like a prayer, 'you are the most beautiful woman I have ever known. Should we find ourselves parted I promise to look for you.'

Again, he hugged me hard and I clung to him, as if drowning. Then he tore himself away. With agility the envy of younger men, in one leap he was on Bess's back. As he gathered the reins, the mare's head came up sharply.

Softly he said, 'I will love you for eternity, Mary. For eternity...' And with that, he kicked Bess into a canter and away up the drive into the fog.

'Please stay, don't go!' I called out into the cool night air.

But there was no reply.

I awoke to a sharp knocking at the front door. Storm was no longer on my lap and through the curtains I could see daylight. I unlocked the door and opened the top half. The postman looked up in surprise.

'Oh, thought you weren't in, what with the curtains all closed. I was about to leave this over at the pub.'

He screwed up the card he was writing and handed me a large brown paper package, casting me an inquisitive glance as I stood dishevelled in my dressing gown. I knew he was just itching to ask.

'Hangover,' I said. 'What time is it?'

'Gone eleven,' he replied with a smirk.

I took the parcel and placed it on the dining table. It had a Dublin postmark. Immediately recognising Mo's handwriting, I opened it carefully to reveal a large box canvas picture. It was one of the photographs she'd taken of me posing as the French Lieutenant's Woman. The composition was stunning. The Cobb took up most of the width of the canvas, diminishing to the horizon, with my lone figure standing at its end glancing back furtively over one shoulder. The photo, itself, had wonderful depth but being printed on canvas gave it an added texture. I picked up the note that accompanied it.

*Dear Maddie,*

*Thought you might like to hang this in your charming cottage – a bit of contemporary to complement the old.*

*Off to New York to see how they do St Patrick's Day*

*celebrations over there!*
    *Keep well.*
    *Your loving sister, Mo xx*

I walked around the cottage, trying the canvas in various locations and eventually decided on the rear wall of the dining room. Having found a hammer and picture hooks, I hung the canvas and stood back to admire my sister's work. Mo was right. Although obviously modern, the colours of that gloriously bright January day and the subject matter captured in the photograph looked perfect in the room.

Realising the day was marching on, I was about to run a bath when the phone rang.

'Is that the delectable Irish lass?' a rich, chocolate-smooth voice enquired.

'Depends who's asking,' I said, hoping I didn't sound too rude.

The man chuckled. 'Charles Bosworth at your service.'

I was taken aback as I'd planned to phone him that very day.

'Helen said you were going to phone me,' he explained, 'but I grew impatient waiting so thought I'd get things moving.'

'This is strange. I was just about to phone you.'

'Well there you are. I pre-empted you. Now, I hear you are a writer "extraordinaire" and that you wish to do a piece on my little patch of organic heaven.'

'Yes, that's the idea.'

'Well, I'm a busy man but I'm sure I can find a slot for you in my hectic schedule.'

I couldn't tell whether he was being serious or teasing.

'My time is currently flexible,' I said. 'You tell me when you'd like me to come over.'

I heard him flicking through a diary. 'What about this Sunday afternoon, say around three?'

I wrote it on the calendar, jotted down the directions to his house and said goodbye. If I ever had the need for a lawyer to represent me in court then someone with a voice like his would be the one to choose; that voice could charm the birds from the trees.

I ran a bath, added a good measure of bubble bath and luxuriated in the silky, warm water, doing nothing more taxing than amusing myself making mountains out of the bubbles and gently blowing them across the surface. In that somewhat meditative state of mind, I returned to my vivid dream.

Hammiton Hall. I couldn't have made the name up, could I? I'd have to look at a map of the area and check if there was such a property in the valley beyond Shipton Gorge. My thoughts turned to Nat. Although Helen hadn't yet shown me the Corbin family tree, my gut instinct told me that he was a direct ancestor. But, there was something more, and a thought began to form in my mind. If true, then my current situation was as sad as the story unfolding for the original inhabitants of the cottage.

Later, I texted Mo and thanked her for her generous gift, telling her the canvas was already hanging in pride of place on the dining room wall.

She texted back:

Knew it would be perfect. Any developments on your research? Are you celebrating St Pat's Day?

I replied:

Story emerging. I have a theory. If true very sad. Working at the pub on 17th.

She texted:

All work no play! Come to New York. Mo xx

I responded:

No time. Writing a book. xx

I stared at my last text message. Indeed, it would be a good idea to write a book about Nat Carbayne and Mary Okeford, if only to keep everything that was happening to me in perspective... As I hit the send button I stopped in my tracks. Mary Okeford – the woman in my dream. The gimmel ring was inscribed NC & MO. I was being so slow! I rushed upstairs and removed the precious wooden casket from the bedside cabinet drawer and stared at the top carved with the letters M C – Mary Carbayne.

'I have found you,' I said softly.

Placing the box carefully on the bed, I lifted the lid and saw Nick's letter lying with the other keepsakes. I took it out but didn't read it, and laid it to one side. I picked up the ring and carefully opened out the hoops. I read each declaration of love and my eyes lingered on the inscription, *NC & MO, 8 May 1635*. Closing the hoops, I slipped the ring onto my wedding finger.

'Mary, show me what happened,' I said out loud. I

imagined I heard an imperceptible sigh. 'Show me and Nat will have salvation,' I whispered.

Was it an illusion or did a warm current of air caress my body?

For a long while I sat stroking the wedding ring and didn't notice the hours pass and the afternoon turn to dusk. I considered everything the cottage had shown me since first moving in. I knew I was linked to The Olde Smithy and that I'd been called here for a purpose. I now believed that purpose was to help Nat's restless spirit find a way to finally be at rest. However, although I had travelled a long way, I still had some distance to go...

# 22

Charles Bosworth's organic smallholding was at Higher Bockhampton, the village formerly home to Thomas Hardy, the writer. Even though Helen had warned me, I was ill-prepared for Charles Bosworth's charm and was surprised at how easy it was to like him. In his mid-forties, he had a pleasant, boyish face topped off by a mop of thick, dark brown hair and the clearest brown eyes, which twinkled at me as I stepped out of the car. As I'd noted before, what was it about these Dorset guys?

'Maddie O'Brien, welcome,' he said in his rich, chocolate-smooth voice with more than a hint of familiarity. I shook the offered hand and experienced a warm, firm handshake. 'You found the little place OK?'

I looked over his shoulder at the imposing, three-storey Queen Anne property surrounded by majestic oak trees.

'Your directions were impeccable.'

He smiled and, immediately taking my arm, walked me around the side of the house. 'First, I will show you around the farm and explain the set-up and what we are working towards. Then I propose to take you to dinner, if you have nothing else planned.'

It was a question; though not. He did not expect an answer.

I nodded and smiled, wondering if this was to be a dinner for two or whether he'd invited me to dine with the family.

Charles Bosworth's smallholding extended to just under twenty acres and backed onto Puddletown Forest. A short distance away from the main house stood a stylish stone building, which I had, at first, mistaken for a substantial range of garages. On closer inspection, however, I noticed the central clock tower stood proudly above a series of dormer windows and four front doors. This, Charles informed me, was staff accommodation, and at the far end stood a large solar array supplying electricity to all the properties.

'We have a back-up diesel generator and there's mains electricity as an option if all else fails,' he explained.

I gazed at the terrace of cottages. If I was one of Charles Bosworth's employees I'd be more than happy with the living arrangements.

'I purchased Pine Lodge eight years ago when I first went into practice with Peter Moore. It was rather rundown when I bought it. A divorce settlement. Actually a client of mine.' He smiled at some memory. 'She'd let the maintenance lapse during the previous five years. Too busy having affairs!'

He laughed, and it occurred to me he could well have been one.

'Anyway, the land was left to do as it pleased but, fortunately, she was into horses and sheep, and the grazing was in good heart. No pesticides or chemical-based products were used for a number of years so I had a good basis from which to start.'

He held open a tall wooden gate set within a high stone

wall and we entered a walled garden situated to the rear of the main house. I gazed across a semi-formal flower garden to the mansion. Along its full length ran a stone terrace with a hot tub situated to one end. On the south-facing garden wall was a large, traditional, wooden greenhouse. Proudly, Charles showed me the vines, fruit bushes, early vegetables and seedlings growing under protection of the glass.

'This greenhouse is heated by low-level, green energy, soil heating via the woodchip boiler located at the end of the staff cottages. The boiler also heats the hot tub – a very popular distraction at dinner parties!'

I grinned. I could so easily imagine Charles Bosworth throwing dinner parties where the guests ended up in that hot tub on the terrace. Dragging my mind back, I concentrated on what he was saying.

'We all benefit from the smallholding's produce. All members of staff have the option of eating what we've grown, but it is by no means compulsory.' He beamed at me. 'It's all part of an effort to make the smallholding more self-sufficient and sustainable.'

'Do you mind if I write and take photos as we walk around?' I asked.

'Please do.'

I rummaged in my bag for a pen and notepad, disconcerted by the positive energy emanating from Charles Bosworth. Perhaps this was what Helen meant when she'd warned me he was a lovable rogue.

I scribbled notes as Charles talked about his plans, the ultimate objective being to reduce his carbon footprint and work towards a more sustainable future. As he talked, we walked, and, presently, we passed through another gate leading out onto a grassed walkway running alongside the walled garden. This overlooked a series of neatly fenced, level paddocks; the furthest bordering Puddletown Forest. In the paddock nearest to us, I saw a large, open shelter and a couple of hen houses. Twenty alpacas of various colours and sizes grazed peacefully in the afternoon sun and a dozen or so rare-breed chickens busily scratched the earth around them. Charles held open the field gate for me. At the sound of the latch, two alpacas broke away from the herd and headed towards us.

'They're inquisitive by nature but harmless,' Charles assured me.

As they gambolled ever nearer, I wondered just how harmless.

'They're only eighteen months old and just testing out their masculine prowess. Don't run, you'll be fine,' Charles said, as the young males circled us.

His words did nothing to reduce my dry mouth or heightened adrenalin. He spoke to the animals in a mellow tone and the larger of the two, a sandy coloured alpaca, cheekily picked up my camera strap in its teeth and pulled.

'Now, Boris, put that down,' Charles scolded.

'Three guesses why you called him that,' I commented.

He laughed. 'They do share the same hairdresser!'

The alpaca continued to pull and Charles firmly removed the strap from its mouth. The smaller of the alpacas, dark fawn in colour, came around to my elbow and nuzzled against me. I stroked its long, flexible neck. I'd not experienced these animals close-up before and was surprised by the softness and thickness of its fleece.

'Did you know that alpacas hate foxes?' Charles chatted on amiably. 'They make excellent guardians for other livestock. Those chickens have nothing to fear from Charlie Fox!'

'Maybe every farmer should have an alpaca or two,' I suggested.

I took photos and tried not to be too distracted by the two youngsters. I had to dodge out of the way of Boris because, having had its game with the camera strap thwarted, it now tried to eat my hair.

'These are third-year offspring,' Charles continued. 'I decided to breed them having first started with just a pair of wethers to make the place look pretty.'

'Wethers?'

'Castrated males,' he explained. 'Then I discovered how easy they were to look after and became hooked. I bought a couple of breeding females and it went from there. I hope we'll have three, if not four, crias this year.'

He looked over at me as I scribbled the information in my notebook.

'That's babies to the uninitiated,' he said, before I could ask.

We crossed the paddock under the watchful gaze of the rest of the herd towards a series of poly tunnels situated on the far side of the fence. The two young alpacas still frolicked around us.

'Do you sell the offspring or just keep them for your own interest?' I asked, trying to keep pace with Charles.

'I sell them from time to time. A good quality male has a very high breeding potential and can be worth many thousands of pounds. There's also the opportunity of high income from stud services and females can be worth anything from a few thousand to ten thousand pounds or more. But I really do it for fun. The law practice can be stressful and this is my release.'

We reached the far gate and, ever the gentleman, Charles held it open for me. I slipped through. The young alpacas watched as we moved into the next paddock and a soft humming emanated from the smaller of the two.

'Oh, that's so charming!' I exclaimed.

Charles smiled. 'Yes, they're very gentle animals and highly intelligent, though spitting is perhaps their least endearing feature!'

'Why do they do that?'

'It's one of the few defence mechanisms an alpaca has and I can tell you it is quite an effective deterrent. It's rare for them to spit at people, though. Normally it's used to sort out the pecking order with other herd members.'

We stood at the fence watching Boris and his friend now scampering around the paddock together.

'Once I happened to step between two squabbling youngsters and received a faceful,' Charles continued. 'I was throwing a dinner party at the time and the old DJ did not come off too well.'

I laughed.

As we walked towards the first large poly tunnel we passed another paddock with a dozen or so Gloucester Old Spots and Tamworth pigs rooting amongst the grass and lying outside their pig arcs. Charles called out, and one of the spotted pigs approached with a grunt.

'Very intelligent these pigs, and kind too,' he said, scratching behind its ear. 'Great pets, though we do rear them for meat. The Gloucesters produce particularly fine bacon and I supply a couple of the local farm shops.'

I tried very hard to ignore the wise look in the eyes of that pig.

As we entered the first poly tunnel, Charles explained it was used as a tree nursery. Through the open rear entrance, I saw a distant paddock planted out with a large crop of maturing Christmas trees.

'You'd be surprised how many people demand organic Christmas trees these days,' he said, following my gaze. 'In the run-up, I make the smallholding available to customers. They can either buy direct from me here or I have a couple of lads who sell them for me at the markets in Dorchester and Bridport. People seem to like buying their Christmas tree from the local solicitor!'

The next couple of poly tunnels were used for growing organic vegetables with the last two filled with soft fruit bushes. Charles introduced me to a young couple working in the furthest poly tunnel.

'Luke and Kerry came here one summer not long after leaving university and, basically, never left. How many years have you worked here now?'

'Coming up four,' replied the young man.

'My helpers are very much a part of the whole process and we have regular meetings to make sure we're all singing from the same hymn sheet,' Charles advised. 'I'm open to new ideas and suggestions, and all contribute. Everyone has a voice.'

'That's true,' agreed the girl. 'We've worked on a couple of smallholdings since uni and this place is like our own. Mr B never plays the big boss.' She gave him a smile.

We chatted a while longer before leaving them to their work. I followed Charles out of the poly tunnel. Once we were some distance away, he turned to me.

'I don't like playing the "big boss". I get enough of that through my legal work. As long as everyone here knows what everyone else is doing, I leave my workers alone.'

Presently, we reached the woodland area at the furthest point on his land. Winding its way out of Puddletown Forest, a crystal-clear, babbling brook fed a lake where a number of wildfowl dabbled in the shallows amongst the reeds.

'Water rates are minimal as this spring feeds a borehole and, as previously mentioned, there's also mains water if necessary,' Charles explained. 'My woodland supplies all the fuel we need for the woodchip boiler and for every tree we fell, we plant two.' He glanced at his watch. 'Well, that's about it and it's nearing dinner time. You will grace me with your company a little longer?'

Again it was a question, but not.

'I'd be delighted to have dinner with you.'

As we walked back to the house, I jotted down an opening paragraph for the article.

*Pine Lodge is a twenty-acre, organically certified, biodynamic, eco-powered smallholding situated in secluded woodland with its own stream and spring water source. The property borders Puddletown Forest and enjoys complete seclusion and privacy where the unique, natural diversity of a practical and replicable lifestyle conserves, recycles and enriches.*

I followed Charles into an impressively large, bespoke

kitchen with a central island. He asked if I'd like to freshen up and showed me to a downstairs cloakroom. He was obviously wealthy and the house reflected this, but it was more homely than ostentatious. On my way back to the kitchen, I stopped to admire the gallery of framed photographs adorning the walls in the hallway. There was one of Charles with a teenage boy and girl; the girl with various ponies and dogs; the boy and Charles skiing and scuba diving; and pictures of a younger Charles with a blonde, aristocratic-looking lady of similar age.

'The family,' he announced from the kitchen doorway.

'Oh, I wasn't prying,' I said, overcome with embarrassment.

'Didn't think you were,' he replied easily. He joined me and pointed to the children. 'My finest achievements. That's Celeste, and this young ruffian's Oliver. And the woman is my wife... ex-wife,' he corrected. 'Deborah.'

'Sorry to hear that,' I said.

'Don't be. We tried marriage but it just wasn't for us. She's living in St Lucia now with her wealthy toy-boy hotelier boyfriend, and good luck to her.' He said it without a hint of bitterness.

'Where are your children?' I asked.

'Both at university. Oliver's at Oxford and Celeste, she's at Edinburgh. They come and visit their old man in the holidays when they're not gadding around the world.' He picked up a set of car keys from the hallstand. 'Ready?'

I followed him out of the front door and around the side of the house to a large, stone-built, detached garage. In it sat a gleaming, midnight blue Audi TT and I waited as he reversed the car out onto the drive. Leaning over, he opened the passenger door and I climbed in beside him.

Cheekily I asked, 'And where does this fit with your lesser carbon footprint?'

Intelligent eyes observed me.

'Good question, Madeleine O'Brien!' His eyes danced with mischief as he put the car into first gear. 'You see, I like the finer things in life and until "they" manage to make petrol out of thin air I will continue to enjoy the fruits of my labours, even if it means putting fuel in its tank.'

I smiled, sat back and enjoyed the ride into Dorchester as Charles expertly navigated the country lanes. His energy was infectious and I couldn't help but like the man.

The restaurant was a charming French bistro in the centre of the market town and Charles informed me that as it wasn't far from the practice, he and Peter often wined and dined clients there. As Charles held open the door for me, the Maître d' hurried towards us.

'Monsieur Bosworth. Good evening.'

'Bonsoir, Jean-Pierre. How is everything this evening?'

'Being a Sunday, not so busy, sir.'

I looked around in surprise. Despite his remark, the restaurant appeared full.

'A table for two?'

'Thank you, J-P. Perhaps the gallery?' Again it was a question, but not.

Jean-Pierre immediately found the exact table Charles requested. I was quickly learning this was how life treated Charles; a charmed existence indeed. The Maître d' took our jackets and then led us upstairs to a galleried area overlooking the main restaurant. As we reached the upper floor I glanced across the room to a table at the back and my heart leapt straight into my mouth. There sat Nick and

Sarah. Of all the nights and all the restaurants… Charles pulled out a chair and I quickly sat down, accepting the menu Jean-Pierre handed to me. My mind went into overdrive and my heart raced. How was I going to handle the situation? Damn Nick! How did he get under my skin so deeply?

Charles took his seat opposite me and ordered a bottle of champagne. As he opened the menu, he casually glanced around the restaurant and his eyes alighted on the far table.

'Nick, my man. How are you?' he asked in an enthusiastic voice.

I made eye contact with Nick and smiled sadly before looking away.

'Good, Charlie. And you?'

'Excellent. And Sarah, my dear, as lovely as ever.'

I glanced at Nick's girlfriend. She was smiling flirtatiously at Charles without a care in the world. Lucky girl. Aware that Nick still watched me, I couldn't help but look at him again before dragging my eyes back to the menu.

Charles was in ebullient mood. 'Nick, you never warned me how ravishing Maddie is!' He winked at me.

I coloured with embarrassment, but it was hard to be cross with someone who embraced life so fully. Shyly, I glanced at Nick. He wasn't smiling.

'Thought I'd let it be a surprise,' he said evenly.

'It certainly is and such a pleasant one at that.' Charles smiled broadly at me before turning his attention back to the far table. 'You must come over for dinner when Peter and Helen return from their travels.'

'Oh yes,' exclaimed Sarah, 'and go in your hot tub again, pleeease!'

So, they had been to one of his outrageous dinner parties...

'Only if you promise to wear that teeny-weeny blue bikini,' Charles teased.

Sarah said she would do just that as she still had the remnants of her Australian tan. Nick said nothing.

'Well, then, I'd better organise a party before it disappears,' Charles said in an amused voice. Turning his attention to me once more, he asked, 'Have you decided what you'd like, Maddie? I can highly recommend the moules.'

We placed our orders and the champagne arrived soon after. It would have been a great evening had I not been so aware of Nick sitting on the opposite side of the room. He and Sarah had obviously arrived just before us and our food arrived almost simultaneously. Charles was the perfect host, toasting me with champagne, his eyes dancing wickedly all the while. His conversation was amusing and accomplished and he was interesting company. If it hadn't been for Nick, I could have fooled myself into thinking I was on a date and relaxed into the evening.

At one point during the evening Charles kissed my hand, his brown eyes looking deep into mine. Flustered, I immediately – and guiltily – glanced across at Nick who sat at his table straight-faced. When my gaze returned to Charles, he looked inquisitively from me to Nick. Smiling warmly, he squeezed my hand and let it go.

'Tell me, Maddie. Is there a man in your life?' He was not prying. He seemed genuinely interested.

I shook my head. 'It's a bit messy.'

'What's a great-looking girl like you doing on your own? How come you've slipped the net?'

I took a deep breath and looked straight into those deep

brown eyes. There wasn't a hint of duplicity in the gaze that met mine.

'I guess I've never met the right man,' I replied, my heart breaking.

'Well, I've never met the right woman but, despite that, I've managed to beget a son and daughter!'

I smiled. 'I guess I could ask you the same question,' I countered. 'Why is a good-looking guy like you on your own?'

'Twelve years with Deborah taught me it's not everything to end up with the prerequisite wife, two children and a couple of Labradors, now deceased... the dogs, that is. But it hasn't stopped me from appreciating the opposite sex.' He looked long and hard at me. 'Oh well, Madeleine O'Brien. There's plenty of time for all that messy business to sort itself out.'

He polished off his glass of champagne with a flourish, topped up my glass and poured himself another. 'Plenty of fish in the sea and, personally, I like fishing.'

I laughed. You couldn't be sad around Charles for long.

Twenty minutes later, Nick and Sarah settled their bill and prepared to leave. On the way to the stairs they stopped at our table. Charles immediately leapt to his feet and started flirting with Sarah.

'You OK, Maddie?' Nick asked softly.

'Yes.'

'No more happenings?'

'Plenty,' I replied quietly. The concerned look on his face tore my heart apart.

Laughing at something Charles had said, Sarah glanced

over at us and a small frown settled on her forehead. Not a solicitor for nothing, Charles noticed everything and quickly smoothed over the situation, engaging us all in conversation.

'Well this has been fun,' he said, 'even if I have been forced into organising another hot-tub party.' He winked at Sarah who giggled in response.

We said our goodbyes and I watched as they walked down the stairs, collected their coats and disappeared through the main entrance. It seemed that I was destined forever to watch Nick walk away from me. The champagne must have gone to my head as, to my consternation, a tear slid down my face. Angrily, I brushed it away. Glancing across the table, I caught Charles observing me thoughtfully.

'Madeleine O'Brien, may I say something?'

Again, it was a question, but not.

Despite my fragile state, I recognised this man would be a force to reckon with in any courtroom.

'You're a lovely lady and I've had a thoroughly enjoyable time. I'd like to think we can repeat it sometime, no strings attached.' He raised a questioning, yet confident, eyebrow.

I nodded. After all, life had to go on and he was good company.

'However, if, in the meantime, you and Nick get it together, well, I will understand.'

I opened my eyes wide. He laughed.

'It's not *really* obvious,' he said, in an amused voice. 'Poor bugger.'

'Who me?'

'No, not you. Nick! There he is, good man that he is.

Been with Sarah donkey's years and doing the right thing sticking with her… and then you come along to upset the apple cart.'

Once again, tears welled up and threatened to spill over.

'It's enough to turn any man's head.'

It was the first time anyone had so openly acknowledged our situation. As he handed me a serviette I had the distinct impression he was well versed in coping with women's emotions. I dabbed at my eyes, thankful that I'd worn waterproof mascara.

'Listen, I understand if you don't want to talk about it but if you do, my door is always open,' he said generously. 'And, Maddie, if there's a bit of advice I can offer, have a little faith.'

I looked at him askance. 'That's what my sister says!'

'Your sister's right and if she's anything like you – and single – I'd like to meet her too.' He laughed, and even his laugh was as smooth as chocolate. 'In fact, she has an invite to the hot-tub party as well…'

# 23

The next morning, with the map open on the passenger seat, I drove to Shipton Gorge. It was a dreary and damp morning, and it suited my mood. Although I'd enjoyed my meal with Charles the previous evening, seeing Nick and Sarah so unexpectedly had made me realise how desperate my situation was becoming. I wanted to live in Dorset, at The Olde Smithy, and I had moved here in the belief that a new life awaited me, but I was beginning to feel downhearted about my circumstances.

My father's words rang soundly in my ears: '*Enjoy the adventure, Madeleine, but don't stay in the wilderness too long*'.

As I drove along the country lanes I considered my options. I didn't particularly want to return to London. With Caro and John's imminent move to Newcastle and Dan now heavily involved with Lucy once more, there wasn't much to tempt me back. And, besides, I sternly reminded myself, I didn't believe in *going back*.

Reaching the inn at Shipton Gorge, I followed the road around to the left and past St Martin's Church. As in my dream, the road led down into the valley beyond. I followed the country lane, keeping an eye out for a road leading off to the right, but a couple of miles further on I arrived at the A35. This was wrong. I pulled over and studied the map. It was a general one without any great detail and I cursed at not having an Ordnance Survey. Putting the car into first gear, I turned the car around and drove back towards Shipton Gorge, looking for any lanes leading off.

After a mile or so, I came across a dirt track to the left. This was certainly no roadway leading to a significant house but there were no other turnings. A car appeared in the rear-view mirror. As I indicated left I saw an old wooden sign, half-hidden in the hedge, announcing Hammiton Farm. At least the name was correct. With an increasing sense of excitement I navigated the track, skirting woodland on the left, and half a mile further on a ramshackle collection of farm buildings came into view. The lane seemed to lead directly into the farmyard.

A sheepdog suddenly appeared. Barking noisily, it ran at the wheels of the car as I followed the track, turning right between the farm buildings and then around a sharp left-hand bend. All at once, and for no obvious reason, my breathing became laboured and my vision blurred. A shooting pain whipped across my forehead. Gripping the steering wheel, I carried on, navigating the car around several large potholes as best I could.

After a while, I breathed more easily and the headache subsided. The lane took me through another series of farm buildings and eventually I arrived at a T-junction. Instinctively I wanted to turn right, but in my dream the turning had been a lane. This was a main road. If I turned left I would come to the A35 again. If I took the right turning, where would that lead? I studied the map. The road led to the village of Swyre and onwards to Abbotsbury, via the coast road. I turned towards the village, though I knew it was wrong. According to the map I was heading away from Hammiton Farm, but something made me want to head south. I had only reached the hamlet of Chilcombe, a matter of half a mile, when the headache returned and I had to stop. I was strangely fearful.

Although it had started raining steadily, I got out of the car, pulled up the hood of my jacket and breathed in deeply, slowly turning around to survey the scenery. Interestingly, I noticed that when I faced south, east or north, the fear dissipated; however, when I looked in a westerly direction I felt decidedly nauseous. Why?

On the far side of the road, a series of fields stretched away to the distance and on a hill to the west I saw the tower of St Martin's Church. I knew I was close, but not close enough. I must have missed the turning. I jumped back as a passing car sped by, sending up a sheet of water from a deep puddle in the road. Open-mouthed, the occupants gawped at me, and I realised I must look decidedly strange standing out in the torrential rain. I climbed back in the car and backtracked, turning left down the rutted lane and driving past the range of farm buildings.

After a mile or so, I came to a bend. As I negotiated it, a rabbit shot across my path and I swerved, stalling the car in the process and ending up in the hedge. I swore under my breath. I was about to put the car into reverse when I noticed the hedge seemed less thick at this point and I could just make out an overgrown track leading off to the left. It was obvious that no one had ventured down it for a very long time and the foliage had grown rampant. No wonder I'd missed it…

Parking the car tightly into the hedge, I stepped out into the rain once again and forced my way through the bushes. On several occasions, I had to disentangle myself from the unforgiving brambles that grabbed at my legs and tore at my waxed jacket. The track was deeply rutted and the rain had turned the mud into a lethal, slippery surface. The going was tough and I scrambled along the path as best I could. My legs turned increasingly leaden, as if I was physically held back, and I had to force one foot in front of the other to make any progress at all.

After five hundred yards, or so, the track petered out. In front of me was an open field, empty of stock and lying fallow. For no reason at all, I started to panic and thought I was going to pass out. The fear was ever-growing. I bent over. With hands on knees, I steadied myself and took several deep breaths. I was oblivious to the rain. A few minutes later, I straightened up and took in my surroundings. Every fibre in my body told me this was where Hammiton Hall had once stood, but here was nothing there now, apart from a curious mound to my right. It was seemingly out of place in the landscape.

I walked to the small hillock and started to pull at the turf, which came away in sodden clumps. With mounting feverishness I tore at the earth, the mud forcing its way under my fingernails. Then, picking up a loose rock, I hacked at the ground and made several deep depressions, which immediately filled with water. After a further fifteen minutes, I broke through to rubble and a square of stonework revealed itself. Scrambling to my feet, I walked a few yards in the opposite direction and stopped. The ground felt stony underfoot, unlike the soft grass and mud in the centre of the track.

Although wet through, I was oblivious to my immediate environment and, once again, I fell to my knees. Cold rainwater soaked through my already saturated jeans. Frantically, I pulled at the grass and, after some time, discovered another square of stonework long buried beneath the earth. Instinctively, I knew these were the remains of the entrance to Hammiton Hall, though the building itself was long gone. In my mind's eye, I saw the great iron gates and the huge stone pillars of my dream.

I got to my feet and walked through the entrance and up what would have been the drive to where the Hall had once stood. With ever-increasing and inexplicable terror, my body began to shake and, suddenly, I was violently sick. I stood in the rain feeling wretched and very alone. Delving deep in my pockets, I found a tissue and wiped my mouth. My face wasn't just wet from the rain; I was crying. Something terrible had happened here and, without a shadow of doubt, I knew it was something concerning me. I forced myself to look around the site, despite being consumed by irrational panic, but there was nothing more to discover. The foundations of the house were nowhere to be seen.

I made my way back to the car and sat for five minutes, waiting for the shaking to abate, before driving down the lane towards Hammiton Farm. As I passed the farmhouse, a man stood and stared from the front porch and called sharply to the sheepdog as it, once again, ran at my tyres.

I arrived back in Walditch and parked alongside the

village green, shaken by my experience. I was cold and wet through, but I couldn't face being on my own and needed some form of distraction, so I went to the pub. Brian did a double take as I walked in.

'Maddie, you look terrible! Come here. I'll get you a drink.'

With my hands still shaking violently and the wet jeans clinging to my legs, I clambered onto a bar stool. Brian set a glass of whisky on the bar in front of me.

'What have you been up to?' he asked. 'You look like you've seen a ghost.'

I looked at him wide-eyed and burst into tears. Swiftly, he came around the bar and wrapped me in a huge bear hug, despite my wet clothes.

'Hey, come on, sweetheart, it can't be that bad.'

'I think it is,' I sobbed.

'No, Maddie. Nothing's that bad. Drink up.'

I shook so much I had to hold the glass with both hands. I took a large mouthful and the whisky burned the back of my throat.

'You know, I don't give any old person my finest single malt,' he said kindly.

I managed a smile, of sorts.

'You just got cold and wet, didn't you?' he said, as if talking to a young child.

The shaking began to subside. 'I guess so.'

Brian would never understand the things that were happening to me. He was a regular bloke without an ounce of 'other worldliness'.

'Good, well now you're here…' He grinned. 'Vera and I have decided on an emerald theme for the seventeenth, so wear anything green. I know you'll look smashing, what with that auburn hair of yours. Oh, and I've risked my reputation once again. You'll be on waiting duties.'

Thank God for Brian bringing me back to the moment.

'I'm getting quite a dab hand at this waitressing thing now,' I said in a weak voice. 'I'll dig something out of the dressing-up box for the evening.'

He scrunched his nose at me. 'That's the spirit.'

I finished my drink and walked back to the cottage. Closing the door on the world, momentarily I leant back against it. Then, with a deep sigh, I changed into dry clothes and opened the laptop to record the latest twist in the sad tale that was unfolding.

# 24

The evening of the seventeenth was crisp and clear. It had stopped raining earlier that afternoon and I ran across the village green, careful not to slip on the wet grass. As I burst through the pub door, Vera – startled by my noisy arrival – acknowledged me briefly before returning to her conversation with Janet. As I hung my jacket on the coat hooks by the door, I noticed someone had lit a fire in the hearth and I glanced up at the painting displayed above it, as I always did.

'Hey, Maddie, I like the skirt,' Janet called over.

I swung round and saw her observing me over the top of her clipboard. In response to Brian's request for the team to wear something green, I'd chosen black leggings and a short pleated skirt in emerald-green tartan, which hadn't seen the light of day since my London media days. With some satisfaction I noticed it still fitted, even though I wasn't now as active as I used to be, when the latest 'rising star' had me running around at their every whim. I'd fixed my hair in a single plait with a green ribbon braided through it, and on my black T-shirt I'd pinned an old Christmas cracker gift – an emerald-green enamelled brooch in the shape of a four-leaf clover.

'Thanks, Janet, and you look great.'

She wore black trousers, a striking green and white blouse and a wide, black patent belt, which accentuated her slim waist.

'The band's already here,' she said excitedly.

I glanced through the archway. On the other side of the restaurant the six-piece Irish folk group were setting up their equipment. She fancied the lead singer and was ecstatic when Brian informed us he'd hired them for the evening.

'How many have booked tonight?' I asked.

'Thirty-six, but we're expecting more.'

I had yet to see the reservations' list and was nervous there might be a table in the name of Corbin, as there had been on Valentine's Night. She handed me the clipboard and I scanned the names, experiencing both relief and disappointment on seeing the surname not listed. However, I did notice Janet had marked herself down for all the tables nearest the band. Charmingly, she blushed when I pointed this out.

The restaurant was transformed with emerald streamers adorning the beams and each table sported a smart green cloth with a small vase of perky daffodils placed in the centre. The musicians had entered into the spirit of the day, and green tassels embellished their instruments. Each band member also sported something green and the young, energetic, lead singer wore footwear of a particularly lurid shade. I watched Janet as she chatted to him, enthusiastically comparing the colour of her blouse to his boots. Trying not to think about my own obsession with a certain person, I hoped that something would come of Janet's infatuation. The group had played at the pub before – a mix of traditional Irish folk and rock – and were very popular. Brian expected a good turnout.

Soon, customers arrived. Although I was busy behind the bar, each time the door opened I held my breath in anticipation. But Nick did not appear. It was ridiculous to be so on edge and I kept reminding myself that I didn't want him to turn up anyway. Sometime around eight, Brian asked me to work the tables for the remainder of the evening. I was pleased to do so; the entrance doors weren't visible from the restaurant and the lively atmosphere would more easily distract me. About an hour later, Charles Bosworth appeared in the archway to the restaurant with Sarah. My heart did a double flip, expecting to see Nick, but it was Becky and Mark who followed them in. Charles approached with a playful glint in his eyes and planted a kiss on my cheek.

'Good evening, lovely lady,' he said, in that chocolate-rich voice. 'I didn't know you could be found here. I may have to change my watering hole.'

I smiled at the compliment. 'Hello, Charles. Have you booked?' I hadn't seen his name on the list.

'No, last-minute decision. Thought we'd come and surprise you.'

I looked past him to Sarah. Her mouth twitched into some form of a smile but her eyes coolly surveyed me.

'A table for four?' I asked.

'Please. Not too close to the band but preferably one with a good view.'

I checked the restaurant bookings. There was a free table over by the window halfway down the room. As requested, it was not too close to the band but still had a good view. A charmed life indeed!

'Hope you don't mind the company I've brought,' he said quietly, placing a hand at my waist. 'I tried to persuade Nick to come too, but he said he wasn't feeling well.' He winked at me. 'Thought that was only ever a female complaint.'

So Nick had bowed out. Some friendship we had...

As they settled at the table, I distributed menus and handed Charles the wine list. Sarah, sitting next to him, appeared animated and excited. True to form, Becky glared at me.

'I'll give you a few minutes to decide what you'd like,' I said.

I cleared away plates from a nearby table. As I walked through the swing doors to the kitchen with crockery piled high, Janet came up behind me.

'That Becky Milner's got a face on her tonight,' she said. 'Probably had an argument with Mark. God knows why he puts up with her.'

Janet and I got on well. Coming from a family of four boys, she treated me like the older sister she'd never had and often confided in me. She'd lived in Walditch all her life and had been at school with both Sarah and Becky.

'Yes, seems to have a bit of an attitude.'

'She's always been that way,' Janet continued. 'Mark must be really spineless to stay. You have to watch your back with her.'

'Have Sarah and Becky always been friends?' I asked.

'Yeah, best mates. Always doing things together.'

That would explain why she was so quick to rush to Sarah's defence over Nick.

I set the dirty dishes on the work surface next to the sink. Vera, plating up, handed Janet a couple of main meals to take through to the restaurant.

'How long have Becky and Mark been an item?'

Janet thought for a moment. 'About five years. She was well pissed when Sarah first took up with Nick Corbin. Really jealous. We all knew Becky had the hots for him. You should have seen her trying to get off with him at Sarah's eighteenth. She was all over him like a rash! But it was her best mate who hooked him. Ended up not only jealous of Sarah but Nick as well.'

'No wonder she's got attitude,' I commented, holding open the swing door for Janet.

She looked at me as she walked through. 'Always had, even at primary school. Used to really bully me.'

I walked back to the Bosworth table to take their orders and noticed that Sarah sat very close to Charles. She gazed up at him with big, round, innocent eyes; giggling and flirting. It was obvious she was on a night off from Nick. Charles, being his usual charismatic self, displayed no particular favour towards her. He was as equally charming to Becky and me... even Mark.

The evening went well and the band played on. At around eleven-thirty, the Bosworth party prepared to leave. On his way out to the bar, Charles approached and put his arm around my shoulders.

'Thank you, Madeleine O'Brien, for a good evening made even more enjoyable by your presence.' His voice was exaggeratedly courteous. 'It could only have been eclipsed had you been seated at my table.'

*That* was the last place I would want to be, considering the company.

'I will phone you soon to arrange a dinner date.' He said it as though it would never occur to him my acceptance of his proposal was anything other than a foregone conclusion. His confidence made me smile. In anyone else it would have been perceived as arrogance, but in Charles... Well, it was very easy to like him.

'I look forward to it,' I responded.

He kissed me on the cheek, before walking through to the bar to join Sarah and Mark who had just passed by. I was about to attend another of my tables when Becky sidled up to me with venom in her eyes.

'Don't think you've got him,' she hissed. 'He's not *that* easily won over.'

I sighed. Why did she think she could treat me like this? Who the hell did she think she was?

'I have no idea what you're on about.'

'Don't give me that shit! Sarah's so sweet she doesn't see it, but I know your game.'

I regarded her coldly. How right Janet was. Becky Milner did have a face on her; an ugly and unattractive one.

'Unlike you, Becky, I've grown up. I don't play games.'

For a moment, I thought she was going to hit me. She wasn't much taller than me but more heavily built. Pulling herself up to her full height, she barged into me and I staggered back. Before I knew it, she had me pinned against the wall. I could smell the drink on her breath.

'What makes you think he'd look at you anyway?' She spat out the words. 'Leave Nick alone! He's not yours.'

Like a spoilt child unable to get her own way, she caught hold of my wrist and viciously twisted, digging her nails into the skin. I winced and tried to escape her hold, but she was surprisingly strong. She dug her nails in further. As luck would have it, at that moment Brian walked through from the bar. He stalled, assessing the situation, and looked enquiringly at me.

'What's going on here?'

'I think one of our customers has had one too many,' I replied, keeping my voice steady. My arm hurt like mad.

Becky still had me pinned against the wall and her elbow now dug into my ribs. She glared at me.

'Don't think you've won,' she growled menacingly, her face very close to mine. 'And you ain't gonna either.'

Brian walked over and faced her. 'Becky Milner,' he said loudly and slowly, 'whatever problem you have with my member of staff I will not have you behaving like this in my establishment, do you understand?'

Over Brian's shoulder, I noticed Mark appear in the archway and look around the restaurant. As his eyes took in the incident, he groaned.

Walking up to us, he grabbed Becky's arm. 'Come on, Bex. Leave it.'

'Don't touch me!' she screamed, flinching away from him.

Fortunately, the music from the band was loud and only a couple of nearby diners looked up. Astonishment registered on their faces.

'Right, that's it! I will not have you causing a scene in my restaurant.' Brian grabbed Becky by the shoulders.

She struggled and tried to break free but, with a firm grip, he frog-marched her towards the bar. Mark trotted behind. However, before disappearing through the archway, Becky looked back over her shoulder at me.

'I'm watching you!' she shouted threateningly.

Fingers of ice reached up from the pit of my stomach.

Janet, having caught the tail end of the skirmish, rushed over. 'Are you all right?'

I nodded and rubbed my wrist. It smarted badly. A red weal encircled it and I saw the beginnings of a purple bruise. Where Becky's nails had dug in, she'd drawn blood.

'You're right, Janet. She is a bully.'

# 25

On the last Friday in March I handed Storm over to Mrs Tomkins' care, packed a weekend bag and headed up to London. I'd not been back to the capital since moving west and was unsure how I'd feel. Would this visit make me yearn for a return to my previous way of life?

I left Walditch around mid-afternoon. It was an easy journey and the traffic wasn't too bad. The nearer I got to London I noticed that most of the cars were heading in the opposite direction, escaping the city. I arrived early evening. Caro and John welcomed me warmly into their home: a handsome, three-storey Victorian house on the edge of Clapham Common. I'd enjoyed many a party there. The couple didn't have children and on every occasion I'd visited, their home was orderly and tidy.

'Oh God, Maddie, I've got so much clearing to do!' Caro exclaimed, as she opened the front door. She hugged me affectionately. 'You'll have to excuse the mess.'

'Looks fine to me,' I said, following her down the hallway and noting how neat it all was. A delicious smell wafted from the kitchen.

'Paella,' she said, over her shoulder. 'Hope that's acceptable?'

'Fantastic.'

At a marble-topped breakfast bar, John sat with an open bottle of wine and a half-filled glass. He jumped up and hugged me warmly.

'Hi, Maddie. You look well. Country air obviously agrees with you.'

I kissed him fondly on the cheek.

'Here, pull up a chair. White OK?' He held up the bottle.

'Very!'

He selected a glass from a glass-fronted wall cabinet and poured the wine. Caro, standing at a huge stainless steel range, checked the sizzling contents of a large shallow pan.

'I invited Dan to supper tonight but he says he's otherwise engaged. He sends his apologies.' She gave the paella a stir. 'However, he is coming to the theatre with us tomorrow.'

'With Lucy?'

'No, she's going to Bristol for some reason. I guess that's why he's allowed out on a Saturday night.'

'You make him sound like a puppy dog,' John admonished his wife.

'Well, she's got him on such a short leash that's what he's fast becoming.'

We had a quiet meal in, just the three of us, and they talked excitedly about their forthcoming move to Newcastle. John was already living there in hotel accommodation for part of the week and he'd brought back a selection of property sales particulars to consider. We spent the evening discussing the various merits of each one, putting them into different piles:

'definites', 'possibles', and 'absolute nots'. Caro and John were charming, intelligent, easy company and I realised I missed this aspect of my old London life.

After supper we withdrew to the sitting room and relaxed in comfortable, oversized settees. It was a grand room with a high ceiling – the central ceiling rose and ornate cornicing still intact – and an original marble fireplace, above which hung a large gilt-framed mirror. The mantelpiece was crammed with framed photos of various nieces, nephews and godchildren and in the centre stood a fancy carriage clock. During the previous summer, Caro had employed professional decorators to paint the house in fashionably neutral colours and original oil paintings adorned the walls. It was a stylish home; one that reflected its owners' good taste.

'So, Maddie, Caro tells me you're writing these days,' John said, as he handed me a brandy.

'Yes, regularly for a couple of mags, ad hoc for others. I can't tell you how excited I was when I received my first freelance payment.' I laughed, recalling how little it was compared to my usual monthly salary from Hawkstone.

'Well, good for you,' he said genuinely. He smiled at his wife and I had the strongest impression he was trying to reassure her in some way. 'I know it's not easy,' he continued. 'Do you think you'll make a living from it?'

'Early days, John, but I hope so.'

'Bet you meet some interesting people,' commented Caro.

I told them about Charles Bosworth and how charming he was, and caught Caro's meaningful look in John's direction. He pretended not to notice.

I laughed out loud. 'Caro!'

'Well, I'm just concerned that you're down there in the depths of the countryside all on your own,' she said sincerely.

If only she knew…

'Thanks for your concern but I'm happy on my own, at the moment.'

Knowing this was far from true, I coloured slightly.

'Better for Maddie to be on her own than with someone who won't let her out of their sight,' said John. 'I'd stick with the occasional charming dinner date if I were you. Far healthier.'

Caro sighed.

'Is it no better for Dan then?' I asked.

'If anything, it's worse,' she said. 'We never see him these days. He's only coming tomorrow because you're here and he wants to see you. Lucy doesn't know, by the way. He said if she did she'd cancel her trip to Bristol.'

How could he stand living with such a jealous and controlling person?

'It will be nice to see him too,' I said genuinely. 'Now, Caro, tell me about this PR launch of yours.'

The following day, Caro and I spent a girlie day shopping in Covent Garden. We had lunch at a wine bar I used to frequent when I worked at Hawkstone Media and bumped into some of the old crew. It was good to see them again. Eagerly, they told me how my replacement wasn't fitting in and Ken Hawkstone constantly bemoaned the day I'd handed in my notice. I wasn't sure this was true, but it massaged my ego. We joined them at their table, polished off a bottle of wine and I caught up on all the gossip. Around mid-afternoon, Caro and I returned to Clapham, heavily laden with our purchases. Dan arrived sometime after five. In all the years I'd known him he'd always verged on the lean, but I was staggered to see him looking so gaunt.

'Maddie.' He hugged me hard. 'So good to see you.'

'Likewise, Dan. But, you know, we do live in the twenty-first century. There are such things as mobile phones.'

He looked sheepish. 'I know, I know. Don't start!'

He didn't look at all well. His hair was long and lank and his skin had a grey tinge, as if he hadn't seen the light of day for some time. Dark circles surrounded strained eyes. We walked into the sitting room where John was quietly reading a newspaper. He immediately put it to one side and rose from his chair.

'Dan, my man. Long time no see.' Brusquely, he hugged his brother-in-law and slapped him on the back.

'Yeah, too long,' Dan said, quickly extricating himself from the display of male bonding. 'Congrats on your promotion, by the way.'

'Thanks. It's a good move up the old career ladder.'

There was a sudden noisy commotion at the door and Caro rushed into the room. 'Come here, baby brother.' Standing on tiptoe, she hugged him and gave him a huge kiss on the cheek.

'Hi, big sis!' With his arms encircling her waist, Dan easily lifted her off the floor.

Caro smiled happily.

How unlike brother and sister they were: one tall and often ungainly; the other so petite and self-contained.

'Oh, it's so good, the four of us together again,' she cried enthusiastically, as her feet touched the ground.

I noticed a shadow pass across Dan's eyes.

'But you're so skinny,' she exclaimed, standing back and critically assessing her brother.

He flinched under his sister's scrutiny.

'Your jeans are falling off. There's nothing of you! Doesn't she feed you?'

'We eat well, Caro. Don't fuss,' he said irritably.

The even-tempered Dan I knew had certainly departed.

John, sensing disquiet, glanced at the clock. 'We'd better get our skates on if we're to arrive in time for the performance. You know what the Underground can be like on a Saturday evening.'

We found our coats and departed for the theatre. Dan stayed close to me throughout the journey and, as the minutes ticked by, the strain lifted from his face.

Somehow, Caro had managed to obtain tickets for the latest musical, which had opened to sell-out audiences and rave reviews. It was a great show. The cast were young and energetic and the songs memorable, and I savoured the theatrical environment once again. Afterwards, we ate at a restaurant not far from the theatre. It felt good to be part of London's bustling nightlife. It was as if I'd been away on a long journey and had returned to a comfortable, familiar environment. However, in my heart I knew I'd moved on and this was but a fleeting visit to a seemingly easier, earlier life.

The tube was packed on the return journey to Clapham Common and there was only one vacant seat. I insisted

Caro took it. The men and I stood crushed together; Dan and John holding the overhead bar, while I held on to Dan. With every jolt he moved closer. Caro's smile did not go unnoticed but, curiously, I felt swamped by her brother's presence.

As we emerged from the tube station she commented how cold it was, immediately linked arms with her husband and walked him smartly up the road towards their house. It was cold, but I knew she was deliberately putting some distance between us. I smiled wryly. I had no intention of rekindling a relationship with Dan, but her heart was in the right place. As we followed in their wake, he put his arm around me. I did likewise, casually placing my arm around his waist. As Caro had noted, there was nothing of him.

'It's good to see you, Mads. I miss our times together.'

'How is it with you?' I asked.

'Oh you know. Much as before.'

I stopped and stepped away from him. 'You don't mean Lucy's "ex" is still on the scene?' I asked incredulously.

'I don't ask. It's easier that way,' he said, shaking his head.

Where was his self-esteem?

'Don't look at me like that, Mads.'

He placed his arm around my shoulders again and we continued up the street.

'But, would you do anything about it if you found out she was still seeing her "ex"?'

'Probably not, Mads. I'm trapped.' He sounded so despondent.

'No one is trapped, Dan. Only you can choose how you want to spend your life.'

Thinking of my own situation, I didn't truly believe these sentiments.

He grunted but said nothing and we walked on in silence. Dan held me close, only releasing me once we reached the house. Through the open front door I saw John busy in the kitchen.

'Anyone for tea or coffee?' he called out.

We said 'yes' to coffee, hung our coats in the hallway and entered the sitting room. Dan sat down on the nearest settee. In order to distance myself from his attentions, I sat opposite. It was quiet and peaceful and I noticed how much more relaxed he was compared to earlier in the evening. Here, before me, was some semblance of the man I'd known and cared about for all those years.

Suddenly Caro appeared at the door. 'I'm bushed,' she announced. 'If you two don't mind, I'm going to bed.'

She came into the room and gave Dan a hug. 'Please look after yourself, brother. Promise to see us at least one more time before we depart for Newcastle?'

He said he would. She kissed him on the cheek and wished me a comfortable night's sleep. As she left the room, I saw her glance towards the kitchen and knew she and her husband were sharing a meaningful communication. A few minutes later, John came through with the coffee.

'I'm knackered so I'll say goodnight. Please switch off the lights when you come up, Maddie.' He smiled at us both and then followed his wife upstairs.

Dan and I were alone in the sitting room once more. I looked across at him and burst out laughing.

'Well, that wasn't very obvious. Your sister!'

He smiled thinly. 'We did have good times didn't we, Mads?'

'Yes we did.' Helping myself to a cup of coffee, I thought back to the many occasions we'd shared.

Suddenly, Dan crossed the room and sat down beside me. 'Do you ever wonder what might have been?'

Careful! Dangerous territory.

'I don't think like that,' I said cautiously. 'I like to look forward in life.'

He nodded. Taking the cup from me, he placed it on the coffee table and then his large hands encompassed mine. 'But if you did, would you wonder?' His eyes searched my face.

'No, Dan,' I said quietly. 'We had plenty of time to sort things out and we didn't.'

He looked so forlorn. 'I'm not happy, Mads.'

'Then do something about it.'

'I can't. I don't know what to do. I need a way out.'

And that's *not* going to be me...

'Just tell her to go.' I removed my hands from his.

He shook his head miserably. 'Can't do that.'

There was that awkward distance between us again.

'Are *you* happy, Mads?'

Loaded question. Where do I start? We'd known each other so well; it was hard not to be honest with him.

'Sort of, Dan,' I replied.

'What does that mean?'

'Well...' I hesitated, and then ploughed on. 'I'm not sure I can stay in Dorset.'

'Why?'

I sighed. It was a long story, which had yet to play its course.

'I don't think there's a life for me there.'

'But, Mads, you gave up a bloody good career to move there!' he said angrily. 'I distinctly remember you saying you were *going home*, although I never understood it.'

'I was. Going home, I mean. But now I'm there it's not that simple.'

He didn't say anything and the silence hung heavily in the air.

'It is... *was* my home,' I said quietly.

He looked at me uncomprehendingly.

'I have something to do, Dan, and then I'll move on.'

It was the first time I had formulated my thoughts out loud.

'Where will you go? Will you come back to London?'

I caught the hope in his voice, even though I'd told him there was no going back.

'No, not London. I've done that. I might go to Dublin,' I said, surprising myself.

'Back to the fold,' he muttered.

'Well, yes, for a while. Perhaps reassess everything and then move on from there.'

Until that moment, I hadn't considered returning to my city of birth. As I toyed with the thought, it seemed not such a bad idea.

'Wherever you go, you will keep in touch won't you, Mads?'

'Bloody hell, Daniel, I've tried,' I said, rather too loudly. 'You never answer your damn phone!'

'I know, I know. But if you moved away for good I would die.'

'Don't be daft, Dan.'

'You know what I mean. It would be final. Knowing you're in Dorset doesn't seem final somehow. Promise me?'

He looked so defeated. Suddenly he leant forward and kissed me. It was a sad, lingering, goodbye of a kiss; full of the memories of happier times.

'Sorry, Mads. Just had to do that one last time. I miss you so.'

The spring sunshine the following morning was surprisingly warm after the cold snap of the previous night. Caro, John and I enjoyed a leisurely breakfast at one of the many cafés in the neighbourhood and then, amidst promises to visit in Newcastle, I wished them a successful move north and headed west once more.

As the suburban roads gave way to open countryside, I felt tendrils of invisible ivy pulling me back to Dorset. Even though I'd enjoyed my visit to London and it had tugged at my heartstrings, I knew it was no longer what I wanted. I arrived back in Walditch with a renewed, unwavering determination to get to the bottom of whatever The Olde Smithy needed me to resolve.

# 26

It was late afternoon and I drove home to Walditch, following another successful visit to 'Strippers'. Amongst all the salvage, I'd found a wrought-iron gate for the front garden and was pleased with my purchase. As I drew up alongside the village green I glanced over at The Olde Smithy and saw a young girl running around the corner of the cottage.

I liked children but it was certainly time to fit a gate; anyone could just wander in. I climbed out of the car, crossed the green and walked up the garden path with the intention of asking the girl why she was in my garden, but when I rounded the corner into the courtyard I stopped dead in my tracks. A faint curtain of mist hung in the air and, through it, I saw Nat with a very young Francis in his arms while Elisabeth, aged about five, ran circles around them. They were all laughing and so happy. Immediately, I thought of the wood sculpture at Nick's workshop and some deeper understanding told me he had captured Nat's family in that piece. I remembered his words, '*When I first started work on the yew I had no idea what I was creating; it seemed to me that the piece had a life of its own.*'

I delighted in the scene before me – all such dearly beloved people – but suddenly they began to fade from sight. Instantly, I was bereft.

'Oh, please don't go!' I called out.

Nat looked questioningly in my direction, but the next minute the figures vanished into thin air. The courtyard was, once again, clear of mist, quiet and empty. I had no control over 'the happenings' – it was like sand running through open fingers.

I walked sadly back to the car, deep in thought. With difficulty, I forced my mind back to the present and carried the gate to the front entrance, propping it against the hedge. Storm called a greeting to me as he scampered across the village green, returning from some secret mission and, together, we walked up the path towards the cottage. From the depths of my bag, I heard my mobile alerting me to a missed message and, once inside, I checked who had texted.

Hi sis,

Great news – Kurt has cleaned headstone pic. Check email. What does it mean?

Mo xx

As the laptop powered up, I made a cup of tea and then settled down in front of the screen. I had about twenty new emails but, ignoring these, I double-clicked on Mo's.

Hi Maddie,

Kurt says he loves a challenge but this particular one has

been quite spectacular! He says this is the best he can do. Does it make any sense to you? Let me know where it fits in with the story.

Love, Mo xx

P.S. Jeff has a friend with a luxury holiday villa in Majorca. We're planning two weeks there. Do you want to come? He can't wait to meet you!

Maybe a holiday would do me good. I would seriously consider it.

I clicked on the attachment and watched as the jpg opened. It was huge so I resized it and as I did, I froze. Mo's friend had managed to decipher the eroded lettering on the headstone in St Martin's churchyard.

*Here Lyeth*
*My Love, My Lyfe,*
*Mary,*
*born twelfth April 1619*
*and beloved daughter,*
*Elisabeth,*
*born thyrd July 1636*
*both cruelly tayken*
*eyghth day April 1644*

Stupefied, I sat staring at the screen. I reread the epitaph half a dozen times. What had happened in 1644 on the 8th April to have taken both Mary and Elisabeth? The question was hypothetical. With sickening dread, I realised that buried deep within my subconscious lay the answer. I found Mrs McKendrick's book and frantically thumbed through the pages. I'd previously read a section referring to skirmishes that had taken place in the area, but their significance hadn't registered at the time. I read a couple of paragraphs but couldn't find what I was looking for. I checked the index for any direct reference. Was this it?

Abbotsbury – The Battle in the Pulpit: page 160.

I flicked through to the page and devoured the following words.

During the Civil War years, the superb Dorset village of Abbotsbury was owned by Sir John Strangways, an ardent Royalist. The village was the site of one of the bloodiest 'misfortunes' of the conflict. In what became known as 'The Battle in the Pulpit', Cavaliers sniped at the Roundheads from the church tower of St Nicholas in October 1644. The pulpit still bears the scars from shots fired by Cromwell's men. After a stubborn resistance in the church and manor house the garrison surrendered, but when the victorious Roundheads entered the house the magazine blew up, completely destroying the house and killing the plunderers.

No, that wasn't it. This incident occurred in the October. However, instinctively, I knew it had something to do with what I was seeking. I fanned through the book and found a previous chapter, which looked more promising.

The neighbourhoods running along the coast of Dorset between Weymouth and Lyme Regis were much affected during the Civil War. In 1644, Sir Edward Walgrave was quartered with his regiment of horse at Bridport when he was surprised by Parliamentarian troops. However, he engaged them near Shipton Gorge, slew some and took forty horses and a cornet. This fighting may have accounted for the two lead musket balls recently extracted from the west door of St Martin's Church in the village.

An interesting epitaph on the south wall of the church suggests that the Roundheads may have pillaged the home of Sir Richard Okeford of Hammiton Hall, close by.

I stared at the last sentence in horror. Not realising the enormity of it, I'd skimmed over this section when first reading the book. There it was, as plain as plain could be. Sir Richard Okeford of Hammiton Hall. I continued reading, dreading what I would learn.

In 1644, there was a fine manor house in the neighbourhood of Shipton Gorge owned by the staunchly Royalist Okeford family. During the first week of April that year, a large Parliamentary force under Sir Anthony Ashley Cooper marched from Dorchester with the intention to rid Abbotsbury of its Royalist garrison, which then commanded by Colonel James Strangways. It would appear that on the way the Parliamentarian troops mounted regular raids and, on the 8th April, lay siege to the Okeford family home. Unfortunately for the Okefords, Sir Richard was overseeing the visit of King Charles I at Maiden Newton at the time and when his wife, Lady Catherine, refused to co-operate with the Parliamentarian troops, the house was ransacked.

The siege of the house itself began with Sir Cooper's men setting fire to the entrance porch whilst keeping up a constant fusillade of musket fire that forced the family and their servants to retreat upstairs. Inside, Lady Catherine bravely refused all offers of surrender and so the order was given that no prisoners were to be taken alive. With the lower half of the house now well alight, screams were soon heard as the flames climbed higher. A second Parliamentary force used grenades, fireballs and scaling ladders to reach the second-floor windows at the rear and, wrenching open windows, threw in bundles of faggots, which set the entire house ablaze.

Lady Catherine's eldest daughter and granddaughter were fatally wounded by musket fire while attempting a daring escape and several of the servants perished before Lady Catherine begged for mercy for herself, her youngest daughter and those remaining. They were spared. As was common practice then, the victorious Parliamentarian soldiers rushed into the burning house to ransack it before it was fully destroyed. Today, nothing remains of the Hall.

Putting the book down, I covered my face with my hands and sobbed. Not only had Nat lost his son to smallpox in 1643 but also his wife and daughter during the course of one day the following year. No wonder his spirit was restless. He'd made a promise to Mary that should they ever find themselves parted he would look for her and, true to his word, this was what he was doing... to this very day.

After a while, as the intense emotions abated, I looked up to find Storm watching me curiously from the kitchen doorway.

'It's OK, boy,' I said softly. 'It's all over.'

As he walked over and jumped onto my lap, I hugged him close.

That night I had nightmares. I was trapped and surrounded by fire. Elisabeth, brave girl though she was, whimpered quietly at my side; her eyes filled with terror. We were in the front room on the upper floor above the porch. Flames crackled around us and the sound of musket shot rang loudly in our ears. The noise was deafening. My mother, the fierce warrior, was determined the soldiers would not take our family home. Charlotte and the servants quaked in fear and kept well back in the room. It was only Duncan who stood loyally at my mother's side.

I held Elisabeth close and told her it would be all right. How could I have lied so? She held tightly on to my skirt and I tried not to show the fear in my heart. Suddenly, above the hiss and crackle of fire, we heard windows being wrenched open followed by thuds, which we didn't fully comprehend until too late. The bundles of flaming faggots took hold and the evil fire licked its way up the curtains, setting light to anything flammable in its path. The roar of fire is a sound I will never forget.

Some of the servants started screaming and if I could

have found my voice I would have joined them. Two maidservants suddenly ran forward away from the fire, which had quickly spread to the rear of the room. Shots rang out and the women fell dead at our feet. Elisabeth screamed and I quickly turned her head away from the horror unfolding before our eyes.

'Mary,' my mother shouted. 'You, Elisabeth and Charlotte go to the next room.'

'It's alight, mistress,' shouted Duncan.

'It will be safer than here above the porch,' she said, hysteria creeping into her voice. 'Oh Richard, where art thou?'

Charlotte stared at me in horror.

'Come now,' I said, holding out my hand to my younger sister.

Paralysed with fear, she didn't move.

'You must,' I urged.

Elisabeth, too, stood rooted to the spot, but I managed to coax her into the next room. Looking back at my sister before we slipped through the doorway, I held out my hand to her once again. She shook her head and her big saucer-like eyes followed our escape.

The glass in the windows cracked and shattered under the fierce heat and there was an acrid stench in the air – the smell of death. I huddled in the corner with Elisabeth and heard my mother bravely shouting down to the commanding officer that she would never surrender her home and they would have to burn us all in it. I had to escape; for the sake of my last remaining child and husband. Speaking urgently to Elisabeth, I told her we would make our way down the stairs and slip out at the back of the house. Fear paralysed my daughter, but I grabbed her hand and she came with me as I hurried towards the door. Flames cruelly licked their way up the stairwell, the wood charred and aglow, but I noticed the far side of the stairs was relatively free of fire. Carefully, we made our way down the burning staircase.

Suddenly an unearthly scream rent the air and I heard my mother cry out, 'Duncan, oh Duncan!'

Without faltering, I continued on down the stairs holding Elisabeth's hand tightly.

It was dark; the air thick with smoke. And it was hot... oh, so hot. We choked and I told Elisabeth to cover her nose and mouth with the hem of her skirt. Avoiding falling timbers, we made our way along the burning hallway and into the servants' quarters, turning right through the kitchens and coming to a side door, burnt through. This was our escape. Sobbing with relief, we spilled out into the stable yard and breathed in great lungfuls of fresh air. The night sky was lit by the orange flame of fire all around but we had made it!

As I felt the cobblestones beneath my feet, I heard two musket shots ring out and watched in disbelief as Elisabeth fell away from me with an astonished look on her face; her mouth open as if to say something. She hit the ground unseeing, her eyes open wide, and a dark globule of blood spilled out of the corner of her mouth. I staggered and clutched at my chest. Through my fingers I felt the warm ooze of blood and watched incredulously as my bodice turned red. As I fell to the ground, a searing pain spread through my body.

Clasping my heart pendant, I whispered, 'I'm sorry, Nat.'

A while later I heard men's voices. 'This one's still alive.'

Painfully, I gazed up into the kindly face of the soldier who had spied us at The Olde Smithy. Recognition registered in his eyes.

'Lie still,' he said gruffly. 'Don't move.'

Fighting for air and with my throat filling with blood, I held out the pendant towards him. Drawing deeply on my last breath, I whispered, 'Please…'

He knelt by my side and removed his helmet. 'What's that you say?'

The pain was unbearable. I could hardly breathe, let alone speak.

'Take this and my ring…' I managed to say. He bent down, his ear close to my lips, and with one final attempt I croaked, 'Farrier… Waldyke.'

My vision blurred, but not before I saw the soldier nod in understanding. Then the black tunnel closed in around me.


I awoke, hyperventilating. The room was pitch black and for a moment I feared I was still in the house of fire. I clutched at my chest. The pain was so intense that I thought I must have died. Confused, bewildered and alone, I sat up and fought for breath. I didn't know what I was doing. I cried for Nat, I cried for Mary and Elisabeth, and I cried for that poor dear boy, Francis, who had never had the chance to know life. I was distraught and the pain in my chest would not go away. Grabbing my mobile phone, I punched in the number. After seven rings a sleepy voice answered. I glanced at the clock on the bedside table – just after three in the morning. I tried to speak but could only manage a deep, racking, drawing of breath. And then his voice, suddenly fully alert.

'Maddie, is that you?'

Again I tried to speak, but still no sound.

'Maddie, breathe slowly.'

I did as he said. Once able to catch my breath, I started to sob uncontrollably.

'Nick,' I whimpered. 'I need you.'

A sharp intake of breath.

'I'm coming over now,' he said urgently.

As the pain finally eased in my chest, I breathed out with relief.

'No, not here. The churchyard at St Martin's. There's something I need to do.'

# 27

The night sky had given way to a sullen greyness and a dense sea mist hung low over the valley. The earth was shrouded in a thick blanket; the silence impenetrable. There was no one around at this ungodly hour, not even the birds, but as I drove into the church car park I saw Nick's silver Nissan. So he had come.

I parked and slowly got out of the car, still shaken by the night's revelations. I walked through the lych gate, up the path towards the church and looked around for him. As I rounded the corner of the West Tower, through the fog I could make out a figure standing at the far side of the graveyard, carefully placing flowers at the foot of Mary and Elisabeth's headstone. It was Nat, his head bowed in sorrow.

I watched for a few moments and then called softly, 'Nat, I have come.'

He raised his head.

'I am here,' I said.

Slowly he turned towards me.

He was older, much older, and I wondered if he

approached the end of his life; one that had been long and hard. His hair was grey and his face deeply lined and etched in sadness. He looked at me in confusion and then disbelief. I smiled and watched as despair began to lift from his eyes and tentative hope take its place.

'Be at peace,' I said tenderly, and my eyes pricked with tears as his face filled with joy.

He took a step towards me.

'Mary's spirit lives on through me.'

He hesitated, consternation settling on that dear familiar face, and I saw the bewilderment as he observed my modern-day clothes.

'Do not fear, Nat,' I called out softly again.

His lovely blue-grey eyes urgently sought mine for confirmation and suddenly I was filled with the purest of emotions. He smiled slowly, our love reaching out across the distance and years between us, and I fought back tears as that dearly beloved man faded from sight for the very last time. In a blink of an eye he was gone.

Nick stood by the gravestone looking at me through the same blue-grey eyes. The love I felt for him was immense and yet I faltered, unsure of where I stood. He watched me hesitate. Taking a step towards me, he opened his arms wide.

'Come to me, Maddie. I won't lose you again.'

The tender look in his eyes told me everything I needed to know. As if in a dream, I walked towards his loving embrace.

'It was always you,' he murmured, taking me in his arms.

We kissed with a passion we both knew we'd experienced

many times before and, once again, I became aware of a sense of well-being and a delicious peace settling upon my soul. Eventually – reluctantly – I drew back for breath.

Away to the east, a pink glow warmed the horizon and burnished gold and silver rays from a rising sun streaked the sky. Filtering up from the valley below, we heard the exuberant chords of an early dawn chorus. All at once there was an easing to the dense sea mist shrouding the earth, and the fog rolled away from the high ground to slowly reveal the church. Suddenly, the subtlest of warm air currents encircled our bodies, as if investigating us. I knew Nick felt it too. Seductively it caressed us – a lingering, tender kiss of breeze – and I had the strongest feeling we were being protected and cushioned from the world; somehow blessed. Then, as quickly as it had arrived, it departed, though the sensation remained.

As I allowed myself to dare believe in this unexpected, yet longed for, turn of events, I gazed deeply into Nick's eyes and recognised fragments of Nat's older soul watching me in wonder.

Holding me close and in a voice thick with emotion, he whispered, 'My love, my life...'

# Epilogue

The sound of gentle rain pitter-pattering on the roof teases me from sleep and I notice the barn is filled with the soft light of dawn. Glancing up through the glass apex, I watch grey clouds swirl across the sky. Turning my head, I see Nick sound asleep beside me. I smile. He looks so peaceful and I don't have the heart to wake him. Snuggling further under the duvet, safe in my cocoon, I luxuriate in the comforting warmth and security I have become increasingly accustomed to. But what a turbulent fourteen months we have lived through to get here!

Understandably, Sarah took it badly when Nick told her of his feelings for me. She was distraught and immediately moved back to her mother's. Since then, we've coped with numerous visits at all times of the day and night, mopping her tears, and as my wonderful man dealt with her in a responsible and caring manner, my already high regard for him grew. I understood his concern was born from an acknowledgement of the not inconsiderable number of years they'd spent together, and his feelings for her were but a spark compared to the leaping flames we fanned. Becky defended her friend. At first, it was stalking and leaving threatening notes on my car windscreen, however, when her tactics escalated to attempts at driving me off the road we had no choice but to involve the police. We didn't want to press charges. She was cautioned and it seems to have had the desired effect; no further incidents have occurred. And then, three months ago, Sarah suddenly announced that she, Becky and Mark were leaving their jobs and going to Australia. She asked Nick if his brother would put them up for a few weeks before they headed to Sydney and he immediately contacted Chris, who generously agreed they could stay. Already, they've been with him three weeks.

It hasn't been easy for us, but dealing with Sarah and Becky has only served to confirm our feelings for each other. As Nick begins to recall past times more clearly and embrace our history together, the pieces of our lives are falling into place.

Last month – on the 8th May – we were married at St Martin's Church. We chose the date especially. We only had to buy a wedding ring for Nick, as we already had mine. The ruby gimmel ring is back in its rightful place and I will never take it off. It was supposed to be a small celebration for family and close friends but with most of my extended family coming over from Ireland it soon turned into a party, which Brian and Vera were only too happy to host at the Blacksmith's Arms. It seemed a befitting venue. However, before leaving the church, Nick and I took a few private moments to lay the wedding bouquet on Mary and Elisabeth's grave. I turn over, trying not to disturb my husband. Even though it's early, I can't get back to sleep. I slip out of bed, grab a dressing gown and make my way quietly downstairs.

As I descend the spiral staircase, Baron and Casper look up expectantly from the couch. Storm, sandwiched between the two large dogs, continues to snooze, and I grin. From day one that cat has made himself at home at Ashton Chase Barn… as have I. Nick's barn always felt like *home* to me. I no longer live at The Old Smithy, but it will never be sold. The cottage belongs as much to Nick as me; it is an important part of our history. Now that Nat's spirit is laid to rest, there are no longer any unusual 'happenings' at the cottage and a particularly tranquil and calming atmosphere pervades. After some consideration, we rented it to a young, local family. I've also left my job at the Blacksmith's Arms and my freelance writing has taken off.

As I enter the porch, the dogs rouse themselves and climb off the couch to follow me. I fill their food bowls and then make my way to the kitchen. Taking two clean mugs from the draining board, I throw a teabag into each and, while waiting for the kettle to boil, I pick up my mobile phone from the countertop and scroll through the latest photos Caro has sent me. Dan and I have not been in touch since our last meeting at Caro and John's London house, but his sister keeps me informed of the latest developments in her brother's life. And what a turnaround there too! I pause at a photo of a smiling Dan, smug-looking Lucy and sleeping baby Archie. Since embracing fatherhood, the troubled Dan has vanished and he looks well and content with his lot. I still can't warm to Lucy, but at least she has given him an important focus and purpose in life other than herself. I suppose I should thank her for that.

I hear Nick get out of bed and walk across the galleried bedroom to the shower room. As I carry the mugs over to the coffee table, Storm eyes me from his supine position on the couch. Now that the dogs have vacated, he stretches out along its length in an ungentlemanly manner. I stroke his belly and he starts to purr.

''Morning gorgeous.'

I turn at the sound of Nick's voice. His hair is tousled and he is casually dressed in jeans and t-shirt. Like mine, his feet are bare.

'Hello sleepyhead. I've made tea,' I say, indicating the mugs on the coffee table.

'Thanks. Have the dogs been fed?' He steps off the spiral staircase.

I nod.

'I'll let them out.' Approaching, he plants a kiss on my mouth and, picking up a mug, takes a large swallow of tea. 'I see Storm's as comfortable as usual,' he remarks with a grin.

I laugh.

As Nick enters the porch, I cross over to the enormous steel-framed glass doors and gaze out over the terraces and the low-lying valley to the sea. The rain has abated but, whatever the weather, I will never tire of this view; it is magnificent. A fine sea mist rises up the valley, making a theatre of the landscape, tantalisingly picking out a bank of trees or a field gate for a few seconds before letting the curtain fall. Increasingly large patches of blue appear in the dense grey canopy and, as the sun peeps out from behind a bank of clouds, dramatic shafts of light break through the dark skies, plummeting to the ocean and turning it liquid silver. As though Nature wants to show off the scenery in all its glory, a double rainbow arcs over the valley.

Suddenly, loving arms encircle me and Nick draws my body to him. Willingly, I lean against him and we stand silently – reverently – savouring the view.

'Look, Maddie,' he says, pointing at the sky. 'Our Guardian Angels watch over us.'

High above, two dark specks fly in a circular formation, their plumage becoming more defined and detailed as the birds of prey glide earthwards. All at once, a third buzzard with slimmer wings and a relatively longer tail comes into view, and we watch as it joins in the dance.

'Looks like a juvenile,' Nick comments. 'It could be last year's offspring, judging by the way the adults are tolerating it.'

'How wonderful,' I sigh.

Nick's hold on me tightens. Softly, he says, 'What do you say, Maddie, to us making babies of our own?'

I glance sideways at him.

'We can give life once more to Elisabeth and Francis,' he continues, the deep emotion obvious in his voice.

I turn in his arms and gaze up into blue-grey eyes filled with love. 'I'd like that very much,' I whisper, and then correct myself. '*We'd* like that.'

He kisses me tenderly. Then, patting me playfully on the bottom, he walks away.

'I'll start breakfast then. After all, we'll need to build up our strength if we're to handle those two rascals again.'

I watch as he moves around the kitchen, at ease in his skin, and I can't stop the wide smile spreading across my face.

At last, I have truly found my way home.

# Acknowledgements

In the beginning, when considering where to base this book my only stipulation was there must be a village green. Memories of childhood holidays spent fossil hunting along the bay at Charmouth guided me to Dorset where serendipity played its part. Due to roadworks, I took a detour and came upon Walditch, and whilst researching the village and its surrounding areas historic events came to light that supplied me with the framework on which to pin my story. Most of the historical elements recorded here are a true account, although I have exercised the writer's 'right' to fictionalise with a slight tweak of location to fit the story.

Many people played a part in helping this book reach publication. My husband, who discovered a time capsule during extensive renovations to our cottage, which set me thinking about past dramas it may have been witness to; the country trader who fired my imagination with a story of her Dartmoor cottage with its internal stained-glass window and unaccountable cold corners; and tutor, Karen Hayes, and the South Dornaford Farm Writers' Group who witnessed my tentative first steps on this particular journey when the novel, yet to be written, was a simple short story.

Big thanks must go to Team Aria for their ongoing dedication in producing and marketing our books; to my editor, Laura Palmer, for her guidance in teasing out the best of this novel; to Helena Newton for her thorough and intelligent copy editing; and to Charlotte Abrams-Simpson for doing a wonderful job in creating the most perfect, softly haunting front cover.

I would, however, especially like to thank Helena Ancil whose continuing support, encouragement and belief in this book kept firm my resolve to see it in print. Thank you, dear friend.

# About the Author

Originally from the Home Counties, Kate now resides in the diverse and inspirational county of Cornwall, which provides a glorious backdrop for much of her writing. Her career has encompassed travel, property and publishing and she currently divides her time between selling fabulous country piles that she can't afford and writing romantic suspense. Together with her ever-supportive husband, a gorgeous Arab horse and a newly acquired 'rescue' cat called Ollie, Kate lives in the beautiful Tamar Valley in a 200-year-old cottage that she (and said husband) painstakingly restored and which proved the inspiration for her third book with Aria.

# Hello from Aria

We hope you enjoyed this book! If you did let us know, we'd love to hear from you.

We are Aria, a dynamic digital-first fiction imprint from award-winning independent publishers Head of Zeus. At heart, we're committed to publishing fantastic commercial fiction – from romance and sagas to crime, thrillers and historical fiction. Visit us online and discover a community of like-minded fiction fans!

We're also on the look out for tomorrow's superstar authors. So, if you're a budding writer looking for a publisher, we'd love to hear from you.
You can submit your book online at ariafiction.com/we-want-read-your-book

You can find us at:
Email: aria@headofzeus.com
Website: www.ariafiction.com
Submissions: www.ariafiction.com/we-want-read-your-book

@ariafiction
@Aria_Fiction
@ariafiction

Printed in Poland
by Amazon Fulfillment
Poland Sp. z o.o., Wrocław

57448046R00199